THE FINAL CUT
David Stanley

PAPER★STREET

Paper Street Publishing

This book is for

Lindsey and Connor,
whether they like it or not...

Also available

Night Passenger

The Dark Halo

The Scapegoat

The Final Cut

1

AT FIRST, HE HEARD nothing. Silence. His ears still half-deaf from the white noise roar of his car's air conditioning. He took a deep breath and held it inside his chest. Franklin Canyon Park in the summer. The air here was fresh, with no hydrocarbon taste of the city. It felt like Los Angeles had disappeared and he'd entered another world. A better world. Surrounded by trees, plants, and animals. People were the problem, no doubt about it. He heard birds singing now, the buzz of insects. It was beautiful really, and kind of a shame that someone had chosen to come here with a corpse.

He walked down Lake Drive past two West LA patrol SUVs that were parked nose-to-tail at the side of the road. In front of them sat an old Ford Taurus with faded blue paint and bull bars. He assumed it was a detective's car, because there was a man in a terrible suit and a three-day beard sitting on the hood eating potato chips.

He took off his sunglasses and introduced himself.

"John Coombes."

"Brad Drake."

In the past, Coombes might've held out his hand to shake the other man's hand, but not anymore. Those times were gone and he wasn't sorry about it.

"Thanks for your call."

"No problem," Drake said. "I guess this wasn't what you had in mind."

"Not even close."

A long time ago, he'd put a note in the system to be contacted should Natalie Simpson Hahn reappear on the LAPD's radar. He'd imagined an arrest, likely on drugs charges, which he'd hoped to use as leverage to get her to revisit an eyewitness statement she'd given him.

A statement he'd always believed was a lie.

"Geek squad took off for lunch forty minutes ago, they'll be back soon."

Coombes nodded and went to inspect the scene while Drake finished eating. He couldn't have timed his arrival any better if he'd tried. It was always his preference to view crime scenes alone, without the presence of another person polluting his senses.

He had no problem finding the dig site, a uniform had erected a whole roll's worth of crime scene tape like they were decking the halls at some Christmas charity function. At the end of the line, he found a neat rectangle cut into the ground, roughly five feet by four.

Hahn was not inside; the hole was empty.

Coombes turned his attention to a line of translucent plastic cases that lay along the edge of the dig site. He walked to the closest container, opened the snap fasteners, and lifted off the lid. The contents of the case were obvious, but he sighed just the same.

Hahn had been in the ground a long time.

She was just bones.

The container held the long bones of her legs spaced out on a soft material like a model airplane ready to be assembled. Coombes thought about the last time he'd seen Hahn. Young, sullen, full of attitude. She'd been a headache for him, a problem that wouldn't go away. Rubbing people the wrong way had been something close to a gift for Natalie Hahn, and it looked like that had finally caught up with her.

He replaced the lid and moved along the line of containers until he found the one holding her skull. It was smaller than he would have imagined, with large eye sockets and the open hole where her nose had been. He tried to imagine that he was looking at Hahn's face and found that he could not.

A skull was not a face.

He saw that there were two different containers at the end of the line and he moved down to take a look inside. The first held a dirty flight jacket, the second a pair of leather boots.

The clothes she'd been buried in.

"Will your partner be joining us?"

The other detective was standing beside him now.

"No, she's attending to some personal business."

Drake frowned, glancing briefly back to the road.

"I'm curious," Coombes said. "How did you make ID?"

"From her driver's license. Wallet was still in her jacket pocket."

Coombes grunted but said nothing.

"I know what you're thinking," Drake said. "A friend could've borrowed the jacket without realizing your girl's wallet was in it. That this could be someone else."

Your girl.

"No, it just seemed careless that the killer didn't check her pockets. I guess if I find her out there still alive, I'll believe this is someone else, but in this job..."

"The simplest answer is usually the truth."

"Right."

Coombes looked around, taking in the location for a second time.

This time, imagining himself as the killer.

It was a good spot, he reflected. Deserted, yet close enough to the city to limit exposure. Nobody wants to get pulled over for a busted taillight with a body in the trunk. There was direct access by road with parking next to the grave site to unload the body and begin work.

The hardness of the earth would've limited how deep the killer was able to go in the time available. Coombes looked at the grave. The hole was shallow. Before it had been excavated, there had probably been no more than two feet of topsoil covering her skull. Despite the low depth, he estimated this represented forty-five minutes to an hour of digging, presumably at night.

During the day, walkers and trail runners used the area for exercise. He knew this, because he was one of them. The thought gave him pause. This wasn't one of his usual routes, but he had to have passed the site at least twenty times in the last few years.

"You never said what your interest was in the victim."

"She was part of a case I worked six years ago. Dakota Lawrence."

The other man's eyes lit up.

"Oh, man. I *loved* her movies. She was so beautiful."

Coombes moved around to the other side of the grave so that his shadow wasn't falling across the grave interior. He squatted down, balancing on the balls of his feet, and studied the exposed earth. Silence fell between them and he waited for the other man to ask his question. Coombes could feel it coming a mile off and even before it arrived, he was annoyed.

"You ever get anyone for the Lawrence murder?"

"No."

He rose again to full height. It wasn't the question that annoyed him, as much as the answer it forced him to provide. He and his partner at the time had dropped the ball, and the murder had gone unsolved.

Thinking about Dakota Lawrence gave him a bad feeling.

He took out his cell phone and opened the camera app.

There wasn't much left of Hahn, but there might be enough.

Coombes returned to the container that held her skull and pointed his lens at it. She'd been in the ground a long time, but her teeth were still better than Drake's. The image swam for a moment, then came back sharp. He aimed his lens at what had been the center of her forehead and took close-up photographs from different angles and distances.

When he was done, he stood and flicked between his pictures.

Looking for something he didn't want to find, but finding it anyway.

Two dark lines overlapping where dirt or blood had been trapped in the bone. It was faint, like single strands of hair forming a perfect diagonal cross. He would need the lab to run tests to confirm his theory, but already he knew in his heart what it was.

They were cuts from a blade.

"Got something?"

Coombes glanced at Drake. "Hard to say, maybe nothing."

He wasn't going to tell Mr. Potato Chips what it meant, because then he'd only fight harder to stay on the case. Coombes put away his cell phone and took out his notebook.

"How was the grave discovered?"

"A dog got off the leash and started digging and barking. It was a couple of days after those heavy rains, so I guess the soil opened up a little and let the smell of decay out. Anyway, the owner had never seen the dog dig like that and called it in. He's an ex-cop and he knew what we were likely to find."

"All right. Tell me about the park's opening hours."

"Park's open 7 a.m. to sunset. There's a gate at the Mulholland end of Franklin Canyon Drive. The gate's automated, opens and closes on its own. There's a keypad that can open it out of hours for park people."

Coombes finished writing and looked up.

"What about the Beverly Drive end?"

Drake nodded slowly. "No gate."

"You're joking. It's completely open?"

"People live down there, they need access 24-7."

Coombes thought every park closed up at night. There were fences and gates all around them like prisons, except L.A. was the prison, not the parks. He supposed this was likely the reason the park had been chosen as a dumping ground in the first place.

"Are there rangers that patrol the park at night?"

"There *are* rangers, but I can't speak to their patrol pattern. I don't know if it made it to you guys downtown, but there were rumors that a couple of the wild fires ten years ago were caused by the rangers themselves. They like to rely on fences and gates now."

"Then whoever did this had all night to dig this hole."

Drake shook his head.

"A couple of kids making out in the back of a car *they* might have all night. A guy digging a hole next to a dead lady? He's got to assume he's about to be popped at any second."

"I like that," Coombes said. "I'll bet you're right."

He put his notebook away and they walked back to the road.

The patrol SUVs had parked sideways, like a screen, but the regular parking was end-on. Coombes figured the killer would've parked that way, with his headlights aimed into the trees so that he could see what he was doing. Drake turned to him.

"You think it's the same killer as Dakota Lawrence?"

"It would be some coincidence if it wasn't, wouldn't it?"

The detective nodded.

"My opinion? If you spoke with Hahn six years ago, I don't think she was walking around too much longer before she made her way here."

"Agreed," Coombes said.

"Did you have any suspects back then?"

"Only one."

Drake gave him a knowing look. One of *those* cases.

"What happened?"

"An eyewitness put him with the victim but we couldn't make it stick."

"Where does Hahn fit into this?"

"She was the witness."

2

As they came through the trees onto Lake Drive, Coombes saw a tall woman in her early sixties walking fast toward him, eyes blazing. She was wearing white coveralls and was towing three bored-looking assistants in her slipstream.

"Are you the asshole who parked in my spot?"

"Probably. I guess that makes you the grave robber, huh?"

"*Archeologist.*"

He smiled at her sour expression. Wind blew her long gray hair across her face and she swept it back behind her ear like she was swatting a bug. Her eyes moved over his suit, then back to his face.

"How many of you guys are they going to send here? We're the ones doing all the work. I suppose I've got to explain everything to you now too?"

"Something like that. Think of it this way, I've not heard all your best jokes yet, so you don't have to come up with any new material."

The archaeologist sighed.

"Very well. This way."

They started to move back toward the dig site and he saw everyone else was coming with them. Coombes stopped and held his hand up.

"No. Everyone else stays here."

The others didn't like that much, least of all Drake, but nobody said anything. The light in the archaeologist's eyes seemed to change and he saw a small nod of approval.

They resumed their walk toward the grave site in silence.

On a second pass, it struck him that the killer had carried or dragged Hahn's body farther than he realized, almost sixty feet. The light from his headlights would've been considerably dimmer during his dig than Coombes had imagined. Perhaps it was a full moon, he thought. The only possible reason for bringing his victim the extra distance, was to increase the gap to where cars regularly parked, and any dogs that might jump out of them.

The exact way that the body had eventually been found.

At the grave now, he saw that he'd left the lids off the containers that held Hahn's clothing. The jacket, the boots. It was pitiful. All that remained of a human life. He turned to the archaeologist and saw that she was watching him closely.

"Do you think she was buried wearing only a jacket and boots?"

"No. The jacket is a synthetic polymer. It's not organic and it doesn't decompose in soil. You could come back here in a hundred years and that jacket would still be there. I figure the victim was wearing jeans, because we found those rivets you get around the pockets. The denim is completely gone though, so you're looking at least five years in the ground. The boots are starting to deteriorate, but the leather's tough and has probably been treated with chemicals. Surprisingly resilient."

"I want to understand how she can be reduced to bones while, in the same timeframe, her boots look like they need a polish."

"Insects aside, the number one thing that causes bodies to skeletonize is the bacteria present within them when they are interred. The digestive system, bugs that live in your skin and hair, the microscopic flora and fauna that live where the sun don't shine...and in that rash you haven't gotten round to treating. We're like ripe fruit, Detective, on the point of rotting down to our skeleton at any moment."

He nodded.

"Some days are more of a struggle than others."

Her mouth twisted in amusement.

"Katie Atwell."

"John Coombes."

They were silent for a moment before he spoke again.

"Have you found anything here I can use?"

"A clue? No. Just what you see here. A forensic anthropologist might be able to give you something. I just *dig 'em up*, you know? See if they have any good jewelry."

Coombes supposed he deserved that.

"I guess you're about done?"

"A couple of hours. We have the big bones, but only about half of the hands."

"*Her* hands."

Atwell tilted her head to the side. "You knew the victim?"

"In a way. I interviewed her about a case."

"But you liked her."

"Actually, no, I didn't. But I saw her alive."

"My team are the best, Detective. We'll look after her."

He nodded and left her to it. Victims were just bones to her, she didn't understand. For the second time he made his way back to the road where Drake and the assistants stood waiting. The other detective glared at him, angry at being sidelined on his own case.

"Show me Hahn's wallet."

"All right."

Drake set off toward the patrol vehicles. The anger was still there in the way he walked, the way he swung his arms. He probably assumed that after Coombes had looked at the wallet he'd be about his way, his interest in the case exhausted.

"You gone through it yet?"

"Only to get ID."

The wallet was in the back of the closest patrol vehicle. The uniforms came out and opened the tailgate then stood next to Drake. Coombes sat on the floor of the SUV and pulled on a pair of blue nitrile gloves. Leaving the wallet still inside the clear bag, he reached inside and examined the wallet carefully.

It was made from a similar fabric to the jacket, some kind of woven polymer thread. The same kind of material that was used to make bulletproof vests. He saw a surfboard icon. It was a fairly masculine item, but that didn't surprise him at all having met the victim.

Coombes flipped it open and saw a clear panel with the driver's license.

Hahn, Natalie Simpson.

Her face looked out at him, just as sullen and gloomy as he remembered. He briefly felt a flare of the anger he'd harbored toward her for her bullshit eyewitness testimony, but it lasted only a split-second. He'd lived with the anger for six years, but for most of that time she'd been dead and buried.

He glanced at Drake.

"License expiry is August 31, 2015. Gives us a partial timeframe."

The other detective nodded; his eyebrows angled downward.

No doubt thinking, *what do you mean us?*

Using his cell phone, Coombes took pictures of the wallet from different angles, still within the bag, then of the license. Hahn's eyes seemed to reach out to him from the picture.

You. You did this to me.

If her testimony *had* been a lie as he'd always suspected, then the obvious takeaway from her being murdered was that she'd known something and had been permanently silenced.

That look she was doing; she was doing it on purpose.

When he and his partner had interviewed her during the Dakota Lawrence investigation, he assumed this angry look was anti-police. But he hadn't taken the DMV photograph, and there she was doing it again. Maybe she was trying for *smoldering* and falling short.

He moved on. Her wallet held four credit cards and three loyalty cards. He only half-slid the cards out, they didn't interest him much. All that mattered was they were made out in her name, and there were none belonging to someone else, or to a company.

None that might lead to her killer.

"I assume you didn't recover a cell phone?"

Drake laughed.

"Afraid not. That would be good, wouldn't it?"

The other cop didn't take his point. Coombes looked up.

"Pretty sure she had one though."

"No doubt. Everyone does."

"Her killer takes the cell and leaves the wallet. Why?"

Drake shrugged.

"Maybe he figures it doesn't matter. He's planning to bury her in a hole anyway, right? Cell phone's different, it can be used to track her. Say he grabs her off the street, smart move is to dump her phone there and then. Could've been days or weeks before he put her here."

"I guess that must be it."

He didn't see Hahn being charmed by her killer into making a stupid mistake like getting into his vehicle. She'd been tough as nails and street-smart. Her guard was never down. If she got into his vehicle, it was because she knew him and thought she was safe.

Coombes turned his attention back to the wallet.

A piece of thin card rose above the top of some dollar bills. The edge had overlapping crescent shapes still embedded in the card.

Fingernail marks.

From the number of times Hahn had pulled it out the wallet to look at it. Carefully, he teased the card out from its hiding place. A black and white image appeared, exactly like he'd imagined.

His heart sank.

"She was pregnant."

Drake swore, and Coombes dipped his head.

Not in prayer, but in defeat. It was a double homicide now. He took a photograph of the ultrasound image, then two close-ups of the information bar along the top listing the hospital, patient name, date, and estimated age of the pregnancy.

The timeline for her murder had firmed up considerably.

Hahn had the ultrasound on June 3, 2015. Based on the wear along the top edge of the photograph, she'd spent around two weeks constantly taking the photograph out her wallet and studying it, then putting it away again.

Which meant it was almost exactly five years since she'd been murdered.

3

HE MADE CONVERSATION WITH Drake for a moment before the conversation went where it needed to go. His theory was that all anyone really wanted was respect, and if you gave them some before you took it away again, it seemed to balance out. That it was just the way things were, and it was nothing personal.

"I think you know what I'm going to say now."

Drake's face hardened.

"I've been on this for three days, Coombes. I called you as a courtesy, not for you to come here and Bigfoot me."

"If this is part of the Dakota Lawrence case, that falls within the RHD purview even without the fact that I already worked the case and know all the players."

"And if it *isn't* linked? I get bounced anyway?"

Coombes had been on the other side of this situation many times and he knew how it felt. The problem was that the case was still sexy for Drake and he needed to make it boring. As soon as that point was reached, the other detective would lose interest. He had an idea about how to make that happen and save himself some grunt work.

"This is *your* patch, that it?"

"You're goddamn right it is."

"All right. Then you work this end, and I'll work mine. If there's no link with my old case, I back out and you take over. No hard feelings."

The other man frowned. "But I've already done this end."

13

"Look around, Drake. What do you see?"

"The park. Trees. What?"

"We're saying some nutcase drove in here, planted a woman at the bottom of a hole like a seed, then drove happily away without a hitch. What do you *think* I'm saying?"

"That if he did it once, he might have done again?"

"*Bingo.*"

Drake stroked the stubble on his chin and looked around, as if measuring up the task at hand. The park was large, and even with a team of dogs it would take a long time to search, time that he wouldn't be under Coombes' feet.

"That's a bit of a long shot, isn't it?"

Coombes leaned forward.

"You wanted a piece? *This* is your piece. For what it's worth, I spent nine weeks on the Lawrence case, a little more than the three days you've put in. But if you find more bodies in here and we solve this, I'll split the collar with you fifty-fifty. That sound fair?"

It was more than fair, and he could see that the other detective knew it. Drake probably also knew that fighting to keep control would only result in it being taken off him altogether.

"I guess I can live with that."

Coombes had a feeling that Drake was about to hold out his hand to shake on their deal, so he put his hand in his pocket and pulled out a business card which he offered instead. They swapped cards. Drake hadn't started a murder book yet, so he promised to email a copy of the incident report and the chronology as it stood.

When he got back to his car he found a woman leaning against it, talking into her cell phone. She smiled warmly at him and wrapped up her call. The woman was wearing skin tight blue jeans, Nikes, and a couture suit jacket that probably cost eight thousand dollars. But what he noticed most of all, was a red spot that appeared in both of her cheeks and spread rapidly out across her face as he walked closer.

"Let me guess," he said. "You just happened to be here."

"Actually, I arrived before you did."

As usual, she was in a playful mood and he didn't have time for it.

"Why are you here, Sullivan?"

"I'm here for the corpse, same as you."

He was right in front of her now. Monica Sullivan, crime reporter for the *L.A. Times*. It was a while since they'd last met and he'd managed to forget how good she looked. Her cheeks were redder than ever. Of all the possible reasons for an emotional response, embarrassment seemed the most likely.

Suddenly he had it.

Drake had asked about his partner and seemed confused when he said she was busy elsewhere. Clearly, Sullivan had spoken to the detective first and allowed him to think they were partners, getting Drake to cough up all the juicy details.

"Impersonating a cop is an offense. I should arrest you."

"Hey, the man assumed, I just ran with it."

"I'll bet you did."

Sullivan was blocking the driver's door and it didn't look like she was in any hurry to move out the way.

"If impersonating a cop is an offense, half the cops in L.A. should arrest themselves."

She smiled at her own joke and he found himself staring at her mouth. It was a *city mouth* and it didn't belong out here, surrounded by nature. It was coated with lip gloss and moved like it had a life of its own.

There was a reason Drake had fallen for her partner act, he'd probably just fallen for her completely.

This was Sullivan's trick; everyone was in love with her.

"I'm still pissed that you never called me back for that drink like you said you would. You shouldn't toy with a girl's heart. We break easy."

He'd never promised to call her, but he let it slide.

"It's great to see you again, Sullivan, but I've got to get going."

"There's no rush, Natalie's been dead for years. Let's face it, her killer's probably dead too."

He said nothing, hoping to draw out more information.

"Look at you pretending to care. I know you're only here for Dakota."

He groaned inwardly. The journalist had the whole thing and she didn't get it from Drake. If she put the burial site's discovery in the paper, the killer could be reading it off the *Times* website before lunch.

"If you run this, you kill the investigation and we never find out what happened to either victim. The story ends. Which means no follow-up articles, no trial coverage. *Nada*."

"You know how I feel about sitting on a story."

"Let's say this case *is* linked to the Dakota Lawrence murder. We could be talking another serial. Give me time to investigate. All you've got so far are some old bones. Nobody's going to care about that, you'll be lucky to get two paragraphs on page five."

She pushed her ass off his door and stepped clear.

"You always knew how to talk to me, Coombes."

"We have a deal?"

"For now. My editor may feel differently."

Sullivan pulled sunglasses out her hair and put them on. The summer sun had turned her brunette hair honey-blonde around her face. It suited her.

"They filmed *Creature from the Black Lagoon* down the road, thought I might check it out while I was here. You want to come with me? I might get scared and need to hold your...hand."

"I'll pass, I've seen it before."

"Maybe I'll show you something new."

"There's nothing new," he said.

Coombes opened the door of his Dodge and climbed inside. There was a tap on the window. The reporter was leaning toward him, giving him an eyeful of cleavage.

She smiled, blew him a kiss, then took off toward the lake.

Sullivan was getting worse. It seemed like she was delivering lines meant for Marilyn Monroe in *Some Like it Hot*, equal parts child-like innocence and femme fatale seduction.

His cell phone rang and a picture appeared. Grace Sato, his partner.

"Hey, Grace, what did the DA want?"

"I've got a problem with an old case. Molly Walker. She was one of my first as a D-1. Her asshole husband drove over her with his SUV and claimed it was her fault. She's been PVS for three years until two weeks ago when she finally went to her reward."

"PVS?"

"Persistent vegetative state. It's like a coma but her eyes were open."

"Okay, go on."

"The thing is, we were lucky to get the case through the first time. Our case is full of holes and her husband was a criminal attorney. He knows how things work."

Coombes nodded to himself.

"Now she's dead, you'll have to re-file for manslaughter or he'll push for a habeas hearing. He'll know you have nothing if you don't. If you can't prove the higher threshold, he'll walk and sue the city for wrongful conviction, loss of earnings, repetitional damage."

Sato sighed.

"For sure. Walker has had an attorney coming and going at Terminal Island all week. He's ready to pull the trigger on a habeas petition no doubt at all. DA's filing new charges within the hour. Try and get a second miracle, keep this psychopath behind bars where he belongs."

It was an unfortunate turn of events, but none of it explained the dread in her voice, the fear. As a junior detective this wouldn't dent her career, probably not even the senior detective. Some cases, you just had to do the best you could with the evidence available.

"What does your partner from back then think?"

"Not much. Sarah Ryan is dead. With her gone, this falls on my shoulders and if he gets out, my career is going to flatline."

That wasn't it.

"What *aren't* you telling me?"

"Sarah didn't die of old age, Johnny. She was shot execution-style in the back of the head coming out her home. Point-blank range, small caliber round. Not three years ago, not last month. Ten days ago. A single day after Molly Walker died."

"Jesus Christ, Grace. Where are you right now?"

"Relax. I'm on Main, I'll be at my desk in five minutes."

"All right," he said. "Be safe."

"I know what you meant to say, Coombes."

4

Coombes drove to the Ahmanson Training Center on Manchester Avenue where archived murder books were now stored. The facility was part of the LAPD's academy and was staffed by recruits who one day might replace him on the front line.

In the homicide archive, he identified himself and gave the case number of the Dakota Lawrence murder book to a bored-looking recruit called Kline. The cadet scratched the number down, then disappeared into the stacks of binders.

There were thousands of them, all unsolved.

Coombes knew that most would never be solved and any that were would first require another person to lose their life to crack the case.

Minutes crawled by.

He imagined Kline out the back of the building somewhere smoking a joint, having forgotten all about the binder he was meant to be searching for on the endless shelves. Eventually, the young man reappeared, holding nothing more than a card.

The recruit had a smirk on his face, like he'd just heard a joke.

"Sorry, Detective, we don't have it."

"I thought they all came here from each of the divisions?"

"They did, unless they were already signed out. Then what happens is that a space is kept for it here, like a library book."

He assumed the card Kline held was a checkout card.

"So, who signed it out?"

"That's kind of the funny part. You did."

More smiles. He'd be telling the boys about this one.

Kline put the card down on the counter in front of Coombes so he could read it. His name was there, along with his badge number, serial number, and a date and time. There was no signature. According to the card, he'd checked the book out of the Hollywood Division archive four months after the investigation was abandoned and it had never been returned.

He glanced up. "I didn't check this out."

"Says you did."

"I see that, but there's no signature."

"Is that your badge number and serial number?"

Coombes glanced down again, double-checking them.

"Yes."

"Are you still at Hollywood?"

"No, RHD."

"Could you have forgotten you checked it out and left it at Hollywood?"

"No. Not with this case. *This* case I'll remember till I die. I'd know if I checked it out because this one gave me goddamn nightmares. Get the picture?"

His voice had become elevated, and the recruit took a step back. A man wearing a uniform appeared. A supervisor. His name badge said Brennan.

"Whatever happened to your book happened at Hollywood, not here. You've got no call to speak to my cadet like that, he was only trying to help."

"You're right." Coombes looked at Kline. "Sorry. This was an important case to me and I never closed it. I'm angry at myself and at this prick who used my ID. I got no problem with you, I apologize."

"All right," Brennan said. "This card is from before we centralized the books, it was a bit of a cowboy operation before. My guess is that it was another detective at Hollywood that used your ID."

This was profoundly unhelpful, but Coombes held his tongue and merely nodded. His anger had got the better of him once already.

"Thanks for looking anyway."

He turned to walk away when Brennan spoke again.

"If you manage to track it down, Detective, be sure to bring it here when you're done with it. We don't like gaps on the shelves."

"If I find it, I plan on closing the case."

"From your lips to God's ears."

Coombes walked back out to his Dodge and stood for a moment behind the wheel deep in thought. It was a gut-punch that someone should take this particular murder book. Of all the cases he'd worked, he would've wanted this book given the most protection.

Brennan was right.

He didn't see a civilian walking into Hollywood Division and taking the book from the archive there, it had to be a cop. His badge number and serial number wouldn't have been that hard to track down, they were on every case he ever touched.

The part he couldn't figure, was why a detective interested in the case would use his ID and not just fill in their own. The only thing that made sense, was if the book had been taken not to solve the case, but to kill it. With no murder book, all the original information was lost and there was no way to rebuild it.

His stomach rumbled.

He'd been on the road and had missed lunch so he decided to take advantage of his partner's absence and eat at the nearby In-N-Out Burger on Century Boulevard. Something about beef, and burgers in particular, put Sato's teeth on edge.

As he drove past LAX, no planes took off or landed.

5

WHEN HE GOT BACK to headquarters he found Grace Sato immersed in her case with the original filing package from the DA spread out before her. The paperwork looked light to his eye, but that was doubtless due to the open-and-shut nature that the case originally presented.

Sato turned to look up at him and made a face.

"What?" he said.

"You've eaten beef."

She could smell it on him, like he was a secret smoker.

"It was delicious, thanks for asking."

"You smell like ass, Coombes."

"Shall I go wash my hands and face?"

"*Please.*"

He'd said it as a joke, but he saw she was serious. Coombes hung his suit jacket on his chair and walked across the detective bureau to the wash room.

Anything for an easy life.

He rolled up his shirt sleeves and began to wash his hands. The soap did not smell good so he made sure to rinse it repeatedly off his skin. His hands were becoming dried-out from all the alcohol gel he was using. The week before, he'd managed to pull off a patch of skin.

Sullivan would let him eat beef, he thought.

Where had *that* thought come from?

Coombes glanced at himself in the mirror and shook his head.

The journalist had given him the smallest amount of attention and his ship was about to capsize. It was pathetic. He dried his hands and walked back to his desk.

He told Sato about the missing murder book over their desk divider.

"Is there another copy?"

"Only what's stored up here."

Coombes tapped the side of his head.

"Can I be brutally honest, Johnny?"

"Sure."

"You're fucked."

"Tell me about it. I was counting on that book for my new case."

"You're certain they're linked?"

"One hundred percent."

"I'm not going to be able to help you, I've got this to deal with."

"I guessed."

He sat in his chair and logged into his computer. No emails from Drake.

This would be because Drake was still in the field. To prevent the other man from forgetting his promise to send what he had, Coombes sent him an email with a friendly reminder on it.

He thought of the seedy-looking West LA detective.

Drake told him he'd been working the case for three days. In hindsight, that seemed like a long window of time for such a small dig site; it wasn't like Hahn's bones were scattered over a wide area, or that they didn't know where to look.

The ex-cop's dog had told them that.

Three days.

The only real question he had, was how much of that time the other detective had been sitting on the Natalie Hahn ID and debating whether to tell him about it.

After finding the note in the system, Drake would've looked him up to see who he was and if he was still working for the Department. Coombes could well imagine Drake's disgust at finding out he was and that he was now at Homicide Special.

So Drake sat on the information for as long as possible, hoping that the extra time would help him hold on to the case. Waiting until the archaeologist was about to pack up her team and head off home. Coombes decided not to get upset about it, as it was the type of play he might've made himself before he joined RHD.

As long as Drake didn't edit the chronology to hide it, he was fine.

He sighed. The Hahn dig site wasn't a crime scene, it was a grave. Beyond the wallet and the cut marks to her skull, there were no leads. He needed to go back to where it started, and find out where Natalie Hahn crossed paths with Dakota Lawrence's killer.

Coombes opened a legal pad and began to write down what he could remember about the Lawrence case, using targeted Google searches to pull additional information from the public domain. The murder had drawn a lot of media coverage due to her rising status in Hollywood, and to some coincidental parallels with the Elizabeth Short case.

Short, dubbed the Black Dahlia by the press, had gained in death a level of fame and immortality that went beyond the dreams of any Hollywood actor. Despite an unprecedented inter-agency task force of 750 investigators, her murder was never solved.

Both women had been perfect victims for the press.

Young, beautiful, and mysterious.

The kind of victim that drew an instant emotional response from the public.

Dakota Lawrence was found on a movie back lot on the last day of January, 2015. She was naked and posed as if she was a doll, her left forearm bent up, fingers closed around a handheld mirror. Like Short before her, Lawrence's pale body was initially mistaken for a store mannikin by a security guard who radioed in for a garbage collection.

The official cause of death was catastrophic blood loss leading to asphyxiation, the result of a six-inch cut to the throat. Additionally, a ligature, thought to be a lamp power cord, had been applied high on her neck and tightened with enough force to almost sever her head.

Although he had become jaded in the time since, Coombes could clearly remember walking toward the crime scene, toward Lawrence's propped-up head and the mark that had been left cut into it.

He worked for two hours, filling ten pages with notes and it was obvious only when he stopped that nothing he was able to produce would replace the missing murder book. To solve both cases, he would need to find the binder and its invaluable data.

"*John.*"

He turned to see Gantz standing next to him.

"My office."

His lieutenant's face was frozen and dark. Unreadable.

"Uh, sure."

She walked away without waiting for him. Coombes frowned, wondering if someone had filed a complaint against him. He immediately thought of Brennan and Kline at the Ahmanson. It didn't feel right, but what else was there?

Was Drake fighting for full control of the case?

He logged out of his terminal and walked into Gantz' office and saw Block sitting on the edge of his lieutenant's desk glaring at him. The desk was causing the fat in Block's legs to stretch his pants to the point where the material was puckered with stress.

Coombes nodded to both of them.

"Cap, L-T."

Block got right to it.

"I assume Sato's brought you up to speed on her habeas case?"

"Looks like Walker's going to walk."

"Cut the shit, Detective. We could be looking at a lot of heat on this. The city's already a powder keg due to the virus. The masks, the stay-at-home mandate. I don't want this asshat getting out his cage and suing us for millions. That could be the spark that sets us all on fire. We need a steady hand to smooth things out. Sato's only a D-I and I want more experience, so I'm putting Wallfisch on it."

Coombes laughed before he remembered Block wasn't exactly a comedian.

"Oh, you were serious."

"Thomas Wallfisch earned his spot here, Coombes. He didn't float in through the window on his looks and a cushy career in the Army like *some* people."

Gantz cut in before he could say anything.

"We're getting a little off track here."

Coombes was having none of it.

"Do you really think Tommy's experience working dead hooker cases twenty years ago will make a difference here? The man hasn't closed a case in four months."

"Watch that tone, Coombes. You're on thin ice already!"

Behind Block, Gantz made a rapid chopping movement with her hand across the base of her throat. Coombes was trying to work out why he was in the room and Sato wasn't, it didn't seem to involve him at all.

"Tell us about your bones case," Gantz said.

Coombes sighed inwardly. He knew *exactly* why she'd invited him into the room and it appeared she'd left Block out of the loop.

He gave them the highlights, emphasizing the victim's link to the Dakota Lawrence case to help justify its place as a RHD investigation. Block grew visibly annoyed and confused, not seeing where Gantz was going.

"Dakota Lawrence...that was what, six years ago?"

"Close enough."

Gantz nodded, like she didn't already know, while Block twisted around to look at her, his eyes narrowed in suspicion.

"And Hahn's been in the ground for all that time?"

"Looks like it."

Homicide Special wasn't a cold case unit, or *open-unsolved*, as the top brass preferred to call them. He didn't need Gantz to tell him that, nor the fact that the state of Hahn's body and clothing eliminated the possibility there would be DNA evidence to take them through to a speedy resolution.

"So," Gantz said. "It seems to me like this Lawrence - Hahn investigation might take a little time to bear any fruit. You might even call it a hobby case. That means you should have no problem fitting it around the Walker investigation with Sato."

And there it was.

Block jumped to his feet, eyes bulging out his head.

"This is *not* what we discussed!"

"I'll do it," Coombes said, more to jam up Block than anything else.

His captain puffed up his chest and glared up at him. It wasn't easy for him, there was a significant height difference between them. It was likely the reason, he thought, why Block had stayed seated for so long in the first place.

"I don't *want* you to do it, haven't you figured that out yet?"

"Like you said, Captain. We could be taking heat on this. TV news, City Hall, the District Attorney, not to mention the 10th floor. If this turns bad, the Department will be looking for a fall guy to take the blame...a limb to cut off to halt the infection."

Something reptilian moved behind Block's eyes. The puffed-up chest relaxed, and his captain took a step back. Block turned to Gantz.

"I think, ultimately, this is your decision, Ellen. Whatever you think's best."

Gantz gave him a plastic smile. "Of course."

Block left the room and neither of them said anything for a beat.

"Sorry, John. I know the Dakota case means something to you but I couldn't put Sato with Wallfisch. He'd crush her spirit like a bug on a windshield."

He knew she was right and it was the only reason he wasn't angry.

"She's not going to take this much better you know. Let me tell her, ok?"

"Get it done soon, John. And what you said about a fall guy-"

She didn't have to finish her sentence; he knew it perfectly well.

"By the way," he said. "Next time you need help with Block, give me a heads-up beforehand and I'll leave my firearm in my desk drawer before I come in here."

Coombes left without waiting for her to reply.

6

COOMBES SHARED AN APARTMENT with Sato on South Hill Street, a short distance from LAPD headquarters. He subleased the property for a fraction of its true value from someone whose life he'd saved the previous year. Due to the appearance of impropriety over the low lease, he had never declared his new address to the Department and had continued using a mail forwarding service he'd been using since his divorce.

Like a hotel, the building had its own gym, bar, restaurant, and pool for residents. However, because of COVID, only the restaurant kitchen remained open, with food being delivered to apartments and left sitting on the doormat in large cardboard boxes.

Which is where he found a delivery when he returned home.

Coombes unlocked the door and carried the food into the kitchen. He could tell what was inside without opening it, the spices seeped out around the edges of the board.

Sato padded in barefoot behind him wearing blue-black pajamas.

"I thought I heard the door."

She came up to him, stood on tiptoes, and they kissed.

Within these walls, they could be themselves with each other. It was a solid second reason for not updating his address with the LAPD.

"I got you firecracker, hope that's okay. If you're not into it, you can have some of my black bean, they always make more than I can eat anyway."

He smiled. Her mood had improved since he'd seen her last.

"Firecracker sounds good, thanks."

He took a beer from the fridge, then carried the food to the breakfast bar, which acted as an informal divider between the kitchen and living area. They ate and made small talk about a cop show they watched the night before and all the cop-stuff that the writers got wrong.

After eating only half his firecracker chicken, Coombes decided he'd had enough, doubtless because of the beer he'd drunk with it to put out the fire. He pushed it to one side and thought about how best to talk about the elephant in the room.

"What are the odds your old partner was targeted due to a different case?"

"Theoretically, high. She's closed a lot of cases, ruffled a lot of feathers."

"But you don't believe it."

"No."

Sato put her chopsticks down and looked away from him.

"Just tell me, Grace, you'll have to sooner or later."

"Okay, there's this other detective. She used to work RHD but she left before I arrived. Anyway, her name is Soto. We look nothing alike, and she's maybe twenty years older than me. Once or twice her mail has come to my desk when no first name is listed."

Coombes let out a breath.

"Soto's dead, isn't she?"

"Actually, no. She saw a reflection of a guy coming up behind her on her car window, didn't much like his face, so she put three holes in his liver."

He felt tension leave his chest.

"I'm glad to hear it."

"As am I, however, it means we can't tie this guy back to Walker."

"Who was he?"

"Some low-level skinhead attached to the Aryan Brotherhood. I guess Walker aligned with them for protection in Terminal Island and now has the clout to get them to do his bidding on the outside. Perhaps helping members with legal stuff to pay his way."

"Or promising them a slice of any lawsuit payout."

Sato nodded. "That too."

"Okay," he said. "We have to assume that word will get back to the shot caller that this guy messed up and someone else will be given the job. You and Soto are still at risk."

"I know. I wore my vest on the way home."

Coombes was quiet for a moment.

If the gunman had the right name, he wasn't sure Sato would've survived. She wasn't gun-orientated; she seemed to believe that it was a part of being a cop that she could leave behind now she was a detective.

"I don't want you leaving here or PAB alone until this is settled."

Sato stood abruptly and picked up her empty plate.

"This is why I didn't tell you anything before, John. I knew you'd over-react. I *knew* it! I actually considered not telling you. I'm a big girl, I can look after myself."

"I bet your former partner thought the same."

Sato pushed past him, toward the kitchen.

"You're insufferable!"

He'd heard that before.

Coombes watched her go and heard her plate smash in the sink. She stood there looking down at it, her hands gripping the counter on either side. After almost a minute, he walked into the kitchen and stood over by the refrigerator, out of range.

"I'd take a bullet for you, Grace. If you took one without me...I'd have to take a different one. That's just the way it is."

"I'm not asking you to do that."

Coombes said nothing for a moment.

He'd like to think that if a skinhead took a run at him, he'd manage the situation, just as Soto had. Sato clearly thought the same, and all he'd managed to do was insult her, perhaps even worry her. That hadn't been his intention.

"I'm sorry for what I said, it was out of order."

She nodded.

"I know why you said it. I think it's easier being the one in danger, you know? I've seen you risk your life enough times to know how *I* feel when that happens. It's shit."

"It really is," he said.

He moved closer and gave her shoulder a squeeze.

"I won't change how I live my life, Johnny. Not for this guy or his Nazi friends. Besides, I have this ex-Army nutcase near me almost all day. He's got too much testosterone but he means well and he's pretty handy in a fight."

Sato looked up at him and he kissed her on the forehead.

They picked up the pieces of her shattered plate and put them in the trash, then went into the living room where he saw she had her notebooks and laptop set up.

"It's strange," he said. "We're both working cases from our past. At least you got your mutt first time around, that's more than I can say about mine. Who knows what mine's been up to instead of rotting in a cage."

She sighed, and her shoulders dropped.

"I might need your help on this one, Coombes."

"I'm glad you feel that way, because Gantz put me on your case. You can probably guess who Block wanted to add to your investigation."

Sato looked like she wanted to be sick.

"Does Wallfisch have pictures of Block naked, or what?"

"No doubt."

"Walker's going to get away with it, I can feel it."

"That's not going to happen, ok?"

Sato wasn't buying what he was selling so he decided to let it go. She sat behind her laptop and pressed the spacebar to wake the screen, then glanced back up.

"Sorry, Johnny, I'm not going to be much company tonight."

"That's ok. I think I'll watch a couple of Joshua Booth movies."

"What will that achieve?"

Coombes shrugged.

"It's been a long time since I worked the Dakota Lawrence case. Everything fades. Memories, anger, inspiration. Without the murder book, the chances of catching her killer are likely zero. Anyway, I figure if I watch her last movie, it will put my brain back in the same state it was in when I worked the case."

"Is there a link between the movie and what happened to her?"

"Our prime suspect was Anthony De Luca. He produced the movie."

"Are you serious?"

"Yeah, but we couldn't make it stick. If we had, Hahn would still be alive."

"That's not on you."

"It *is* on me, Grace. That's how this gig works."

7

COOMBES LEFT SATO TO deal with her case and moved over to the sofa units. Their apartment was largely open plan with different areas for different functions. To compensate for this, he had purchased a pair of wireless headphones that allowed one of them to watch television or listen to music without disturbing the other.

He turned on the TV and put the headphones over his head.

They subscribed to four different streaming services and it took him the best part of fifteen minutes to discover there were no Joshua Booth movies on any of them. Instead, they were all on a high-end movie service apparently aimed at people who drank cognac and wore bow ties. Rather than sign up for another service he'd forget to cancel, he just bought the two movies he was interested in.

Fallen Idol and *Carnival of Delights*.

The movies Booth made before and after Dakota Lawrence's murder.

He cued up *Fallen Idol* then walked through to the kitchen and got himself a beer from the fridge. Coombes sat his notebook and pen on the table in front of him in case he wanted to make some notes and pressed play.

The movie opened with a back shot of Dakota Lawrence standing looking out a window wearing a thin nightdress. He'd read that the shot was inspired by the Salvador Dali painting *Girl at a Window*. Art was a huge influence in Booth's work, with the result that every shot looked like it could be printed out and framed.

When Lawrence turned away from the window the camera moved forward, closing in tight on her head and shoulders. Her eyes were red and tears were running down her face, smudging her make-up. The camera held on her face, feasting on her distress.

Her face was alive with emotion and all of it looked real.

Even like this, Dakota Lawrence was stunning, a classical beauty.

The lighting changed from soft to hard and her tears stopped.

She walked out the room and through an apparently empty Spanish Colonial mansion, her bare feet silent on the tile floors. A distant voice could be heard and she moved toward it. An older man stood on a balcony wearing a white suit, talking on a cell phone and holding a cigar with his other hand. He seemed to sense her approach and turned to face her. His skin was deeply wrinkled and leathery. Old enough to be her grandfather.

He smiled at her. It was a nasty smile, a sick smile.

Not her grandfather.

She ran toward him arms wide as if to embrace him, then at the last second brought her arms forward and pushed him over the stone balustrade into space. The camera followed him out over the edge, where he hung briefly in super slow-mo before returning to normal speed and falling fast onto a Ferrari, blowing out all the windows and setting off the alarm.

Lawrence sighed with near-sexual satisfaction, then walked down a staircase into the courtyard where his body lay smashed against the car. The sound of the alarm faded away, replaced by the husky sound of her breathing, and the steady beat of her heart.

She walked to the Ferrari and angled her head to look into the old man's sightless eyes one last time. Blood was pooling next to his face. She reached out and moved her fingers through the blood until they were thickly coated with it. Lawrence raised her hand in front of her face and studied her fingers as if she thought it might all be a dream. After a moment, she brought her fingers up to her lips and put them inside her mouth.

The opening titles rolled.

Booth knew how to open a movie, that was for sure.

This would be the fifth time he'd watched *Fallen Idol* but none of those times overlapped with when Dakota Lawrence had been alive. Every time he'd seen it, he carried the knowledge of her grim death. The way she looked at the crime scene, and the way she looked with her chest cut open, organs being lifted out to be weighed.

From movie star, to the morgue table.

It was impossible to reconcile the two versions he had of her, so he did what he always did, he drank some beer. For the next hour and forty-eight minutes, she was alive, if only on his television.

When the movie ended, Coombes found that he'd written nothing in his notebook, the same as every other time he'd watched it. Nevertheless, the fire to catch her killer was once again, furnace-hot so he didn't view it as a waste of time.

He cued up *Carnival of Delights*, then went to get another beer.

It seemed to him like he might need the beer, for an entirely different reason. The reviews for the movie were terrible. As he walked back past Sato, she looked up at him, a look of concern on her face.

"You haven't got *Laura Syndrome*, have you?"

She was asking if he'd fallen in love with the victim.

"Some get under your skin more than others."

"Want me to take your mind off it for a while?"

"No, I'm going to watch another movie before it gets too late."

"Damn. I just can't compete with a dead girl."

He leaned down and they kissed. It felt like the first time, it always did. Probably that meant something, he thought, as he sat back down in front of the television.

Carnival was universally acknowledged to be Booth's worst movie and because of that, Coombes had never made any effort to see it. At its premier in Cannes, the audience had famously cheered as it started and booed when it finished. Many had walked out before it ended. He wondered how much of it he'd sit through himself and why, if it was such a lemon, it had cost him almost twice as much to buy as Booth's gothic classic *Fallen Idol*.

Within a minute, his purchase had paid for itself.

Improbably, his dead eyewitness was the star of the movie.

8

WHEN COOMBES LOOKED AT his notebook the next morning his excitement of the night before faded and the significance of his dead eyewitness in *Carnival of Delights* became obscured. Anthony De Luca now had two more names beneath it.

Joshua Booth.

Scott Peters.

He saw that Sato was ready to go and he walked with her to the door. The apartment no longer had a peephole as it had been removed in order to fit a doorbell camera, so he had to pause and look at his cell phone to check that there was no Nazi assassin waiting outside the door ready to strike.

The hallway was empty.

Since they'd moved in, the hallway had always been empty. He'd never seen any of his neighbors coming or going to the elevator. The walls were so well soundproofed it felt like they were the only ones who lived in the building.

Coombes put away his cell phone and, with his right hand resting on his Glock, opened the door with his left. They walked out into the hallway and Sato locked the door while he fixed his eye at the blind spot next to the elevator, the next place where an assassin could be waiting.

"Johnny, this is ridiculous."

He said nothing and walked along the hallway, drawing his Glock and aiming it down at the floor. Using his arm, he indicated for her to hug the wall closest to the elevators so that he was on the far side. If a skinhead was standing in the blind, he would see him first and Sato would be hidden by the wall.

There was no one there.

Coombes started to relax. It was possible the Aryan Brotherhood didn't know where she lived, few people did. Maybe they were waiting outside the address Sato had filed with the Department.

"Just wait there until I check the elevator."

"You're pissing me off, Coombes. I didn't agree to this."

Nevertheless, she stood short of the corner and waited for him to press the call button. A single elevator served the whole building. If there was a fire, they had to rely on stairs around the other side of the building to get out.

The elevator pinged and the doors opened.

A man stood there with a bald head and a leather jacket.

He lifted his Glock and aimed center mass. The man froze, his eyes wide. It took Coombes a second to process that the man was old and he was holding a small dog in his hands. It was one of his neighbors.

He lowered his weapon and holstered it.

"Sorry, Mr. Mayor."

"I'm not the mayor anymore, son. You're the cop?"

"Yes, sir. I mistook you for someone else."

The former mayor glanced across at Sato, who was wearing her bulletproof vest over her suit jacket.

"Have the coyotes located the henhouse?"

"Something like that," she said.

The elevator doors began to close and it seemed to bring everyone back into the moment. The former mayor caught the closing door with his free hand and they swapped positions so that they were inside the elevator and the old man was in the hall.

"There was a man on the first floor when I got on, looked like he was waiting for someone. Just thought I'd mention it."

"A skinhead?"

The old man smiled a little.

"No, a Latino. A bike messenger maybe."

Coombes nodded.

"Thanks anyway."

The doors closed once again and they plummeted toward street level.

Inside the elevator he again had Sato stand to one side so she did not present an immediate target to anyone waiting in the lobby. It was possible the Brotherhood could've handed off the job to an outside contractor after the failure of their previous assassin.

To his disappointment, the doors opened and the lobby was clear.

"See, Johnny? I'm fine. They hit Sarah Ryan two weeks ago. If they'd wanted me, they would have come for me before now."

"I think you're right."

The parking garage was also clear. This came as no surprise to him, as in some ways, it was more secure than the lobby or the apartment building. They climbed into the Dodge. He left his seatbelt off in case he needed to quickly get out the vehicle and placed his sidearm under his left leg where he would be able to easily draw it.

The car's bucket seats blocked his holster.

He drove around to the exit and the transponder clipped to the sun visor automatically triggered the rolling metal shutter that kept undesirables out the garage. There was a convex mirror mounted high up on the corner to assist residents getting out onto the street.

South Hill was quiet. It was early, and the virus had removed more than half the traffic. He got straight out and let out a sigh. They were in the clear.

He pulled his seatbelt across and clipped himself in.

As he glanced across to his side mirror to change lanes, he saw a black Ford Explorer that had been parked half up on the sidewalk drop down and fall into line behind him. The back window of his Charger was covered in a film of city dirt, he could see nothing of the SUV's driver or license plate.

He turned on 9th Street and again on Main.

The Explorer came with them.

For a tail, it lacked subtlety.

"I told you we'd be fine," Sato said.

Her face had lost the tension from the apartment and the spark was back in her eyes again. He decided not to mention the Ford for now.

The light changed on him at the 6th Street intersection. He considered coasting through the red to trap his follower on the other side, then decided against it. That would simply alert his tail that they'd been made and the next time it would be a different vehicle.

Better to know a threat than to be blind to it.

"Tell me about Dakota Lawrence."

He glanced at Sato.

"You didn't read about the case? It was everywhere."

"I meant tell me what *wasn't* in the papers."

"Some creep knocked her out, then tortured her. But that first blow? It was so hard that it would've killed her no matter what happened after. So, technically, the murder weapon was not the blade that cut her throat, but that first weapon, whatever it was."

Sato was silent for moment.

"Then our cases have a lot in common."

He didn't know what this meant, but he nodded anyway.

The Explorer followed them all the way to the Police Administration Building and only left them when their car dropped down into the underground parking structure. The SUV went around them and he slowed more than usual so that he could catch the other vehicle's license plate which he committed to memory.

"I have an errand to run before I look at your Walker case."

Sato's mood had cleared and she was her normal bright self.

"That's fine, Johnny. Now the DA's re-filed we've pushed back the time-line, got this guy on the back foot."

He dropped her near the elevator and re-holstered his weapon. This done, he made a quick note of the Explorer's license plate to check later. Coombes looked up from his notebook in time to see Sato turn back and see him watching her.

She made a shooing gesture for him to go away.

Coombes drove back out onto the street. There was no black Explorer waiting for him. He decided it didn't matter if they changed the Ford for another vehicle. His guard was raised now. Whatever they used, he was certain he'd pick it up quickly.

He headed to Boyle Heights.

9

COOMBES KEPT A FADED yellow Post-It Note stuck to his monitor. Before that, it had been on three previous monitors, as he made his way through the ranks to RHD. The note acted as a constant reminder to help focus every investigation. It said simply:

Who benefits?

Correlation does not imply causation.

Means, motive, and opportunity.

He supposed that *motive* and *who benefits* were the same, but he liked the purity of the separate version at the beginning of a case.

It was hard to look at a studio photograph of Dakota Lawrence's perfect face and think anyone could *benefit* from her death, but it was far more likely than being murdered by a random psychopath for no reason.

Statistically, the person who killed her was someone she knew.

A best friend, a lover.

Someone close, above suspicion.

Lawrence's body had been found on a studio lot where access was controlled by a gatehouse and a guard. To gain access, you had to have a right to be there. However, the first time Coombes and his partner cruised up to the gate they'd been waved straight through without a challenge.

He assumed the guard simply recognized them as the detectives they were, or had seen the internal police strobes mounted next to their rearview mirror, but the incident forever caused him to question the studio's security.

Since statistics favored a killer that was already known to Lawrence, and her body was found in a controlled area, it was assumed her killer either worked for the studio that owned the lot, or one of the production companies that rented space there.

The 6th Street Viaduct had been removed due to bad concrete, so he crossed the L.A. River using the 7th Street Bridge, and turned up onto Whittier Boulevard.

Nobody was following him, either because he wasn't the target, or because his quick turnaround in the parking garage was unexpected.

His mind turned back to his old case.

Joshua Booth and Dakota Lawrence had dated during the filming of *Fallen Idol* and there were multiple reports of heated arguments between the pair both on and off-set. It wasn't hard for Coombes to imagine one of these arguments taking a dark turn, nor of the director framing her murder as the work of a psychopath as a misdirect.

On the face of it, Booth was good for the crime.

Then, almost overnight, he was eliminated as a person of interest.

Two eyewitnesses placed Lawrence at a party held at Anthony De Luca's home hours before she was found dead. The last sighting of her alive. They said she spent most of the night in a room alone with De Luca, who appeared to be plying her with alcohol.

Booth was not at the party.

Neither, said De Luca, was Lawrence.

Natalie Hahn and Scott Peters had taken the crosshairs off Booth's chest and it never returned. It didn't feel anywhere close to a coincidence that both eyewitnesses appeared in *Carnival of Delights* or that Hahn was now dead.

He parked outside the address listed on Peters' driving license and killed the engine. Like the rest of L.A., the street was full of cars. Residents were home, not at work.

Coombes stepped out and glanced quickly around as he shut the car door.

He walked up to Peters' front door and rang the doorbell. After about half a minute, a black man weighing at least 300 pounds appeared wearing sweatpants and a vest. His body almost perfectly filled the door frame.

"Fuck are you?"

"LAPD," Coombes said, tapping his badge. "Who are *you?*"

"You come to *my* house and you ask who *I* am? Get lost, cop."

"Let's try this another way. I'm looking for Scott Peters. I know that's not you, but this is the address I have for him."

"I've lived here for three years, man. Just me, no dudes."

"Who owned the house before you?"

The other man laughed and Coombes took a step back as he imagined an invisible COVID dispersal cloud that he'd seen on the news.

"Are you for real? I don't own this place. Who owns anything in L.A.? I rent, same as everyone else. I don't know who rented it before me."

"You never got mail addressed to the previous tenant?"

He could see he'd scored a hit.

"Actually, yeah. But it was junk. Credit card applications, like that."

"And the name listed was Scott Peters?"

"It could've been, I don't remember. I saw it wasn't for me and binned it. That kind of mail I toss even if it *is* for me, you know what I mean? Nobody opens that shit."

Coombes nodded. He knew it.

"Any of your neighbors likely to remember my guy?"

The big man glanced briefly over Coombes' shoulder.

"The old bat across the street. Bitch spends all day looking out her window. If anyone knows, it's her. Probably got it written down, license numbers, times, descriptions."

"Thank you for your time, sir."

"Wait a minute. You're a detective, right?"

Coombes turned back. "That's right."

"He's killed someone, hasn't he? The guy that lived here."

"No, I just need to locate him to get a statement. To be clear, however, I don't want you putting something on your socials that we're looking for him. If you tell someone else and *they* put it on *their* socials the shit rolls back to you, ok? Obstruction of a police officer is good for a year in county or $1,000 in fines."

"What happened to the First Amendment?"

"All freedoms come at a cost."

Coombes crossed the street to a bungalow with an orange tile roof. The front door was sheet metal with an iron gate in front of it. He wondered if the big man had sent him to some gangbanger's house for a laugh. Whoever lived here, took security seriously.

He raised his hand to the doorbell when a voice came through the steel.

"What do you want?"

The old bat had seen him approach. She really did spend her day at the window.

"LAPD, ma'am. Open the door."

"You got a warrant?"

"I need your assistance, you're not in any trouble."

He heard locks being turned and the sheet metal part of the door opened, leaving the bars in place. A SWAT team couldn't get past this woman. She stepped to the side so that a strip of sunlight fell across her face and the left half her body. She was black and somewhere between 80 and 800 years old. Her skin looked like fossilized leather.

"Hold up your ID card, not the badge."

He sighed and did so. It was her right to ask.

"All right, Detective John Coombes, what do you want?"

"Before we get to that, I want you to put down the weapon and put both your hands on the bars where I can see them."

He'd only guessed about the weapon, but he saw her arm straighten at the shoulder like she was propping a shotgun against the door frame. Her hands came up onto the bars.

"Ask your question, son. I'm missing *MacGyver* for this."

"I'm looking for Scott Peters, used to live across the street."

"I remember. Didn't really fit into the area, know what I mean?"

"Because he was white?"

The woman grinned at him. Half her teeth were missing.

"That, and the other reason."

"Which was?"

"He was queer. Brought men back here all the time. Only, they *weren't* men. They were skinny Mexican boys that looked like they were 12 years old. Weighed less than me, those boys, and I'm just bone."

Coombes let a couple of seconds drift by before continuing.

"Ma'am, we're trying to locate Mr. Peters and the man across the street said you might be able to help."

"Yeah? How's that?"

"I was hoping you might remember the last time you saw Mr. Peters. Perhaps even the day he moved out. Was he coming and going all day with a car, did he have a van, or did he just disappear in the middle of the night? That's what I'm after."

"One moment, I'll get my book."

The woman disappeared into her home before re-emerging with an inch-thick notebook. She turned the pages quickly, looking for the information. It looked like the pages had been well-thumbed, the corners were turning up with wear.

"Here we go. February 18th. Pervert finally moving out," the woman glanced up. "That's what I called him, The Pervert."

"I got that, thanks."

The woman continued to read.

"Pervert got his whole life in a tiny U-Haul. One trip."

"He hired a U-Haul? That's good. Anything else?"

The woman grinned again.

"I spelled 'whole' without the w."

Coombes closed his own notebook and nodded.

"I'll let you get back to *MacGyver*."

After dead bodies, dealing with people was the aspect he hated most about the job.

IO

Joshua Booth ran a production company called *Son of a Gun* out of an anonymous glass-and-steel building on Barton Avenue in Hollywood. Coombes parked on the street in front of the building and saw that there were plenty of spaces. The last time he'd been here, he'd had to walk several blocks from an almost-full parking lot. Now there was room to land a light aircraft. It occurred to him that with the film industry in shutdown there was a good chance that Booth might be at home, or trapped somewhere overseas.

So be it.

He took off his sunglasses and stepped out his Dodge.

The sun was blazing and there was no breeze to move it around. Coombes crossed the street and entered the office building which was cool enough to store fruit. He took the elevator to the top floor and approached the company's reception desk.

A nervous-looking woman stared at him, like she expected him to rob her.

"I'm here to see Joshua Booth."

"Do you have an appointment?"

Coombes never called ahead, even though that sometimes meant he arrived at a location when his target was elsewhere. Phoning ahead was like playing poker and letting your opponent see your cards.

"No. Tell him John Coombes is here, he'll see me."

The receptionist nodded, reassured by his friendly confidence that he wasn't a writer, or some other type of psychopath. She lifted her telephone to her ear then moved the mouthpiece down to speak over it while she waited for Booth to pick up.

"What company do you represent, Mr. Coombes?"

"The Los Angeles Police Department."

Her eyes opened wide in surprise. He heard a man's voice through the telephone handset which was still at an angle. *Booth*. He was in, she couldn't pretend he wasn't.

"There's a...Detective John Coombes here to see you."

He smiled at her for guessing *detective*, he hated when people introduced him as a *police officer*, although he was that too. The call was short, no more than a couple of words before she hung up the handset.

"If you'd like to come this way."

He followed her down a hallway and she held open a door for him. She didn't offer him a coffee, or a bottle of water, she just closed the door again and left. Fair enough. He'd finessed his entry to prevent from being stonewalled, but she didn't have to like it.

"Just give me a minute to finish up and you'll have my full attention."

"No problem."

Booth was seated at his desk, head down, hands busy with something in front of him. There was a scraping sound and Coombes took a couple of steps closer and looked at what the director was doing. He saw sheets of paper spread across the wood and long rectangles filled with dark pencil drawings.

Storyboards.

Booth was working on a new film. Imagining scenes, camera angles. Nobody was shooting movies and the theaters were all closed, but work continued in the background, preparing for the day when reality could resume.

Coombes frowned.

When he'd got out his car, he hadn't put his mask on. After wearing masks for months, he'd simply forgotten it like it was from another lifetime.

He thought back to the dig site the day before and realized he hadn't been wearing one then either. It was an outdoor space; it didn't matter so much.

"You want me to wear a mask?"

The director spoke without looking up.

"Don't bother. Everyone's going to get the virus, Detective, it's inevitable. A piece of fabric over your mouth isn't going to change that. In fact, I've had it three times already."

Booth echoed what Coombes had been thinking for months now. Whether a mask worked or not, nobody was prepared to wear one for the rest of their lives. It wasn't tenable. Therefore, the only point to debate was when the mask mandate was going to end.

Coronavirus was out there and it wasn't going away.

While he waited for the director to finish up, he looked around the room and thought about what he was going to ask the other man. Booth's office was exactly as he remembered it. One end had his desk setup and the other end had a four-seat sofa opposite a large television. It looked like the director took frequent naps on the sofa.

The end wall contained three rows of eight framed movie posters of the great man's work. Coombes walked over for a closer look at the posters.

With two exceptions, each one was a masterpiece.

"Apologies. When I'm in the zone I like to finish what I'm doing."

He turned to see Booth standing just behind him.

The man moved silently, like a panther. It was the first time since he'd arrived that he'd seen the director's face.

Joshua Booth had a three-day-old black eye.

"I understand," Coombes said. "I'm the same way."

"How you do anything is how you do everything."

"I *like* that."

"Not mine, I'm afraid." Booth paused. "Were you popular in high school?"

"Not really. I didn't fit in with any of the tribes."

"You were an outlier."

"I guess. I was big for my age so I could've been a jock. I was on the football team, maybe that makes me one regardless. I hated those guys; they were all bullies. They knew to watch themselves around me. I caught them picking on someone, I'd kick their ass."

Booth seemed to like that answer and nodded enthusiastically.

"You watch movies?"

"Sure, who doesn't?"

"I suppose you like all those superheroes?"

"No, that's not me at all."

Booth smiled. "And why's that?"

"I don't believe the heroes. All light, no shadow. Nobody is like that, people are complex. Anyway, I always found the villains more interesting and believable."

Booth clapped his hands loudly together.

"Exactly right!"

The office door opened and the receptionist stood in the gap looking more nervous than ever. It was clear to Coombes that she'd been standing at the door listening, that she hadn't run all the way from the front desk.

"Everything's fine, Janice."

The door closed again.

"Jesus, I can't react in any way without her thinking I'm under attack."

It was an obvious point to ask about the black eye, but he left it alone.

"Why did you ask me about high school?"

"Just testing a private theory of mine."

"Which is?"

"People who were popular at high school care less about the underdog, because they just can't imagine themselves in that position. They see that person as weak, pathetic. Well, I *was* that person in high school, Detective.

I was bullied. Every movie I have ever made is about an underdog, because that's who I am."

Coombes said nothing, the other man was on a roll.

"I saw you looking at the posters. The good guys, the bad guys. It's a cliché of course, but all of them are me. I empathize with the most twisted killers because to a man they were all badly treated as they grew up. It only takes a couple of setbacks to change the course of a man's life from one as a cop, to one as a killer, or perhaps, a movie director."

Coombes nodded.

"We're all capable of murder if the right conditions are met."

"That sentence is pretty much why I'm here. Why are *you* here?"

He hadn't expected that, but Coombes let nothing show.

"Are you good with faces, Mr. Booth?"

"Not too bad, why?"

"But I take it you don't recognize me."

"No, sorry. What context should I know you?"

"The context of me standing right here in your office six years ago."

The director's face darkened.

"You were one of the detectives that investigated Dakota's murder."

"That's right. I assumed you would remember my name."

"I drank a lot back then. Both before and after. Especially after. I drank to forget, but it didn't work the way I wanted. I still remember what I'd rather forget, but I have forgotten things I should remember. I made *Carnival of Delights* and I cannot remember a single thing about it, not even visiting the sound stage. One minute I'm doing auditions, the next I'm on a press tour in Cannes trying to talk about it."

It seemed that Booth was more interested in explaining his memory lapse, than finding out why a homicide detective was back in his office.

"I was the junior detective back then and my partner was kind of toxic, so I don't blame you if your focus was on him."

The director sat heavily on the sofa and rested his elbows above his knees. It was a stable position. If someone thought they were about to pass out, they sat the same way. Elbows on knees, head dipped, leaning forward.

"It doesn't look good, does it? That I didn't ask about Dakota, or if there have been any developments. I mean, why else would you be in my office?"

Booth wanted to be reassured that he wasn't a suspect, but Coombes merely nodded and took out his notebook.

"In fact, I'm *not* here about Dakota. Well, not directly."

"No? What then?"

"I'm here about Natalie Hahn."

Coombes watched Booth closely. His face looked pale, and there was a vibration to the end of his little finger that hadn't been there before.

"What about her?"

"Well, she's dead. I'm a homicide cop, remember?"

"Oh, god."

"You probably won't remember on account of the drinking, but back then, Natalie came forward to place Dakota Lawrence alive two days after she left your home in Silver Lake. Both she, and another actor called Scott Peters, said she was at a party held by your producer up in Laurel Canyon."

Both of Booth's hands were vibrating now, his eyes moving around the room as if for a script he could pick up and start reading lines of dialogue to replace the words that were missing from his throat.

"You think the murders are connected?"

"Of course."

"And what is the connection?"

"You, obviously."

Coombes smiled and he saw Booth wither.

"Surely you don't think I killed Dakota and Natalie?"

Coombes ignored this.

"Who's in charge of casting your lead actors?"

"Me, Tony, and Fran."

"Tony being Anthony De Luca?"

Booth seemed to shrink before him. "Yes."

"All right. Who's Fran?"

"Fran Knudsen. She's casting director on all our projects."

He wrote this in his notebook, even though he knew who she was and her job title. The main thing for an interviewee to understand was that when they said something, it was for keeps. It was in the notebook. Changing the story later, whatever story that was, would be noticed. Coombes looked up.

"I find it interesting that Hahn and Peters were in *Carnival of Delights,* the movie you made after Lawrence's murder. After that, they never acted again, not even in a dog food commercial. I saw the movie last night and both of them sucked. In hindsight, it looks like they got their parts as a thank-you for lengthening a victim timeline to make it appear that you were not the last person to see Lawrence alive."

Booth stared at him, swallowing repeatedly.

"How do I disprove something that isn't true?"

Coombes nodded. It was a problem he faced all the time.

"With Hahn dead, I'd normally re-corroborate her story with Peters..."

He let his voice trail off and shrugged, like the other man would know the problem.

"What? *Scott's* dead too?"

Booth's voice was almost hysterical. He made a note of it.

"Let's just say that I'm having difficulty locating him. I was hoping that you might be able to point me in the right direction. His address would square this away very quickly."

He heard a chirp and Booth dug out his cell phone and began to type away on it, ignoring the fact that he was in the middle of a police interview. None of this surprised Coombes, it was just the world they lived in. Being rude didn't mean you were a murderer.

When Booth finished typing, he stood up.

His cheeks were pink again, the vibration in his hands gone.

The brief session on his cell phone seemed to have restored the director's composure and confidence. It was too bad. Coombes preferred interviewees on the ropes, struggling to breathe, as they tended to make more mistakes.

"Detective, I make small movies by industry standards, but each one employed 30 to 60 people. Spread across twenty-four movies, that's a lot of addresses to expect me to keep track of and, the truth is, being a director does not make you a lot of friends. You can't care about actors' feelings *and* make a good movie. I shout at them for 12 hours at a time. They don't want to see me again at the weekend for a barbecue and beers, they just want paid."

"I don't *expect* you to remember an address, Booth. I *expect* you to have it on a computer somewhere, perhaps even on your cell phone. Then, I *expect* you to give me the addresses, or any other damn thing I ask for, without a warrant. Because you want to help me solve this before this killer strikes again. Your address details for Peters are likely no better than the one I already ran down, but that's *my* call, not yours."

It was the first time that he'd lent on Booth and it worked.

"Of course! I'll have Janice provide you with whatever you need."

Coombes looked at the movie posters again to let his anger dissipate.

When he'd looked up information on each movie, he'd used IMDb. The Internet Movie Database held a wealth of movie information. He'd seen cast lists, descriptions, box office numbers, and movie stills. But he'd not seen the movie poster that came out to promote each movie, nor had he seen them all side-by-side like this.

Between separate browser tabs, a blind spot had appeared.

In each movie, the female lead was a blonde with shoulder-length hair. Some had a curl in their hair, others not. In either case, they could all pass for sisters. It was doubtless why they'd been chosen by Booth, if not by their killer, assuming the two were not the same.

He turned to face the director.

"Did you have a sexual relationship with Natalie Hahn?"

The question was out of left field and Booth rocked back on his heels. An easy ten seconds drifted by before the director nodded.

"Just like you had a relationship with Dakota Lawrence."

They'd covered this last time around.

"Yes."

"How long were you in a relationship with Natalie?"

"Three months? Something like that."

"Just to save me some time here, should I assume that you form intimate relationships with *all* your leading ladies?"

"That would not be accurate."

"Come off it, Booth. I'm going to find this out anyway. If you block me then it looks like you have something to hide. That's not something you want to do in a homicide investigation. So, tell me who else."

The director thought for a moment before walking over to the wall to point at women on four different movie posters.

"You slept with those four as well?"

Booth shook his head.

"No. *Not* those four. The others. It's how I work, they become my muse."

Coombes sighed. Hollywood was a gutter bigger than the L.A. River.

"I'm going to need to photograph these posters."

11

COOMBES STOPPED AT A roach coach on the way back to the PAB that he knew served coffee. A lot of bricks-and-mortar stores remained closed due to the pandemic and, judging by the line of uniformed cops, the food truck was doing good business serving the LAPDs needs. When he got to the front of the line, he ordered his coffee and took it over to one of the tables set up around the vehicle.

He took out his iPad and brought up the *L.A. Times* website to check that his cold case remained buried from the public eye. He saw no trace of it and felt himself relax.

The table vibrated against his hands and he looked up.

Monica Sullivan sat opposite him with a big smile on her face. She was closer than the last time they met, and he noticed for the first time that a constellation of light freckles ran across her cheekbones and the top of her nose. It looked like an artist had sprayed them on with an airbrush.

Fairy kisses, that's what his mom used to call them.

The freckles were beautiful and he allowed himself to look at them for close to ten seconds. Again, Sullivan's cheeks grew red. For a journalist, she had no game face at all.

"What now, Sullivan?"

"It's just...you haven't looked at me like that for a while."

He told himself to forget about the damn freckles and took a mouthful of coffee, his gaze drifting off to the other tables. He saw no patrol cops he knew, but most probably recognized him from the *Ferryman* case the year before which had put him on the nightly news on several occasions.

"Don't get me wrong, Coombes, I could get used to you looking at me like that."

He closed the cover of his iPad so that she didn't see what he'd been looking at and placed it on the table next to his coffee. Sullivan's perfume was rolling across the space between them now, he was breathing it in.

"You shouldn't be this close to me, Sullivan."

She leaned closer still, over the table.

"Because you're *attracted* to me?"

He sighed. "Because of COVID."

Her voice dropped to a low whisper.

"I'll risk it. You look healthy."

They were a foot apart. If he leaned forward the way she was, he could kiss her. Coombes sat back in his seat to recover some personal space. He was falling for her stupid flirty act, the same as every other loser.

"I suppose you being here is a remarkable coincidence."

"Not really," she said. "I followed you from Booth's office."

His face must've fallen, because she smiled again.

Maybe his own game face wasn't that good either. He supposed that she had a black Ford Explorer and that another mystery was solved. When he said nothing, she continued.

"I take it from your expression that he's a suspect?"

"I can't comment on an active investigation."

Sullivan laughed. It was a honking, goofy laugh that was somehow charming. He saw the cops sitting at other tables turn their way.

"So," she said. "How many of his movies have you seen?"

"All of them."

"Then you're a fan?"

"His stuff's different, I like that. You never know what you're going to get."

"It's not generic."

"*Right.*"

"How many of his movies did you see at a theatre?"

Coombes didn't have to think about it.

"None. I watch them on TV. Usually late at night with a beer."

Sullivan nodded.

"That doesn't surprise me. Everybody knows his movies, but almost nobody pays to watch them. Most are flops at the box office. A couple are in the black by single digit millions on high double-digit costs."

"People don't go to the movies to think."

"He makes art, not money. That's one of his expressions by the way. He doesn't even try to be commercial. He caters to a small die-hard fanbase that go to see all of his movies, he would never dream of selling out and making a big blockbuster. It would probably give him a stroke."

Sullivan was going somewhere and Coombes wasn't certain where.

"Why are you telling me this?"

"What's the obvious question, Detective?"

"Why would investors continue to give him money he's certain to lose?"

"Correct."

"So, what's the answer?"

"That I can't tell you, but I do know that the IRS has taken a frequent interest in his finances. I'm told he paid $20 million for his new home. It doesn't take a genius to know that something's not right."

"Follow the money," Coombes said.

Sullivan said it right back to him, like it was an incantation.

"Thanks, this has been helpful."

He stood, picked up his coffee and tablet, then walked toward his car. Sullivan got around in front of him on the sidewalk, blocking his way.

"I'm not here to be helpful, Coombes. I want in."

"How would that work? You told me once before that there was no sitting on information anymore. I tell you something, the next minute people are reading about it on the *Times* website? That doesn't work for me."

"The crime beat is dead right now. The virus has squashed everything flat. You know the expression *if it bleeds, it leads*? Well, nothing's bleeding. The populace is sitting at home getting fat and watching TV, nobody's out there murdering people. Your investigation is all I'm interested in right now. I figure that we might be able to help each other out."

He reflected that with Sato tied up, Sullivan could be helpful.

"What is it you think you could offer the investigation?"

"Before I worked the crime desk, I worked entertainment and celebrity. I have a lot of background on the people you're looking at, not to mention contacts that don't talk to cops and resources within the *Times*. We'd be a good fit you and me."

There was a real sparkle in her eye now.

"I'll think about it."

"*Think about it* means no, say yes."

In the most casual way possible, she touched his bare forearm and gave it a squeeze. Her hand was warm and the hairs on his arm stood on end.

"If we do this, you need to stop doing that."

"What?"

"The flirting. I like you Sullivan, probably more than I should, but I'm in a relationship. This right here, is going nowhere."

"I like you, too, cop. This is just who I am. I'm *bubbly*."

Her hand was still on his arm. The heat of it was surging around his body.

"Dial it down or we have no deal, ok?"

Sullivan removed her hand and stepped back. "How's this?"

She was still smoldering.

"Outstanding."

"Do we have a deal? I already held up my end at Franklyn Canyon Park."

He supposed that if he said no to this deal then there was a chance that Sullivan would go back on the previous deal and release what she had about Natalie Hahn and her link to the murder of Dakota Lawrence.

"All right. But you don't investigate anything I don't ask you to, you don't publish anything before we get to the end, and you stop pretending that you're a cop."

She squealed then rushed forward and put her arms around his neck, their bodies pressed together. He had a coffee in one hand and his iPad in the other, he couldn't detach her. After a beat she released him and stepped back.

"Sorry! No touching, got it. I'm just so excited."

"*Right.*"

He walked on to his Dodge, trying to forget the way her body felt against him and hoping she would leave. Instead, she fell into step next to him. He glanced across at her and saw she was smiling again. There was something predatory about the way she smiled and he knew he'd made a mistake agreeing to her partnership.

"What do you want me to do first?"

He saw that if he didn't give her something, she'd only continue to follow him around, potentially giving away a lot of his investigation. He would never have told her about Booth, but now that she had his name, she might as well work on that.

"I thought we decided. Follow the money."

"You want me to do what the IRS couldn't?"

"Sullivan, you could get blood out of a stone. You've got this."

He put his coffee cup on the roof of the Dodge and dug the key fob out his pocket. He unlocked the car and stood half-in half-out of the Charger as he grabbed his coffee off the roof. When he finally turned back to the journalist, he saw that she was staring at his left hand, sitting on the driver's door frame.

"I notice you don't wear a wedding band anymore."

He turned away from her, it was easier that way.

12

IT WAS 12:30 BY the time Coombes got back to the detective bureau and he'd achieved next to nothing. Interviewing Booth so early in the investigation was unusual but he wanted to see the other man's face when he heard the news about Hahn. If he interviewed him later and the news about Hahn had already broken, Booth would've had time to prepare.

Instead, he'd seen surprise, fear, and a partial shutdown.

In Coombes' experience, bad people always prepared for the day they were discovered. When that moment finally arrived there was no fear or surprise, only a face that said:

So, this is what that moment feels like.

Because he didn't get that, Coombes was inclined to look elsewhere for a suspect. Yet if Booth had been waiting on this discovery, it was also possible he could prepare himself for how to act in order to appear innocent. Coombes knew well enough how good the director was at shaping a narrative onscreen. Booth's favorite theme was the *unreliable narrator*, a hero that lies to everyone, including themself.

Sato glared at him as he approached.

"You said you had an errand, Coombes. It's after 12!"

He held up a paper sack.

"I come bearing gifts."

She spoke to him in Japanese for close to a minute. Coombes didn't speak Japanese, but if tone was anything to go by, she wasn't happy with him. He nodded and waited for her to finish, just as he would if she was speaking English. When she was done, he continued like everything was normal.

"How about we go across the road and eat this in the park?"

"*Fine.*"

She grabbed her suit jacket and he walked back across to the elevator. Inside it, she came close to him, then immediately shrank away, her face turned toward the doors.

They crossed 1st Street and walked into Circle Park. It looked like there'd been a purge of homeless people since his last visit, because the place had been cleared out. He sat on the steps leading up to City Hall and began to sort through the food in the sack. When he passed Sato a container of noodles, he saw she was almost arm's reach away.

They ate in silence, anger sitting between them next to the gyozas.

He turned and saw she was glaring at him again.

"Can you turn off the high beams? I'm here now."

Sato turned away and stared into the trees.

"I paid a visit to the hospital where Molly Walker was in her almost-coma. Actually, I paid a visit to the parking lot, I wasn't allowed in due to the virus. The place is chaos. Anyway, I eventually got one of the nurses that knew her on the phone. She said that Carson Naylor visited Molly every day."

The business partner.

"He loved her," Coombes said.

"That was my take."

"Does that change anything?"

"I always suspected, based on how he looked at the scene."

"And how was that?"

"Like he wanted to catch the next flight out and be with her."

Coombes nodded, but said nothing.

"Walker tricked me, Johnny. I fucked up. Every time I think about it, I feel stupid. The worst mistake of my life, you'll never see me the same way."

"Tell me."

"I told you about the dashcam footage, how it was disallowed by the judge? I didn't tell you why. *I'm* why."

"Just start at the beginning and lay it out for me."

She ate some noodles while she put the timeline together in her head.

"Ryan and I got to the crime scene fast, within minutes. Paramedics were still pulling Molly out from under that bastard's SUV. He'd dragged her along underneath for about twenty feet. Somehow, she was still alive, if that's what you want to call it. I go to the sidewalk where a patrol cop had the husband. Walker had this big smile; he just couldn't stop. I wanted to shoot him right there, it was like a fever burning inside me."

Forty feet away, a man wearing a suit and sunglasses lined up a cell phone and appeared to take a photograph of them. If the man was trying to take a picture of City Hall, his cell wasn't tilted far enough back.

"The uniform tells me Walker is high, that he was sitting in his vehicle getting baked, waiting for police to arrive. Sure enough, there are leftover joints on the road and in the footwell of his Mercedes."

Coombes nodded and waited for her to continue.

The man taking pictures of them moved around to the left, perhaps to capture his good side. Coombes wondered if he was an investigator working for Walker's attorney, trying to discredit Sato ahead of the re-trial.

"I don't think Walker was as baked as he let on, I think he was playing me from the start. The patrol cop went to bring his vehicle over to transport Walker to the station, but he gets blocked by the ambulance. I turn to watch Molly's smashed body getting loaded into the back by paramedics.

"My eyes were off him for seconds, but that's all it took. He bolts into his SUV and I see him reaching for the dashcam. I figure he's trying to delete evidence, so I drag him out. We land in a pile on the street and he reaches his foot up and kicks the door shut."

Coombes sighed, seeing it.

"You went back for the dashcam."

Sato nodded.

"He wasn't trying to delete anything; he was goading me into retrieving the dashcam without a warrant. If he *had* erased it our people would've just brought it back. The judge said that because the door was closed, my search was unlawful. Walker got me and the judge to destroy evidence for him."

Coombes said nothing as he thought things over.

Walker had played a game on her for sure, but it had been for nothing as he'd been convicted anyway. If there was one thing juries hated more than cops, it was smug lawyers.

"After it happened, did you think you'd make it to RHD?"

"No."

"Every cop has a story like this, Grace. You have to shake it off and move on. The law is an ass that often only seems to serve the guilty."

"The dashcam footage was thrown out of court, but we still have a copy. I think you need to see it before you tell me to *shake it off*."

The anger was back and it wasn't going away anytime soon.

He nodded, then packed up the remains of their lunch.

Coombes saw no sign of the man in the sunglasses as they left the park and walked back to headquarters. It was possible, he reflected, that the man had simply been taking pictures of Sato because she was a beautiful woman and there was no agenda behind it.

Once they were back at their desks, Sato set up the dashcam clip for him to watch. The footage had sound so she plugged in her headphones and stepped to the side so that he could sit in her seat.

Coombes put on the headphones and pulled her chair in close to her desk so that the smaller window of the footage filled his vision and clicked play.

A wide street with trees and high hedges. Beverley Boulevard. A cross street came up that said June. Walker was in Hancock Park, headed toward Oakwood.

The Mercedes turned on Hudson Avenue, the speed dropping away.

Walker started talking to himself.

Fucking bitch, where are you?

Come out, come out, wherever you are.

He was looking for her car, Coombes thought.

Huge mansions lay on either side. The view from the dashcam was limited, but Coombes had been on the street before and knew what it was like. Unlike many similar areas, the huge properties either came close to the sidewalk or were only a short driveway away.

He could imagine Walker driving along, his neck craning to the right, then to the left, searching for his wife's car. A new voice cut in, a woman's.

In three hundred feet, you will arrive at your destination.

Stephen Walker began to laugh.

Fuckin' A.

There was less than fifteen seconds of playback left on the clip.

Vehicles were parked along the road. Mid-range cars and flatbed trucks. Doubtless belonging to staff for those living in the huge properties.

A flatbed with groundskeeping equipment was parked with its tailgate down. Walker moved across to give it some space. Right in front of it, Molly Walker stepped out into the street, took several quick steps, then froze when she saw her husband driving toward her.

Now Stephen Walker began to really laugh.

He hit the gas and his Mercedes surged forward, smashing into her body sending a spray of blood across the windshield. It was over in a split-second.

She was there, and then she was gone.

Walker continued to laugh as he hit the brakes and came to a stop. The laugh was high-pitched like a little girl. After a beat, the rain sensor activated the windshield wipers, cleaning the blood away like it never happened.

The clip ended and Coombes sat back to think about it for a moment.

He saw Sato watching him from his side of the partition that separated their desks. Her mouth was angled down at the corners, and tears were running down her face. She didn't have to be watching to be emotionally involved by what happened.

Coombes grabbed the playhead and scrubbed back from the end of the clip to the moment where Molly Walker appeared on the road.

She didn't turn her head to see if it was safe to cross, she just stepped out.

Even on a sleepy street like Hudson Avenue, that was crazy. It wasn't like Walker drove a whisper-quiet electric car, he was driving a monster SUV.

Those Mercedes were like tanks.

He let the end play again until just before the moment of impact. There was no timecode on the clip, however, the media player indicated that two and a half seconds passed between stepping out and impact. It was longer than he thought.

Why did she just stand there?

Even with her husband accelerating toward her, there had still been time to get back behind the truck. Something didn't fit. He took off the headphones and looked up at Sato.

"I want to see everything."

13

FOR THE NEXT FIVE hours, Coombes poured over every inch of the original murder book, the filing package submitted to the District Attorney, and the case workup the prosecutor had created in preparation for the trial. In what appeared to be a genuine coincidence, the original prosecutor was also dead, leaving Sato as the last one standing. As he'd already noted, the filing package was thin. The investigation was of the open-and-closed variety.

Stephen Walker drove over his wife with intent to kill.

But proving intent is a high bar.

Notes early in the murder book indicated that Sara Ryan, the senior partner, believed that Walker would confess if correctly prompted. A confession would seal it all up.

In the interview, Ryan made repeated mention of the incriminating dashcam footage. Again and again, Walker claimed what happened was an accident. At one point, he claimed to be as much a victim as his wife.

When he said that, his wife looked like boiled fruit in a Ziplock bag.

Coombes had seen the footage, seen the Mercedes surge forward, and heard the suspect's laughter. It was hard to argue with the point of view that Walker tried to kill her. Yet, he felt an unease deep down.

Something else was going on, he could feel it.

When talking about the footage didn't get the job done, Ryan and Sato had played the clip back for Walker on a laptop and urged him to admit what he'd done in return for a more favorable sentence.

Walker didn't budge, he claimed to see only an accident.

He appeared to be in denial, unwilling to accept the bind he was in.

With hindsight, it looked to Coombes like Walker had allowed them to build their entire case around evidence that he knew he could get thrown out at pre-trial, hoping the case would collapse without it.

At trial, things had gone another way.

Walker had been unable to explain why he was driving on that street, why his GPS system was pointing at Molly Walker's business partner's address, and why there was an unregistered firearm under his seat.

They were also able to prove that he had accelerated prior to impact by comparing Walker's speed as he passed an earlier street camera with the speed at the time of the collision, calculated by tread left on the asphalt as he braked.

He'd intended to kill her one way, then killed her another.

The jury bought it, but Coombes wasn't there yet.

"Well?"

He looked up and saw Sato watching him.

"I don't like it. This is half a case. Where's the other half?"

"What are you talking about?"

"He was driving the Mercedes at the time of the incident, no argument."

Sato's face hardened. "*But?*"

"The intent to kill is weak. I'm surprised the DA let you put it to bed like this. Obviously, this was before the dashcam was tossed, but relying on a single piece of evidence is risky at the best of times."

"We caught him in a lie. He said he just happened to be on that street, that he used it all the time as a shortcut. We got his story nailed down before we showed him the dashcam footage. You can clearly hear the GPS telling him that he has reached his destination."

"All right. Maybe he lied because he knew how that looked, but that's not the same as lying because he was there to kill her. That's a big leap, Grace, and that's the part that you need to shore up at trial, he'll be attacking that."

"You saw the footage! He did it!"

"I saw it, but the jury didn't. The next jury won't see it either."

Sato lifted her hands off the partition and held them up in front of her.

"I can't deal with this; I need a moment."

She turned and headed for the restroom.

He sighed. Sato was getting her wires crossed. The case against Stephen Walker was not that he struck his wife with his SUV, but that he did so deliberately, with intent to kill. She saw the immediate bloody aftermath and that was clouding her judgement.

Accidents happened all the time, but is that what this was?

He turned to a blank page of his notebook and wrote down potential issues based on the assumption that Molly Walker was a victim of an accident.

GPS destination.

Acceleration before impact.

Unregistered firearm.

Behavior after the incident.

Coombes didn't add anything about the trick Walker pulled on Sato related to the dashcam as it added nothing. The man was a criminal defense lawyer, he saw how damaging the footage would be, so he dealt with it.

Objectively, it was a smart move.

Walker's erratic laughing and smiling could be dismissed as shock or a side effect of being high. It was a fact that in moments of stress the wrong emotion could come out and no guilt could be drawn from it.

Coombes scored out *behavior.*

The GPS information and the discovery of the firearm were both the result of a second search of Walker's vehicle. Performed under a search warrant, this was not part of Sato's impulsive early search. However, Walker almost got this search tossed too on the basis that the contents of his car were not responsible for his wife stepping out onto the road.

The judge, having previously sided with the defense over the dashcam, decided to allow the second search in a balancing move. At retrial, the next judge would feel no such obligation and Coombes felt that the firearm might also be disallowed.

That would leave the prosecution with a forensic technician talking about tire tread ablation under heavy braking, and a mathematics professor explaining the science of extracting vehicle speed from video playback.

The standard defense play would have Walker produce his own experts who had an alternative read of the same data and the science would be neutralized.

The only thing that moved the needle was the gun, and there was no way to tie it to Walker or that he even knew it was there. He had reacted with confusion and believable outrage when he was told about it under questioning.

The case was pure air.

It was obvious to Coombes that he was going to have to start again from scratch and be open to the possibility that Stephen Walker might actually be innocent.

14

THE RIDE HOME WENT about the same as the ride in. He got two blocks before he noticed the Ford Explorer in his rearview mirror. It had been parked illegally at the side of the road waiting for him. He had purposefully cleaned the Charger's back window before leaving the parking garage, but the driver was hidden from him by the glaring sun. He put on his sunglasses and when they stopped at a traffic light, he turned to look back between the front seats and tilted his head. The sunglasses were polarized and the glare of the windshield vanished. He saw a single figure sitting in the Explorer. A silhouette.

Broad shoulders, with short stubby hair.

Not Sullivan.

"What is it, Johnny?"

He faced forward just as the light changed.

"We're being followed. A black Ford Explorer."

"Shit, a Nazi?"

"Hard to say. Maybe."

He turned off 6th Street onto South Hill Street. Sato turned to him.

"We need to lose the tail, Johnny. Can't let them know where we live."

"No point. That SUV was parked across the street from our building this morning. It followed us all the way to work. Whoever it is, they already know where we live."

"Why am I just finding out about this now?"

"I didn't want you to worry."

"I've had my guard down all day you asshole! I thought I was safe!"

"You're right, I'm sorry."

They drove in silence, Sato gripping the door handle tight. He turned in at the parking garage. There was always a delay between the transponder triggering the barrier and then the barrier being sufficiently open to drive under.

It was an obvious spot for an ambush.

There was no sign of the Explorer behind, but his mirrors were pointed in the wrong direction. The barrier started to open. It was a roller with folding metal strips, not a boom arm. The roller prevented unauthorized pedestrians as well as vehicles, but operated more slowly. He looked past Sato through the passenger window and onto the sidewalk.

Nothing.

He powered under the barrier then stopped, his hand sitting on the gear shifter in case the Explorer tried to follow them in. Any sign of that, he'd slam them into reverse and block it outside until the barrier timed out and closed.

He saw that Sato had her sidearm out.

Finally, she was getting it.

It occurred to him that the transponder was holding the barrier open so he crawled forward another five feet. Now the barrier closed and he'd never been so glad to see it.

He drove around to their assigned parking.

"Check the glovebox," he said. "I think there's a scope in there."

"A *scope*?"

"A telescope. About four inches long, black rubberized casing."

When he parked, she had the scope ready.

"What are we going to do?"

"I'm going to see who this A-hole is. Stay in the car until I come back."

He saw her face as he stepped out. She was seething with anger. *Good*, he thought. She needed to be angry right now. If someone was coming for her, she needed to be in the mood to put holes in them until they were dead.

Hopefully, that person wouldn't be him.

He drew his weapon and ran through the garage, toward the exit. Twenty feet from the opening was a spot where you could see out onto the street without breaking cover. It was a vantage point he'd located on the day he moved in, as if he'd anticipated this exact scenario.

Army training, he supposed.

He got to the spot and re-holstered his weapon.

The Ford was exactly where he thought it would be, the same space it had been in that morning. There was a dip on the sidewalk that made driving up onto it easy. Coombes directed the scope at the driver's window. The sun illuminated a stripe of the driver through the heavily tinted glass.

White male, fat, light blue shirt.

There was something immediately familiar to Coombes about the man, but the strip of light was too narrow to make any kind of identification.

Neck, jawline, collar.

Coombes directed the scope down at the front tire and saw it was significantly flattened at the bottom. The driver was heavy even by SUV standards. He thought about charging across the road and the potential of getting into a firefight with the man in the blue shirt. It would be messy, with every chance that either he or a passing motorist could be killed.

There was no back exit from the building, no way to get out and go around the block and approach the driver from the other side. From where the Explorer was parked, the driver could see both the front door and the parking garage, the only ways in or out.

Coombes was still debating what to do when the SUV rolled forward off the sidewalk and drove away. He walked back to his car, unsatisfied by the outcome. Adrenaline was still pumping around his system and the garage appeared brighter than on the way out.

Someone was keeping tabs on them.

Assuming they were home for the night, the follower had simply driven away. Waiting for a better time to hit them, a time when the odds might be more in the other man's favor.

He saw through the Charger's rear window that Sato wasn't in the car. His heart leapt and he spun around to see her next to the wheel of a Range Rover on the opposite side of the row, left knee on the concrete, right raised to brace the gun in both her hands.

"You're dead, Coombes."

"That's not funny, Grace. I thought I lost you."

She said nothing to that and stood, holstering her Glock.

"What happened to our friend?"

"I chased him off. We won't be seeing him again."

Sato laughed, but there was no humor in it.

The Ford driver was a problem, but one he hoped to sort out the following morning. They walked toward the stairs that linked the parking structure and the apartment building.

"By the way, Coombes, tell me to stay in the car again and I *will* shoot you when you come back. I'll say the gun just went off or something."

He glanced at her and said nothing.

THEY SHOWERED AND CHANGED into casual clothes then sat at the breakfast bar and picked at a large pizza that neither of them felt like eating. To take a break from the Walker investigation, Sato asked him about his case. He told her about the wallet with the ultrasound picture, and the mark the killer had left on Hahn's skull.

"An X?"

"Not exactly," he said. "An X is narrower than it is tall, this would evenly divide a square, not a rectangle."

"Okay. And both victims had the mark?"

"Same mark, same place."

"All right, here's the part I don't understand. If he's going to bury her, why mark her at all? Where's the payoff for him if she's never found? Either he wants people to see what he's done, or he wants to conceal it. Am I wrong?"

Coombes shrugged.

"Some of these guys, an idea gets inside their head early on and over time it gets stronger and stronger. It's like hearing music you hate and humming it for the rest of the day. They can't tune it out. Eventually, it gets to the point where they're forced to act on it, just to make the music stop.

"This cross is part of what compels him, it's not something thrown in at the last minute. From the first moment, he's imagining people dead with this thing on their face and working backward to the start point to make it happen."

"Jesus. Some people are so screwed up."

Sato looked depressed. The nature of their job seemed to weigh more heavily on her than it did for him. Not for the first time, he wondered if Homicide was where she belonged. Being a gifted cop wasn't enough, you had to protect yourself to stop the dark getting in.

He decided to mix things up.

"Do you remember Monica Sullivan?"

Sato became still, like she'd gone into a trance. He prompted her again.

"*Times* reporter, covered the *Ferryman* case?"

Sato turned to look at him, her gaze cool.

"Yes, Coombes, I remember her. I actually remember *every* woman who is in love with you, it's like this gift I have."

Coombes laughed awkwardly. It had been a mistake to mention the journalist, he could see that now.

"That's ridiculous."

"Uh-huh."

He went back to reading the notes he'd written in his notebook. The conversation was eerily similar to one he'd had with his ex-wife, who had accused him of being in a relationship with Sato long before it happened.

"Was there a reason why you mentioned Sullivan?"

"Oh. She's covering the bones case."

"I guessed that much. My point is, so what?"

"She agreed to not publish the story as long as she gets an exclusive."

Sato looked at him for a long beat. "What else?"

"Sullivan wants in. Work part of the case."

"Johnny, tell me you didn't agree to that!"

"I'm not missing a second chance to catch Lawrence's killer."

"Surely it's illegal? She's not a cop. If it comes out at trial-"

"Relax, she'll only be doing research for me. We're not going on stakeouts together or breaking down doors. I only have one kick-ass partner."

"You're insane if you think you can trust her."

"What was the right choice? Allow her to publish and let a killer go free?"

Sato had no comeback to that, as he knew she wouldn't. He'd made the best of a bad deal, and in doing so had gained a measure of control over Sullivan that he would never otherwise have had. Silence fell between them and to help cover it, Coombes ate a couple more slices of the pizza. It was stone cold and the mozzarella had turned to rubber.

"You said we have half a case before, what did you mean by that?"

He tossed a bit of pizza back in the box, grateful for the interruption.

"Judging from the filing package, you planned to show that Walker intended to kill his wife by showing the jury the dashcam footage. He calls her bitch beforehand, establishing pre-existing anger toward her, then we have him accelerating to hit her. Intent."

"Right. We wanted to file for attempted murder. Ryan thought the case met the malice aforethought trigger due to the cursing, the GPS, and the handgun. The DA didn't agree, so we filed for attempted manslaughter."

He nodded.

"All right, but your argument, whether you use the dashcam footage or not, was that he planned on shooting her and that it was some kind of divine providence that he was able to hit her with his G-Wagon first. But there's no motive in your paperwork. Was she having an affair? Had he been violent with her in the past? Were there financial problems? *That's* the half that's missing. It should've been there whether you had the dashcam or not."

Sato's face turned red.

"Listen, we were working three other cases at the time. We were *swamped*. This case was a walk in the park, we wanted it cleared as soon as possible. How were we to know the dashcam footage would be thrown out?"

He sat back.

"Why do you think she stops?"

"*What?*"

"Molly Walker. She practically runs out into the street without looking then stands frozen like a deer in headlights. All she had to do was step back."

"She obviously wasn't expecting to see her husband. If he was there, maybe he knows about her affair. She shuts down. She's in shock."

"An *alleged* affair. We don't know anything was going on."

Sato rose and walked to the window.

She wasn't looking at the view, she'd seen it before.

He took the remains of the pizza through to the kitchen and got himself a beer. When he came back through, he saw Sato was still standing at the window. He supposed he'd pushed her too hard, forcing her to see mistakes and nobody likes to see that.

Coombes sat sideways on one of the sofa chairs on the other side of the room where he could keep a discreet eye on Sato. He finished the bottle before she spoke.

"I think we should take a break."

"We are taking a break, Grace."

"No," she said. "I think we should go back to being just partners."

"Are you kidding me?"

"You've been a real peach today, Coombes."

He went over to her at the window.

"Look, I'm sorry if I've been tough with you about this case, but it's nothing compared to what's coming from a defense attorney. We need to be ready."

"It's not just this case, Johnny. I've been thinking about this for a while now. The two of us are partners first, if it got out that we were in a relationship, we'd be done."

Coombes took a deep breath and let it slowly out.

The first twenty-odd things he felt like saying to her would only put him further in a hole so he kept them to himself.

"I'd rather lose you as a partner than lose you like this. How about that? You could partner up with Gonzalez, she's good."

"Don't make this more difficult than it has to be."

He'd heard *that* line before. Coombes said nothing. It was obvious that her mind was made up, there was nothing he could say to change it. She didn't even want to listen to him try. Maybe there'd be a time for that some other time, but it wasn't now.

"This is awkward, Johnny, but can I stay in the spare room until I get a new place. I gave up the lease on my apartment a long time ago."

"I guess giving up is what you're good at."

15

It took Coombes less than forty minutes to drive to the prison at Terminal Island, located near Long Beach. The traffic was the lightest he'd ever seen it, his journey time governed more by the weight of his right foot than lines of cars in his way. He could definitely get used to what the virus was doing to his travel time, although he knew he shouldn't.

Coombes parked up and secured his firearm in the gun safe in the back of the vehicle. He didn't like leaving it with anyone out of his sight, no matter how trustworthy they were. His visit had been arranged with prison officials ahead of time, but the deputies still messed him around for twenty minutes so that he would know who was in charge.

He pretended not to care, taking the time to mentally compose what he wanted to say to Stephen Walker and why he was there. Eventually, he was led through to the room where prisoners met with visitors, through a sheet of glass and via a telephone handset. Walker was already seated at one of the stalls. There were no other prisoners and no waiting visitors.

He sat opposite Walker and picked up the handset. The other man made no move to pick up his so Coombes put his badge down on the counter and used the handset to knock on the glass. Walker picked up his handset.

"Detective Coombes, LAPD."

"Where's the *other* cop?"

Walker was talking about Ryan, not Sato. There was amusement in his eyes. He had ordered her death and was letting him know it.

"I'm here to get your side of the story, I'm in charge now."

"Oh, no, my friend. You guys *had* your chance, I'm the one in charge now."
Coombes leaned forward.

"By now you've no doubt heard that the DA has re-filed. If you lose the next one, you could be moved from this holiday camp up to the supermax at Pelican Bay. We'll keep filling until we get one that lands."

"If you're so confident, why are you here?"

"My orders are to save the city money. If you're innocent, in the long run it's cheaper to drop the new charges and not oppose your habeas petition. The DA that put you here is no longer around. The current DA loses no face letting you out, you'd be a mistake of the previous incumbent. It's all politics. I don't have a dog in this fight either way."

"Tell me the part where I should care."

"Obviously, if we don't oppose your petition then you save a bunch of time in here, and you won't need to cut a lawyer a huge slice of any payoff down the line. If you're not interested, I'll let you get back to whatever you were doing before I arrived."

Walker said nothing, he was thinking about it.

Coombes decided to give him another push.

"Every hour you spend in here is an hour you could get shanked, sexually assaulted, or given COVID. I hear Coronavirus is ripping through the prison system. No masks or vaccines for you. No social distancing. That's why we're in here, by the way, not in an interview room. The glass protects me from whatever's coming out your mouth."

"You're running this now?"

"That's right. Soto's out the picture."

Walker didn't even blink.

Coombes had used the wrong name on purpose and the other man didn't react. This told him that the incorrect name had come from Walker, the dead skinhead hadn't made the mistake.

"What do you want to know?"

"Simple. Tell me what happened that day."

"This is bullshit. I told that Chinese detective what happened, nothing's changed since I've been in here."

"I'm guessing that you missed something out, Walker, because what you told Soto helped put you in this box in the first place."

Walker glanced away, an effort to hide a flash of anger.

"It started a couple of weeks before. Notes under my wiper blades. They were typed, no handwriting. I thought it was a joke at first, a friend messing with me."

"What did they say?"

"First one said, *How well do you know your wife?* A couple of days later, there was another, this time it's *Your wife gives the best head in LA County.* It goes on like this getting worse and more perverted until the last one, which was just an address and a time."

"You went there to see what was happening."

"I could *guess* what was happening."

"Right. How is it that you think any of this helps you?"

"I know how it looks, like I went there to kill her. That's why I never told the other detective. My point is, I was *lured* there and the next thing I know I've killed her. She's right in front of my car and I've gone over her."

"They found a firearm in your car, that looks like intent to me."

"A gun I never saw before. My fingerprints weren't on it."

"Gloves."

"Listen, someone put it there. If it wasn't one of those cops, it was the person leaving the notes."

"That might work if you walked in and found them shot to death and your fingerprints were all over the scene, but you ran her over with your SUV. I've seen the dashcam footage. You *accelerated* toward her."

"An accident. I hit the gas instead of the brake!"

"You were laughing."

"I was *high*. I'd been smoking weed all morning. I was expecting to find them in bed together, you know? I thought the weed would make it easier. Think about it, if the weapon *was* mine wouldn't I have tossed it down a drain or something before the cops arrived? I didn't because I didn't know it was there."

Coombes said nothing for a moment.

Walker was a scumbag; he'd probably *always* been a scumbag. He was a defense attorney after all. In prison he'd found bottom and aligned with human waste. Maybe he'd done only what he had to do to stay alive, but he was still responsible for the death of Sato's old partner.

Nevertheless, his story sounded real.

"These notes you received; did you keep any of them?"

"No, but they were worthless anyway. Anonymous typewritten notes? You people would just say they went to motive and use them against me."

"Say I believe you. Who could've planted the gun?"

"I've been thinking about that. I figure it had to have been while my car was valet parked, being detailed at the car wash, or while it was being serviced. My Mercedes was serviced like the week before this happened."

"And the last time it was detailed?"

"This is a long time ago now. All I can tell you, is that I don't need to get it detailed *after* it's been serviced, those Mercedes guys do all that as part of the deal. If I know there's a service coming, I don't bother getting it cleaned because I know it's going to be taken care of anyway. I suppose you're talking about a month before the service. Why?"

"The firearm was found under your driver's seat. If we're saying someone put it there then it had to be during your service, or at a valet parking place after that. If it was done at the detailing before the service, the Mercedes guys would've found it."

"Son of a bitch, you're right!"

"So did you use valet parking after the service?"

Walker took a moment to think about it.

"I can't remember, it's too long ago."

Coombes decided to move things along.

"You were a criminal attorney, should I assume there were a long line of disgruntled clients that would want you in here?"

"Every day, I think *who would want me in here?* It's true a couple of clients have come to mind, but they would come at me directly. Shoot me, or firebomb my home, not try and frame me like this. There would be no breadcrumb notes, who thinks like that?"

"How about outside of your work. Were you in dispute with anybody?"

"My neighbor's dog kept shitting in my yard, but I don't think the owner framed me for my wife's death."

Coombes nodded. He was done here.

"All right, Walker. I'll look into all this, see what shakes out. I expect you to leave me to my work, but I'm happy to put as many of your Nazi friends into drawers as you can spare. I'm a combat veteran, not some delicate flower for you to prune. You feel me?"

"I don't know what you're talking about."

"The Brotherhood might protect you in here, but outside is *my* world. There's no payout from the city if you're *dead*."

Walker had no comeback to that, but Coombes let the silence run for about ten seconds before he hung up the handset. He eyeballed the lawyer as a sheriff's deputy came over and took Walker away.

Coombes stood, pulled up his mask and left.

Out in the parking lot, he took a long moment to clean his hands with an alcohol hand wash. He hadn't been exaggerating the COVID situation just to get Walker to talk.

Sometimes, nothing hit harder than the truth.

16

THE INBOUND LEG OF his trip took a little longer than the outbound and it was approaching 11 a.m. by the time he got back to the PAB. Sato was still buried in her old murder book where he'd left her, looking for fresh angles. She looked up as he took off his jacket and hung it on the back of his chair.

"Let me guess, our boy's still unrepentant."

"Still innocent, actually."

Sato shook her head.

"What about Ryan? Did you draw him out on her murder?"

"Didn't really have to, he as good as rubbed it in my face."

Coombes gave her a quick outline of his interview with Stephen Walker. As he spoke Sato's expression hardened and when he finished, she practically exploded.

"Are you telling me that you believe this piece of shit? He's been in there two years and the best he can come up with is that a mystery man sent him some dirty notes?"

"What he said about the gun holds true, don't you think? If he knew it was there, he would've ditched it before the uniforms turned up."

"*Or* he was so relieved the deed was done that he forgot all about it. Forgive me, Johnny, but I think what he said about his wife cheating on him is steering how you feel about this. You became sympathetic...you've been where he is."

"That's a low goddamn blow, Grace."

Coombes sat in his chair and logged in to his computer.

Was she right? Or was she trying to cover an investigation mired down with tunnel vision and dashcam footage that appeared to make their case a slam-dunk?

"I'm sorry, Johnny."

He didn't look around at her.

"Yeah. So am I. By the way, I used Soto's name twice during the interview and he never corrected me or showed any reaction. I think you're in the clear, but you might want to advise Soto to watch her six for a while."

"*John.*"

He looked at her, leaning over the divider. Her eyebrows were pitched up in the middle and her eyes were fat with tears ready to go. She'd thrown the grenade, why did she get to be the one upset about it?

"You would never have said that to me before, Grace. Is this really how you want it from now on? Is this better?"

"It's Walker, he hits my buttons. I didn't mean to hurt your feelings."

"All right, forget it."

Sato took a moment to get back to where she started.

"If you help prove his innocence, he gets a free pass on having Ryan killed. We can't tie him to that. He comes out smelling of roses and gets a million dollars from the city, is that what you want?"

"We swap murders, that it? Look, if Walker's not responsible for his wife's death, then someone else *is* and they've never been caught. I can't let that stand, can you?"

"How can he not be responsible? We know he killed her."

"If someone jumps in front of a train, is the driver responsible?"

Sato opened her mouth to say something, then closed it again.

"You and Ryan did a deep dive on Stephen Walker right to the bottom of the Pacific, but there's nothing in the file about Molly Walker except the injuries she sustained. That was a basic mistake, even if the husband did it. I want to know about her and her business partner, everything from soup to nuts. Were they having an affair? Were there problems in the business, all that. If it *wasn't* her husband, then dollars to doughnuts it was her partner."

"You think she was *pushed* out in front of her husband?"

"It's possible."

"And if she was, what happens to Walker?"

"He told me he was high at the time of the so-called accident and *that* was why he was laughing on the dashcam footage. That was a mistake. All we knew before was that he got high *after* he hit her. I just checked NCIC. Walker has a previous DUI charge *and* a hit for drug possession in 2016. That means we can re-file for DUI murder which carries a fifteen-year term. Even if time served is deducted, he's still looking at thirteen years in a hole."

Sato looked crestfallen.

"You think that's enough? Ryan's dead. She had two kids, a husband."

"It's not going to matter. When the Aryan Brotherhood realizes that there's no payout coming to Walker from the city, they will deal with him themselves. He got one of their soldiers killed and these guys take that seriously. He'll be dead inside a month."

Sato didn't like that answer any better.

"And you can live with that?"

Coombes shrugged. "Apparently."

His cell phone pinged on the desk next to his hand. A text message. He glanced at the screen and read the message before the screen went dark.

I need to see you! xxx

He glanced at Sato and saw she'd read it, upside-down. She sighed and sat down behind the divider. Sullivan's joking around was becoming a chore. He picked up his cell and texted back.

Where are you?

A three-dot animation played.

Times building. You?

Across the street. Get me a coffee, I'll be 5 minutes.

An emoticon of a face appeared, blowing a kiss. He was too old for this shit. Coombes stood and pulled on his suit jacket, his eyes falling on Sato.

"Sullivan's got something," he said.

"My money's on gonorrhea."

Coombes laughed and laughed; he couldn't stop. It was like a hurricane passing through that he just had to ride out. Shelter in place, that's what they called it. A couple of detectives looked at him and, after a beat, Block stuck his head out of his office and stared at him with a sour expression. Coombes didn't care, Sato's expression had brightened.

"*That's* the Grace I want back," he said.

"I'll see what I can do."

Coombes rode an empty elevator down to the first floor then exited onto Spring Street where he walked down to the crossing. He walked quickly, making good time. He realized that he was looking forward to meeting the journalist.

A smile and a pretty face, was that all it took? He thought.

There were a lot of empty seats when he arrived in the *Times* canteen, but that didn't stop Sullivan from standing and waving. Coombes nodded and walked to her table, where he saw his coffee was waiting. She lifted up her elbow to touch and he did the same. A COVID handshake. It was the first time he'd ever done it, and it was with Sullivan.

"You may as well take that thing off, you've already inhaled me."

He pulled his mask down and let it hang around his neck.

"I honestly wasn't sure how I was going to drink coffee with it on."

He unfastened his jacket button and they sat down.

"I guessed black," she said. "All cops take it black, right?"

"Right. What've you got for me?"

"No chit-chat? No, *I had a dream about you last night?*"

Inwardly, he sighed. She continued to work him, even when he was voluntarily seated across from her. His eyes again fell on her freckles.

Goddamn, they were cute.

"We're trying to catch a killer, Sullivan. Can we focus on that?"

"All right, Mr. Straight-to-business. I located Chad Evans, the IRS agent assigned to Booth's tax audit. He screens all his calls and didn't reply to any of mine. I decided to visit his home in San Gabriel. He was out when I arrived, so I set up in my car across the street and waited for him. There's a tall gate guarding his property and it got me curious about why he might need it. About an hour later, Evans returns in a beat-up old Honda. The gate slides open and he drives this Honda inside. That's when I see it."

Sullivan smiled at him, but she couldn't hold it, and laughed.

"*What?*"

"He's got a bright red Ferrari on his driveway."

"Evans is dirty," Coombes said. "Taking bribes."

"That's for sure. I get half a dozen pictures of it with my long lens, then I'm out my car and across the street before the gate closes. I'm inside as Evans steps out with his groceries. You should've seen his face; he knew he was busted."

"Look, Sullivan-"

"Monica."

She had her charm turned up to 11 again.

"Look, *Sullivan*. I'm not comfortable with you putting yourself at risk like that. You're not a cop. You were vulnerable. I didn't know where you were. Cornered people do crazy things to survive."

"That's sweet of you, Coombes, but I can take care of myself. Anyway, you want to know where Evans got to with Booth before he got a new car?"

"Sure."

"*Son of a Gun* is a front. He's washing mob money for De Luca and he's doing better than we thought. Booth has his own special effects company called *Assassin FX*, which he uses to inflate costs. Say a movie makes $100 million at the box office and it cost $90 million to make, Booth bills *Son of a Gun* $15 million from *Assassin* and suddenly he's lost money."

Coombes nodded. "And special effects are impossible to quantify."

"Exactly. The IRS has no way to prove anything and he's such a small player that he's practically under the radar anyway. So, he pays no tax on his movies and probably clears ten million a pop. On top of that, he sold his back catalog to an exclusive streaming service for forty-five million *and* gets thirty percent of physical media sales."

"Nobody buys physical media anymore, do they?"

"Enough to make a difference. He spent the last year and a half creating 4K restorations of all his old movies. He has a small fanbase, but they are generally wealthy and into the high-resolution thing. Those 4K Blu-rays start at $25, more for limited editions."

It was good intel, and it amazed him that Sullivan had turned up the information in less than 24 hours, but it was obvious to him that none of it advanced his case in any way.

"Sounds like Booth's making more money than De Luca."

Sullivan shook her head.

"Even ignoring the special effects skim, every one of Booth's movies return a minimum of 92% of invested capital. That might be terrible for a normal investor, but for laundered money, getting north of 65% is amazing. De Luca will be very happy with the arrangement."

Following the money hadn't given him the result he'd expected.

Based on this information, De Luca seemed a better fit for the killer, just as he had the first time around. Sullivan's smile faltered.

"Why so glum, Coombes?"

"Based on what you said, Booth's nothing but a fraud who wants to make artistic movies with low box office potential. That doesn't bother me. In fact, I kind of admire it. I don't care how much tax he pays; I'm looking for a killer and none of this adds up to murder."

Sullivan nodded.

"You still like Booth for this?"

She wasn't mocking him, she just wanted to know.

"Hard to say," Coombes said. "If it's not him, it's someone close. He's the starting point, the center of the wheel. We follow the leads out to the killer."

"Do you know what NLP is?"

"Never heard of it."

"Neurolinguistic programming," Sullivan said. "It's a pseudo-science popular with con men and politicians. It uses language prompts to get inside another person's head."

"And Booth's into this NLP?"

"He did an interview with *Rolling Stone* last year about how he believes NLP links with his theory about muses in the creative process and the power of the subconscious mind."

"Uh-huh."

"Anyway, an NLP user will ask an apparently random question when you first meet. Like, *are you a dog person or a cat person?* How you answer dictates everything that follows. You're just making conversation; they're working out what makes you tick."

"You think he used NLP on these women?"

"I'm saying he uses it on *everyone*. What's the first thing he said to you?"

Coombes took a moment to think about it.

"Something about high school, if I was a jock or a nerd, something like that. Then he asked me if I liked superhero movies."

"There you go. He's trying to work out how you'll best respond to answers, if you want him to be weak, or aggressive. I bet he said he was bullied, right?"

"That's right."

Sullivan smiled and her eyes seemed to sparkle.

"Afterward, did you think he was innocent, or guilty?"

"About the same," Coombes said. "That he was my best suspect."

"*But?*"

"I guess I wanted him to be innocent because I like his movies."

"And because he presented himself as sympathetic or even *pathetic?*"

Coombes nodded but said nothing.

"Guys like Booth always get what they want. Be careful with what you think you know about him, because everything he's shown you about himself is a fiction."

It didn't feel good to think he'd been taken in by a con man.

"Ok. But none of this means Booth's a killer. If he's into this stuff like you say, he's just as likely manipulating me out of habit to make the awkward questions go away."

She smiled.

"I like that about you, Coombes, that you're smart. It's an attractive quality."

He looked at her face for a long beat. Her eyes, her mouth, the freckles.

"It is, isn't it?"

Sullivan laughed again and he felt warmth spread out inside him. A tangible bond was forming between him and the journalist. She was becoming important to him.

"You don't think it's Booth, do you?"

Sullivan shook her head.

"No, I don't. He's got something to hide, sure, but it's not that he's a murderer. He's likely worried your investigation will expose his financial situation."

She was probably right, but he wasn't done with Booth just yet. Nothing so far explained why the director had chosen to put Natalie Hahn in a movie. The most logical explanation, was still that it was a pay-off for lengthening Dakota Lawrence's timeline. He needed to find Scott Peters, the other eye-witness.

"I followed the money. Now what?"

It was a good question. Coombes had nothing for her. But giving Sullivan nothing would result in her going off on her own, sticking her nose where it wasn't wanted, like into Anthony De Luca's mob business.

He reflected that Sato's investigation wasn't the only one with tunnel vision. His approach so far had been to replicate the same mistakes he'd made the first time around. If he continued, he'd only replicate the same result.

It was time for a new approach.

"All right. I want you to go through the *Times* archive looking at Dakota Lawrence. Find out if she had problems with drugs or alcohol, who she was in a relationship with before Booth, any conflicts in her life."

"A background packet."

"Right."

"I could get the *cleaner* to do that, Coombes. I want something sexy."

"Then take a selfie. This is policework. It's not sexy, it's a grind."

She smiled at him.

"*What*, Sullivan?"

"You basically just said I was sexy."

"Oh, for god's sake! Like you don't know that already."

"I knew it. I just wasn't sure you did."

17

WHEN HE GOT BACK to his desk, he saw Sato had her big headphones on and her gaze was fixed on a legal pad she was filling with handwriting. He stood looking at her over the partition for an extra beat, waiting for her to notice him but her head didn't move. She clearly didn't want to look at him in case she saw something on his face that she didn't want to see.

Excitement at spending time with Sullivan, he supposed.

Hadn't she broken up with him?

He made some notes about his meeting with the journalist and the revelation that Booth was a tax dodger. Not such a big surprise, he reflected, the rich never paid their share. He found himself thinking about the black Explorer. For a while he'd assumed the Ford was Sullivan's vehicle and had let the matter drift. He flipped back a couple of pages in his notebook to where he'd written down the SUV's license number the morning before.

It was time to find out who'd been following them around.

Coombes entered the plate number into the DMV portal and the page refreshed. He sighed, seeing that it was a fleet vehicle. No owner was listed. He stared at the fleet operator.

City of Los Angeles Police Department.

Shit.

Coombes ran his hand back and forth through his hair for a moment then impulsively stood, pulled on his jacket and walked to the elevator. The guy in the blue shirt was a cop, one of his own. Internal Affairs, he assumed. But why were they after him?

This was the advantage the guilty had over the innocent.

Innocent people never saw it coming.

The elevator doors opened and he got on. Internal Affairs operated out of the same building, setting up a tail would've been straightforward and require little planning. But if it was easy for them, it was easy for him.

Easy goes both ways.

In the parking garage, he walked along the rows looking for the Ford. The garage held a mix of personal vehicles and the usual city rides for detectives on rotation. Chargers, Mustangs, and Impalas. Car manufacturers had shifted production away from sedans in favor of mid to large-sized SUVs and the LAPD had been forced to follow the trend.

Ford Explorers, Chevy Tahoes.

In hindsight, he didn't know why he hadn't made the connection.

He knew where Internal Affairs parked their vehicles. The garage wasn't randomized, detectives grouped together in their departmental cliques even when they parked. He saw eight black Explorers in the IA section, and none of them had the license plate he was after.

There'd been no tail following them that morning.

This indicated that whatever their interest in him had been, it was now at an end and the detective in the blue shirt had been assigned elsewhere. At that moment, he was likely bothering some other hard-working detective, instead of pursuing criminals like a real cop.

Coombes decided he'd wasted enough time on the issue and began to walk back the way he'd come. He felt contaminated, just standing where IA parked their vehicles.

His cell phone rang an unfamiliar melody. Not a call, but an incoming connection from his doorbell camera.

A live video feed appeared showing two Asian men at his front door. They didn't ring the doorbell; the camera had been triggered by vibration and facial-recognition software.

The man closest to the lens worked the lock, while the other stood facing down the hallway, keeping watch. The door opened within seconds, the viewpoint of the lens turning with the door to face the wall inside.

Both men filed past.

A message appeared asking if he wanted to save the clip to the cloud. Coombes clicked *yes*.

He wasn't being robbed; he'd seen both men before. The man who worked the lock was called Wang or Zhang, and the lookout was Liu. Both men worked in Internal Affairs.

It seemed like IA weren't finished with him after all.

He thought about what they might do in the apartment. There was no computer for them to try and access files. Sato had a laptop and they both had tablets, but they had taken them with them when they left for work.

That left taking photographs and planting listening devices.

He stood staring at his cell phone, waiting for the camera to activate when his guests left, then realized this wouldn't happen. His doorbell would suffer some kind of malfunction and fail to capture the IA detectives as they left. They would hope the malfunction wouldn't be noticed so they could come and go in the future without worrying about it.

He sighed and put his cell away.

The structure filled with the throbbing sound of a vehicle coming his way. He went to the rail and looked up and saw a flash of black door mirror. His gut told him that it was an Explorer, he knew well enough what they looked like now, even as a glimpse.

He ran to safe position and ducked down behind a Mustang.

The odds of this being the SUV he was looking for were impossibly remote, but not zero. There were a finite number of vehicles that used the parking structure at any one time and he was looking for one of them. One that was currently missing.

The vehicle shot past, toward the RHD section.

He stuck his head out to watch as it braked.

It *was* the correct license plate. This was his guy.

The SUV turned front-end into a parking space and the engine died. Coombes ducked back behind the Mustang so the driver wouldn't see him as he stepped out. He heard the Explorer's door open, then slam shut. The driver walked toward the elevator.

Leather-soled shoes, wooden heels. *Heavy.*

He realized the driver would have to walk past him to get to the elevator.

Coombes was wearing a suit that had cost him $1,400. There was no way he was going to destroy it scurrying under the Mustang like a cockroach. It was doubtful he'd even fit under there. On the other side was a 20-year-old BMW. Gantz' personal vehicle. The BMW was practically lying on the asphalt, panting; he'd have to be an ant to get under it.

He was trapped.

The other man was nearly at his position, he had to do something. He looked down and saw his shoe. He smiled and undid the lace then held the ends like he was about to tie it. The shoelace gave him a reason to be bent down, other than trying to conceal himself.

He kept his head dipped forward, using his black hair to blend in with the shadow between the two cars. The other man cruised past with no change in the cadence of his walk.

Coombes re-tied his shoelace and stood up.

He watched the Explorer driver walk down the line of vehicles like he'd never seen him before. Fat, short hair, it even looked like he was still wearing the same blue shirt as the day before.

This time, there was no mistaking the identity.

It was Block.

18

Coombes needed to get away for a while and decided to take Sato to the scene where Molly Walker met her fate. No matter how well he knew an investigation, nothing compared to visiting a crime scene for himself. It was an option unavailable to him for Dakota Lawrence and Natalie Hahn, who were both murdered at an unknown location.

He stood looking at the former home of Carson Naylor, the business partner. It was huge, a mansion. Over ten million dollars, easy. Naylor's business had made decent money before it all went wrong. It felt like the property was trying to tell him something, but what that was he couldn't say.

With nothing coming to him, he turned to face the street.

Sato was wearing mirrored sunglasses instead of her normal polarized sunglasses. It wasn't hard to figure out why. The location brought back bad memories and she didn't want him to see her eyes.

He could relate, he really could.

Using measurements taken from the incident report, they used chalk to mark the three major points of interest: where Molly Walker stood; where Stephen Walker's SUV was when she first appeared; and the position of the Mercedes when he floored the throttle.

While they got set up, Coombes told her about Block and the two IA detectives. He expected her to get mad, but instead she was silent and let her sunglasses do the talking. When they were done, Sato drove the Dodge back down Hudson Avenue, turned, then nosed forward to line it up at the first marker. He walked into the road and faced the Charger.

This was the starting position.

It surprised him how far away the car was and how small Sato's face looked behind the wheel. No bigger than his smallest fingernail at arm's length. If he didn't already know it was her, he wouldn't have known from a quick glance.

He replayed the dashcam footage in his head.

Molly Walker had appeared fast, then drawn to a sudden halt like she'd been running for a train, only to see it pull away. She had then shot a look back toward the sidewalk, before finally turning to the SUV.

Her face had shown instant recognition. Coombes walked back to the sidewalk and dummied several runs of stepping out and glancing up the street, then the way he'd do it, which was the opposite.

Look first, then cross.

He didn't like the scenario for two reasons.

First of all, nobody crossed a road like that. They looked to see it was safe to cross before stepping out, they didn't wait until they were already in the middle. Second, who wasted time looking at the *driver* when two and a half tons of steel was hurtling toward you?

He thought for a moment.

The Mercedes was a distinctive-looking vehicle and there weren't many around. It was chunky, it had an exhaust that went up next to the windshield, the thing was ready for a safari. It was possible that simply seeing the *type* of vehicle was enough for Molly to take the extra step of identifying the driver. It explained why she froze.

If she was having an affair, her thinking was easy to guess.

Not you, not here.

Her husband being there could only mean he knew about the affair and she was in trouble.

On the day of the incident, a flatbed truck had been parked at the side of the road limiting her view, forcing her farther out onto the street than normal.

Sato thought this explained why she didn't sense the approaching danger by limiting her sight lines until it was too late.

Coombes didn't buy it.

The flatbed might have blocked her view, but it also offered her protection. All she had to do was step back behind the safety of the truck. In his own experience, the presence of an obstruction always made him more cautious than usual, not the reverse.

In reality, the moment had existed for only a split second.

At this point, Stephen Walker had been driving at a pedestrian 22 mph. He was approaching his destination, and he had slowed to look for his wife's car.

Coombes beckoned Sato on.

She drove forward to the second position they'd marked on the road. This was the point where Walker hit the gas, or as he would have it, hit the gas instead of the brake. A single second had passed and Walker had traveled thirty-two feet in that time.

At this distance, he could easily see Sato's face through the windshield.

While prepping for the original trial, Sato had conducted a test to see if Walker could've stopped if he had hit the brake. The prosecutor believed the defense might argue the collision was unavoidable either way and that Molly Walker was the agent of her own destruction. Since the test relied on reaction time the test was inconclusive. In six out of ten simulated accidents, Sato stopped without hitting a dummy, with the remaining four times being a hit.

Walker, of course, had not hit the brake.

It took the Mercedes two and a half seconds to cover the remaining 188 feet to where Molly stood. On impact, the SUV broke both her legs, her pelvis, her right arm, half her ribs, her collarbone, and fractured her skull as it hit the road. Then, by some unfortunate miracle, she hadn't died.

He decided he'd seen enough and beckoned Sato once again. She drew up alongside and he opened the passenger door and climbed in.

"Did you get what you needed?"

He shook his head.

"I thought seeing it in person would make the pieces fit, but I have more questions than ever. Nobody crosses a road like that. It reminded me of the shower sequence in *Psycho* where Janet Leigh gets into the shower stall *then* turns the water on. Who does that? You'd get a minimum of thirty seconds of cold water before the heat came through."

"You're living in the past, Coombes. I see people crossing without lifting their eyes from their cell phones. Sometimes they're doing a video call or live streaming. Nobody is 100% in the moment anymore, their mind is on their socials, the news, their personal life."

He supposed she was right.

"Okay," he said. "She'd just been with Naylor. She's happy, in love, and she's already in the middle of the road before she thinks about where she is and the danger she's in."

Sato smiled, her first of the day.

"*Exactly!*"

He turned to face forward, to look at an intersection a short distance away.

No matter how in love or happy he'd ever been, he'd never forgotten how to cross the road. Some things were just hard-wired. As an Angeleno, he basically assumed he was about to get creamed by an SUV at all times and lived accordingly.

"I suppose you're right, Grace. What else explains her actions?"

"She makes a mistake and he takes advantage. There's no mystery to solve."

It was a point of view she doubtless shared. Not long after he'd run over his wife, Walker tricked Sato into making a mistake and he again took advantage. The man was on a roll.

"What now?" Sato said.

"It's time we had a chat with Carson Naylor."

19

THE CURRENT ADDRESS LISTED in the DMV for Molly Walker's business partner was on Bronson Avenue in Larchmont, a little over a mile from his former address. A family home, instead of a castle fit for a king.

Carson Naylor opened the door and flinched. *Interesting.*

"Detectives Coombes and Sato, LAPD."

Naylor stood in the doorway his hands gripping the frame on either side like he was working himself up to parachute out an airplane. It was a posture Coombes had seen many times before: Naylor didn't want to let them in.

Instinctively, Coombes disliked the other man.

"Of course," he continued, "you've already met Detective Sato."

Coombes was pushing him already; he couldn't help himself.

"It's true then, there's going to be another trial."

"That's right, Mr. Naylor. Now, are you going to invite us in?"

Naylor muttered something Coombes didn't catch, then stepped aside. As he came through the door, he turned so his back wasn't toward Naylor as Sato passed him. She gave him strong eye contact, no doubt confused by his aggression.

The door closed and the space became dark, amplified by dark furniture and bare wooden floorboards. Naylor walked them through into a large media room with open patio doors out into a yard. The light here was perfect. He sat down without asking, crossed his legs and took out his notebook. Naylor sat opposite him in a worn leather Eames chair.

He said nothing and let his eyes move over Naylor.

The other man's face was pale and beaded with sweat, his eyes sunken and dark. Naylor looked sick. He'd seen drug addicts look the same way, like they were haunting their own body.

Disliking someone wasn't exactly a new experience for Coombes, it was practically his default setting. Often when this happened it turned out that the other person was no good so he'd learned to listen to instinct rather than dismiss it.

Sato, though, was having none of it.

"You moved house," she said. "Why don't you tell us about that?"

"I had to. Every day I was looking at the spot where it happened. When I went to work, I didn't want to go home. When I did, I'd stand there looking at the road unable to breathe."

Naylor answered Sato's question while looking at him.

Coombes' opinion of Naylor dropped still further.

"I see," she said. "And how have you been since then?"

"A couple of months ago, I saw another one of those G Wagons. I threw up all over the sidewalk, my shoes, my suit. I just couldn't stop. I thought I was going to pass out. Seeing this thing took me right back to that day."

The conversation wasn't going anywhere useful, so he cut in.

"Where were you when it happened?"

Naylor glanced at Sato, then back to Coombes.

"We covered this last time; she knows all this."

"This is a new trial, Mr. Naylor. Fresh charges. Everything is reset, we have to prove the case all over again and Stephen Walker knows how the game's played. The jury doesn't get to know that he's been in prison for the last two years. I like to start fresh. Understood?"

Naylor nodded. He looked broken.

"Do you think that monster might get away with it?"

"He might. How about you answer my question?"

"I forgot what you asked."

Coombes turned to Sato.

"Have you got a copy of the overhead on your iPad?"

"Sure, just a second."

Sato opened her tablet and located the picture he was after. It was a simplified drawing that had been produced to show jurors the sidewalk, the road, the outline of the flatbed truck and a cross where Molly Walker had been standing when she was struck by the SUV.

He held the tablet in front of Naylor.

"Where were you standing?"

Naylor pointed to the side, just off the screen.

"My house was here. I wasn't wearing shoes, so I stood in my doorway to watch her go. *Why didn't I put on my goddamn shoes?*"

The man had been spinning this story about his shoes since day one and Coombes was tired of it.

"This isn't going to work if you're feeding us a bunch of BS."

"What do you mean?"

"You didn't *watch her go*; you kissed her goodbye. The two of you were lovers."

Naylor's face turned scarlet. "Who told you that?"

"Molly was sexually active prior to what happened in the street. A sample of semen found in her body was collected and processed for DNA. Are you really going to make me come back with a warrant for a cheek swab?"

There was no sample, no DNA.

Naylor tilted his head forward and sobbed.

Coombes didn't have to look to know Sato was glaring at him.

"We were in love. She was going to leave that pig and we were going to get married. He must've found out. That's why he did it, isn't it? If he couldn't have her, nobody could."

Coombes wrote this last expression in his notebook.

"If that's so, how do you suppose he found out?"

Naylor looked up. His eyes were bloodshot.

"Because she was happy. When I met her, she was miserable all the time. She drank, took pills, slept half the day. After a couple of weeks, she changed. There was a chemistry between us, we made each other laugh. She quit the booze, the pills, she got into exercise. He couldn't have missed it, he had to know why."

"Did she mention if he was ever violent toward her?"

Naylor nodded.

"Not long after they got married, he began pushing her around, hitting her. She said he once punched so hard that she blacked out and fell through a glass table. After that, it was just verbal abuse, controlling behavior, all that. She was terrified of him."

"I'm surprised he let the two of you work together."

"He didn't want to but he'd had his bar license suspended on a drug charge. He needed money to pay the bills until he got his license back. By the time he did, I guess he got used to his wife making more money than him."

"Did she need medical treatment after the incident with the table?"

"I assume so. Molly said she came to and there was blood everywhere. He was just sitting looking at her, drinking a beer. Like maybe he thought she was dead and he was working out how to get rid of her body."

Coombes made a note to check ER records. A prior history of violence toward the victim could help close the case.

"Tell me about your business."

"I'm a jeweler. The way it worked was I designed the product and Molly was the face of the company. She had a regular slot on one of the home shopping networks. People just loved her; she was like the best friend they never had. Everything would always sell out; we couldn't keep up with demand."

Coombes nodded.

"How's the business going without her?"

"It's not. She *was* the business, without her, sales dropped to zero."

"Isn't it true that the business was in trouble long before the accident?"

Naylor jumped out his seat, coming straight at him.

"It was *not* an accident. Don't you dare call it that!"

The man's eyes were bulging, crazed. Naylor was standing over him, close enough to take a swing. Coombes hadn't used the word accident by mistake, it was a test.

"Sit down, Mr. Naylor. You won't like what happens if you don't."

Naylor balled his fists in frustration, his jaws clamped tight while he considered his next move. He sighed and the tension went out his body. Coombes continued.

"Your business was failing, it's a matter of public record. Two thirds of your staff had been fired and you started working from your address on Hudson. So, when you say that you didn't want to come home from work and pass the spot where it happened, we've immediately got a problem, no? You're telling us a lie."

Naylor held his hands out at his sides.

"What's it matter now? The sector collapsed. We couldn't compete with Chinese imports; they were practically giving it away. Only the premium brands survived."

Naylor sat back down, defeated.

By the conversation, by the way the world was now.

Coombes had some sympathy for Naylor's situation. He'd seen a lot of businesses go under to the faceless horde that was globalization. Being beaten on prices, when the other guy was using slave labor as a workforce.

"Should I assume that these business problems were causing friction between you and Molly in the days leading up to what happened?"

"We were worried about it, sure, but we had a strategy that would've saved the company. If you're suggesting we fought, that's not what happened. If anything, it brought us closer together. We were a team."

Coombes looked up from his notebook.

"And this strategy you mention, what was it?"

Naylor hung his head.

"Import Chinese product ourselves and re-brand it."

"What about your US employees?"

The other man didn't answer and turned his face away in embarrassment. A wild animal will chew off its own leg to escape a trap, business was no different.

He turned a page in his notebook and left a gap before continuing.

"So," Coombes said. "The big money stops rolling in. Maybe her husband figures he no longer wants to turn a blind eye to what the two of you have been getting up to, decides to do something about it."

He saw relief on Naylor's face.

There shouldn't have been relief.

"Molly's money was paid into a joint account. Her husband was spending it like nothing had changed, like the market would bounce back. It was the only money she had, if she was going to divorce him, she would've needed that money for herself."

Coombes frowned.

"You think he meant to catch you in the act?"

"What did *you* mean?"

"We think he came here to kill you. He had a gun."

Naylor's eyes widened.

"Can't you use that against him?"

"It goes to motive, but it's circumstantial. The gun wasn't involved in what happened. We have to prove the case that's in front of us."

"That's ridiculous!"

Coombes glanced at Sato to see if she had any more questions and saw Naylor follow suit. It was the first time he'd given her any attention. She got straight to it.

"If I could just go back for a moment to expand on something my partner asked before. Aside from the state of the business, how was Molly generally in the weeks before the events of that day?"

Naylor's head tilted back, his eyes going up to the ceiling.

That's where the memories were, up and to the left.

"She was on a big health kick. Special nutrient shakes, a *lot* of fruit and veg, expensive vitamins. It's the way she was, she didn't do anything by half, she was all-in every time. She even started getting into all that crystal stuff. Some of her friends were hippies or whatever they call them now. I didn't judge, it seemed to be working for her."

Sato sighed quietly, like she knew what was coming.

"And how *exactly* did it seem to be working?"

"She lost weight," Naylor said. "Look, I thought she was perfect the way she was, but she'd poke her chin and cheeks all the time, ask me if I thought she should get work done. I *didn't* and I told her so, but with this new regime she managed it without surgery."

"Was she happy and pumped up with her success?"

Naylor shook his head.

"No. She never mentioned her weight loss to me. After all the times she complained about her supposed imperfections, suddenly, she didn't want to talk about it."

Both he and Sato made notes of this. His handwriting was terrible and Sato finished long before he did and asked another question.

"Any new tensions between her and her husband that you know of?"

Naylor's face screwed up in a snarl.

"Same as ever. Threats, bullying, throwing her stuff around. The last couple of weeks she got super-nervous. If we went out for lunch, she'd worry he was going to catch us together. I didn't get that. I mean, we work together, why wouldn't we eat at a restaurant? She'd pull out her cell phone and look at her socials for a moment, it seemed to relax her."

Sato nodded and turned back to Coombes.

"We understand you were a frequent visitor to Molly in hospital."

Naylor frowned at him. "And?"

"Every day for two hours. How did you spend the time?"

"I talked to her. I thought she could hear me and that she might follow my voice back out the dream world to where we were."

"What did you say to her?"

"For the first half hour or so I'd tell her about what was happening in the world. I'd read her news from the *Times*. Then I'd read her sections of *Sharp Objects*, her favorite book. It's not exactly a ray of sunshine that novel, but I was trying to reach her, you know? I thought familiar words, a familiar voice...something might activate in her head. I must've read that book to her three times."

Sato leaned over and whispered to him.

"Where are you going with this, Johnny?"

She was right, the hospital was an irrelevance.

"I think that's everything for now, Mr. Naylor."

They got to their feet and Coombes put his notebook away. Naylor remained seated, his thoughts apparently still thinking about Molly in her hospital bed.

"You weren't called to the stand last time around, but it's safe to assume that won't be the case this time. If you lose your cool in court like you did with me then all you do is help this creep get out of prison. I want you to take some time to get your head straight."

Naylor stared blankly up at him; his expression unreadable.

"We'll show ourselves out."

They walked back the way they'd come.

Naylor might have come down in the world a little, but he lived in a pretty nice home for a man that was unemployed. Maybe one point five million. It was a long way from sleeping under a bridge, that was for sure.

Coombes supposed Naylor had some equity built up in his previous home to transfer to the new property. The failed business explained his move here as much as any desire to escape what happened on Hudson Avenue.

They got back into the Charger. He'd parked in the shade, but the interior was still over a hundred degrees. Coombes started the car and cranked up the air-conditioning.

"Naylor's hiding something," he said.

"Yeah, but what? Something that matters, or something that doesn't?"

"Whatever it is, I want to know before the trial."

"That stuff about the DNA, you made that up?"

He held his hand over the cool air pouring out the vent and moved his fingers back and forth. It always seemed more cooling if you moved your hand.

"I might have exaggerated a little."

"Johnny, you lied."

"I played a hunch, Grace. It's part of policework, it's not illegal."

"What if they *hadn't* had sex, what then?"

"Then I would've apologized and said I was mixing the case up with another we're working. As it was, I confirmed the theory she was loved-up and happy, possibly explaining her distraction as she crossed the road. He was never going to tell us that otherwise."

"You're a piece of work, Coombes."

"I am whatever the work needs me to be."

———

SATO STOPPED AT A Drive-Thru on Romaine and he bought lunch, paying a masked server with a card reader on a pole. They parked in the regular restaurant parking and began to eat, engine and AC still running. The conversation with Naylor had left him without much appetite, but the spices on his chicken wrap brought it back and he finished it in less than a minute. He took a drink, then picked at his fries. Sato turned to him.

"How's your bones investigation going?"

"Not good, Grace. I have no leads, no crime scenes, a missing murder book, and no interest from anyone in command that I pursue the case, never mind solve it."

She said nothing for a moment.

"The person that took the murder book knew your badge number and serial?"

"That's right."

"You're talking about another cop."

"Definitely. Someone that fitted in and knew my digits like the back of their hand."

He ate some more fries. They tasted like cardboard. Was it worth it, living longer, if this was the price? He knocked them back with a mouthful of Coke, at least that still tasted good.

"I think you're intentionally creating a barrier to finding it."

He turned to face her. She knew, it was there on her face.

"Why would I do that?"

"What if you find this murder book and see something you didn't see before. The killer was right there and you missed it. You had him and let him walk. Now he's killed again, maybe more than once. If you don't find the murder book, maybe you never find out. It's easier to live with not knowing."

"Jesus, Grace."

She picked up her Diet Coke and sucked on the straw, causing her mouth to pucker around the end. He found himself staring at her lips.

Sato pretended not to see it and put the cup down.

"Okay, a cop took the book but it wasn't official or they would've used their own name when they checked it out. They used your name to hide theirs. You worked the case, it looked natural that you would have it, agreed?"

Coombes nodded. "That makes sense."

"Let's say for the sake of argument, that the person who took it *wasn't* trying to block a future investigation, what does that leave?"

"But that *is* what they're doing."

She held up her hand. "Bear with me."

He knew what she wanted; he'd thought about it before.

"It leaves someone trying to solve it."

"Of any cop in L.A., who other than yourself was as invested in the Lawrence case and, as you say, knew your digits like the back of their hand?"

Coombes closed his eyes and sighed.

"Oh, man," he said. "That asshole!"

"I mean, when you get right down to it, Johnny, the only digits I know as well as my own, are yours."

20

EDDIE WILLARD OWNED A bungalow five streets from Coombes' former address. Despite this proximity, neither one of them had ever visited the other's house the entire time they were partners. Coombes rang the bell. He hadn't much liked Willard, who had been brimming with unjustified confidence and unwilling to accept input from others. Two fatal character flaws for a detective and, to his mind, a contributing factor to Dakota Lawrence's killer escaping justice.

Coombes pressed the bell again, this time for a five-count.

Old bastard's probably still asleep, he thought.

Willard's car sat on the drive; he was definitely home.

He glanced back to the Dodge and saw Sato inside, working on her tablet. It wasn't just command that wasn't too interested in his case.

Coombes raised his hand again, ready to give the bell a ten-count push. Nobody enjoyed being on the receiving end of one of those. At the last second, he saw light shift through the narrow glass panels in the door and stepped back.

Willard opened the door wearing boxer shorts and sandals, his formerly paper-white skin now tanned to a deep bronze by years of retirement under the Californian sun. Coombes saw curly white chest hair and a beer belly as tight as any pregnant woman. Willard smiled.

"Hey, rock star. It's been a while."

Inwardly, Coombes sighed. He hadn't missed *that* nickname.

"Almost five years."

Willard glanced at Coombes' suit and tilted his head.

"I don't see you in the rat squad, I guess you made RHD?"

"That's right. Are you going to invite me in?"

The door opened wide and his former partner waved him in. Willard was holding a thick glass tumbler in the hand that had been hidden by the door. There was a quarter inch of amber liquid at the bottom.

They walked into a living room. The air felt like it had been in there a while. A television sat in the corner, a small black rectangle. Maybe thirty-two inches. Willard wasn't spending his retirement in front of the screen like a lot of people did. Like *he* would. Coombes had his eye on an eighty-five-inch TV. Like going to the movies every day.

He saw Willard's detective shield in a cube of resin on a bookshelf. A reminder from the Department of his years of service, and a reminder that it was in the past.

Coombes turned to Willard.

"I'm sorry I didn't make it to Nora's service. I hope you know I would've gone if I'd heard about it in time. I'm just not in much contact with any of our old network."

Willard gave a small nod.

"I appreciate that, brother."

They stood awkwardly. He wasn't sure how to begin.

"All right, John. You're not here for me and this isn't a social call, so I guess this is about an old case we worked. Am I right?"

"I'm looking at one of our unsolved cases. When I checked the archives, I found that the murder book is missing. Apparently, I checked it out, when I know for a fact that I didn't."

Willard's left eyelid twitched.

"I don't know what you're talking about."

"Come on, Eddie, I know you took it. I'm not here to make trouble for you. I need it back."

They stood in tense silence, like a couple of wild west cowboys ready to shoot each other in the street. Willard sighed, his chest deflating. It was hard to play the tough guy when you were only wearing boxer shorts.

"Walk with me."

He followed Willard down the hallway, his head turned sideways, looking at framed photographs on the wall, anything rather than the untanned scar tissue in front of him. The pictures were all of Willard's wife. Smiling, happy. Before her diagnosis. Willard opened a door opposite the kitchen, then held the door open for Coombes against an automatic closer.

Inside, the lights were already on.

This was where Willard had been when he'd rung the bell.

It was a large double garage which had been converted into office space. On the wall against the house, five cork boards had been mounted vertically, lining the space from floor to ceiling and from the door into the house to the double door to the driveway outside.

It was an evidence wall, and it was covered.

At the top of the middle cork board was a photograph of Dakota Lawrence. A studio headshot, not one from evidence. She was beautiful, with a hint of something behind her eyes. Mischief, intelligence, *something*.

Coombes stood looking at the wall, processing the evidence.

As before, Willard was focused on Anthony De Luca as prime suspect. To this end, there were many pictures of him that looked like they'd been taken recently with a long lens. Recently, because De Luca was wearing a neck scarf pulled up over the lower half of his face in a half-hearted attempt to comply with the mask mandate.

"I know what you thought of me, John. That I was a washout, that I didn't care anymore, that I was just waiting to pull the pin. The worst part, was that you were right. But the Lawrence case..."

Coombes turned to Willard.

"It got under your skin."

"Yes. I needed it. To solve it, to catch that bastard. When we didn't, I couldn't do it anymore. I left the Department the first chance I could."

"Cut yourself a break, you were wounded in the line of duty."

"That was my own fault. My negligence got me shot but it served its purpose and gave me a way to retire early. I took it, man. I guess you didn't like me taking disability when others have been wounded worse than me, but I was no use to anyone with a badge."

"I never thought any less of you for that."

"It allowed me to be with Nora at the end. I'm grateful for that."

Willard finished his drink and held up his glass.

"Can I get you a Scotch?"

"I'm good, thanks."

Willard poured himself another glass from a bottle that was sitting on the workbench next to him. Three fingers.

"You back on Lawrence officially, or unofficially?"

"A bit of both. My lieutenant knows about it, but I'm working another case."

Willard's eyes moved over him, working it out.

"You identified another victim, but it's old. A cold case."

"That's right."

The side of Willard's face rose up in a snarl. No surprise, just anger. They had always assumed Lawrence's murder wasn't a one-off. A killer that took the time to mark his victim was proud of what he'd done and was going to do it again.

"What do you want from me, John?"

"The murder book for one. Then I want everything on this wall behind me and anything else you've turned up since I last worked the case. I'm taking it from here."

Willard's face fell.

"Don't shut me out of this, rock star. I need to be a part of it."

Coombes had anticipated this reaction. The other man had invested a lot of time into catching Lawrence's killer. Without a sense of ongoing involvement, Willard might not be cooperative about the evidence he had or hold a vital piece back for himself, as he often had in the past. But Willard had to know who called the shots now.

"I don't know. You've got no standing, you're not a cop anymore."

"I'll do anything, ok? Grunt work, surveillance, whatever you need. Not being a cop means I can poke around without a warrant. Go where you can't go."

"That's kind of what I'm afraid of, Eddie. If we get this guy, we get him right. We give nothing to a defense attorney except an unwinnable case."

Willard's face lit up. "You said 'we'."

"All right. Look, there will be some legwork you can help me with, particularly since I'm working this other case. How about we see how that goes and take it from there?"

"You got it, John."

"None of this is official. My lieutenant will know nothing about you."

"I get it. Helping to catch this guy is my reward."

"A couple of things that are non-negotiable. If you're on the case, you're off the sauce. I don't want you working this with a glass of Scotch in one hand. This isn't *The Rockford Files*. Also, there's this great invention called clothes; you need to look into that before I see you again. Finally, cut the 'rock star' shit, that got old a long time ago."

Willard put his glass down and held up his hands in surrender.

"Whatever you need."

Coombes dug out a business card and passed it to Willard.

"Make copies of all this stuff and send it to my email. The good stuff, the bad stuff, the meaningless notes. Let *me* decide what's important, just send it all over. I'll work up a list of tasks for you. Some of them you might already have covered."

"I've been on this for a long time. I covered a lot of ground."

He spotted a blue binder on the workbench, next to Willard's ass.

"I'll take the murder book now," he said.

"Take it, I got another copy saved up here."

Willard tapped his right temple.

Coombes took the binder then shot a last look at the wall of evidence.

Booth was on it, way over to the side. There were no paparazzi-style shots of him getting in or out of his car or home, as there was for De Luca. He kept his head moving in case Willard saw where he was looking. Natalie Hahn was up there too, for the role she played as an eyewitness, foreshadowing her role as a victim.

When he was through, Willard pressed a button on the wall and the large double door began to open, flooding the garage with daylight. His old partner walked with him down the path, then across the street to where Sato was parked.

A car honked its horn as they crossed the road.

"I'm not the man I used to be, John. I'm back in the zone."

Coombes put on his sunglasses and opened the passenger door.

"That would be more believable if you were wearing pants right now."

Willard laughed. "Same old John."

He lowered himself into the car, nodded to Willard, then closed the door.

Willard hadn't changed, he just wanted Coombes to forget his true nature. Nobody changed, not really. Not him, not Willard, not the sick twisted waste of skin that cut a cross into Dakota Lawrence and Natalie Hahn.

The only time anybody changed, was to get worse.

21

WHEN THEY GOT BACK to the apartment, Coombes found his doorbell had a flashing light which indicated that the IA detectives had performed a factory reset on the device in an attempt to erase everything. Since files were stored in the cloud anyway, all they'd really done was delete his internet connection and account information.

With the Aryan Brotherhood situation not yet resolved, he needed to get the camera back up and running as soon as possible.

Coombes walked around the apartment to make sure nobody was lying in wait. The apartment looked exactly as it had when they'd left, yet somehow everything seemed different. Two men had broken in and made themselves at home. Co-workers.

People that should have his back.

He found the first device in the kitchen, stuck to the underside of one of the high-level units. It was dull, black, and anonymous. Nothing to say what it was, or who had put it there. It was shaped like an old-fashioned pack of gum, the kind you ripped the end off and there were seven sticks inside.

Coombes left it where it was and straightened up.

It dawned on him that IA might also have installed video surveillance. His eyes went up, scanning the corners of the room, then the pendant light that hung down from the ceiling. He saw no cameras, but there was another device in the pendant. This one looked like a three-inch long hotdog except it was white, no doubt to blend in with the light fittings.

A backup microphone, or some kind of signal booster.

Placement of the microphones would be governed by where IA expected to capture conversation. The kitchen was small and intimate. Coombes had always felt safe here, able to be with Sato as he wanted, away from the rules of the Department. It was a good spot to pick if they wanted to catch him with his guard down.

The next obvious target, was the breakfast bar where he and Sato spent time eating, sometimes having a drink. He left the kitchen and explored the underside of the breakfast bar. He found another anonymous pack of gum.

It was too easy.

But he'd only found the devices because he was looking for them. Coombes supposed his visitors would want to be in and out as quickly as possible in case they were interrupted.

He found the same type of device on the underside of the coffee table in front of the TV, and on the low desk where Sato worked with her laptop. That just left the bedrooms. He figured that the bathroom, the walk-in wardrobe, and the cupboards were all safe.

Dread built in his gut.

What would it mean if the bedrooms were bugged?

As a cop, he lost a lot of the protection afforded to a private citizen. A judge might hesitate before signing off on the bugging of a bedroom, but if he was under suspicion by the Department, no judge was involved. The IA had the right to come in here, that was their job.

This was Block coming at him.

He'd made his captain look like a clown on national television the year before and Block wanted payback.

Coombes took off his suit jacket and got down on his knees, checking the underside of his bed, using the flashlight on his cell phone to reach into the dark spaces. Nothing. Next, he looked on the back of the headboard, then the bedside lights. All clean.

He glanced at the nightstands on either side of the bed.

The obvious places were the backs, the side that faced the wall; or underneath, facing the floor. The tops and the sides were visible, no hiding place. Coombes reached underneath and swept his hand blindly across the bottom. He found a black sock under his nightstand, and a stud earring under Sato's. Lastly, he stood and checked the backs, facing the wall.

Still nothing.

A microphone had to be unobstructed, it couldn't be inside a drawer, yet he found himself pulling out each of the drawers to check them just in case. He sat on the edge of the bed and took a deep breath. The other bugs he'd found almost immediately, if there were any in the bedroom, they wouldn't be that hard to find.

He looked at his nightstand and the items on it.

A lamp, a handset for the landline, a cord to charge his cell phone, and a clock radio. He turned over the radio and saw a flat disc stuck to the bottom.

For the first time, Coombes felt angry. This crossed a line.

Were they trying to catch him and Sato in bed together?

He walked into the living room, caught Sato's eye and tilted his head toward the door. They walked silently out the apartment and into the hallway.

"Everything's bugged," he said. "I didn't check your room, but I'm sure there's one there too. They're small, so I doubt they can transmit far. Either they're using our own Wi-Fi, or they storing up recordings to be reviewed at a later date."

"Is this about you and me?"

"I don't think so, it doesn't feel right. Block hates me and wants me gone. Somehow, he found out about this apartment and thinks this is his best shot to even the score."

"Johnny, if they looked in my nightstand next to our bed-" Sato flushed pink when she realized what she'd said. "Shit. *Anyway*, there's a bunch of my things. They'd know it isn't yours, it's girly stuff."

"Relax. At best it proves I'm in a relationship, there's nothing there with your name on it. Your little setup in the spare room will convince them that we're on the level. It's funny, but this might actually help us down the road."

"All right, but what do we do about the microphones?"

What he wanted to do was box them all up, walk into Professional Standards, and dump it on one of the IA detective's desks as the man sat there open-mouthed. It would be satisfying, but would gain him nothing. They were in his grill because they thought he was up to something and returning the bugs would do little to make that go away, it might even lead to him getting suspended.

This was part of what he'd signed up for, he'd always known it.

"For now? Forget about them, we've got murders to solve."

"Are you *serious?*"

Coombes shrugged.

"You broke up with me, there's nothing to hide."

He moved to pass her and she put her hand on his chest, stopping him.

"I hit pause. I *didn't* break up."

"Let's just focus on our cases, work out where we're at later, ok?"

She nodded, and let her hand drop away.

22

It was close to nine p.m. by the time he had his first look at the murder book that he'd taken from Eddie Willard that afternoon. The first thing he discovered, was that for every section in the book, there was a second version added by Willard as he continued his unofficial investigation. It surprised him that his old partner had respected the integrity of the original documents not to mess them up with potentially inadmissible content.

With the addition of Willard's new files, the binder was three inches thick and weighed about four pounds. It was the most extensive murder book he'd ever seen, and it both impressed him and made his heart sink.

This was what failure looked like.

Coombes opened the binder to the first section, the chronological record, and began to read. Every entry had a time and date listed against it, and each summary description entered had the surname of the detective who completed it.

As with most cases, the bulk of the entries were at the beginning of the investigation, where time was usually a factor, with fewer and fewer entries going forward as leads came to nothing and the investigation stalled.

The chrono showed that the body of an unidentified white woman was discovered at 07:18 on 01/31/2015 by Carl Smith, a security guard working for Aquarius Studios. Smith was following up on an earlier report that a store mannikin had been dumped on a vacant lot on a section of the sprawling studio known as Avenue Forever.

The Watch Commander contacted Willard, the senior partner, at 07:32 and by 08:15, both he and Willard were on site. When they arrived, the body had already been identified by a passing secretary as Dakota Lawrence.

Coombes frowned: the secretary's name wasn't listed.

All he remembered was that everyone at the scene already knew who Lawrence was when he and Willard rolled up. He had, after all, recognized her himself once he got over the fact that she was naked, drained of blood, and her head was almost severed by a power cord.

A canvass of the area revealed nothing as the majority of movie people were not morning people and didn't normally arrive before 09:00 at the earliest. Of those working late the day before, none had noticed any unusual activity, or unfamiliar faces.

There was no security footage.

The Coroner Investigator and forensic technicians took control of the scene at 09:16 and Lawrence's ID was officially confirmed with a portable fingerprint scanner. The investigator was unable to give a precise time of death beyond an eight-hour window as the blood loss was so complete as to skew the metrics for liver temperature, rigor mortis, and lividity.

The eight-hour window meant that sometime between 22:00 - 07:00 the killer drove up, posed the body, then drove away. No blood, hair, or fibers were recovered from the scene; however, a cast was taken of a size 9 Adidas Ultra Boost.

Coombes sat back.

Somehow, he'd managed to forget about the shoe print left at the scene. The small size and light impression weight indicated that it likely belonged to a woman of no more than one hundred twenty-six pounds. From these two facts, it had further been supposed that the print hadn't been made by the killer.

Dakota Lawrence was removed from the scene at 10:05 and forty-eight minutes after that, Willard and Coombes left to perform death notification to Dakota's mother.

Coombes flipped forward to Willard's new chronological record and noticed that he'd started with copies of the original and handwritten notes on top. Willard had written *Melissa Claybourne* next to the missing secretary's name with a cell phone number. Next to the window of death, he'd written *possibly up to 48 hours - Ron Goldstein, ME*. Finally, by the shoe print, he'd added *M. Claybourne, size 7*.

He recalled that one theory behind the shoe print was that it had belonged to the secretary who'd identified the body. Taking the time to eliminate this thread impressed Coombes, and he decided to work exclusively from Eddie Willard's new versions going forward.

His former partner claimed to be a changed man. Based on what he'd seen so far, he was inclined to agree. Sato's case would use up a lot of his time. Instead of splitting his focus between Booth and De Luca, he'd have Willard continue his surveillance of the producer, while he pursued what he thought was the more worthwhile lead.

Let them each follow their own instincts.

Coombes turned the corners of following pages with his thumb until he got to the end of the section. He sighed. The chronological record was 34 pages long. He'd only read the first 9 pages and it had taken an hour and a quarter.

A murder book was just facts. Times, descriptions, names. There was no emotion on the page, but as he read it, the emotion came back to him. All the details he'd tried to remember when the murder book was missing came flooding back, unlocked with a few facts.

Mostly what was unlocked, though, was the rage he'd felt that first morning in the studio lot. A desire burned like never before to catch whoever was responsible and for whatever form justice took to take place.

"You're tired. Look at it in the morning."

Sato was standing next to him in black satin pajamas.

"You're right," he said, hearing the truth of it in his voice.

Coombes didn't move, thinking that a good place to take a break in the chrono was after he and Willard first met Booth. He'd long held this idea that if he worked on something before he went to bed his subconscious would continue to work on it while he was asleep and the answer would be there for him in the morning.

"John. You always tell me not to work tired, that I'll miss things."

"Using me against me, that's not fair."

"It is what it is," she said.

23

EARLY THE NEXT MORNING, Coombes parked outside an ochre-colored Spanish Colonial on Stearns Drive and killed the engine. Until recently, this was where Stephen and Molly Walker lived. He opened the door and stepped out onto the street.

It was not immediately obvious to him why he'd come here, except for the fact that he thought Walker's neighbor might know a little about the state of the couple's relationship. He stood on the sidewalk and stared at the Spanish Colonial, then turned to look at the houses on either side. He didn't know which neighbor Walker had mentioned during their interview. Potentially, a neighbor could include houses on the opposite side of the street.

He discounted that for now and walked to the house to his left.

The houses were all different styles, this one looked like a brick and had white walls and fussy fences all around. It didn't feel right. Coombes walked back the way he'd come to the house on the other side, walking past Sato who stood on the sidewalk with a hand propped up on her hip.

The house on the right was smaller and there was no fence marking the boundary with the Walkers' lawn. This was it, he thought. Next to the path he saw a small sign.

Beware of the dog!

This was *definitely* the place.

Walker had complained about the neighbor's dog shitting on his lawn.

He gave the doorbell a polite two-second press. A moment later, a large man opened the door wearing a red robe and his face covered in shaving foam.

The man allowed himself a visual inspection of Sato's chest before turning to Coombes.

"I'm not buying anything."

Coombes drew his suit jacket aside, exposing his badge.

"Trust me, we're not selling. Coombes and Sato, LAPD."

"Oh yeah? What's this all about?"

"We'd like to talk to you about Stephen Walker."

"What a scumbag. I don't know what to tell you, man. I never met him. I only moved in here on Monday. It's Bill Perry you want to speak to, not me."

"Really."

It wasn't a question; Coombes wasn't used to being caught flat-footed.

"Oh yeah. I picked this place up at an amazing price, it wasn't even listed on the market. Perry reached out to a couple of people, word got back to me, I bought it. Simple. Best deal of my life. Must've saved two hundred grand."

Inwardly, Coombes sighed.

"I don't suppose you have a new address for this...*Perry?*"

"As it happens, I do. He moved next door!"

The man in the robe laughed. With the red robe and the white foam beard, he was quite the summertime Santa Claus.

"Next door, as in *Stephen Walker's* home?"

"The very same."

Coombes wasn't sure what to think. Molly Walker was dead and Stephen Walker was in prison. Who sold the property?

"Thank you for your time, you've been most helpful."

"No problem."

Coombes let Sato go ahead of him so that Pervert Santa was unable to stare at her backside as she walked away. He thought over the situation. It seemed strange after the way Walker spoke about his neighbor during their interview that he would then turn around and sell his home to him.

Not that disliking someone meant you disliked their money.

"What do you make of that, Johnny?"

"Sounds like Walker is liquidating his assets on the down low. Either to pay for his legal team, or in preparation for an escape."

"*An escape?*"

"Historically, most prison breaks happen out of courthouses. Defendant wears a suit, acts normally, fits right in with everyone else. It's not such a stretch, you know? I have no doubt at all that the Brotherhood has a foothold in the Sheriff's Department. This whole trial could be nothing more than a ruse to get Walker out the Island."

Sato laughed. "A *ruse?*"

"A trick, a strategy."

"I know what it means, Johnny. I just wasn't expecting you to say it."

Coombes thought she was about to crack a joke about their five-year age gap until it dawned on him that partners didn't have age gaps, only people in relationships.

"I don't know about you, Grace, but I can't *wait* to hear what Perry has to say."

Sato's smile fell away as they approached the place Molly Walker called home. The property was at least a third larger than the one next door. He could see why Perry would be interested in making the move, it was a significant upgrade.

No car sat on the driveway in front of the house.

He looked through a gate at the two-car garage that lay beyond. In his experience, nobody kept their car in a garage unless they were on vacation, or unless the car was a stone-cold classic and likely to be stolen. This was particularly true if the garage lay beyond a gate, it was just too much hassle for a daily routine.

He cupped his hand to shield his reflection and stared in Perry's front window. He saw two long sofa units facing each other and a large screen TV in between on the wall. Not an ideal viewing setup, he thought. His eyes went to the chairs, then down to the floor.

Nobody sitting, nobody dead on the floor.

Despite the early hour, it appeared Perry was out.

Coombes went to another window. This one looked in on a kitchen. He saw a large chrome coffee machine, a hob with a stainless steel extractor hood, and an island unit with a countertop that looked like a butcher's block. His eyes caught a fast movement and a second later teeth were snapping on the other side of the glass with a bark he could feel in his bones.

He jumped back. "Jesus!"

Sato looked over. "Are you all right?"

"I found his dog. It is *not* friendly."

"Sounds like the two of you have a lot in common."

"Not enough belly rubs?"

Sato shook her head, as if at a child.

"Do we wait for this joker, or circle back later?"

"Circle back," he said.

They got back into the Dodge and he pulled quickly away.

His heart was still racing from the dog's barking and he felt wired, ready for anything. He thought about Stephen Walker selling his home, about the timing of it. If Walker believed the state had no case and he was going to be freed, then the sale of his property made no sense.

On the other hand, if Walker assumed the new trial would go as badly as the first, then a quick sale made sense for two different reasons. To fund a life on the run after an escape; or to protect his greatest asset from a wrongful death lawsuit by Molly's family.

A quick sale implied guilt and a belief he faced an unwinnable case.

"Do you believe me now?"

He turned to Sato. "What's that?"

"Walker selling his house like that...I don't care how you slice it, Johnny, that makes him Molly's killer. It was no damn accident."

He was quiet for a moment. It was hard to disagree with her, yet he couldn't help but feel there was something else going on.

"I'm still hung up on the way she comes out on the street."

"Come on, Johnny. She was distracted, that's all."

"Say she wasn't. That leaves tripping, or being pushed."

"You're over-analyzing literally two seconds of her life. She made an odd movement, we probably all do occasionally, but there's no camera there to record it."

"Picture this. Molly and Naylor are kissing goodbye, but it isn't at his door like he said, it's in front of the flatbed. The truck hides him from the dashcam *and* from Stephen Walker. Naylor pushes her into the street but he's way too early. The Mercedes is slower than he expected, because Walker is looking around for his wife's car. Instead of the impact being instantaneous, she's left hanging in the middle of the road before she's hit."

"And I suppose Walker *accelerating* to hit her is irrelevant?"

Sato was playing on his dislike of coincidence.

"Or an accident, just like Walker said. He hit the gas instead of the brake. I don't believe it, but it's possible. In any case, being pushed explains why she turns toward the sidewalk. She was surprised, shocked. The speed she came out, he must've shoved her pretty hard."

"You didn't hear this scumbag laughing at what he'd done, Johnny. If you'd heard that, you wouldn't waste a second thinking that he wasn't responsible."

Coombes nodded.

"You're right, but what I'm saying is they're not mutually exclusive. Walker went there to kill; I have no doubt. For the sake of argument, let's say the windshield notes were real. He's angry, he doesn't question *why* someone is feeding him this information until later. He gets a gun and heads over there. Time to make them pay, right?"

"This is thin, Coombes. Desperate, even."

He ignored her and kept going.

"On the drive over, Walker has to realize that killing them will cost him everything. But he doesn't turn back, he hangs in there. The anger remains. Now, cut to the moment on the street when she appears in front of him. From his point of view, it's a gift from god. He realizes he can kill her and pretend it was an accident. He *grasps* that opportunity."

Sato thought for a moment before replying.

"The way Naylor has it, he and Molly were having an affair for a long time. Years. Despite that, she's still not left her husband. Maybe he thought the only way they'd be together is if Stephen Walker divorced *her*. So he baits Walker with the notes, then gives him a time and a place where he plans to let Walker catch them kissing. It doesn't occur to him that Walker might have a gun *or* that he was crazy enough to drive over his wife."

It was a solid interpretation of the same facts and maintained Naylor's saint-like status. Sato had managed to give the windshield notes a less incriminating background. Coombes smiled. He was impressed, she almost had him convinced.

"That's pretty good, Grace."

"Why would Naylor want to kill her. It makes no sense."

Who benefits?

Suddenly he knew what that guilty look was on Naylor's face, and the look of relief about a question he hadn't asked.

"Naylor's home on Hudson Avenue had to be eating him alive. I can't imagine what a mortgage payment looks like for a place like that. With the business failing, he's screwed. The fact that he isn't living there anymore bears this out. It has to be about money."

"And how would Molly's death change that?"

"I guess he had a life insurance policy."

"But they weren't married."

"Doesn't matter. They were business partners and she was vital to that business, he said as much in the interview. Naylor probably imagined Molly's husband killing her long before it happened and realized what that would mean for him."

For the first time he saw doubt on Sato's face.

"If Naylor did what you say, I don't know if I can be a cop anymore."

"What are you talking about?"

"If I can be fooled like that, then I need to do something else. I believed him then; I believe him now. If we find an insurance policy, I'll still think he's innocent. I can't explain it, Johnny. I see a man whose life's been torn apart, not a killer."

"All right, but what's that got to do with being a cop?"

"I'm American, but I'm also Japanese. Shame is different for us, there is nothing worse. I should've quit the first time after Walker tricked me."

Coombes could tell that she meant it.

Her reaction puzzled him, since her view of Naylor was so different to his own. They didn't often have a difference of opinion about potential suspects, but it happened sometimes. She had never threatened to quit before.

Did she want him to turn a blind eye to Naylor?

"I never asked you," he said. "What was Molly's cause of death?"

"Respiratory failure."

He imagined Naylor holding a pillow over Molly Walker's face and keeping it there until she stopped breathing. For Coombes, that was more romantic than reading someone the same book over and over.

Naylor could've pushed Molly in front of any vehicle, at any time or place. The only reason for involving her husband was to give the police a better suspect. A jealous husband made a pretty good patsy.

Sato was right about the notes, he thought, it had to be Naylor that left them, but not for the reason she said.

The notes manipulated Stephen Walker to kill his wife.

But it was for nothing, Molly hung on to life for two more years. Naylor's business folded, he had to sell his mansion, and his rich life ended.

Sato turned to him.

"I suppose you spun all this out of his *shoes* story?"

"It smacks of bullshit, Grace. The way he used the same words with us and with the uniforms at the scene. Over and over. That's the sign of a lie right there."

"Or he draws comfort from the words when he thinks he could have saved her, they're like a prayer."

Coombes didn't get irritated with Sato for holding on to her belief in Stephen Walker's guilt, a good partner provoked discussion.

It did, however, lead to a dilemma.

If both men were equally responsible for Molly's death, then he knew there was zero chance of a successful conviction for either. If the DA got wind of the situation the new murder charge would be quietly dropped and the habeas petition approved.

Coombes might have to choose which man would pay the price. Since one man was already paying, it seemed the choice had already been made.

24

THEY SAT IN SILENCE in the Dodge as they made their way back to head-quarters, each of them lost in their own thoughts. It was his practice to drive without music or the radio playing. He liked to travel with just the thrum of the engine, the hiss of the AC, and the rolling purr of rubber hitting the road. This was his calm space, and it helped him think in a way that just wasn't possible under the crackling florescent tubes of the detective bureau.

After a moment he heard Sato speak.

"What are you grinning about?"

"I was just thinking about the business partner, about how he said Molly would look at her socials to relax. If they were at a restaurant, she'd be across the table from him, right?"

"All right, so he didn't see her screen. Does it matter?"

"I don't think she was looking at her socials. I think what she was doing might help keep Walker behind bars."

"Tell me," she said.

He laid it out for her and to his surprise, she didn't laugh.

"Let's do it."

Twenty minutes later, they rolled up outside Property Division's huge se-cure storage warehouse where case evidence was stored on a semi-permanent basis for trials, re-trials, and appeals. They got out the Dodge quickly, both of them sensing a potential break in the case and keen to button it down.

Coombes gave the property officer the case number for the box he wanted, then turned to look at Sato while he waited. Her face was flushed, her eyes bright. She was excited, maybe nervous about what they might find.

It was a good look on her, he hadn't seen it for a while.

The sign-out sheet showed that the box hadn't been checked out since it had arrived almost two years before. If Sarah Ryan had checked this avenue of investigation and not told Sato, her name would be on the sheet.

Coombes realized Molly Walker's cell phone would have a flat battery and he had no way to charge it. He glanced at the property officer and saw his name badge said Billings.

"Billings, you got an iPhone power cord back there?"

"Sure do."

Billings opened a drawer and pulled out a cable attached to a socket adapter and laid it on top of the storage box. Coombes nodded his thanks, then carried the box over to an inspection table and gloved up.

To prevent accusations of evidence tampering, Sato video recorded what he was doing on her cell phone. She started off tight on the box to record the labels and the unblemished seal, then stepped back for a full frame of him and the box.

A year before, a cop show used evidence tampering as a plot device and defense attorneys routinely raised the issue in court like it had actually happened. It was exactly the kind of bullshit move he expected from Stephen Walker and he wanted to be ready.

Using a small pocket knife, Coombes cut the tape sealing the box and placed the lid to one side. He decided to narrate what he was doing for the benefit of the video.

"Property box for Mary Gardner Walker, DOB 28-06-84, DR18-445615. Inspection carried out by Detective John Coombes and witnessed by Detective Grace Sato."

The box contained clear plastic evidence bags, with the largest containing the summer dress that Molly had been wearing at the time of the incident. There was so much blood on the dress that Coombes paused when he laid it to one side. It seemed impossible that anyone could've survived the injuries or the blood loss for more than a couple of minutes, yet Molly Walker had fought to live for almost two years.

Coombes found her cell phone.

He turned it over in his hands, still inside an evidence bag.

A screen protector had been applied to the display and there was both a diagonal split from corner to corner and a spiderweb high-impact fracture. Coombes hoped that the phone still worked.

"Cell phone. Apple iPhone X or 10 if you prefer. Device is damaged and powered-down, battery likely depleted. Attaching power-only cord to charge."

He attached the lead Billings had provided and plugged it into a socket. Sato came close to show the screen. It stayed black for almost thirty seconds, then the Apple logo appeared. Nothing seemed to be happening, just the logo in the middle of the screen.

"Do you want me to stop recording, Johnny?"

"No, keep it running, it needs to be uninterrupted."

At least a minute went by then the logo cleared and the screen lit up. A default background picture that came with the device. One percent battery. He swiped up from the bottom and a keypad came up, asking for Molly's passcode.

"All right, here's where we find out if we wasted our time. Trying passcode suggested by Carson Naylor, coworker." He typed five-two-four-three and the lock screen cleared. He couldn't help but smile. "That's it, we're in."

Coombes saw a standard grid of apps that he recognized from his own cell phone, almost all of which now had new icons. The tracking app was on the first page, likely indicating high frequency of use. The same app was on his own phone; it was the market leader.

"Decedent's phone has a family tracking app installed. Opening."

He selected it. Sato moved in close until their shoulders pressed together.

An alert appeared stating that there was no cellular connection. He dismissed the message and brought up a list of people that Molly tracked using the app. There were nine entries; her business partner, her husband, and seven women who he assumed were close friends.

It was exactly as he hoped, but it was the next part that was important.

The app recorded events such as phone use while driving, hard braking, and rapid acceleration. For nervous parents to keep an eye on their children.

The log file showed that Stephen Walker had performed the exact acceleration and braking pattern defined in the prosecution case against him. This was no wooly scientific extrapolation from speed camera footage and tire tread left on the road, this was cold, hard data.

Walker was done.

Sato brought her phone in across his chest to line up with the screen of Molly Walker's iPhone. The picture washed out for a second, then came back perfectly exposed.

"App data corroborates eye-witness statement and forensic evidence already on record. Grace, pass me the phone and step back, you should be on this too."

He aimed Sato's cell at her and rotated his free hand to get her to speak.

"Detective Grace Sato, Robbery-Homicide Division."

After a beat he stopped the video and laughed.

"That was *inspired*, Grace. Surprised you didn't give your badge number."

"Fuck you, Coombes! We got what we needed, didn't we? We *own* his ass!"

"For sure."

He re-packed the evidence then carried the box back over to the property desk. Billings seemed amused by the video recording he'd just witnessed.

"For the record, Detective, there is a security camera in here."

"Can it pick out what I was doing on the victim's cell phone?"

"Probably not."

"Do I get to take a copy away with me?"

"Not without clearance from the Chief."

Coombes tilted his head a little.

"Any other questions?"

"Did you turn the cell phone back off? We don't want fires back here."

"Shit. Just a second."

He was still gloved up so he opened the storage box and quickly located the cell phone again and went through the steps of powering it down. He angled Molly's cell phone more toward him than necessary while he re-entered the passcode.

You never knew where the Aryan Brotherhood could reach.

His screw-up with the iPhone restored the balance between them and Billings nodded as the box was passed back through to him.

"Thanks again for the power cord, Sergeant."

"Not a problem, Detective. Have a good one."

As they walked back to their car it felt like some kind of tension had broken between him and Sato. The end was in sight on her case, and confidence of a good result was returning.

25

Coombes decided to drop Sato at headquarters and go back out to pay a visit to Booth's casting director, Fran Knudsen. His concern was that once they finished the Walker investigation, they would be put back on rotation for new cases. The last thing he wanted was another case taking priority over his Lawrence – Hahn investigation. If that happened, Gantz might decide to give his case in its entirety back to Drake.

Knudsen had an office at *Son of a Gun* but he decided to try her home address first since he figured there wasn't much for a casting director to do when they weren't casting.

He pulled up behind a red Mini and cut the engine.

When he stepped out onto the sidewalk, he saw a British flag was painted on the roof of the small car. Only when he saw the flag did he realize he'd seen the vehicle before, when he worked the original Lawrence case.

Knudsen had never been interviewed and he realized now that was a mistake. If anyone knew Booth's heart of darkness, it had to be her. He'd come here more or less on a whim, but as he saw the flag a line of questioning formed, as it often did.

Knudsen answered the door, half a smile already on her face, cheeks flushed and an apron tied in front. The smell of home baking hit Coombes in both nostrils and his stomach rumbled. To his surprise, her smile didn't go away when he identified himself.

"Josh said you might visit me. Come in."

She led him into her bungalow, toward her kitchen.

"Once I get these out the oven, I'm all yours."

At that, a buzzer sounded and she put on a pair of gloves and pulled two trays of muffins out the oven, kicking the door shut with her foot behind her. He watched her tip the muffins out on a wire rack to cool.

"I just have a couple of questions about-"

"Can I get you a coffee, Detective?"

"That would be great, thanks."

She sucked crumbs off her thumb and forefinger, her eyes on his.

"How about my muffins? Help me out, won't you? I can't stop baking. I'll die of diabetes long before COVID gets me. They're real blueberry, not that fake shit."

"That's kind of you, ma'am."

"It's funny, Josh never mentioned that you were a cutie."

Coombes nodded seriously.

"I'll have to speak to him about that."

Knudsen took two mugs over to a pod coffee maker.

"Go through and take a seat, I'll be with you in a moment."

He walked into to a media room with a sofa and chair positioned next to a low coffee table. Coombes chose to sit in the single chair in case Knudsen sat next to him on the sofa and started sucking her fingers again.

Knudsen placed a coffee and a plate with two muffins on the table in front of him. His stomach growled so loudly that he wondered if she heard it.

"Give them a couple of minutes to cool before you eat them. I assume this is about that poor Lawrence girl again? Has the case been re-opened?"

"I thought I'd take another run at it, see if I can't get a better result."

"And how can I help you?"

"I don't know how the movie business works, and I was hoping you could explain to me the casting process at *Son of a Gun*. Who does what and when."

He smiled at her, then dropped his gaze to his coffee and picked it up.

"Well, it's just like how it is on TV shows. We have auditions then choose the ones we like the best. There are no big stars in our movies, we use actors that don't have any baggage for the audience. Except for background artists, everyone is auditioned."

"Is Booth present for that or is it just you?"

"It varies, you know? We do the leads one day, then everyone else on maybe two or three other days. Josh and Tony are always there to cast the leads, but secondary characters they more or less let me decide."

"They trust you."

"Exactly. I know what they're looking for as much as they do."

Coombes nodded.

"I'll be coming to that in a moment. But the leads are different?"

"Of course. You get the leads wrong; the whole movie is in trouble."

Knudsen adjusted her hair, sweeping strands behind her ear.

The hair adjustment seemed like a tell to Coombes.

That she had caught herself thinking about Natalie Hahn and the effect her performance had on *Carnival of Delights'* box office.

He said nothing, knowing Knudsen would fill the void.

"It all comes down to how well they can act and their personality. You can't tell any of that from a headshot or a promo video, you have to be there and see how they move, how they speak, their unscripted mannerisms. Josh knows what he can pull out with a lens."

"All right," he said. "So how are these casting sessions initiated? Are they open for people to just turn up, or are actors invited to audition?"

"Josh did an open casting call on his first movie. It was a disaster. People came still in their work clothes and acted out scenes from *Grey's Anatomy* and *Lost*. Like Joshua Booth would watch either of those shows. It was painful. After that, it was invitation-only."

"I see. And was it the same for these invitations? That Booth and De Luca would select who was invited to casting calls for leads and you would choose secondary actors?"

Knudsen smiled. "That's exactly right."

"This is through actors' agents I assume?"

"Yes, you see profiles for different actors, headshots, sometimes a short video clip and then make contact. It's kind of like using a dating website."

An interesting analogy, he thought.

Coombes took a bite of muffin to disguise how interested he was in his follow-up question.

"Then you are told who to invite?"

"This initial selection process is time-consuming, so I take care of that and present Josh with a shortlist of headshots in hard copy for each role and he signs off the ones to invite for audition."

He wasn't getting what he wanted.

"Let me ask this another way, Miss Knudsen. I noticed that the leading ladies are fairly similar. Long blonde hair, pale skin, dark eyes. Even their height and weight are similar. I'm wondering if that's because you're subconsciously choosing women that resemble yourself, or if this comes from a preference communicated to you by Booth or De Luca."

Knudsen smirked.

"It's like this, Detective. When we started, I'd present Josh with blondes, brunettes, red heads. Whoever could've fitted the role. Hair color is never mentioned in scripts. Over time, I noticed that only blondes were selected so I stopped including the others as they were just taking up space and wasting my prep time."

"Booth chose the final shortlist and then the three of you together would select who got the role based on the audition?"

"Yes."

It was clear to him from this comment that Booth was in charge of choosing the leads and that De Luca probably only turned up to mouth breathe while beautiful women went through their routines. Aside from the producer having lavish parties with the cast and crew, he'd uncovered no sign that De Luca had ever had a relationship with anyone on set.

He finished a muffin, then the remainder of his coffee.

It was getting to the awkward end of the conversation.

"As I'm sure you're aware, Mr. Booth has gone on to have sexual relationships with almost all of these women-"

"All consensual."

She jumped in before he even asked his question.

Booth was a class-action lawsuit waiting to happen. The days of behaving like this and getting a free pass were long gone. Talking these young women into his bed, making them think it was their idea. One day, maybe they'd realize it *wasn't*. That they were pressured into it.

At the very least, Knudsen was enabling a sexual predator, at worst, a killer.

"Does it not bother you that he's using you to get laid?"

Knudsen jumped to her feet and pointed at the door.

"Get out. This conversation is over."

Coombes stayed seated and straightened his shirt cuff.

"How long were the two of you in a relationship?"

Her arm drifted slowly down to her side and her face went slack. Seconds ticked by, but he said nothing. He didn't move, just let time do his work for him. Finally, she sighed.

"We dated in high school, then re-connected after university."

"You were together when he wrote *Last Night, Before I Died*?"

"Yes."

"Then you were his first muse."

Knudsen sat down like a bag of laundry and stared at the floor.

"I always hated all that *muse* crap."

"He pays you to find women that look like you did when you left university. When you inspired him. Then he sleeps with them and tosses them away like garbage when he's finished with them."

"I know, Jesus, I'm not stupid. I saw through it after the second movie."

"Why do you put up with it?"

Tears rolled down Knudsen's cheeks and she wiped them angrily away.

"Because I'm still in love with him."

It always amazed him the amount of abuse people would tolerate because their heart couldn't accept what their brain already knew. In this way, perhaps, he was no different.

Wasn't he doing the same thing with Sato?

Knudsen spoke into his silence.

"We all eventually become whatever Josh wants us to be."

Coombes stood.

There was one more question, but he thought she'd only answer it if she thought he was leaving. She walked him toward her front door.

Knudsen's home was as sterile as a hotel room. Her life was on pause, waiting for her great love to take her back. He wanted to tell her that Booth was never going to change and that she should stop hanging on to the past and move on with her life.

But he was a cop, and none of those things were any of his business.

"Was Josh ever aggressive or violent?"

Her foot made a misstep and she almost fell over. He didn't think it was because he'd called Booth by his first name.

"Not exactly."

They had reached the front door and he turned to face her. His body casually blocking the door, preventing her from opening it. A trick he'd learned from Sullivan.

"What then?"

She didn't want to answer but there he was blocking the door. She was almost rid of him, just one more answer. Coombes didn't feel good about the situation; he was a foot taller than Knudsen and twice her weight but he needed her answer.

Potentially, more lives were at stake.

Her shoulders sunk down and she dipped her gaze to the floor.

"When he left USC he was different. He'd put his hands around my throat while we made love and tighten his grip until my vision went dark at the edges. The first time he apologized after, said he didn't know why he did it, something just came over him. But I knew he'd liked it. Soon, he was doing it every time. I had to start wearing a scarf to cover the bruising. For a while in my life I thought Josh would go too far, but it was worth it just to see the way he looked at me while he choked me."

Coombes had no response.

Some people are just too damaged.

26

THE INTERVIEW WITH THE casting director had opened a couple of unexpected doors so he sat for a moment in his Dodge making notes and thinking about the best way forward. It was obvious to him that Booth's interest in choking dates was certain to have continued with the women that followed Knudsen. If he hadn't got what he wanted, he would've gone back to her in a heartbeat. The fact that he hadn't, told Coombes that the director had the situation handled. He looked at his notes so far.

Original muse, strong resemblance to female leads and victims.

Childhood sweethearts, still in love with Booth.

Submissive.

Booth wasn't looking for a woman that would allow him to do whatever he wanted, he was looking for someone that would fight like her life depended on it. A strong woman that he would overpower and almost kill with his bare hands at the moment when she was most vulnerable. To replicate the terror he'd seen on Knudsen's face the first time.

He thought of Natalie Hahn.

Hahn was no church-going innocent from a cornfield state, she knew the way the world worked. Together the pair made a dangerous combination. Booth had a darkness that he only let out at night, while Hahn's was on all the time. She was a muse that might've lasted him the rest of his life.

He glanced across and saw Knudsen watching him from her window.

Her face was devoid of emotion. It was a look he hadn't witnessed during her interview. Had she seen something new in Booth's relationships with Lawrence and Hahn?

Had she killed off potential rivals?

It was hard for him to imagine Hahn being transported to her grave in Knudsen's tiny vehicle, never mind the casting director carrying a body and digging a hole in the earth.

Still, though.

Knudsen had access to the studio lot where Lawrence was found, and neither woman would have seen her as a threat. The victims would've climbed into any vehicle she asked them to.

The casting director was still watching.

He gave her a friendly smile and a little wave and he saw her shoulders drop a little as she relaxed. Coombes changed his earlier note.

Submissive...or an act?

Then added:

Jealousy motive to kill?

He didn't really see it, but he preferred to write ideas down before they flew out the other side of his head and were forgotten.

A more likely scenario, was that Booth tied a power cord around Lawrence's neck to hide bruising that he knew would identify him. The uniform petechial hemorrhaging caused by the power cord effectively erased finger marks caused by choking.

As much as he wanted to follow up on the sexual violence angle with other actresses that he knew Booth had dated, Coombes decided to get back to his delayed hunt for Scott Peters who had the potential to clear Booth of the murders, just as he had before. With his friend Hahn dead, and no potential movie role on the horizon, it would be interesting to see if Peters' story changed this time around.

The address for Scott Peters provided by the *Son of a Gun* production office had matched the one listed with the DMV in Boyle Heights. That left him with an address off Victory Boulevard in North Hollywood that Peters had given to U-Haul as his destination.

He entered the address into his GPS and put his gear selector into drive.

———

WHEN HE ARRIVED, HE saw signs that appeared to be permanent attached to the side of the building stating it was For Rent. This indicated to Coombes that the residential turnover was high and that the chances of still finding Peters there were low.

He parked up and killed the engine, then stepped out into the street. The area looked a little rough-and-ready so he elected not to fasten his suit jacket so he could draw his weapon fast if he needed it.

The building was a two-floor structure like a motel with multiple apartments and an outside walkway for accessing apartments on the second floor. He'd been part of a raid on a place with a similar layout during his days on patrol and knew that the manager usually lived in the first unit.

He pounded on the door and stepped back. The door opened and a short, roundish-looking woman that he took to be of Russian heritage stood there glaring up at him.

"You police?"

"That's right."

"I called three weeks ago and *now* you come? I already fixed damage! I had to pay out of my own pocket because you're in a doughnut shop."

Coombes took off his sunglasses and stepped forward, crowding the woman in the worst way possible. He wondered if working Homicide was making him into a monster or if he'd always been one. This was who he was without Sato to keep him human.

"I'm not here about any *damage*, ma'am. I'm looking for Scott Peters."

A normal person would've stepped back but the Russian stood her ground. Peasant stock. Thick skin, wide shoulders. She was probably carrying a blade for potatoes or whatever else. If he wasn't careful, she'd open out his intestines and arrange them over his shoes.

"I don't know who you're talking about."

"A *guest*. Moved here six months ago."

"No," she said, shaking her head. "Never heard of him."

She was stoic and anti-police, but he sensed that she believed what she was saying. It occurred to him that if Peters had moved from Boyle Heights because he felt threatened, he might be using an alias. Coombes stepped back out of the woman's airspace.

"You mind if I show you a photograph?"

She nodded, then shot a look behind her into her home like there was someone back there in the darkness. A man who didn't like cops, perhaps. A husband, a son.

Someone with their own legal problems.

Coombes realized that he'd left his tablet in the car. Instead of going back for it, he pulled out his cell phone and brought up Scott Peters profile page on IMDb. There were only three photographs and none were as good as the studio headshot on his iPad. A monochrome picture that could've been anyone; a picture of Peters with another man on set; and a picture taken during the press junket in Cannes promoting *Carnival of Desires*.

He enlarged the last one and turned the screen for her to see.

"What about this man?"

"That's 4B."

Coombes angled the screen so he could see it. The picture had jumped back to the previous image with the other man, he must've brushed it with his finger as he turned his cell.

He pointed at Peters on screen.

"This man is a guest here?"

"No, the *other* man. With the shirt."

Coombes looked at the man standing to the left of Peters. He had golden skin and wore a puffy white shirt that was unbuttoned all the way to his chiseled abdominal muscles. He clicked on a small information button.

Scott Peters and Trevor Gaines.

"What about this other man? You ever see him before?"

The woman shrugged.

"Men come and go. I don't keep track. He's not a guest."

"All right," Coombes said. "Mr. Gaines is in 4B?"

"That's right."

Her face twitched. Amusement, maybe.

The Russian woman was wasting his time. She began to close the door on him so he put his left hand out to stop it.

"He's not there, is he?"

Another micro-expression. *Disappointment.*

"Taco Bell on Oxnard."

"What? He eats there a lot?"

"I guess so. He's the manager."

Coombes walked back down the side of the building.

As he approached the street, a man with a shaved head and a double lightning neck tattoo walked past and approached his Charger in a half-crouching run. The man was holding a pistol low and was positioning himself in the blind spot of the Dodge.

Coombes eased his Glock out its holster and moved from the sunlit path into a shaded area under a tree. The man with the tattoos reached the Charger and crouched down behind it. He glanced up the road and appeared not to see Coombes, looking only for traffic. Seeing none, he made his way quickly down the side of the car and pointed his automatic at the empty driver's seat.

If he'd been sitting there, the man's approach might've worked.

"Hey, asshole!" Coombes shouted.

The skinhead turned sharply around, the gun arm coming up between them. Coombes put a hole right through the other man's forehead. For a millisecond, all that seemed to happen was a pink mist appeared around the Nazi's head. Then time seemed to resume and the man fell slackly onto the hood of his Charger and then onto the road.

The car alarm filled the air, the turn signals flashed.

Coombes walked over to look at the dead man.

The road behind him sparked three times before he realized he was taking fire from a second shooter. He noticed a slight figure in tight black clothing firing backward from the seat of a motorcycle. Having failed to hit him, the motorcyclist accelerated away, weaving from side to side to throw off his aim.

Coombes bent down on one knee in the middle of the road, slowly let out a breath, and fired a single shot. He was using the center-mass concept, imagining he'd hit something vital to the motorcycle. Instead, the round went through the rider's thigh and he heard a scream over the sound of the car alarm.

A *woman's* scream.

The motorcycle wobbled, as she fought to bring it back under control, then she turned off Beck onto Erwin Street and disappeared. Coombes stood. He knew it was pointless to give pursuit, he'd never catch a motorcycle.

He turned and saw that he had Nazi brains all over the hood of his car. The Charger was black and absorbed every watt of energy that the sun put out.

The brain tissue was already cooking, he could smell it.

27

It took a patrol unit ten minutes to arrive, then another hour for an officer-involved shooting team to come from downtown to take his statement and walk him through the scene. The Russian woman came out onto the street to see what all the fuss was about and stared in open-mouthed surprise at the corpse lying on the road and the man standing over it.

By the time he cleared the scene, it was almost two o'clock.

The Taco Bell had limited seating due to the pandemic, but if there was a lunchtime rush, he must've missed it because there were only eight other customers when he walked inside. The casting director's home-made muffins were long gone so he ordered a burrito, a crunchy taco, and a cherry Pepsi; all of which he decided to eat before speaking to Gaines.

If the Russian woman called to warn Gaines, so be it.

He held his food carefully with a napkin despite extensively washing his hands with alcohol gel in the parking lot. His right hand felt dirty in a way he couldn't describe.

The man he killed was Joseph Wright and he was 34 years old.

He stared into space as he ate, thinking about the irony of his life. His entire function was to catch killers, yet sometimes he was forced to kill others himself. Weren't they simply different sides of the same coin? Hadn't he provoked the man into aiming his gun at him?

The detectives had asked three separate times why he chose to confront the armed man and not wait for an opportunity to capture him alive. It was the kind of garbage that only someone who hadn't been in the situation themself would think of, yet there was a truth to it.

With Wright dead, there was again no way to tie the hit back to the Aryan Brotherhood, or Stephen Walker. It was pretty clear that the former lawyer had passed on his name and not the message to let him work the case. This told him that Walker was vulnerable about something and was trying to kill not only him, but the investigation.

Coombes finished his food and drank some Pepsi.

He felt nothing for the dead man, only a numbness in his head and a dirty feeling about the hand that held the gun. A member of staff was cleaning a nearby table so Coombes told her that he wanted to speak to the manager. She sighed, rolled her eyes, then walked through to the back of the restaurant.

An easy five minutes passed before Trevor Gaines walked over to his table. The chiseled abs from the set photograph were in the rearview, replaced by a thirty-pound belly.

"Was there a problem with your order, sir?"

Gaines was standing well back from his table. Social distancing. If it continued, it was going to make their conversation difficult. Coombes unclipped his shield from his belt and let the manager have a look at it without other customers seeing.

"I need to have a conversation with you, Gaines, and not about the food. How about we take this outside?"

Gaines moved closer, his voice dropping to a whisper.

"Am I under arrest?"

"I just have a couple of questions. You can answer them in the parking lot, or downtown handcuffed to a table. Any preference?"

"The parking lot."

They walked outside and away from the restaurant windows. Coombes positioned himself so that Gaines was facing into the sun. In general, people who asked if they were being arrested had something to hide, so he decided to start there.

"You know why I'm here asking questions?"

Gaines shook his head and a couple of his chins.

"No idea, I swear."

People who added *I swear* definitely knew something.

"All right. Tell me about Scott Peters."

The name hit Gaines like a gut punch.

"He's dead, isn't he?"

"Unknown. I'm trying to locate him."

He remembered the comment about men coming and going, a phrase he'd overlooked the meaning of until now.

"The two of you were romantically involved I take it?"

"I thought he was the one."

Coombes took out his notebook without breaking eye contact.

"What happened?"

"After the movie came out things took a dark turn. He thought someone was trying to kill him. He moved house, changed his name. Scott kept looking behind him to see if we were being followed. It was infectious, we became totally paranoid."

Coombes could relate, he was closing in on paranoid himself.

"Who did he think was going to kill him?"

"The producer of the movie, he's a mob guy from Vegas."

"He thought *Anthony De Luca* was going to kill him?"

"Him or his bodyguard. His bodyguard is crazy."

"You happen to remember this bodyguard's name?"

"Nico Abruzzo."

It was horseshit, but Coombes wrote it down anyway.

"When was the last time you saw Scott?"

"The day after he moved in with me, he just vanished. It was like the ground swallowed him. None of our friends saw him, his cell phone didn't connect. His car was still parked on Beck until it was towed away. If he'd left on his own, he would've taken his car, right?"

"And you think De Luca or Abruzzo is responsible?"

"What else? He thinks someone's out to get him, then he disappears."

"Did he share his story about mafia hit men with any of his other friends?"

Gaines shook his head.

"No, just with me. He knew how paranoid it sounded."

"Here's what I think, Gaines. The two of you had an argument, things got out of hand and the next thing you know, Scott's dead. *You* killed him."

"No!"

"Yes. You saw him with another guy, you got jealous and you killed him."

"Stop saying that! I *loved* him."

"Why would a movie producer want *Scott* dead?"

He said it like Peters was pocket lint to a man like De Luca.

"Because Scott lied to the cops to protect a friend."

"What friend?"

"Natalie something, I can't remember."

"*Natalie Hahn?*"

Gaines nodded. "That sounds right."

"What did they tell the cops?"

"They said they'd seen a woman at a party with this producer dude and that he'd been trying to get into her pants. Natalie made it all up, it wasn't true. Anyway, the woman was murdered so the story basically framed De Luca."

Coombes kept his face calm as he wrote in his notebook.

"Uh-huh. You know why they said it?"

"All I know is Natalie was into that director big time, she was obsessed. Joshua Booth this, Joshua Booth that. She and Scott used to run together, going to Hollywood parties trying to get parts. I guess they were sleeping around, Scott never talked about it. Somehow, the story they told the cops translated into them getting starring roles in Booth's next picture."

"Where you met Scott."

"That's right," Gaines said.

"There's something I'm confused about."

"What's that?"

"Scott frames an innocent man and gives the killer a de facto alibi, yet he thought that the person that wanted him dead is that same innocent man, not the killer? Do I have that right?"

Gaines flinched. "*Right.*"

Coombes put away his notebook. He'd had about enough of Gaines and was already imagining his drive back to headquarters. The rumble of the road, the cool hiss of the air conditioning, and a glass-and-steel bubble around him containing precisely no other people.

He'd had more than enough *people* for the day.

Gaines swallowed nervously.

"Is there any chance that Scott's still alive?"

The man had been right before, Coombes thought. No one left their car behind. Not in L.A. If Peters was gone and the car had remained, then Peters was dead.

"I'm sorry," he said. "I don't think so."

Coombes returned to his Dodge and sat in the still heat of the car. After a moment, beads of sweat appeared on his skin. The display said 112 degrees.

He started the engine and cranked up the AC.

Without Peters, it would be impossible to dig into Hahn's statement or ask how that story had come about. It mattered little after what Gaines said. A new thought came to him.

What if Hahn's fictitious account inadvertently framed the correct man?

Coombes was no fan of coincidence, but the person Natalie Hahn had chosen as a foil in her story made a great suspect in his own right. He would've been a person of interest regardless of her statement. Like Booth, De Luca had no alibi.

He called Willard and a voice came at him like a machine gun.

"I'm not buying anything, get lost."

Must be tough to be a salesman in this world, he thought.

"Eddie, it's John. I've got a job for you."

"All right! About goddamn time."

"It's going to involve a drive. Does that wreck of yours still roll?"

Willard laughed. "Last I checked. What do you need?"

"As it happens, you *are* going to have to buy something, but I'll pay you back. What cell carrier do you use?"

He outlined his plan to Willard. On the one hand, it was work suitable for a rookie, on the other, it had real-world potential for the case.

"What do you think, Eddie?"

"I'm a little embarrassed I never thought to explore this angle already."

28

It was after three by the time he got back to the PAB but it felt more like eight at night, the way the day had dragged out. As he walked through the detective bureau, RHD detectives stood and clapped, some with phones pinned to their ear. He acknowledged it with a nod and a reluctant smile.

Internal Affairs might not have his back, but these guys did.

Even Wallfisch and McCreary, two detectives that liked to noise him up, were there front and center with big grins on their faces. A shoot-out cut through the petty politics, you were brothers and sisters in blue.

"Thanks guys."

Sato wasn't clapping or smiling. Her eyes tracked him as he walked through the squad room toward her. She looked like she was ready to cry or maybe throw up. He got to his desk and hung his suit jacket on the back of his chair, an uneasy silence building between them. After a beat, Sato leaned toward him until her forearms lay across the top of the partition between their desks. There was fire in her eyes.

"Your phone was ringing off the hook. After a couple of minutes, what I am assuming is the same caller, called me. Monica Sullivan. She asked if you were ok. I had to hear from her that someone tried to kill you."

"How did she find out?"

Sato made a face like *you tell me.*

"I've not been in touch with her today, Grace."

Sato shook her head in disbelief.

"New rule, Coombes. If someone tries to kill you and I'm not right next to you, you call me the first chance you get, you hear me? I don't want to hear about it from a journalist."

He nodded. "I'm sorry, you're right."

"By the way, you gave *Sullivan* my number?"

"Of course not. She dug that up on her own. Anyway, did the judge sign off on the warrant for the app data?"

It took Sato a moment to change subjects.

"Yes, and I already got the data from their servers. It's exactly the way we want it. Shows Walker accelerated right into his wife and didn't hit the brakes until after the job was done. I'm finishing up the filing package and we have a meeting with the new prosecutor in about forty minutes. Give me five and you can read what I've got."

He nodded again, then sat down and checked his cell phone.

There were 18 missed calls and 23 text messages.

Twelve text messages from Monica Sullivan, eight from Sato, one from Gantz, and two from an unknown number. He opened the text from his lieutenant first.

SIS have approved your transfer paperwork.

Coombes smiled at Gantz' grim sense of humor. Special Investigation Section had a dark reputation and had been nicknamed *the death squad* due to the frequency of fatal shootings.

Next, he opened the unknown number.

He was disappointed to find it wasn't from a Nazi shot caller in Terminal Island, but Detective Kennedy. The texts stated that Force Investigation Division was opening an investigation into the shooting of Joseph Wright and he had a second interview at 9 a.m. the next day.

Great.

He'd been through the wringer several times before, and with each pass it became more difficult. From previous experience, the second interview established whether the Department would suspend him pending the culmination of the investigation. Coombes sighed. The timing of the FID investigation was less than ideal, since he already appeared to be under investigation by Internal Affairs.

The first four texts from Sato were about the case. In good spirits about the warrant going through, then about the data that followed. Then the journalist had clearly got through to her.

Johnny, are you ok? Please call me.

I don't like how we left things. You know nothing's changed.

You better be dead, Coombes, to ignore me like this!

I didn't mean that. Call me.

He turned to the partition between them, imagining Grace on the other side. She thought he might've died, yet she was still carefully typing what she wrote to him in case it got back to the Department and hurt her career.

Sullivan's texts were different, she didn't hide anything.

Her texts were long, clearly written fast on her computer, not typed into a cell phone. Interspersed through the text were emojis of hearts and kisses. Coombes decided not to read the messages at all and instead typed back:

I'm fine, cell phone was muted.

He clicked send and wondered what it meant that the only person he'd replied to was the journalist. Before he had too long to think about it, Sato passed him the filing package on Stephen Walker. She'd captured the whole thing perfectly, yet he felt his confidence in the case fall away as he read it.

The case was still a bunch of hot air.

He glanced at Sato, and saw she again had her excited face on.

"Come on, prosecutor wants to see you too."

He pulled on his suit jacket as they walked through the detective bureau. The elevator was empty and they rode it down to street level in silence. It was about as quick to walk to the Hall of Justice as it was to drive. She looked into his eyes, trying to see something.

"You want to talk about it?"

"About what?"

"Come on, Johnny. You don't have to pull this *macho* crap. I know you're thinking about that guy. It's not your fault, ok?"

"I was thinking about it, but not how you think."

"What then?"

He waited until they were at the crosswalk before continuing.

"There's a connection between everything. Because one thing happens, another thing happens. A hidden pattern. Most of the time you don't see it, but every now and then you catch a glimpse and it blows your mind."

Sato said nothing, waiting for him to get to the point.

"All right," he said. "I was thinking how things would've gone if I *hadn't* left my iPad in the car. I would've used Peters' studio headshot, got no ID, then returned to the Dodge two minutes earlier, where some mouth-breather would've shot me to death while I waited for the AC to kick in."

He could tell that this wasn't what Sato wanted. She wanted him to be wracked with guilt about the man he'd killed. That's what a normal person does, a person that isn't a psychopath.

Coombes wasn't there yet.

The light changed and they crossed 1st Street and took the diagonal footpath down the side of City Hall toward Spring Street.

"If you don't want to talk to me, talk to someone else."

He stopped and turned to face her.

"You know on cop shows when the hero kills a bad guy and starts hitting the liquor. His wife doesn't understand him anymore. He starts going to strip bars, maybe picking up hookers. That sound about right? It's bullshit."

"*John-*"

"No, listen. I'm not *sorry* this asshole is dead, I'm not *happy* he's dead. I just don't give it a second's thought. He put himself in that position. If I hadn't got him, he would've got me. That's the truth. After me, he would've moved on to someone else. *You.*"

Sato looked like she wanted to put her hands over her ears.

"I can't listen to this, it's too ugly."

She wanted him to talk about it, but only if he said what she wanted.

They resumed their walk to the Hall of Justice in silence.

Between the Army and the LAPD, Coombes had now killed fifteen men. He felt guilt for only one, a man who had once been a friend. He knew what remorse felt like, and he'd never feel it for an assassin with SS tattoos.

As they crossed Temple, Coombes spoke again.

"I didn't kill him, Grace. He volunteered for the morgue and I accepted."

THE NEW PROSECUTOR, GABRIEL Reyes, was a pencil-thin man in a tight shirt and thick, black-framed eyeglasses. Reyes was typing into his computer as they came in and he didn't stop typing as they stood over him. It seemed like a power play by the deputy district attorney, so Coombes sat without being asked and crossed his legs so that his ankle was resting on his right knee.

The edge of his shoe had blood on it and it didn't look recent.

He glanced around the room while he waited.

Reyes' office had previously been a jail cell back when the building had served as the county jail. Those days were long gone, but it was still clear what the intended use was of the room. The LAPD got a shiny new building, but the city had put its attorneys in an old jail. It was perfect. Coombes wanted to shake whoever set that up by the hand.

The prosecutor stopped typing and turned to look at him.

"All right, how about you tell me what we've got on Walker."

Coombes gave Reyes a quick summary while the prosecutor skimmed the filing package.

When he finished, Reyes was quiet for a moment as he processed the information. Finally, he shook his head.

"It's not enough. This tracking app...it's not evidence, it's *data*. On the stand this guy will say his phone fell off the dashboard and hit the floor. Acceleration, followed by impact. Hell, if he goes all-in on the accident angle then this proves nothing. He hit the gas, not the brake. An accident. The data supports that interpretation too. It doesn't show intent to kill. No doubt this is part of the puzzle, but it's no magic bullet. The judge might not even allow it into evidence."

Coombes thought of another problem, but kept it to himself.

"What about the eyewitness?" Coombes said. "He saw the whole thing. His story backs the data from this app. His word alone was good enough the first time."

The prosecutor nodded, but his mouth was angled down.

"By your own admission, the supposed eyewitness was having an affair with the victim. That relationship makes his word count for nothing, you know that. Unless you find something better, I'll be forced to recommend to the DA that we drop the homicide charge and go for vehicular manslaughter. I could land that plane with my eyes closed."

"You wouldn't dare!"

"The DA only wants to fight battles that can be won. I don't know if you know this, Coombes, but the courts are backing up. The virus is causing chaos. Trials are being pushed back or pleaded out. Find something by tomorrow afternoon latest, I want to finalize this over the weekend before the pre-trial hearing on Monday."

Tomorrow. What could he find in such a short timeframe?

Coombes wanted to punch the lawyer right in the middle of his face. Sato glanced at him, then back to the prosecutor.

"That's *it?*" She said. "Have you seen the dashcam footage?"

"No, Detective, I haven't. We can't use it, so I didn't watch it. I'm sure I don't have to remind you *why* we can't use it?"

Sato jumped to her feet, knocking her chair over.

"You son of a bitch! You're a goddamn coward!"

Reyes spread his hands.

"I'm just the messenger here. It's a buyer's market. It was a miracle he served any time in the first place. The way things stand, those two years are likely all Walker will serve."

"He murdered his wife!"

Reyes closed the folder and pushed it back across his desk.

"Then prove it, because this is a steaming pile of garbage."

Coombes grabbed the folder and left the room. He'd known the case was hopeless from day one. After a beat, Sato followed him.

"Johnny! What the hell was that?"

Coombes realized that his face was burning so he elected to take the stairs rather than stand and wait for the elevator. Behind him, Sato said something in Japanese that didn't sound friendly, before switching back to English.

"Johnny, come on. I never saw you fold like that before."

"He's right, Grace. We're lucky he called us on it."

Sato was struggling to keep up.

"Will you stop for a second, I'm in heels."

He stopped and allowed Sato to draw level.

She saw the heat in his face but said nothing and dropped her gaze down to his chest. Sato knew about shame and embarrassment; she'd told him as much. Her own cheeks colored in sympathy.

"We messed up, Grace, and that little errand-boy didn't even know why he hit the target. Think about it, if Walker knew he had an app on his cell phone pinpointing his wife's exact location, why would he need someone to send him notes *or* use a GPS to get there?"

Sato tilted her head over.

"Molly Walker was tracking him without his knowledge or consent."

"That's right, and there's something else. I've used that app before. The operating system periodically warns that you're being tracked. If she installed it on his phone, it hadn't been there long or he would've known about it."

"What does it all mean?"

"I don't know, but that's not a question that points to Stephen Walker."

He resumed his descent of the stairs, this time at a slower pace. Sato moved with him, her heels like tiny gunshots. They passed the next floor exit before she spoke again.

"Then she tracked him because he scared her and she wanted to know where he was. How does that hurt us? We feed that in with Naylor's story about Walker knocking her out and her trip to the emergency care facility. It's all part of the same pattern, no?"

"That ain't it, not even close. I promise you, it's worse."

It seemed there was no chance at all that they were going to find what Reyes wanted by close of play the next day. Their best option now was to use what little time still remained to build a case for DUI murder and keep Walker off the streets.

"Three pieces of advice, Grace. Don't eat yellow snow; don't dry your face with the middle of a towel; and never trust a deputy district attorney."

His cell phone rang as they stepped out onto the sidewalk.

"Coombes."

"John, where are you?"

It was his lieutenant.

"Hall of Justice. What's going on?"

"10th floor has been on my ass. Jackson wants to see you."

"Now?" Coombes said, to amuse himself.

"If you can make it *yesterday*, that would be better."

Gantz disconnected.

29

COOMBES RODE THE ELEVATOR to the 10th floor, his head full of questions. Had the chief heard about his friction with Block? With Internal Affairs? Was he being suspended while FID investigated the death of Joseph Wright? Jackson was a hard man to get a bead on. One minute he was serious, the next jovial, but for sure he hadn't called Coombes in to tell him a knock-knock joke. The elevator opened and he stepped out.

The chief's outer office was empty and still. His adjutant not at her usual station and Jackson's door was ajar. A full mug of coffee sat steaming on the assistant's desk.

The scene looked off and without thinking about it, his right hand rotated five degrees so that it lined up with his firearm. He moved over to the hinge side of the part-open door and reached across to lightly knock with his left hand, his right bent, ready to draw if need be.

"Chief? Everything ok?"

"Come on in, Detective."

He opened the door and walked into Jackson's office. The chief was sitting on the edge of his desk while his assistant stood on the other side of the room like she was taking notes.

"Sorry, you're in the middle of something. I saw the door-"

Jackson glanced at Coombes' hand, the way it sat next to his gun.

"You thought something was wrong and came to help me."

Coombes felt his face grow hot for the second time in an hour.

"Yes, sir."

The idea seemed to amuse the chief, a smirk forming on his face, his head giving a small nod as if Coombes had just unknowingly confirmed something for him. Jackson stood and walked around his desk to his chair.

"Take a seat. I've been expecting you."

Coombes sat, the adjutant hovering somewhere behind him.

"You've had an interesting day, Detective. Were you injured?"

"I followed official policy, sir. It was a good shoot."

Jackson smiled.

It was a secret weapon, Coombes thought, for putting people at ease.

"I have no doubt about that, that's not why you're here. There are a couple of things I wanted to discuss privately with you."

"Yes, Chief."

In private, with your assistant.

"What's our exposure on this Molly Walker case?"

"The husband's a piece of shit. There's no doubt he ran over his wife, he claims she stepped out in front of his SUV and he couldn't stop in time. The dashcam footage the judge excluded shows him accelerating toward her."

"I know that, Coombes, I read the file. What else?"

"The location of the so-called accident was outside Molly's business partner's home. Walker now claims he was lured there by a third party who informed him that his wife was having an affair through a series of anonymous notes. He claims he went there to confront them, or catch them in some kind of compromising situation. It's unusual for someone pleading innocence to cough up a possible motive like that, never mind a former defense attorney, so my feeling is that there's something there."

"Even so, the notes didn't make him drive over her."

"Exactly. There is also the matter of the unlicensed firearm in his vehicle. It's possible he planned to kill them if he found what he expected. He maintains that the gun was planted."

"Then you're saying that she just *happened* to appear in the street directly in front of his vehicle and he decided to drive over her instead?"

"Pretty much. Means, motive, and opportunity. He had all three. The business partner has confirmed the affair. Walker probably intended to shoot them but sees a way to make it look like an accident and hits the gas."

"Can you prove any of this?"

"We're still working it."

"I have some concerns about your partner. She made some mistakes in the original investigation, things that could hurt us now."

"Grace Sato is a fantastic cop, you've got nothing to worry about."

He'd let some anger slip out and a small smirk appeared on the corners of the chief's mouth. It gave Coombes a bad feeling.

"Detective Sato. You and her are close?"

Here it comes, he thought. The warm-up speech wasn't why he'd been summoned, it was just the chief getting in some practice swings before he stepped forward to receive the ball.

"Yes, Chief."

"How close?"

"She's my partner and my best friend. We share the same apartment."

Jackson showed no surprise, which meant he was in the loop with the apartment surveillance operation.

"The apartment on South Hill?"

"That's right."

"You mind telling me how a D-III can afford an address like that?"

Coombes took a deep breath. He had been practicing some version of this speech since he'd first moved in and he wanted to get it just right.

"It belongs to Amy Tremaine. She previously rented the apartment to a friend of the family who was then murdered. Well, I'm sure you remember how I came to meet the former governor's daughter."

Jackson nodded and indicated for him to continue.

"After what happened to her at the hands of those kidnappers, she offered me the same deal as her late friend - the use of the apartment in exchange for paying the mortgage for her new place in MacArthur Park."

The other man tapped his tented fingertips together, his eyes going up toward the ceiling. Coombes took this to mean that the chief was trying to decide if this financial arrangement passed the smell-test, or if there was a case to answer for a *conduct unbecoming* charge.

When Jackson looked back down, he knew he was in the clear.

"I won't need you any more, Jean."

"Yes, Chief."

The assistant left the room.

She'd been there as a witness, Coombes thought. They way she'd held her notebook, she could've had a cell phone recording everything.

"Block's got it into his head that you're dirty. He's personally followed you home a couple of times. He's had IA keeping tabs on you."

"I know."

Jackson laughed. "You aren't meant to."

"Can I speak candidly?"

"Why stop now, Detective?"

"I have a doorbell camera. I saw those clowns break into my apartment live on my cell phone. They wiped the local recordings, but like I say, I saw it live. You can't delete live. It took me five minutes to find their listening devices. Those guys were not bringing their A-game to my apartment, I'm afraid."

Jackson had a grin on his face.

"You're a straight-shooter, Coombes, I'll give you that much."

"I've got nothing to hide. The apartment's not a bribe, I pay to live there. Maybe not the going rate, but enough to give me a nosebleed every month."

The chief was silent for a moment.

By flat-out admitting that he lived with Sato there was no lie to be caught in. His transparency, he hoped, would indicate to Jackson that they simply shared an apartment. There was no rule against that. The way things were with the price of accommodation, sharing living space with other cops was likely the norm within the rank and file.

"What is it between you and Block?"

"If I pushed him down a flight of stairs he wouldn't know how to fall."

Jackson laughed again, rocking right back in his chair.

They were becoming a couple of buddies.

"Leave the IA investigation with me, Detective. I'll deal with it."

"Appreciated."

There was a moment of silence and Coombes hoped the conversation wasn't going to return to the exact nature of his relationship with Sato.

He'd heard that supervisors were discouraged from asking direct questions about the sexual relationships of those beneath them, whether it was against regulations or not. He had no way to confirm this, or if that even applied to the chief.

"You made D-III in a little over five years. What now?"

"Chief?"

"I've been looking into your background, Coombes." Jackson glanced at a stack of paper in front of him as if to illustrate the background check. "West Point, very nice. You were a captain in the Army before you moved to CID, but left after only eight years. That's a short stay for a West Pointer. You mind if I ask why you left?"

"Boredom."

Jackson sat back.

"Are you bored here?"

"No, sir."

"Your whole life has been dedicated to serve. First your country, now your home town. That service is why you moved up the ranks so quickly."

Coombes wasn't sure where Jackson was going with this.

"I am where I want to be, Chief."

"Your head's hitting the ceiling, Coombes. D-III is all you get as a detective. I want you to switch to command track. You could be L-I this time next year, C-1 four years later. You already did the work, why not get paid for it?"

"And if I made lieutenant or captain, that would still be in RHD, right? Taking murderers off the board, not working in Juvenile Division or Professional Standards?"

"Well, no. You would be posted to wherever we needed you. But I think you know that, don't you, Coombes? You're making a point."

"I'm a detective not a bureaucrat. Managing budgets, COMPSTAT meetings...that's not what I'm about. I'm here to catch bad guys."

"Old school, huh?"

"I guess so."

"Look, we've got a lot of dead wood needing to be cleared out and I want people I trust coming through the ranks. Job satisfaction doesn't last forever, I want you to know you have options. That shoot-out this morning could've gone another way. Think about it."

"All right, I'll think about it."

He wouldn't think about it, not even for a second.

Coombes walked toward the door.

The conversation had reminded him of something important, something he'd been overlooking for a long time. There was a way out for him and Sato and the chief had given him the keys.

"Coombes, one more thing. I know they keep you pretty busy downstairs, but find the time to update your address with the Department. That mail divert makes it look like you're hiding something, even if you aren't. Same for Sato. Keep it above board."

Everybody's hiding something.

"Right, Chief."

30

COOMBES AND SATO DROVE home together in silence. It seemed likely that detectives who planted listening devices in his home might also think to wire his car. The Dodge belonged to the Department, which meant that they could do what they wished with it. He had performed a basic search to no avail, but he knew how little that meant. Microphones, even cameras, could be made so small that they were barely noticeable.

Yet the devices in his apartment had not been hard to find. All sound, no visuals. No spy-style pens or picture frames. For his own sanity, he could see that he was going to have to buy a surveillance wand and sweep his car and apartment for further devices.

He pulled his Dodge up to the barrier and waited for it to open enough to drive in. The spot felt vulnerable now, a location where he could be ambushed. The barrier rolled slowly open, then he drove underneath and around to his parking spot. He parked up and they got out the car and walked toward the stairs into the apartment building.

"Jackson said he'd shut down the investigation."

"Do you believe him?"

It was a fair question. If IA realized the surveillance operation was blown, the obvious next step was to tell him it was all over and allow him to drop his guard. But would Jackson really have made the pitch for him to switch to command if he still harbored doubts about him?

"Yeah, I guess I do. I think he likes me."

Sato laughed. "What's not to like, eh, Coombes?"

The laugh brought a spark back into her eyes that he hadn't seen for several weeks. He reached out and held her hand then glanced around at where they were standing, as if noticing it for the first time.

"You kissed me here once, do you remember?"

"I remember."

"You said you wanted to know if it was still there. What did I say?"

"Come on, Johnny, let's not do this."

He softened his voice. "What did I say?"

Sato sighed. "You said it would be there until you were dead."

"It *is* still there, Grace. Is it not for you, is that it?"

"This hasn't been easy for either of us."

"So why are we doing it? Nobody knows about us. Nobody cares."

"You know why."

"I do. We're happy together and you're scared about what comes next."

"That's the point! *Nothing* can come next. You're in my chain of command, Johnny. That's always going to be between us. The only way it won't, is if one of us leaves. I don't want to leave RHD, do you?"

Sato dropped his hand and pushed past him, climbing the stairs in front of them. He had to smile a little, she was so feisty.

He followed after her, taking the stairs three at a time.

They reached the top at around the same time and he held the door open as she exited the stairwell into the lobby area of their apartment building. The concierge sat behind a large curved desk, he saw them and nodded.

As they waited for the elevator, she turned to look at him.

"Why are you smiling? You think our situation is funny?"

"It's just that today I realized how simple the solution was."

"Yeah. We don't tell anyone we're seeing each other, I'm familiar with the ins-and-outs of this masterplan. We tried it, remember?"

"What if I told you this problem will resolve itself?"

"Everything goes from bad to worse, you know that."

"Once you make D-III we'll be the same rank. Chain of command rules fall away. Do the work, take the tests. Done. The chief pinned a medal on you Grace, they can't say you don't deserve it. After that, we're a digit apart. You could make D-III in eighteen months."

Sato's mouth fell open.

"Then we could go public?"

The elevator doors opened and they got on.

"Do you know Perez and Lowe in Major Crimes?"

"Can't say I do."

"They're married. Both are D-IIIs. If they can do it, so can we."

Sato was silent a moment as she thought about it.

"I don't know. You made D-III in five years; I've been in six already and I'm still on the bottom rung. Not everyone is a rock star like you, Johnny."

He regretted sharing Willard's nickname with her.

"That's what no one seems to understand. I *didn't* make it in five years. I was in the Army for eight years beforehand. I was a thirteen-year veteran when I was promoted. The difference between us is that I didn't make it to RHD until I was already D-II. Homicide Special gets all the best cases. It's easier to get promoted when you are closing cases that are in the news."

"Then we wait."

"For what?"

"For me to make D-III like you said. I want to be with you, Johnny, but I don't want to hide it anymore. I feel like we're having an affair and I can't do it. I don't *want* to do it."

COOMBES SAT AT THE breakfast bar and opened the Lawrence murder book. He was almost through it now, and he sensed there was nothing in it to move the investigation forward.

Willard had started well, hunting down extra details, and attaching names and cell numbers of people he'd spoken to in case he needed to get back in touch. The problem was that Willard was committed to De Luca as her killer and that steered everything he did.

After about an hour, he set the binder to one side and began to look through material that Willard had sent from his evidence wall. There were eight pages torn from a notebook that Willard had pinned up, presumably because he thought they were important.

The one that caught his eye, related to the killer's signature.

He and Willard had spent a long time trying to figure out the significance of the cross cut into Lawrence's face, if it was a random design chosen by her killer, or something that could help identify him.

Willard had again pondered this question and arrived at a new idea.

That it indicated rejection.

Since De Luca attended auditions, Willard hypothesized that actors that didn't make the cut had a cross placed on their studio headshots. Coombes found this idea intriguing, because it was something that worked just as well for Booth who had ultimate say on casting.

Where it seemed to work for De Luca, was the belief that Dakota Lawrence rejected the producer's sexual advances at the wrap party hours before her death. Willard had later discounted this idea, scoring a line through it and writing *never mind* in angry or drunken script.

Willard had presumably interviewed other guests at the wrap party and accepted that Lawrence was never there; that the eye-witness story from Hahn and Peters was bullshit.

From Coombes' point of view, it didn't matter.

What *did* matter, is that Willard didn't try to see if the idea of rejection worked for anyone else, he just dropped it and never went back to it.

He imagined Booth with a Sharpie, drawing a cross on photographs of actors he rejected. It was a strong visual, but it didn't work. Booth regularly re-auditioned actors he'd previously rejected. An actor that wasn't right for one part, might be a good for another.

When it came to Booth's women, age appeared to be the only form of rejection that was final.

Sato appeared next to him.

She was wearing the long T-shirt she wore to bed. The hem came down to the top of her thighs, which were bare. Sato stepped on a foot rest on the side of the barstool and swung her right leg over so that she was sitting on his lap.

She smiled, amused by his confusion, then kissed him.

It felt good, and he allowed himself to get lost in the moment. Coombes could feel himself being restored, like some inner battery was being charged after heavy use.

When the kiss ended, he placed his index finger vertically on his mouth to remind her of the Internal Affairs microphone under the table.

They walked into the hallway outside their apartment.

"I thought we broke up?"

"No," she said. "We're hitting pause, there's a difference."

"What's the difference?"

Sato turned away from him, her gaze directed at the floor.

"You're still mine. You don't get to move Sullivan into my spot."

Sullivan. All the drama that occurred between them had happened since he'd told her he was using the journalist to work the case.

"Come on, Grace. That's ridiculous."

"I've seen the two of you together. You *like* her, I'm not imagining something. I could smell her perfume on you, I saw her message with the kisses. I'm not stupid."

"All right, I like her. She's an excellent investigator. If she wasn't a journalist, she'd make a damn good cop. Is she a flirt? Sure, but it doesn't mean anything. She's the same with everyone, it's how she gets information. I do nothing to encourage it."

Sato fixed him with a stare, her eyes ready to cry.

"How do you know what she's like with other people?"

He realized that he *didn't* and thought again about the way the journalist's face kept flushing scarlet. No matter how big a fake you were, some things you can't control.

"Right now, our goals are the same. The case and the story about it are linked. No case, no story. As soon as that changes, I have no doubt she'll disappear over the horizon."

Sato said nothing and turned to go back inside.

"Hey," he said. "We never finished our kiss."

"Not all kisses end that way, Johnny."

31

AT EXACTLY 9 A.M., Coombes was led into an interview room and told to take a seat. The suspect side. He sat and looked at the two FID detectives. Kennedy and Stills. They were his age, still young, hungry. From his point of view, that probably wasn't a good thing. A camera was mounted on a tripod, the cable going off through the wall. For some reason, it hadn't occurred to him that his interview was going to be recorded.

He wondered if Block was watching via the camera.

It felt different being on this side of the table.

Kennedy sat a file folder down on the table, then began to pace the room from side to side like a big cat at the zoo. The folder had his name on it and was half an inch thick. He was a little disappointed it wasn't thicker.

Stills checked his watch and looked up.

"Have you got a union rep coming?"

"No," Coombes said. "I've got nothing to hide."

Kennedy stopped mid-pace and came over to the table. His hair was cut down to a thick dark stubble that covered his cue ball head and wrapped around his chin. He wasn't losing his hair; this was just a look he was after.

Nothing to grab him by in a fight.

"This is your fourth officer-involved shooting in eight years, Coombes. That's got to be some kind of record. You know, some detectives manage to go their whole career without drawing their weapon."

"Is there a question coming?"

"All right, Coombes, let's get to it. How about you run us through what happened, starting with when you arrived at the location."

A cop interrogating another cop had to at least suspect they were wasting their time. Both sides knew the game, the moves, and where they went.

Kennedy had his suit jacket off; his shirt sleeves rolled up. He was standing, his body angled over the table toward Coombes, his gun hanging from a chest holster over his heart. It was a power position, meant to intimidate him into making a mistake while he locked in his story.

Coombes sat back, out of range of Kennedy's breath.

He'd already told the story three times at the scene but he knew how it worked. Coombes re-told his story, making sure to add some new details to keep it fresh. Repeating the same story word-for-word was the sign of a lie.

If he knew it, so would Kennedy.

Coombes included some details from his interview with the landlady and the implications for his case, then his trip back toward the road where he first saw Joseph Wright making his attack run on his Dodge.

When he finished his interviewers looked irritated.

"How about you try that again, and put in the part you missed out."

Kennedy's response came as no surprise to Coombes. Repetition was one of the tools in a detective's toolbox, and was part of the process of nailing-down a story.

Coombes calmly went back to the beginning and started over. He just had to wear them down with the truth so he could go about his day.

When he finished again, Kennedy smiled a little.

"You claim Wright was approaching your vehicle, gun in hand?"

"That's right."

"How far out do you estimate he was from the bodywork?"

Coombes thought for a moment.

"Maybe three feet?"

"When you fired, was he at the same distance, or did he move toward you?"

"He turned around, if he moved closer it wasn't by much."

Another smile.

"That's when you shot him through the head?"

"He was there to kill me, Kennedy, I didn't have a choice."

"Just answer my question, Detective."

Coombes thought about it.

"He turned and aimed his gun at me and I shot him...no, wait...he dropped down onto one knee first, *then* I fired."

Kennedy's smile disappeared.

"He wasn't standing?"

"I was aiming center mass, the only reason I hit his head is because he dropped down. If I'd shot him standing his brains would've ended up on the other side of my hood."

The two detectives stared at him in silence.

"Oh," Coombes said, understanding. "You thought I'd shot him in the middle of the street then dragged him over to the car to support a story about him trying to sneak up on me?"

"Any reason you didn't mention this before?"

"Didn't I? I guess I forgot. I definitely mentioned it to the uniforms who were first on the scene. They were wearing body cameras, pull the footage if you don't believe me."

"We'll do that," Kennedy said, straightening up.

Kennedy was an ass, he thought. It was probably in the job description. He turned to Stills. Sometimes the quiet ones were the ones you had to watch.

"What about the woman on the motorcycle?"

"No ER treated a female with a gunshot wound yesterday. If she's Aryan Brotherhood, they might have a tame physician. Gangbangers have their own healthcare system."

"What about the murder of Sarah Ryan and the skinhead Soto put in the morgue? Are you looking into that?"

"We're not here to answer *your* questions, Coombes."

"It's all part of the same puzzle, Stills. You can't look at a single piece and expect to see the whole picture."

"We're only concerned with if this was a good shoot, that's it."

"And if the Brotherhood keeps sending assassins to kill me, what then?"

"Try not to kill the next one. It's difficult to question a corpse."

He was hitting his head off the wall.

Kennedy began to unroll his shirt sleeves. Coombes assumed this to mean the interview was at an end. He glanced toward the camera and used his index and middle finger of his right hand to brush imaginary lint off his left shoulder. Two bars.

A little message for his captain.

"Are we done here, fellas?"

Kennedy picked up the unopened file folder and shoved it into a briefcase. Either the folder was a prop, or it contained photographs showing where Wright's brains had landed and a spatter analyst's report on where the Nazi had to have been standing to replicate it.

"This is just part of a larger conversation, Coombes."

Wasn't it always.

"I'm happy to answer any questions now, get this all wrapped up."

Kennedy glared at him.

"We'll be in touch, Detective."

As he came out the interview room, Combes glanced at his watch. A little over twenty minutes. On previous occasions, second interviews by FID had removed an hour to an hour and a half of his life. They had invested everything in the idea that he'd moved Wright's body and when he blew that out the water, they had nothing left.

The shorter-than-expected interview gave him a window of opportunity and he didn't feel like wasting it by returning to his desk.

32

ACCORDING TO MONICA SULLIVAN, the mansion in front of him had cost Booth twenty million dollars and had incurred the wrath of the IRS who couldn't figure out how he could afford it. Coombes drove his Dodge around the turning circle in front of the building and parked next to a midnight blue Navigator bearing the *Son of a Gun* decal of Booth's production company. He killed the engine and stepped out.

Joshua Booth stood in the doorway wearing running gear, an oversize watch, and a pair of sneakers whose gold laces matched the color of the watch. Booth smiled warmly, like they were old friends meeting after a long absence.

"Good morning, Detective! Come in, let me show you around."

Coombes locked the Dodge and walked to where Booth stood.

"Were you expecting me, Mr. Booth?"

"Oh, very much so. Come in."

Coombes saw only darkness in the other man's eyes. The smiles and the bonhomie were no more than a mask Booth was wearing. It wasn't hard for him to imagine those same dead eyes calmly watching the last moments of life drain away from his victims.

Past the doorway, a marble entrance hall opened out to reveal a curved staircase with gold handrails. It looked like a scene from *Fallen Idol*, except everything was pristine, without the cobwebs, dirt, and decay from the movie.

Though she'd never been here, he imagined Dakota Lawrence sweeping down the stairs, her perfect face somehow both emotionally torn and serenely at peace.

The walls were bare, save for a square of darker wallpaper with two picture hooks in the center. Until recently, a painting had been mounted on the wall.

They walked past a door held open by a gold statue.

Coombes turned his head to look at it as they walked on.

"Is that real?"

"I have five Oscars, Detective. Since none are for Best Picture or Best Director, they are all basically doorstops. Don't tell the Academy I said that."

"I'll give you fifty bucks for it."

Booth gave a small laugh and continued down the hall.

Coombes decided to adopt a bumbling detective persona worthy of *Columbo*. The last time they'd met he'd leaned a little on the director to get answers but if he kept doing it Booth would hide behind a lawyer and he was in no position to take things further right now.

He needed to build rapport with Booth, and tease the information out.

They entered a large room with a wall of glass that looked out along the coastline below and across the Pacific. Coombes took in the view for a moment. He had a nice view himself, but this had him beat.

He turned to face the room.

Most of the space was taken up by a swimming pool. A deck area sat on all sides with loungers and chairs. The end wall had a bar with shelves of spirits at the back and taps for beer at the front. Six chrome and leather barstools were sat along the edge.

"This is *nice*," Coombes said, exaggerating the last word.

"Thank you."

Booth brought his conquests here, he thought. First, he'd soften them up with liquor, then he'd use the pool as a device to introduce nudity into the mix. Perhaps there was cocaine somewhere to get things going, then he'd get what he wanted.

"When I become a millionaire, this is what I'm getting."

Booth smiled, barely holding his contempt at bay.

Artistically, the director was a success, but Booth's box office numbers and tax returns didn't support the lifestyle Coombes saw around him. The man was a fraud in every sense.

"Can I get you a drink? I saw you looking at the bar."

"Tempting, but I'm working."

"An espresso then?"

"You know what? I'll take you up on that."

They moved to the bar, with Booth going behind like a bartender as Coombes slipped onto one of the stools. He wondered how many women had sat where he was sitting, and if any of them were dead.

Booth's black eye looked worse, with purples and yellows creeping in.

The director made two espressos and slid one across the counter.

"You look like a no-cream man."

Coombes nodded and took a sip. It was perfect. When you bought coffee in a store it was served at close to boiling point and you had to wait for it to cool down before you could drink it. The high temperature destroyed the flavor and burnt your lips. But not this coffee, this he could drink immediately. He finished his cup and put it down on the small saucer.

"That machine right there, that's going on my list."

Booth smiled. "Of things to buy when you're a millionaire?"

"That's right," Coombes paused. "It's actually a pretty long list."

"I'll bet. How can I help you today, Detective?"

"Let's go over by the window where the light's better, I want to take notes."

In fact, he wanted to see Booth without the bar in the way, providing the director with either physical support or potential sources of distraction to delay answers.

Coombes chose a spot away from the loungers so that Booth couldn't sit down, then took his notebook out his pocket and flipped to a blank page.

"Talk to me about Natalie."

"What do you want me tell you?"

"What was she like. Was she funny, moody, did she light up the room. Did other people turn to look at her when you were together? Anything. I want a sense of who she was."

Joshua Booth stared into space.

It looked like Booth could hardly remember the murdered woman, but just as he was about to prompt the director again, he spoke.

"She was dark. It felt like something bad happened to her in childhood that she never wanted to talk about. I know this sounds strange, but it was this *damaged* part of her that first drew me to her. She could be funny too, but in a shocking way. Natalie was no cheerleader, that was for sure."

Coombes nodded and made notes. It all fitted with the young woman he'd interviewed and her sullen stare. He wrote down *childhood trauma?* and underlined it.

"You dated for twelve weeks. When did it start and why did it end?"

"You're not going to like my answer to that."

"I'm not here to be amused, Mr. Booth."

"I was in a bad place after what happened to Dakota. Like I said before, I started drinking a lot. I met Natalie in a bar. It was the day after they found Dakota and we just clicked. I took her home and we had sex. She was like a wild animal, scratching and biting. Pulling my hair, you know? It was exactly what I needed, an escape from reality."

Booth paused, but Coombes waited for him to continue.

"Anyway, the way I am, she became my new muse when I was working on my next project, her darkness shaped the story. After the movie wrapped, I didn't need her anymore, so I got rid of her."

"You got rid of her."

"A poor choice of words. I meant I ended the relationship."

"That's what you do is it? You date women, extract something from them to make a movie, then toss them aside like garbage?"

"I told you that you wouldn't like it."

"You're a piece of shit, Booth."

"Yeah, I know."

"If you know, why don't you change?"

Booth shrugged.

"Because I don't want to. Look, this is my creative process. These women, they know what they're in for with me, it's no secret how I work. Other directors, in stable relationships, they make the same movie over and over again. All my movies are different, because the muse that powers them is different."

Coombes took a moment to make a note of this in his notebook then looked up. The detached manner that Booth described his relationships made him a good fit for a sociopath. He thought of Natalie's performance in the movie.

"You met her in a bar. Should I assume she wasn't an actor?"

Booth crunched up his face, obviously a sore point.

"*Carnival of Delights* was her first movie. She was paid as an actor therefore she *was* one. It's the way the union works. You can't replace an actor with someone off the street and pay them peanuts, it's against the rules. Everyone has to start somewhere."

"She got the part because the two of you were sharing a bed, true or false?"

"True."

"Not because she was blackmailing you because you murdered Dakota."

"Oh god, no."

"But you can't prove that, can you?"

Booth threw up his arms in frustration.

"How would I prove that? That's crazy. I dated Natalie after Dakota, that's all. After Natalie I dated someone else, then someone else."

Coombes grunted vaguely and made a lot of notes, most of which were garbage. He'd noticed that every time he wrote something down, Booth tensed up. The longer he wrote, the more Booth became uptight. Finally, he looked up.

"All right. Was Natalie seeing anyone else while you were dating?"

"Not as far as I know. I wouldn't have been with her if she was. Call me a hypocrite; I don't mind *being* a slut but I won't date one."

Coombes laughed, then wrote Booth's line verbatim into his notebook.

"Will you stop writing things down, it's getting on my nerves!"

"Did you and Natalie use contraception?"

The question didn't faze the other man at all.

"Sure. She was on the pill. I don't want children."

"You didn't use condoms?"

"The whole muse-thing doesn't work through a rubber bag, Detective."

"Uh-huh. You ever see her take the pill?"

"No, why? I saw them in her bag once, I don't get involved in all that."

Coombes found himself thinking about Sato.

They had never discussed protection either and, like Booth, he was relying on her to take care of it. Unlike Booth, he'd never seen any evidence that she *was* taking care of it.

He made eye contact as he asked his next question.

"You didn't wear a condom and Natalie didn't see other people, yet she was pregnant at the time of her death. What would you think, Mr. Booth?"

The director frowned.

"I've not seen Natalie in years, why would any child be mine?"

"Because Natalie's been dead in a hole since you broke up."

Booth paled visibly and put his hand against the window to brace himself.

"Then you *do* think I killed her."

"You just told me that you don't want children. Her being pregnant is a motive for you to kill her even if she *wasn't* blackmailing you for Dakota's murder. If you don't want children, it follows that you also don't want to pay child support. Either you had one reason to kill her, or you had two. You still had *a* reason and one is all it takes."

"Except I didn't kill Dakota and I didn't know Natalie was pregnant."

"I'm inclined to believe you, Booth, but past experience has taught me that two victims linked to one man makes that man their killer. It's basic cop math."

"I guess this is the point where I get a lawyer."

Coombes closed his notebook.

He'd strayed off the path of the bumbling detective and this was the result, he'd shot himself in the foot. Sometimes he couldn't stop being who he was.

"You never asked me before if I liked your movies."

Booth's eyes lit up. He was interested, despite himself.

"And?"

"You're a despicable excuse for a human, Booth, but I have seen all of your movies, most three of four times. That won't mean anything because you don't know me, but I can't say the same for any other modern director."

The compliment was filling up the other man like a balloon.

"All things being equal, I'd rather get someone else for this. I *like* your movies. But questions need to be answered, you must see that. If you lawyer-up it makes me think there's something there. See? You automatically become prime suspect. So I keep investigating until I get my answers a different way and you better believe that I will get them."

"I didn't hurt these women, I couldn't. I'm not wired that way."

"Let's say I believe you. How about you tell me again what happened the night you last saw Dakota, because the version that you gave me and my partner was a total lie."

Booth's face twisted awkwardly.

"The truth is not always straightforward. I missed something out, that's all. I never lied. You see, none of the women I've been with have slept with me. We have sex and then they leave. They don't stay the night."

"Why would any woman put up with that? You're treating them like prostitutes."

"I have a phobia, Detective. I can't sleep unless I'm alone."

"Why's that?"

"You won't believe me. It's stupid."

"I hear a lot of stupid, I'm used to it."

Booth sighed and stared at his hands.

"I'm afraid my eyes will be poked while I sleep. That I'll be blinded."

"No kidding."

"I thought you were going to laugh at me."

"As it happens, I have a phobia of my own."

"Really?"

"If I'm drinking from a can outdoors, I wonder if a yellow jacket has flown inside while I wasn't looking. That it will sting me when I take a drink. On my lips, or inside my mouth. Now that I think about it, I have a similar one about drinking from a cup of water on my nightstand. It's dark, I can't see the surface, and there's a spider floating there. I drink it."

Booth raised his hands, as if to ward off an attack.

"Please. I'm sensitive to this stuff."

He thought about how this changed Booth's original testimony.

Booth had claimed that the last time he'd been with Dakota Lawrence they'd dined at an upscale restaurant before returning to his home where they spent the remainder of the evening drinking and having sex.

He and Willard had both inferred that Lawrence had stayed the night when, in fact, she'd been ejected and had driven home alone, presumably intoxicated.

At the time, the difference in her timeline would've meant little. His eyewitnesses placed her alive at a party held by Anthony De Luca two days later. From that point on, De Luca became the focus of the investigation and Booth fell away, an early person of interest.

"I find it interesting that Natalie was at a wrap party for a movie she wasn't in, and the director of the movie wasn't there. Then, forty-eight hours later, she happens to meet that same director in a bar where they hook up and begin a relationship."

Booth shrugged.

"I hate those parties. By the end of a shoot, everyone dislikes me. I'm not a nice person. I treat actors in a way that will give me the performance I want from them on camera. Those parties are for the cast, every director knows that."

"A coincidence that Natalie was there, then at the bar you met in?"

"She went to the party to find me. When I didn't show, she staked out a bar I'm known to frequent. She was a fan, Detective, it's happened before."

Coombes decided to move the conversation on.

"I suppose I should ask what happened to your face."

"I got mugged."

"A *woman* mugged you?"

Booth glanced up sharply. "What are you talking about?"

"I can see the marks of her knuckles in the bruise. A small hand, bones close together. Strong though. She's done a real number on you."

"It doesn't matter, I'm not pressing charges."

"One more question. What does this mean to you?"

He held up the piece of paper he'd shown Sato.

"A letter X?" Booth shrugged. "Roman numeral for ten?"

"What else?"

"It's not really my style, but some people use them as kisses."

A kiss. Coombes nearly groaned out loud. Is that what it represented? A kiss goodbye? He looked at the way Booth was staring at the symbol.

Did he see pride? Recognition?

"All right, what about specific to you, or to movies."

"Am I still a suspect?"

"For now."

"Why would I help you tighten a noose around my own neck?"

Coombes thought of damage to Dakota Lawrence's neck.

"Do you care at all about what happened to these women?"

"Sure, I care. I bore easily, but that doesn't mean I'm dead inside."

"So far, the facts all point in one direction. If this isn't you, it's someone close to you. A friend maybe. Don't you want to know who that is? I know *I* would. If getting justice for the victims doesn't do it for you, I'm sure the experience will be great material for a movie."

Booth eyed him carefully.

"A letter X was found near Dakota and Natalie?"

Coombes nodded, but said nothing.

"Don't you see? I dated both women. They're my *exes.* I'm being set up."

"I don't take you for a stupid man, Booth. If you were the killer, I don't think you'd announce your link with the victims. Also, since Natalie was buried, the concept of a frame goes out the window. Why put a frame in place when the body might never be found?"

"That question right there? *That's* your movie."

33

Sato watched him walk across the detective bureau, her head turning, locked on target. She had her headphones on and they completely dwarfed her head. The headphones, he'd discovered, often meant he was in the doghouse. Sato's head continued to follow him. Her gaze was piercing, her eyes unblinking. He was busted. Coombes put his tablet computer on his desk and slipped off his jacket.

She pulled the headphones down around her neck.

"I suppose you were away seeing your *little friend?*"

From the death glare, he assumed this was a reference to Monica Sullivan, who was actually six inches taller than Sato.

"If you mean Joshua Booth, then yes."

"Johnny, what the hell? Walker has to be filed *today.*"

"I just had to get out of here for a while."

"Block came looking for you about ten minutes after your interview ended. He was *not* pleased with you, Coombes. Next time you decide to pepper spray the captain's asshole I'd really appreciate if you hung around for the fallout because I'm sick of dealing with it."

Block *had* been watching the interview.

"Sorry, Grace. The guy brings out the worst in me."

"When I apply for D-II he'll be on the review panel. You realize that, right? This war you have going on has nothing to do with me but it will be me paying the price, not you."

"Sorry, I hadn't thought about that. I'll try and cool it down."

She nodded without enthusiasm and pulled her headphones up over her ears. It was like hanging up on a call. From her point of view, the conversation was over. He tapped on the partition and she sighed and flipped a headphone off her right ear.

"What are you working on?"

"Plan B, the DUI murder. Just like you suggested."

"Need any help?"

"Yes, Coombes. I need you to do Plan A."

"Right."

He sat down and flipped back through his notebook to his original notes after watching the dashcam footage. On the other side of the partition, Walker being high at the time of the incident worked in their favor, on this side, it worked against them.

Intent to kill disappeared in a cloud of smoke.

Slow reaction times, even hitting the wrong peddle, all explained by the drug in Walker's system. No malice aforethought, just an accident, one of over 6,000 that year.

Without the dashcam footage, there was no Plan A.

He opened the murder book to the medical examiner's report. There were photographs of Molly there that he hadn't seen before. Until now, his only visual of the victim had been her DMV photograph and the video of her walking out onto the street.

The before pictures, not the after pictures.

Two years had passed since her husband had run her over, but the damage was still there, still raw. This was how Sato had seen Molly.

He wondered how Naylor could go to the hospital to visit her day after day and look at someone he loved like this. If it had been Sato lying there, he would've put a pillow over her face and ended it, come what may.

Maybe that *was* what happened, he thought.

He turned to the autopsy report and found it was missing. When he looked over his partition to ask Sato about it, he found she was also missing. Her screen was showing the login window. That usually meant that she was in a meeting or had left the building.

Coombes called the Medical Examiner's Office and identified himself to the administrator on the other end.

"How can I help you today, Detective?"

"I need some information on a Mary Gardner Walker, D.O.D. 18th June of this year. I believe cause of death is respiratory failure, I just want to check that's correct."

"One moment."

The line went quiet, with just the soft clicks of a keyboard.

"All right, I have the file. Your cause of death is a little off. Respiratory failure might be true, but officially it's COVID-19."

Sato had lied to him and buried the autopsy to hide it.

"No kidding."

"The virus hits people with a compromised immune system harder. Most victims of this disease are near the end for some other reason, COVID is just the final straw."

He nodded, even though the other man couldn't see him.

"One more. Do you know who handled the funeral arrangements?"

"You want the funeral director, or the lawyers?"

"Lawyers."

Coombes wrote the details down in his notebook, signed off, then dialed the number for the attorney. A woman's voice came on the line, young, probably early twenties.

"Finch and Finch."

"I'd like to speak to someone about the Mary Walker estate."

"Are you a family member, sir?"

He knew from previous experience that he could expect nothing from a law firm without a warrant which he had no probable cause to get, so he decided on another tack.

"No, ma'am, I am not."

"We can't discuss client matters-"

"I was told a property on Sterns Drive was available for a cash sale and this was the number I was given. If I have the wrong number, I apologize. My handwriting is not the best."

There was a pause and the voice came back softer.

"I'm afraid the property has already been sold."

"Oh," Coombes said, putting it on thick. "That's too bad."

"It went very quickly. I've had calls all week about it."

"Well, thank you for your time, ma'am."

"You're welcome."

He hung up the telephone. The obvious conclusion was that the house on Sterns Drive had been in Molly's name and became part of her estate when she passed away.

The pieces were starting to fall into place.

Stephen Walker had been sued for malpractice in 2016. The case was settled out of court, but it would've been a wake-up call for Walker. The case was against him personally, not his firm. He could've lost everything.

It would make sense that he would transfer his property to Molly to firewall his largest asset from forfeiture.

Two years later, the windshield notes start to appear.

After the anger of Molly's betrayal had passed, Walker would've realized how vulnerable he was. The property was hers. To protect it from forfeiture, the title deed transfer had to be iron-clad. Which meant he had no claim to it in any divorce settlement.

The only way Walker could get his multi-million-dollar property back was if Molly died and the ownership passed back to him through her will.

But it hadn't worked, Coombes thought.

He'd seen estates tied up in probate for months, even years. The property could not have passed back to Stephen Walker while he was serving time for attempting to kill her. It was therefore clear that Molly had changed her will and Coombes had a good idea about who the new beneficiary might be.

He grabbed his jacket and headed out.

———

CARSON NAYLOR LOOKED AT him warily from his doorway without speaking. After a beat, his eyes flipped to the side, looking for Sato. There was obvious disappointment on his face when he saw Coombes was alone.

"I guess you know why I'm here, Mr. Naylor."

"I don't know what you're talking about."

"Look, you wasted my time. You made me come back here when you could've been straight with me. If you're going to continue the bullshit, we can continue this downtown. I'm through being nice, I've used up my quota for the week."

Naylor sighed and held the door for him to enter.

Coombes was wearing a mask, but he found himself holding his breath as he walked past the other man. Naylor looked worse than last time. Coombes kept his distance as he followed him to the kitchen where they'd sat before.

The door to the yard was open and a breeze was coming in.

"How about we do this outside where it's more ventilated?"

"*Ventilated?*"

"I know you've got the virus, Naylor. You gave it to her."

"Molly died from COVID?"

"That's right."

"You're saying *I* killed her?"

Coombes said nothing and instead walked into the yard. It was a peaceful space, with no city noise. He pulled his mask down and watched as the other man came out.

Tears were running down Naylor's face.

On the drive over, it seemed possible that Naylor could've deliberately infected Molly Walker with COVID by coughing repeatedly near her face. He would've known that the virus would be enough to take care of things and that her death would raise no red flags with the hospital or with the authorities.

What better way to hide a murder, than in thousands of other deaths?

Naylor's tears looked real. It was hard, particularly for a man, to fake tears. Coombes decided to start with a simple question.

"She told you she changed her will, didn't she?"

"We talked about it; I didn't know she'd actually done it. Her husband was drinking more, getting more violent. She planned to show him a copy of the new will so he knew that he stood to gain nothing from her death. It was to protect her."

"If he saw your name, wouldn't he figure out you were lovers?"

"The plan was to deny it. I was just her best friend, someone she trusted. Bottom line, I thought I could handle him if he came at me. I suppose I also thought it would lead to them getting a divorce faster and that she and I could finally get married."

"How so?"

"Molly had him over a barrel with the house, right? It was a bargaining chip. She wasn't trying to steal it from him, she just wanted what was fair. He'd been spending her money from the business for years; she wanted it all back."

"When did you find out that the new will was in effect?"

"Last week, when I got a letter from Finch and Finch."

He saw no deception on Naylor's face.

"Why didn't you mention this last time I was here?"

"Are you kidding me? I know what this looks like, it looks like a motive to kill her. Next, you'll be saying I pushed her in front of his car!"

"But you *didn't*, right? Because you didn't know she'd changed it yet?"

"If that's the only answer you'll believe, so be it. I wanted to spend the rest of my life with her, Detective, maybe you don't know what that feels like. We were soulmates."

Sato had eaten this up, she was a true romantic.

"Molly hadn't told you that she'd changed her will. Is it fair to assume she had also not told her husband? Probably not an easy conversation to start."

"I hadn't thought about it, but that makes sense."

"Let's move on," Coombes said. "Tell me about the life insurance policy."

Naylor closed his eyes and groaned.

"That's got nothing to do with anything! We set those up the second year we were in business. One for her, one for me. My financial advisor suggested it. I forgot all about it."

"What was the value of the policy?"

"Five million...ten in the event of foul play."

Coombes whistled.

"You just keep landing on your feet, don't you Mr. Naylor?"

"I'd set it all on fire to have her back."

"Her husband claims someone left a series of messages on his windshield in the days leading up to the incident. Was that you?"

"No."

Coombes believed him, but a jury might not.

"If Walker gets wind of any of this, the case is over. It's reasonable doubt. It might even be grounds for mistrial. He'll be out on the streets faster than you can brush your teeth."

"I did nothing wrong!"

"Look, I wasn't here today, ok? We didn't talk about this and if you say that we did, I'll deny it. Walker will hire an investigator. You need to call Finch and Finch, tell them to stop talking about the damn house on Sterns Drive. Do you understand what I'm telling you?"

"Yes."

"Well, hallelujah for that."

Coombes pulled up his mask and walked past Naylor, back through the house. The other man followed along behind him like a scolded puppy.

"Why are you helping me, Detective?"

"Sometimes justice comes down to choosing a side. My partner believes in you, that's good enough for me. Her heart is bigger than mine, she knows this stuff. Also, since you've not tried to have me killed, that puts you out in front of the other guy."

Coombes opened the door and walked down the path.

He was done with Naylor, that only left Walker.

As he lowered himself into the Dodge, he remembered the missing autopsy report. He assumed Sato had hidden it to protect Naylor. Perhaps believing that the jeweler deliberately infected Molly with COVID, just as he had. But that that didn't scan.

Sato told him that Molly had died from respiratory failure which fit just as easily with Naylor ending her life.

There was something else going on.

34

As he drove back downtown, he considered what it all meant. Assuming that Walker hadn't invented the windshield notes during his incarceration, things narrowed very quickly. It wasn't a big case, only three people were directly involved. Naylor said he hadn't left the notes, and for sure Walker didn't leave them for himself, who did that leave?

Logically, only one person.

Molly Walker.

She had access to Stephen Walker's SUV to plant the firearm and his cell phone to install the tracking software. Suggesting that she used the windshield notes to lure him to her business partner's address, where she deliberately stepped out in front of his vehicle.

It was a suicide.

Molly knew her life insurance would pay double if it looked like her husband killed her. She also knew everything would be caught on the dashcam, sealing her husband's fate.

Coombes thought again of the odd stumbling way that Molly came out onto the road. It was the one piece of the puzzle that never fit for him. She'd had to force herself to do it, he thought, to fight her body's natural desire to live. The glance back toward the sidewalk was to take one last look at Naylor before the end.

Because she loved him, not because he'd pushed her.

Coombes would've seen it for what it was if she'd stepped out just prior to impact. That's what suicides looked like, there was never any gap. A split-second between deciding to end it all, and the lights going out.

Four or five seconds, they could last a lifetime in the wrong situation.

Molly's plan had to have two parts; give her husband a reason to kill her, then give him an opportunity. The plan relied upon the impact being clearly avoidable and Walker being so enraged that he took no action to stop.

The administrator at the Medical Examiner's Office said she died from COVID because she was compromised. He'd assumed that was a reference to the injuries she sustained when her husband drove over her in his SUV, but that didn't explain her suicide.

More likely, she had a pre-existing condition with a prognosis she was keen to avoid. A condition that made you lose weight fast without wanting to brag about it. Something that would be listed on the missing autopsy report.

He sighed.

Sato had known the whole time.

She interviewed hospital staff while he was busy with Booth. That was *before* she saw the autopsy report, which meant she knew what was coming and didn't want him to find out about it.

Any time he'd come close to the truth, she'd steered him away.

He pulled up at a traffic light and watched a woman cross in front of him. Her head down, eyes never leaving her cell phone. Sato was right, no-body looked before crossing anymore. It was a miracle that pedestrian deaths weren't higher than they were. All it took was a driver looking at their cell phone at the same time as the pedestrian.

Coombes thought about where all this left Stephen Walker.

He was both murderer and victim.

It would be impossible for Walker to prove that his wife had installed the tracking software on his cell phone without his permission. Since there was also no proof the windshield notes ever existed, all the evidence pointed to him using the app to track Molly's movements, then following her to her lover's home to kill her with the gun.

Coombes felt no sympathy for Walker, nor did he intend to help him.

Molly had paid a steep price for what she did and had served a sentence of her own that was almost as long as her husband's. Whether she initiated it or not, nobody had the right to do what Walker did. She deserved justice.

It was midday Friday and he was only now caught up with where Sato had been on Monday morning. She'd wasted his whole week with noise, a week he would rather have spent investigating Joshua Booth.

Coombes parked his Dodge.

They now had a maximum of five hours to find something concrete on Walker they hadn't found all week. He knew that wasn't going to happen. Nothing had changed. Without the dashcam evidence, Walker would be out on the street.

He saw Cahill, another Robbery-Homicide detective, waiting for the elevator. He was talking into his cell phone, his back toward Coombes.

"What do you mean it just went black? There was no error message...I'm sure it's not *gone*, honey, it'll be there somewhere...You've been working on that screenplay for months, you must've saved it. Come on. I don't think you're stupid, I'm trying to reassure you."

Cahill turned and saw Coombes then shrugged his shoulders, as if to say *what are you going to do?* The elevator doors opened and they got on.

"Then you've got nothing to worry about. The document folder is backed up to the cloud every hour, there'll be a copy up there. You've only lost an hour's work, that's all."

Coombes found himself listening to the conversation. It made him remember his video doorbell, and the incompetent IA detectives who broke into his apartment.

"I can't do anything from here, sweetie, I'll take a look tonight, ok?"

Honey and *sweetie*, from Cahill. He never would've guessed.

The other detective finished his call just as the doors opened. Cahill glanced at him, embarrassed to have been overheard on a personal call.

"Computer problems at home."

Coombes nodded. "I gathered."

They walked through the detective bureau to their desks.

Cahill's mundane telephone conversation had caused his anger with Sato to fade and his focus to return. As he took his jacket off, his eyes connected with Sato's on the other side of the partition. She could see that he knew the truth, it was there on her face.

"Don't be angry with me," she said.

"We need to talk, Grace, but now's not the time."

"All right."

She sounded two inches tall. Defeated. Coombes sat and logged into his computer, then opened the Walker murder book to the property report. There was a tightness across his chest that was either a heart attack, or the last vestiges of hope.

He'd promised to be fair with Stephen Walker during his interview at Terminal Island, but the man had added his name to a hit list anyway. This told him that Walker knew there was evidence against him if he just knew where to look.

Coombes opened what turned out to be an eighty-eight-page document he'd downloaded from the internet. Cases were made and lost in the details and there were a *lot* of details.

Twenty minutes passed, but Coombes barely noticed. Blood was in the air, and there was a smile on his face.

"What are you doing?"

He turned from his screen and saw Sato watching him.

"I decided to look at the technical specs of Walker's dashcam. Turns out it was a top-end model. Great resolution, low light, parking monitor, all the rest."

"So what? The footage was disallowed."

"The judge ruled the camera and the memory card inside it were the result of an illegal search. Basically, what you reached in and grabbed with your hand. *Not* the footage."

"The footage is *on* the memory card, Johnny."

Coombes smiled and pointed at his screen.

"Which leads me back to the technical specification. Did you know, for example, that in the event of an accident, a backup copy of the current files can be automatically sent to the user's cell phone."

Sato's mouth fell open.

"And *those files* would be admissible?

"You never touched his iPhone, right? That was recovered as part of the legitimate search of his vehicle. His cell phone was the top-named item on the search warrant."

Sato was quiet for a moment.

"You said 'can be', you're saying it might not be there?"

"The user has to install an app and create an account first."

"What are the chances Walker did that?"

"Pretty good actually. About half the camera features require the app to work. I don't see him shelling out $500 then not setting it up properly. He loved his SUV, he got the best to protect it, right? Otherwise, he'd just buy a no-brand dashcam for $80."

Sato's eyes were huge, wanting to believe it.

"I need this, Johnny. I really need it."

"There's more. This dashcam had three lenses: the standard one pointing through the windshield; one recording the cabin interior; and lastly the view from the tailgate. We heard Walker laughing on the original footage. I figure if we play front and interior clips side-by-side in court he's done. How can any part of it be an accident if he's laughing?"

Sato paused to acknowledge his omission of Molly's share of the blame.

"What do you want me to do?"

"Write up a warrant for a file system extraction on Walker's cell phone, say that we believe it contains a recording of the murder. Let's not rely on the previous warrant, we don't want to leave anything to chance."

"*Right*," she said.

Coombes turned back to his screen in time to see a new email notification. He smiled. Eddie Willard had come through for him. He made a quick calculation in his head. De Luca's office was in the Financial District, not Hollywood.

The producer was close.

"Hey, Grace, I need to interview an old suspect on the Lawrence case. Shouldn't take more than an hour. Can you handle the warrant?"

"Sure. I don't think judges go for your scowling face anyway."

"I hear that."

35

A PAINTING HUNG ON the wall behind Antony De Luca's desk. It depicted a man in a suit and tie glaring defiantly out from under the low brim of a fedora. One of his eyes looked a little off, like it had started to roll back inside his head. The painting was based on a photograph Coombes had seen before. The man in the suit was Benjamin 'Bugsy' Siegel.

De Luca saw where he was looking.

"You like my painting?"

"A hero of yours?" Coombes asked.

"I know what people say, Detective. That I'm some sort of gangster just because my cousin is part of the Bellucci outfit in Vegas. They want to believe it so they can say they met a made man, so I play along a little. That's all Hollywood is, a dream."

"Wasn't much of a dream for Dakota Lawrence."

"I had nothing to do with what happened to that poor girl."

Coombes' cell phone began to buzz in his pocket.

There was a substantial difference between *vibrate* and *silent* and he smiled awkwardly at the producer and declined the call from his smart watch.

No *saved by the bell* for you.

In fact, it was the other way around.

"The day we found Dakota, it took us almost five hours to track you down. Your cell phone was unavailable, your people didn't know where you were. Later, you said you were up in Big Bear and had no cell service."

"Uh-huh."

"Is that still your story, Mr. De Luca?"

"Yeah. I remember because I had to buy gas and it's the wrong place to run out."

"Let's stick a pin in that, come back to it later."

"Okay."

De Luca looked uncertain, off-balance. Coombes hadn't seen that before from the producer and it encouraged him. To keep him on his toes, he changed the questions around.

"All right, you and Booth, how did that come about?"

"I was at *The Biltmore Grill*. Literally my first meal after arriving in Los Angeles. Josh was at a table twenty feet away with a beautiful woman. He was drunk, loud, and rude to staff. From where I was seated, I could hear every foul thing that came out his mouth. He was intolerable, yet hilarious. When management finally kicked him out, something made me go out onto the street after them and give him my card."

"Why do you think you did that?"

De Luca shrugged.

"I was new in town, I thought we could be friends. That probably sounds strange now, with social media, but back then you made friends organically. Anyway, people who amuse me are few and far between. I hadn't laughed like that in years."

"He didn't know you were a producer?"

"I *wasn't* a producer. I was a financier, I specialized in leveraged buy-outs and IPOs. I had one lunch with Josh and he sold me on producing his movie. The rest is history."

Coombes made a note of this and looked up.

"And the beautiful woman with Booth was Fran Knudsen?"

De Luca picked up a cigar and cut the end off.

"Got it in one."

"I wouldn't light that if I were you. This is an office, not a residence."

Anger swept over De Luca's face. It was exactly what Coombes had hoped for, to see beyond the curtain.

"Why are you here? You want me to admit to killing the girl, that it?"

"That would save everyone a lot of time."

De Luca laughed.

"You're like a dog with a bone, aren't you? We did this dance six years ago and you got nowhere. All that's changed is you got a better suit. You want me to take a polygraph? I'll do it, I've got nothing to hide."

Coombes smiled.

It was barely a day since he himself had used the *nothing to hide* line. The comment about his suit intrigued him. Most of the time, nobody noticed that his suit was anything special and if they did, it was rarely a man.

To the untrained eye, suits had a way of looking the same.

Coombes glanced at De Luca's hands as they played with the unlit cigar. The nails were manicured, the skin free from cuts, or any other sign of everyday wear-and-tear.

"Are you married, Mr. De Luca?"

"I assume you know that I am not. What of it?"

"Josh dates many of the women in his movies, I was just curious if you do the same. I'm told that you like to go to the auditions, watch the actors go through their routines."

"If this is about that bullshit story about me with Dakota-"

Coombes waved that away.

"I know that's garbage, relax. I guess what I don't understand is why, when this came up before, you didn't blow it out of the water when you so easily could have."

"I'm not following you."

"That story about how you met Booth, it missed something out, didn't it? The reason you went out onto the street after him is because you were *into* him. You found him attractive."

"It's time for you to leave, Detective."

"We're both adults, Mr. De Luca. Men of the world. In hindsight, it explains why you left Vegas when you did. Those mob guys are not very progressive, are they?"

"If you don't leave, I'll have my security guy eject you."

"Nico Abruzzo? Go ahead. I'll tell him what I know on the way out. Five minutes later, he'll be on the phone to your cousin. Is that what you want? I mean, you call him *your* security guy, but I don't need a pie chart to see he works for Vegas."

De Luca fell silent.

"How does it work? Booth chooses the women and you choose the men?"

The producer looked out the window.

"Not like Josh, but every now and then someone will catch my eye and we'll have a little fun. It's how things work around here. One person wants something, another person wants something else. Both get what they want one way or another."

"Dangerous for a man in your position. To stop that secret getting out."

"Not really. They think I'm a gangster."

"Scott Peters."

De Luca sighed. "Off the record?"

Coombes put his pen down, like *off the record* meant something to a cop. "We can do that."

"I met Scott at a party years ago. After we did our thing, I discovered he was underage. I panicked. I loaded him up on ecstasy and coke then dropped him in North Hollywood. He was so wasted I thought he wouldn't remember what happened. When he walked into that audition, he looked at me and smiled. He had me, I had to give him the role."

"That must've led to tension on set."

"It didn't. He bore me no ill will. In fact, we reconnected."

Coombes shook his head.

It was amazing any of them found the time to make a movie.

"*Then* what happened?"

"Same as what always happens. He realized he didn't need me anymore and went off with someone else. Another actor. I don't take it personally, Detective. These are young guys, to them, I'm an old man. A dinosaur. I wouldn't be with me either."

No kidding, Coombes thought.

"All right then, Big Bear. It might interest you to know that I had an associate drive up there with a bunch of burner phones from different carriers. The cell coverage was uniformly excellent with no dead spots."

De Luca shifted in his leather chair.

"If I said I was at Big Bear, that's where I was. I have a place up there; I don't remember saying anything about a cell phone. If it wasn't bad service, then the battery was flat."

Coombes laughed.

"Let's see if I have this straight. The star of your movie is murdered, you're nowhere to be found *and* unavailable via cell phone. This time due to a flat battery. It's *almost* like you turned your cell off while you killed her and dumped her body."

"Look, the truth is, I don't go to Big Bear because I *want* people to be able to find me, I go up there to get some peace and quiet. We finished our movie, we had the party, then I split town the same as I always did."

"As it happens, I believe you. But I'm still going to need his name."

"*His name?*"

"Come off it, De Luca. You went up there to sit in your hot tub with some kid you picked up at the party. And don't tell me it was *a long time ago*; you remember your alibi's name like it's your first love because you know one day it might save your life."

De Luca sighed.

"Robbie Ellis. He's represented by Gersh, you'll have to get his contact details from them, I don't have them anymore."

Coombes wrote this down, then stood.

The idea that De Luca had a hitman following Scott Peters around was laughable. The last thing he wanted was for the mob to know how he spent his time. A more likely scenario, was that Peters figured out who killed Dakota Lawrence and was silenced by her killer.

The producer walked him out. He didn't stop at the door to his office like Coombes expected, but instead walked him all the way out to the street door, where he hesitated.

"What we discussed; it goes no further?"

"No," Coombes said.

"It doesn't go into any reports or anything?"

"Only if it becomes relevant. I don't see that happening."

"I wasn't kidding about the polygraph. You want me to do that, set it up with my secretary and I'll be there. No attorneys, nothing like that."

Coombes put on his sunglasses.

"I'll bear that in mind. If this is the last time we speak, De Luca, I suggest that you check the age of your dates going forward to avoid future legal problems."

"I learned my lesson, Detective."

Coombes nodded, unconvinced, and walked to his Dodge.

The only scenario he could imagine De Luca killing Lawrence, was if she caught him in a compromising position with one of his young men. Killing her, to stop his secret coming out. This didn't work for Coombes for the simple reason that De Luca's sexuality had to be an open secret on set and Hollywood in general.

De Luca was no killer.

The only remaining loose end was why Booth appeared so frightened of De Luca during their interview when it appeared the men had been friends for close to two decades.

The answer was obvious, Sullivan had given it to him.

Son of a Gun was laundering mob money through the box office and Booth was skimming off the top using the special effects company. Booth wasn't just defrauding the IRS and the American tax payer; he was stealing from Bellucci crime family.

As he approached the Dodge, Coombes remembered the call that came in while he was with De Luca and saw he had voicemail.

He played the message back.

Detective Coombes, this is Valentina Sanchez. I've found something on your victim that you're going to want to see. I'll be in my office until four o'clock.

Coombes smiled. The anthropologist had come through for him. They were almost ready to file the Walker investigation, now this.

His luck was finally turning.

36

He got into his Dodge and started the engine. There was an odd smell inside the cabin that he couldn't place and he assumed a detective from another rotation cycle had left food under one of the seats. Something meaty, with garlic. It puzzled him that he'd been driving the car for a week and not noticed it before now. He turned up the air conditioning to try and clear it out, then glanced up at the windshield.

The rearview mirror was angled down, at his knee.

Coombes frowned and angled it back up.

A man was seated behind him with a skull bandana tied across the lower half of his face. A gun was aimed at Coombes' chest. This would be the bad smell, he supposed.

The muzzle of the gun dug into his side.

"*Drive.*"

"Where?"

"Someplace private."

Physically, the man was a solid match for Nico Abruzzo.

Coombes pulled out of the parking spot and drove down the descent ramps toward the street exit. He didn't know there *was* anywhere private in Los Angeles, the parking structure they were in already seemed pretty private to him.

The exit toll was fully automated, so there was no one to distract the gunman, or provide any kind of help. He inserted his ticket, then tapped his credit card. The barrier opened and they drove out onto Flower Street.

The man in the mask leaned forward.

"I'm going to make this real easy, Detective. Go for a gun or make any sudden movement and you're going to be sucking milkshakes for the rest of your life."

He hadn't spoken to Abruzzo while he'd been in De Luca's office, only seen him through a glass window. It seemed likely to Coombes that the purpose of going somewhere private was to provide the other man with a good spot to kill him and dump his body.

"Which direction?"

"Take 9th to Olympic. It's just across the river."

Coombes thought about his gun and imagined the steps required to use it. His holster access was restricted by both his suit jacket and the car's bucket seats. Even if he got his hand to his Glock, he still had to draw the slide back to load it, not to mention turn and aim.

All before the guy behind him could pull the trigger.

Coombes turned onto 9th Street and glanced at the rearview.

"What do I call you?"

"You don't call me anything, jackass. I'm just a messenger."

Coombes nodded.

"I'm going to call you *Bob*. You look like a Bob to me."

The gun hit his head and orange sparks floated through his vision.

"Keep it up, funny guy, see what happens next."

Coombes was in no rush to get to his destination, but COVID had cut the Friday traffic in half and less than ten minutes later he was driving over the Olympic Boulevard bridge.

"This is it. Take a right and right again. Park under the bridge."

A low, windowless concrete building sat on the left, with the bridge on the right. Both were covered by graffiti. It was exactly the kind of place where you'd find a body. The sound of traffic on the bridge above also meant a gunshot inside a car would never be noticed.

Coombes slowed, looking for a good spot.

Other vehicles were parked under the bridge, most of them old, ready to be junked. He chose a space wide enough for two and parked so that the passenger side was close to a white Toyota pickup, leaving space for him to exit the vehicle.

Coombes turned toward the back seat, using his shifting proximity to disguise moving the gear selector into reverse.

"Let me ask you something, Bob. Have you even *heard* of breath mints?"

The man tried to hit him again, but Coombes was way ahead of him, and pressed the gas pedal hard to the floor. The car surged backward and the man in the mask flew forward into the narrow gap between the front seats, his gun arm twisted awkwardly to the right. Coombes brought his elbow back sharply into the man's face with a crunch, then hit the car's brake and bailed out the Dodge, rolling onto his back to reach for his gun.

He found nothing, not even a holster.

Coombes' heart sunk.

The FID detectives had taken his Glock after the shooting the day before. His personal weapon was in the glovebox.

The back of the Dodge flew open and the gunman was on top of him, kicking him in the stomach and chest. After five or six blows, Coombes did something his training told him never to do.

He drew himself up into a ball and waited for it to end.

The blows slowed, then stopped, his assailant out of breath. People never talked about how much work it was, kicking someone to death.

"You want to *hear* the message, cop, or do you want to *be* the message?"

So, he hadn't been brought here to be killed.

Coombes ran his tongue around inside his mouth. His teeth were all present and correct. He turned and spat blood onto the cracked concrete next to him. There was something familiar about the other man and the way he was holding himself.

"I know you, don't I? That's why you're wearing the mask."

"I'm just a cog in a machine, Coombes. You don't want to be caught in that machine, so don't bother looking for me. I'm protected, understood?"

The sooner he heard what the guy had to say, the sooner he'd be gone.

"And the message?"

"We need you to kill the Walker investigation."

Coombes laughed and felt flashes of pain from his ribs and back. A tide of nausea rose up inside him, but even that couldn't stop him laughing.

It was a relief to know the guy was a Nazi, not a mobster.

"That's funny to you?"

He'd miss all this excitement if he was a lieutenant.

"There's something you need to understand, *Bob*. I don't know what Walker told you people, but he's broke. As in, not a goddamn penny. His multi-million-dollar property is gone. If he gets out of Terminal Island and wins compensation, he's not been inside long enough to make that worth your time. I've run the numbers. He'd get a little over a hundred and fifty grand and he'll likely burn through all of it pursuing a repetitional damages case. If you're helping this guy for financial gain, you're never getting paid."

The masked man was silent for a moment.

"I'm not involved in that side of things."

"No doubt, but not getting paid is the least of your problems."

"What are you talking about?"

"One of you assholes killed a cop; attempts were made on two others. Whoever set that up is going in a hole forever, make no mistake. Walker has one move left and you already know what it is. He'll deal the Brotherhood down the river without a thought."

This seemed to hit home and the other man bunched his shoulders like he was about to start kicking him again.

"I'm not here to *take* a message, asshat, I'm here to give it."

"Right. Kill the investigation, got it."

The other man straightened and took stock of his position, looking one way, then the other. It was a move Coombes had made many times.

It was a cop move.

This didn't surprise Coombes much. He thought he'd recognized something about the man. Since almost everyone he knew was either a cop or victim, the chances of him being anything else were low.

He wondered what it took for a cop to do this to another cop.

The man had been told to deliver a message, but that didn't mean he knew about the Brotherhood's previous activities. Like any large organization, gang members were not given the full picture, only their tasks.

"You going to do what we want, or not?"

Refusing might bring him back to being the message again.

"I tell you what. I'll think about it."

Think about it means no.

"I knew you'd say some shit like that, Coombes. Play us for fools until it's too late, then jam us up in court. They can't say I didn't warn them."

The man brought the gun down on Coombes' head.

When Coombes came to, he found himself lying face-down next to his Dodge. The car's engine was still running, the front and back doors open. His tongue felt thick and his mouth tasted of blood. He stood slowly, his hand grabbing the car for support.

The man in the mask was gone.

His pocket was vibrating, it was probably what roused him. Coombes pulled his cell out and saw a picture of Sato's smiling face. These days, it seemed like the only time he saw her smile was when she called him.

"Yeah?"

"I hope you don't mind, but I got the warrant signed and decided to take the phone for extraction myself to save time. It's all there, Johnny. We've got this prick. Thank you for this. Thank you, thank you, thank you!"

Coombes slumped down into the driver's seat.

"That's good, Grace."

Sato paused.

"What's happened? You sound funny."

"One of Walker's goons caught me by surprise and laid me out cold."

Her voice became hard, businesslike.

"Where are you? I'm coming to pick you up."

"Never mind that. This guy is a cop, I'm certain of it. He was wearing a mask so I didn't recognize him. Might even work in our building. I'm pretty sure I broke his nose so if you see someone in a suit with a broken nose be ready for anything."

"You think the *Aryan Brotherhood* has someone on the inside?"

"Seems that way."

Sato said nothing and he heard the squad room behind her.

"Look, I'll be back in twenty minutes, see you then."

Coombes disconnected.

He glanced out the side window and saw his sunglasses lying smashed on the concrete. They were carbon fiber, with polarized lenses, and they had cost him nearly $300.

Stephen Walker was getting no favors from him.

37

As he made the short trip back to headquarters his thoughts drifted from his ambush and the gunman's identity, back to the Lawrence - Hahn investigation. To his mind, the interview with De Luca had eliminated him from his enquires. Coombes felt no disappointment. He'd never seen the producer as a viable candidate for a sadistic killer. He'd invested nothing in it, unlike Willard who had believed every gangster vibe that De Luca had sent out.

A would-be gangster with no alibi, who was known to the victim, and had full access to the restricted studio lot where her body was found.

On paper, not a bad suspect.

Coombes decided not to tell Willard about De Luca's alibi, at least, not until after he'd had a chance to track down the actor in question and verify the story. Aside from anything else, De Luca made a nice juicy target for Willard and kept him out of his way.

He descended into the parking garage and parked up.

The elevator opened as he approached and Block came barreling out. He appeared to still be wearing the same button-down blue shirt he'd been wearing since Monday.

Block barely managed to stop without hitting him.

"You little shit! Didn't they have *chain of command* in the Army?"

He supposed that Block and his Internal Affairs witch hunt had just been slapped-down by the chief.

"I was in CID, Captain. I could've arrested a general."

He smiled at Block and gave it some wattage.

"You think he's going to be there to bail you out next time? Jackson's the fourth chief I've had, he's not going to be here forever. He's ambitious. This is *basecamp* for him, Coombes. In a couple of years, he'll be gone."

He remembered his promise to Sato to defuse things with Block.

"Look, how about we start over?"

Block's face was scarlet.

"Fuck you, Coombes! This will *never* be over. You feel me? Far as I'm concerned, you're done here. I'm talking to a ghost."

Block pushed past him, then turned back.

"Clean yourself up, man, you look like a hobo."

Nice.

Coombes stepped into the elevator and sighed.

He was 36 years old. In nine months, he'd be 37 and would pass the age limit for joining the FBI. He'd never wanted to be anything but LAPD, but the clock was against him for a career change. Block was right about one thing. Jackson *was* ambitious.

Before returning to his desk, Coombes stepped into the washroom and went over to the sinks. It was the first time he'd looked in a mirror since the gunman's attack.

His face was dirty across one side, like the dark half of a crescent moon. This would be from lying passed-out on the dusty concrete under the bridge. There were a dozen small cuts from stones that had impacted with his face and an inch-long comet-trail of blood that came down out of his hairline and stopped on his forehead.

He carefully reached into his hair and flinched.

Coombes pulled his hand back and saw blood on his fingertips.

He cursed, then began to wash. The cuts on his face began to bleed as he washed them, so he used small pieces of toilet wipes from one of the stalls to halt the flow, then began to wash blood out his hair. When he was through, he used his still-damp hands to brush dust off his suit jacket and pants.

As he walked through the detective bureau, he met Wallfisch.

"Hey, Coombes, did you cut yourself shaving...your entire face?"

The other detective laughed.

Coombes reached up. He'd forgotten to remove the pieces of paper from his cuts. He had no comeback ready for Wallfisch and merely nodded in response, his face coloring with embarrassment. Today was just getting better and better.

When he got back to his desk, he saw that Sato was reviewing the filing package ahead of their visit to the prosecutor. She glanced up at him and he saw her mouth pop open.

"I don't want to hear it, Grace, it's been a long day."

Sato went back to what she'd been reading.

He saw that the desk behind his, belonging to a detective called Niedermeier, was empty. Coombes went across to it, his body lowered behind the cubicle wall. He glanced both ways, just as the gunman had less than half an hour before, then tried the desk unit.

The top drawer rolled open.

Niedermeier had broken four fingers several months earlier when a suspect had shut her car door on her hand. Coombes scanned the top drawer, then checked the one below.

Nothing.

He pulled the top drawer open again. There was a plastic pen tray on runners at the top of the drawer. It was pushed all the way to the back of the unit. He pulled the tray forward and found a white pill bottle. Bingo.

Dihydrocodeine.

Coombes smiled. He grabbed the container, slid the pen tray back where it was and closed the drawer.

If Niedermeier didn't want her painkillers stolen, then she shouldn't have left them in an unlocked drawer, inside a building full of cops.

He glanced up as he was sitting down and saw Sato watching him, her face pinched with disapproval.

He dry-swallowed two pills, then winked at her.

———

GABRIEL REYES SAT AT his desk looking through the filing package on Stephen Walker. A heavy line formed on the prosecutor's face as he read, and judging by the way he was turning the pages, he wasn't happy. Finally, he put both his hands palm-down on the desk and looked up.

"Is this a joke, Coombes? The dashcam, again? It was already thrown out."

"Sure, the dashcam was, but not this *copy* of the footage from his cell phone. It's all right there if you don't skim over it."

"Oh, I read it." Reyes said. "It's bullshit."

"If it's bullshit, why did the judge sign off on the extraction?"

Reyes twisted awkwardly in his chair.

"There's no way the DA is going to pursue a case like this in the current climate. If the new judge takes the same stance as the first then we're left holding our dicks."

Coombes stood and leaned across the prosecutor's desk.

"Since another judge already greenlit the evidence, that won't happen. It would be instant grounds for reversal at appeal. No judge wants that, it makes them look stupid. Now, either we go with the case my colleague has outlined for you, or we go to the DA and get her opinion direct."

"Step back from my desk, Detective."

Coombes turned his head to the side.

"Grace? Step out the room and close the door."

She rose silently and left. Reyes eyes darted nervously between Coombes eyes and his damaged face.

"You think you can muscle me, Coombes? I'm a deputy district attorney!"

"Given the jail cell you work out of, you're a *very* deputy district attorney. As in, your career's going nowhere and you're destined to sit here for all of it rubber stamping dead-end cases with no chance of convictions. The DA's office is like an Apple Store and they have you here in the dungeon. You *like* that?"

"What's that got to do with anything?"

"Think about it. You were given this case because it was seen as problematic. If it tanked your career, so what? Nobody else wanted it because they thought the video footage was gone.

"I have a friend who works the crime desk at the *Times*; I give the word and she'll be all over this. A rich lawyer running over his wife? The whole of LA wants to see justice."

Reyes said nothing, his eyes going down to his lap.

He was thinking about it.

Coombes reached into his pocket and put a memory stick down gently on the desk between them.

"You never looked at the footage, Reyes. As soon as you do, you'll see what a slam-dunk this case actually is. We have not one but two search warrants covering us this time, the video will be admitted. Now, you and me are going to watch it."

Coombes resisted adding that he had two copies of the footage and his next stop would be the *Times* building. Another threat and he'd lose all his progress with the prosecutor.

Reyes looked up. "All right, show me."

Coombes set up the footage on the prosecutor's computer. The view through the windshield on the left, view of Walker driving on the right. He set both video players to loop the footage then pressed play on both as close together as he could. The clips were short and they looped three times before Reyes cracked.

"Turn it off, turn it off! I'll do it. This fucker's staying in prison."

38

As he parked up outside the Coroner's building on Mission Road, he noticed Sato's head was down, looking at something on her iPad. Her mood had been flat since they'd left the Hall of Justice which often happened after a case had been filed. The Walker case wasn't just any other case to her, and if she was anything like him, she probably resented the fact that she'd needed his help to get it across the line.

"Are you coming in?"

Her head remained down, her fingers working the screen.

"I think I'll stay here, Johnny. This is your thing, not mine."

She didn't know how to be with him anymore. Perhaps she was dreading going back to their apartment and being stuck looking at his face for the rest of the evening.

"If you want to shoot off, take the car and I'll make my own way back."

"That's ok," she said. "Do your thing. I don't like the smell in there."

His case was nothing but a *thing*, an obsession.

Coombes nodded and got out the car.

She's right about the smell, he thought, even outside the morgue. He slipped off his suit jacket, left it on the driver's seat, then shut the door and walked across the near-empty lot into the building.

The anthropologist's door was open and he saw her facing away from him at her desk. He knocked lightly on the door with his knuckle. Sanchez turned to look at him over the top of some reading glasses.

"You said you had something for me?"

"Detective! Yes, come in."

She stood, then hurriedly took of her glasses and threw them on the desk behind her.

Sanchez had twenty years on him, but her skin was flawless. The eyeglasses were the only sign of aging, and she appeared to be sensitive about it.

She put on a pair of gloves, her eyes never leaving his face.

"What happened to you?"

"I was too handsome, I had to have some of it removed."

Sanchez smiled.

"I got the hospital records you sent me; they were quite enlightening."

"How so?"

"Let me show you."

She walked to a steel table where bones had been laid out like a flat-pack skeleton. This was the closest he'd been to seeing Natalie Hahn since their last interview. It was a pitiful sight. He looked up at Sanchez and saw there was a spark in her eyes, like she was in the middle of telling a joke and the next part was the punchline.

"The cause of death appears to match your previous victim, Dakota Lawrence. Namely, a contusion to the upper rear of the head by a rounded object, possibly a champagne bottle."

Coombes hadn't expected the murder weapon to match up, as it originally seemed like the killer had grabbed whatever was nearby to hit Lawrence. Nevertheless, a similar m.o. helped to link the cases as it was a detail that had never been revealed to the public.

"All right," he said. "But you didn't invite me here to tell me that."

She held up her hand in a *give me a moment* gesture.

"I found an old injury on the right ulna...that's the smaller bone of the forearm."

Coombes nodded; he knew what an ulna was.

Sanchez lifted the bone off the table with both hands and carried it over to her desk. Using both hands was a sign of respect. Her desk had a light on a boom with a magnifying glass set into the middle of it. She sat the bone on a black cloth and lined up the magnifier, then stepped aside so that Coombes could step up close to see.

She pointed at a faint line on the bone with her gloved finger.

"You see this? That's a heal line. At some point in her childhood, this bone was fractured then perfectly healed. Since most people are right-handed, it is common for injuries to occur on the right arm as it is the first to be thrown out in the event of a fall, or raised to ward off an attack. There is no matching heal line on her radius, so I'm guessing this was from a fall."

He turned from the magnifier and found the anthropologist standing surprisingly close to him. Coombes ignored it.

"You said perfectly healed, I assume that means she went to hospital?"

"Correct. The quality of this heal guarantees it."

There was something about Sanchez's voice. An implication, something.

"There should be records of that, I get it, but there aren't. It happens."

"Actually, Detective, it doesn't matter that her records are incomplete because the x-ray from 2015 was of the same arm. Look."

Sanchez took an x-ray film from the folder that were part of the hospital records and put it on a light box. She held up the bone below the image for comparison. Sanchez watched him closely, waiting for him to see it.

His eyes moved along the x-ray, then along the ulna.

Carnival of Delights had experienced a troubled shoot with four on-set accidents, one of which involved a special effects rig falling on Hahn's arm. Her injury was superficial, but she'd been taken to hospital as a precaution.

"It's not there," he said. "The previous break should show up, right?"

"*Right.*"

"Then...you're saying it *wasn't* Natalie Hahn in that hole?"

"I don't know whose arm that is, but it wasn't Hahn's."

He couldn't believe it, they'd lost ID.

Without the Hahn identity, the link to Joshua Booth became tenuous. Then there was his own position to consider. Since he'd never told Brad Drake about the killer's signature, the West LA detective would push for the case outright, and Block might give it to him as an act of revenge.

Sanchez was watching his face.

"That wasn't what you wanted to hear, was it?"

"From the point of view of my investigation, no."

He had to control the flow of information to Drake.

First, he had to bring the other detective up to speed on the diagonal cuts, then, maybe a couple of days later, reveal that the victim was not Natalie Hahn after all. The killer's signature would keep the cases linked and therefore his role in them.

"Can you do me a favor?"

Sanchez's face hardened.

"I can't hide this, Coombes."

"And I'd never ask you to. What I'm saying is, it's Friday. Send me the report on Monday. This woman has been dead for over half a decade, give me the weekend to get my ducks in a row."

Sanchez thought it over for a moment.

"I'll meet you halfway, Detective. I'll send it on Monday, just like you want. But I'll put today's date on the document and if it comes up at trial I'll say exactly when I told you."

"Good enough."

Coombes returned to the steel table with the bones on it.

Not knowing who lay before him made the hunt for her killer that much harder. He had no starting point, no threads to pull on.

Without the Hahn ID, the investigation was doomed.

The smart move on his part would be to let Drake take the case and walk away, but he couldn't do it. He'd let this killer escape him before, he wouldn't do it again.

Sanchez moved alongside him and put the ulna gently back into place.

His victim was now a Jane Doe.

Historically, unidentified victims were given zero priority within the system. He was Homicide Special, RHD. The cream of the crop. Block would never sanction him wasting time on an unidentified bones case.

"Is there any way to identify her, Doctor?"

"Dental records are a possibility, but she was young and had perfect teeth. No cavities, no extractions. I doubt there are x-rays or molds of her teeth on file. We might be able to extract genomic DNA from her molars, but I'm sure you see the problem there."

"We have nothing to compare it to," Coombes said.

"That's right."

He stared at the Jane Doe's bones. Sanchez spoke again.

"I can tell you that she was white, five foot eight, and of Northern European descent. German, Dutch, Scandinavian, or British. It's not much to go on. I'm afraid, Detective, we'll probably never know who she is."

Coombes didn't like hearing that, and he almost forgot to say goodbye to Sanchez before he left and walked angrily back out to his car.

39

COOMBES WOKE EARLY ON Saturday and decided to get out of bed, instead of mindlessly doom-scrolling news on his cell phone. Because he was working, he put on a suit and tie as if he was going into the office. Dressing casually while he was on a case had never worked for him. He needed to look the part of the detective even if there was no one around to see it.

Since Sato was still asleep, he brewed coffee using a French press which made none of the grinding and pumping noise of his machine. While it was infusing, he ate a bowl of cereal then set himself up at the breakfast bar.

He was now half-way through the Lawrence murder book.

Coombes re-read the notes on the first interview with Booth.

Because Willard was primary detective, he'd handled both the interview and the subsequent reporting of it in the murder book. It was obvious to Coombes now that Willard had never taken Booth seriously as a suspect, even when they had no one else.

Subject relaxed throughout interview, showing no signs of guilt or deceit.

During the next interview, Willard's tone softened still further.

Subject is personable, funny. Eager to help.

Finally, the third and last interview.

Subject is no longer a person of interest.

Coombes frowned. At the time of the interview, Booth was very much a suspect. Hahn and Peters' account of Lawrence at the wrap party didn't surface until the next day.

He finished his coffee and poured another.

The only logical explanation was that Willard had added the *person of interest* note later, in which case, he would've expected to find it below a note on the interview commenting on Booth's demeanor. He had never seen Willard not leave one of these comments, which led him to believe that the original line had been removed and replaced with another.

Willard had immediately believed De Luca was the killer.

That being the case, it seemed possible to Coombes that Willard had sanitized the murder book to remove doubt and eliminate an alternate suspect theory for a defense attorney to divert a jury. As it stood, they investigated Booth with routine questions in line with procedure and dismissed him as a suspect.

Had anything else been removed?

He took a drink of coffee from his fresh cup.

Coombes thought of a storage box where he stored his old notebooks. Notes he would've taken during those interviews, anything Willard might've omitted would be in there. The box was on the floor of his wardrobe at his previous home. He could clearly visualize it in his head but he knew that *in his head* was the only place the box now existed.

His ex-wife was not the sentimental type.

Sato walked past, yawning.

"He didn't do it," she said, without stopping.

"How do you know?"

"*Finding a suspect is like falling in love,* that's what you said to me once. You don't believe this guy did it, I can tell. No boner."

Coombes watched in silence as she left the room. It took the running water sound of the shower a moment later to break the spell of her words.

First Willard, then Sullivan, now Sato.

Nobody believed Booth was a killer.

He was no better than Willard. Stuck on an old suspect, unable to move on. And how could he criticize his old partner for sanitizing a murder book when he had basically done the same thing in the Walker case the day before.

Omitted facts that would help Walker get a fair trial.

He had phoned-in his Walker investigation so that he could return to his primary focus, a cold case from six years ago.

Rock star, what a joke.

Coombes stared at the Lawrence timeline and shook his head.

It was based on Booth's last date with Dakota and her supposed appearance at the *Fallen Idol* wrap party two days later. Since he knew now that Lawrence had never been at the party, that section of the timeline vanished. The last verified sighting of Lawrence alive was from restaurant staff where she'd eaten with Booth.

He took out his cell and dialed a number from his notebook.

A voice rolled down the line, thick with sleep.

"Go for Josh."

"This is Detective Coombes. I have a quick question."

"Wait, what time is it?" He heard the other man groan. "Oh my god! It's not even 8 o'clock. What the hell's wrong with you?"

Coombes ignored this.

"In light of our conversation yesterday, I wanted to check the timeline I have for your last night with Dakota." He paused, but Booth said nothing. "Let's see. I have you leaving your former home in Silver Lake around 9, dining at *Saffron* in Beverly Hills until 11, before returning home at 11:45."

"That sounds right."

"You then had some drinks, before taking things to the bedroom."

Coombes avoided saying the phrase Booth used at the time.

"We had sex, if that's what you're asking, although I don't remember how good it was or how long it lasted. We knew it would be the last time, that always makes it special."

"What time did Dakota leave? Ballpark guess is fine."

There was a pause, perhaps as the director worked out what sounded less incriminating, most impressive, or as he just plain tried to remember which woman was which.

"After two. Two-thirty, max. I wanted to start editing the movie the next day while it was fresh in my mind."

"What kind of state was she in at the time?"

"She left with a smile on her face, Detective."

Rage swept through Coombes' body and he had to bite his teeth together to hold it in. There had been no smile on Dakota's face when he saw it a short time later.

"I *meant* was she sober?"

"Is that a joke? No."

"What about drugs?"

"We did some blow, sure, nothing serious. I doubt she was feeling any of it when she left if that's what you're getting at, that stuff disappears fast."

"But she *was* drunk when she drove home, yes?"

"No. I had my car pick her up and take her home. I always do."

"What *car* is this, Mr. Booth?"

"*Son of a Gun* has a contract with a limo service downtown called *Fletcher's*. They use classic Lincoln Town Cars. The girls love getting transported around in style, they feel like the President or something."

Coombes made a note in his notebook.

Fletcher's / Lincoln Town Car.

"That's pretty fancy...though I guess it's all deductible?"

Booth laughed.

"Don't hate the player, hate the game."

"Would it be fair to say that the reason these women are driven around in the first place is because they are frequently intoxicated and unable to drive?"

"It's not like that at all."

He pictured the scene. The car drawing up and Lawrence being loaded into the back, three sheets to the wind. If she was driving herself, being drunk was an argument for staying the night and Booth didn't want that.

"The limo allows you to control when they leave."

"Right. Look, if you're serious about dates and times for Dakota and Natalie's coming or going, the limo company have all that. Everything's logged. When a car picks up a client, when they're dropped off. I'll call them, tell them to give you full access."

Booth disconnected.

Coombes stared through the floor-to-ceiling glass at the building opposite.

It was hard for him to believe that Booth didn't realize the significance of the limousine evidence. Why, then, had he not mentioned it before? The log, the driver, they would both establish that Lawrence left Booth's home alive.

Not an alibi, but close.

Booth could've mentioned the limo in the first interview without mentioning his phobia about being blinded in his sleep. On the night in question, his relationship with Lawrence was allegedly coming to an end anyway, reason enough for her not to stay the night.

The case against Booth was over.

40

SATO WALKED PAST HIM, toward the kitchen. Like him, she was wearing her business suit. His head turned to watch as she began to prepare breakfast by cutting fruit into a bowl. A peach, a handful of strawberries and blueberries. Offensively healthy.

She sat opposite him and began to fork the fruit into her mouth.

"What's happening, Grace?"

"We're partners, Coombes. You helped me, now I help you. Let's face it, you need all the help you can get. So far, you've not been able to find your ass with both hands."

He smiled. Sato was back.

"Welcome aboard."

He watched her eat and thought about his next move.

Somehow, he needed to identify his Jane Doe.

A search of missing persons would be impossible without a name or a face. If she was in the system, it could've been from years before she was murdered. This left Coombes with no clear path to identifying his victim and moving the investigation on. He had no doubt that a plan would form in his subconscious as long as he was busy doing something else.

It was the way his mind seemed to work.

Until then, he had two outstanding tasks: checking De Luca's alibi with actor Robbie Ellis; and verifying Booth's story with *Fletcher's* limo service. Since Ellis lived in the valley and *Fletcher's* was eight blocks from his apartment, the limo company became his first stop.

With the Aryan Brotherhood situation still unresolved, their trip out the apartment and down to the parking garage was once again tense. It was only when they were making their way down South Hill that the tension began to ebb away.

"How long do we keep that up, Johnny?"

He hadn't thought about it. Walker would be arraigned on Monday. He had the right to a trial within 60 days, but this timeframe might be problematic with delays caused by COVID and the need for social distancing. Since a speedy trial was a Sixth Amendment right, the District Attorney would be forced to drop any cases that went beyond this timeframe.

Was Walker counting on that? He thought.

"I don't know," he said. "Let's see how Monday goes and take it from there."

"It'll be five weeks before his trial if we're lucky. Monday changes nothing. I can't live like this, Johnny. If you insist on it, I'll have to leave."

Coombes said nothing. He thought she was leaving anyway.

Threatening to leave, he reflected, was one of those things that only really worked the first time. After the second or third time, you developed an immunity. If she was so willing to leave, then logic told him there was nothing between them worth saving.

Several minutes passed before he turned onto Venice, then again onto Broadway and into the parking lot that belonged to *Fletcher's*. Eight immaculate Lincolns were parked side-by-side like a dealership of old. A thick-set man with a receding hairline and a square jaw was working a cloth over the nearest car.

"What are we doing here, Coombes?"

"Booth told me this morning that he uses this firm to drive his girlfriends around. He claims there will be a record of when women left his property and where they went."

"He was sitting on that the whole time?"

"So it seems."

Coombes killed the engine and stepped out of the Dodge. Opposite, the man with the square jaw turned away from them and squatted down, suddenly consumed by detailing a section of a Lincoln's fender.

Watching them in the chrome as he worked.

It was hardly the first time he'd been made as a cop, something about the way he moved gave him away. For a long time, he'd wondered why one person or another cared when the cops came visiting, but no longer.

He waited for Sato to cross the front of the Dodge and they walked across the lot to the office door, marked by a logo with *Fletcher's* written in a looping cursive typeface.

He should have been here six years ago.

Why *had* Booth held this back?

The interior was like a theme bar with memorabilia on the walls, in this case, golden-era Hollywood. Three rows of framed photographs of actors in iconic action. Marylin Monroe on the subway vent; Fred Astaire with an umbrella; Cary Grant fleeing a crop duster. The pictures covered the walls in every direction.

"Help you?"

Coombes turned and saw a man had come out a back room. He was wearing a shirt and tie and had thick black braces holding his pants up. He looked like he'd walked out of a Laurel and Hardy movie.

"Detectives Coombes and Sato, LAPD. We need to see your Joshua Booth files, lists of his pick-ups, passengers, times, destinations, all that."

"You got a warrant?"

Inwardly, Coombes sighed.

"I spoke to Booth earlier, he said he'd tell you guys to give me access."

"Fair enough, but he's not called yet."

It wasn't hard for him to imagine Booth hanging up and immediately going back to sleep, he'd barely been awake in the first place. Coombes took out his cell and re-dialed the director from his recent calls log. It rang eight times, then went to an answering service.

He disconnected without leaving a message.

The little shit was ducking his calls.

Coombes looked at the guy behind the desk.

"Mind if I use your line? I think he's avoiding me."

"Knock yourself out."

He punched Booth's number into the man's landline and listened to the same answering message. The timing of the second call would be enough to tell Booth who was calling even if his cell identified the *Fletcher's* number.

This time, he left a message.

"Mr. Booth, this is Detective Coombes. I'd appreciate if you could call me at your earliest convenience. I'm here at *Fletcher's.*"

He hung up and glanced back at Sato.

To his surprise, her hair had become tangled and messy and two extra buttons had become unfastened on her shirt. Her bra was now clearly visible. She angled her head to the side, indicating that he come over. When he did, her voice dropped to a low whisper.

"I've got a warrant here somewhere, maybe this guy will find it."

"This isn't a cop show, Grace. We have to do this the right way."

"What have we got to lose?"

Sato stepped around him and approached the man with the thick glasses. She sat on the edge of his desk and leaned way across the wood like a cabaret singer in occupied France.

"Look, we have the details already, but it's just what he remembers. Turns out he'd been drinking, having a good time. Facts become a little fuzzy and we need to sharpen them up before we put them in our reports, you understand."

Coombes had never seen this side of Sato before and he decided it didn't suit her. This was Sullivan's arena, leveraging her looks to get what she wanted. Sato had an edge underneath the charm that suggested a door would get kicked down shortly.

"I believe you, but I can't do what you're asking. I'd lose my job."

"Perhaps we can do this another way," she said. "We need to speak to the driver that Booth uses. These would be late calls, not during the day. Can you tell me who that is?"

The man nodded; his gaze fixed on her chest.

He typed into his computer, then did a little laugh.

"Lucas Dillon."

"How about you give us his address so we can have a word with him."

"Not necessary, he's in the lot washing the cars."

The square-jaw guy. Coombes saw an opportunity.

"Perfect. Can you get him for us?"

"I guess that's ok."

The man rose from his desk and went through the back. He was barely out the room when Coombes was sitting in his chair. A screensaver prompted him for a password. He glanced at Sato who had been watching the man at the keyboard.

"Password."

"His password is *password?*"

"Yes."

He typed it in and the screen cleared. A project management database was open. Booth's name already filled in. Two drivers were listed; a day driver and a night driver. He clicked on a button to fetch the records and a new window appeared with a list of entries spanning 34 pages.

He heard a door slam, then voices coming through the back.

The receptionist and the man with the square jaw.

Coombes put a thumb drive into the computer and dumped it all across. The file size was small and it transferred almost instantly. He pulled the thumb drive and put it back in his pocket then cleared the results window, taking them to the original screen.

"Put the mouse up to the top left corner," Sato said.

He did so, and the screensaver came back on.

Coombes moved around the desk to where he'd been before. He turned side-on to the approaching men and looked down at his cell phone like a teenager, in what he hoped was a vision of boredom and of someone innocently passing the time.

To use anything from the computer records in court they would have to come back for it with a warrant and hope that the data they were after was still there.

"This is Lucas," the man said.

Lucas Dillon stared at Coombes with open hostility.

"What's this all about?"

Though he was into his late fifties, Dillon's body was wide and muscular, like a quarterback. As the years passed, it was hard to maintain muscle mass so Coombes figured he was a dedicated body builder.

"Good morning, Mr. Dillon. Detectives Coombes and Sato, LAPD. We're looking into an old homicide case, Dakota Lawrence."

"Man, that was a long time ago," he said. "What about it?"

Coombes took out his notebook.

"You drive the midnight shift here, is that right?"

"Nine p.m. to nine a.m."

"How long have you been doing that?"

Dillon shrugged and glanced at the man in the black glasses.

"Eight years?"

He didn't break eye contact with Dillon as the other man confirmed it.

"Have you always worked nights?"

"No, I was here for a couple of years before I moved to the night shift."

"And why did you do that?"

"It's more peaceful, clients are more chilled out, not rushing to be someplace. I don't need that kind of stress. Anyway, I've always been kind of a night owl."

"And yet you're here now, 10 a.m., polishing cars."

Dillon's shoulders became taut as he flexed his muscles.

"COVID, man. We're practically shut down. I came in to help out any way I could. This company's been good to me, I want to do what I can."

Coombes wondered how polishing cars helped keep the company afloat, but skipped it. The purpose of the question had been to provoke anger and he'd got that.

"So how does it work? You leave your personal vehicle here, take a Lincoln and drive your shift, then bring it back here at 9 a.m.? Or do you park the Lincoln at home while you sleep and bring it back later?"

"I bring it straight back here after my shift. Look, are you trying to fit me up for that dead girl? I had nothing to do with that."

"These are just routine questions. It turns out that you are likely the last person to see Dakota alive. That alibis Mr. Booth, that's why we're here. He was dating the victim. You picked her up from his home, she's still alive, we can stop looking at him as a suspect."

"Second last," Dillon said.

"Excuse me?"

"Her *killer* would be the last person, not me. I just drove her home."

Coombes nodded as if correcting himself, though he was well aware.

"All right, anything significant happen that night?"

"No. I drive up, she gets in, I drive her home. That's it."

"Did you talk to her as you drove?"

"We're not a taxi, man. We're a limo. I think she spoke to someone on her cell, I can't remember. I don't eavesdrop on private conversations."

Coombes knew for a fact that she made no calls, he'd checked her cell records.

Sato spoke for the first time.

"The midnight shift, you must have a lot of free time on your hands where you're sitting around waiting for clients to drive them, is that right?"

"That's the part I like. I find somewhere quiet, park up and listen to my audiobooks, wait for the call to come through. You get to know the best spots, where you'll be left alone."

"While you were waiting for Mr. Booth to call, did you see anyone that looked like they were hanging around waiting? Someone that didn't belong."

Dillon thought for a long time, then shook his head.

"No, sorry."

Coombes cut in, excited by Sato's line of questioning.

"What about at *Lawrence's* home?"

"Actually, there was something, but it was a couple of nights before. When I arrived at her home in Glendale this car takes off like it's the Indy 500. A couple of minutes later, it comes back on the other side of the road. Like they didn't want to be seen and thought I'd be gone."

Coombes looked up from his notebook.

"Why weren't you?"

"I was filling out a timesheet and listening to the end of a chapter on my audiobook. I prefer to listen when I'm parked; I can't lose myself in a story if I'm focused on driving. Anyway, nobody got out the car and the headlights stayed on. It was still there when I left."

"Could you see inside the car?"

"No."

"What kind of car it was it?"

"One of those tiny cars, you know the ones I mean? Looks like a kid's toy. I used to see the same car around the studio lot before when I worked days. Has a flag on its roof."

Fran Knudsen's car.

"Was it like the cars in *The Italian Job*?"

Dillon nodded. "Exactly!"

"All right, Mr. Dillon, you've been very helpful. Anything else come to you, give me a call, day or night. I'm a bit of a night owl myself."

He gave the driver his card and closed his notebook.

Coombes and Sato walked out into the parking lot and crossed over to the Dodge. He would need to replace his sunglasses soon; the sun was remorseless. They sat for a moment in silence and watched as Dillon emerged and went back over to the line of Lincolns. He turned to look at them and Coombes lifted his hand off the top of the steering wheel in a half wave and got a nod from the driver. Sato spoke.

"The car he mentioned, that mean something to you?"

Coombes started the engine and cranked up the AC.

"It's the casting director's car. Fran Knudsen. She used to date Booth."

"You think she could've done it? A jealousy thing?"

The possibility seemed remote. A more likely suspect, was the muscle-bound man in front of him. If Knudsen had killed Lawrence, then she didn't drive her body to the studio lot in the back of her car. It just wasn't possible.

"If the Jane Doe was killed after being mistaken for Hahn, then this clears Knudsen. She knew Hahn by sight, no doubt about it."

"Unless it *was* no mistake," Sato said.

"*Right.*"

"You think Dillon made it up to get us off his back?"

Coombes thought for a moment.

"No, it sounded genuine. But he's still the better suspect."

"That's for sure, the guy gives me the creeps."

41

AS HE DROVE BACK out onto Broadway, Coombes thought about his planned next stop: chasing down Robbie Ellis, Anthony De Luca's alibi. He did some quick calculations. It would take them forty minutes to an hour to get there, the same back with maybe fifteen or twenty minutes for the interview. The thought didn't appeal. De Luca had never been a suspect for him and the trip to the valley was nothing more than a huge waste of time.

He decided to hand off the alibi-check to Eddie Willard, who would relish getting more involved in the investigation and for whom time was in abundance. Since Willard was no longer a sworn police officer, his interview would be no more legal than the data he had just taken from *Fletcher's*, but Coombes was certain it wouldn't matter. Should things unravel in an unexpected way, he could always redo the alibi-check himself.

Coombes thought of Booth's production company.

He'd focused on the director while he was there but he realized that he shouldn't have. If Booth was the center of the wheel, the connection he was looking for was almost certainly recorded within the company somewhere.

In a filing cabinet, or a computer hard drive.

Coombes shared his thoughts with Sato, but she said nothing.

He took the 10 to the 110, then the 101 toward Hollywood. The traffic was light and they moved quickly. As they dropped back down onto surface streets, Coombes reached into his pocket and dug out the painkillers he'd stolen from Niedermeier and shook out two more. Only four left. He closed the lid and knocked them back with some bottled water from the center console.

The label said *one tablet every six hours*.

Pharmaceutically, he was well into next week.

Sato was watching him closely.

"Why do you think that guy took you to the spot under the bridge?"

"To make me to feel isolated, I guess. In a place where anything could happen. The parking garage might've had security cameras, or an eye witness. He wanted me to think he was prepared to kill me so that I would take him seriously. I did."

Sato nodded.

"Ok, so he picks you up in the financial district. We can assume he didn't call dispatch for a pick-up or get an Uber back to his car. Therefore, he had to have a partner."

"For sure. But I never saw anyone else, so it doesn't really matter."

"It *matters* that there are two of these idiots, not one."

He saw that her hands were griping her knees tight and the true nature of the conversation became clear to Coombes. She wasn't asking about his assault with a view to catching the perpetrator, she was thinking about her own safety.

If his assailant *was* a cop, then it followed that the subterfuge over her identity was over. The chances of him having a regular partner called *Sato* but was working this case with a detective called *Soto* were zero.

The Brotherhood knew who she was now.

"I don't think you need to worry, Grace. The prosecutor has all he needs from us, taking us out now wouldn't change a thing. This was a last throw of the dice. The court case will move forward now and they will just hope Walker skates on the charges."

She dipped her eyes down, embarrassed.

"You think he will?"

"No. Do you?"

She said nothing and he turned back to look through the windshield.

After a couple of minutes, he parked on Barton Avenue. He had wondered if there would be anyone there, but he'd worried for nothing. The *Son of a Gun* windows were illuminated and Fran Knudsen's Mini was parked in front.

"Check it out: the casting director's car. Small world, huh?"

"Hmm."

He noticed Sato's bra was still visible.

"Not that it doesn't do it for me, Grace, but you can probably fasten your shirt again. I'm probably the only red-blooded male in a five-mile radius."

Sato glared at him as she re-fastened.

"Sometimes, you're a real asshole, Coombes."

"No doubt," he said.

They got out the Dodge and entered the glass-and-steel building.

Being in the same space again reminded him of his last visit and his hand unconsciously went up to his face. He'd forgotten to mask-up again. Coombes glanced at Sato and saw she hadn't forgotten hers. Masks were part of Asian culture; you have an illness; you wear a mask to protect everyone else. It was an ethos that didn't cross the Pacific.

In America, it was every man for himself.

She was right, he *was* an asshole.

They rode the elevator to the top floor where they found the lobby deserted. Close by, there was a low rumbling sound that became a shrill squeal before stopping. It was a sound he was familiar with; a document shredder. Coombes followed the sound to an unmarked office with a frosted glass door and opened it wide.

He saw the receptionist, the casting director, and man he didn't recognize surrounded by piles of documents. They jumped with fright as he burst in, faces freezing in horror. Knudsen was standing with a handful of paper about to shred some more.

"I gotta say," Coombes said, "this doesn't look good."

"This isn't what it looks like," Knudsen said.

It was a line he'd heard before.

He bent down close to the shredder. It was a cross-cut shredder, there would be no piecing anything back together like they did on TV. The container underneath was almost full. Next to it, was a half-full trash bag that he guessed held more shredded documents.

He stood up and gave Knudsen his full attention.

"Really? You're not destroying evidence?"

"Screenplays."

He glanced at the paper in her hand. Even upside-down he could tell it was no screenplay, he could see columns of numbers, names. It was financial information.

"Why would you shred screenplays?"

"We shred used scripts to stop leaks about upcoming movies, and we shred unsolicited scripts without reading them to prevent unintended copyright theft."

Knudsen's hand shook and the papers rustled. Her knuckles were bruised. *From punching Booth*, he thought.

Coombes glanced at the receptionist and the man he'd never met before as if noticing them for the first time. He smiled a little.

"You two, get lost. But don't go too far in case I want to have a conversation with you next. If I have to come find you later, you will regret it."

They scuttled out the room and Coombes turned back to Knudsen.

"What's *really* going on here?"

"That's none of your damn business," Knudsen said, eyes blazing. "We didn't invite you in here, so unless you have a warrant, you can beat it."

She recovered fast. Inside, she was made of steel.

He studied her for a moment, trying to put it together. These days, shredding paper was old hat, everything was digital. Documents were rarely printed-out, most were simply consumed on-screen. So what was it that was so damaging?

The clue was in her hand. Financial information.

Son of a Gun was cleaning house, which could only mean they were expecting a visit from the IRS, Feds, or the Vegas crime syndicate that produced all their movies.

"Look, we already know about your tax evasion operation; the pay-off to the IRS agent; *and* the skim Booth's running on the Bellucci crime family. If you're doing all this because of us you're doing it for nothing. We're *homicide* detectives, that's all we care about."

Knudsen's body sagged like a week-old balloon and her hand dropped down a fraction. The documents she was holding entered the top of the shredder, causing it to activate with a scream and mechanically eat the paper.

It sounded like the documents were being murdered.

"Sorry," she said, when silence returned.

But he wasn't, he wasn't even mad. The brief interruption had made him realize what they needed from *Son of a Gun*. He just hoped that it too hadn't been shredded.

"I want to see the selection work-ups that you presented to Booth. The headshots, all that stuff from before actors auditioned, plus any audition notes if you have that."

Knudsen's eyebrows went up.

"For which movie?"

"All of them."

They moved to a meeting room with a long cherry wood table. After a couple of minutes, Knudsen returned with the young man, each carrying a cardboard box file. There were twelve binders in each, one for every one of Booth's movies.

Coombes lifted the binders out and spread them out across the table, sorting them into chronological order. He noted that the earlier folders were thicker and he knew that would be because Knudsen hadn't yet realized that Booth was looking for a younger version of her.

Booth made a lot of noise about how his movies were different because they were all driven by a different muse, but to Coombes, it was nothing but a joke. The man was repeatedly choosing a different version of the same woman.

His muse was Knudsen.

What did he get out of using these proxies that he couldn't get from the real deal? Booth had to know that she was still in love with him. Was he afraid of commitment, or was there something else?

Sato waited until they were alone before speaking.

"You think the killer's another actor?"

"No. I think our Jane Doe is in one of these binders. We know she was a similar size to Hahn, possibly similar enough in appearance to be mistaken for her by her killer. We don't need to search the whole of LA County for this missing person, someone already did the prep work and rounded up all the candidates."

Her face lit up.

"Johnny, that's genius!"

"Knudsen told me that female actors who didn't make the cut for one movie would be re-considered for a different movie until they aged-out."

Sato's lip curled.

"Booth is a pig; did I say that already?"

He didn't disagree.

"We're looking for a woman who auditioned unsuccessfully and who didn't return to a casting call for the next movie, or any movie after that. The Jane Doe has been in the ground six years, so we need to look at years on either side of 2014."

Each binder contained both male and female actors, separated by a divider. On top was a list of names for all those auditioned. Coombes noted that the list for *Carnival of Delights* was thin had Natalie Hahn's character name was typed next to her. He supposed this was because her audition had taken part weeks earlier in Booth's bedroom.

With the lead cast, no Knudsen stand-ins were auditioned.

Coombes wondered if this was the first time Booth had done this and he quickly found that it was not. Dakota Lawrence's name was also typed-in on the *Fallen Idol* list. He'd never discussed with Booth how he'd met Lawrence and assumed that he'd met her at an audition. This, clearly, was not the case.

He picked up the binder for *The First Day of Night*, Booth's next movie.

Billed as 'a spiritual prequel' to his first movie, *First Day* was seen as a blistering return to form following the disastrous *Carnival of Delights* and Booth's second-best overall after *Fallen Idol*. In the space of a single movie, Joshua Booth had recovered his reputation among fans, and his position within the industry.

Without *First Day*, there would've been no streaming deal.

A line was drawn through the names of three women on the audition cover sheet with *no show* written at the end of the line. It was exactly what he was looking for. He looked at the call list for the next movie to see if any of the names reappeared, but there was no mention.

Failure to turn up was enough to eliminate you from all future work.

He studied the names. Sally Fenn, Adrienne Strömberg, and Jess Stone.

Fenn's profile listed her height as 5'10", two inches taller than the estimated height for his Jane Doe. Height estimates from skeletal remains were not wild guesses, they were hard science. If Sanchez said his victim was 5' 8", that's how tall she was.

That left Strömberg and Stone.

Both women were 5' 8" and viable candidates.

They had auditioned for *The Body Double*, the movie Booth made before *Fallen Idol*. Because he hadn't auditioned either Lawrence or Hahn for his next two movies, *The First Day of Night* was the next casting call for a lead.

In the meantime, eighteen months had passed.

It was possible both women had lost interest in Booth after *Carnival of Delights'* critical reception, or because of Lawrence's horrific murder the year before. Still, it was something.

Coombes put headshots for both women side-by-side in front of him, then looked from one to the other and back. Their heads were exactly the same size in the frame.

"They could be sisters," Sato said.

He nodded.

"All these women could, Hahn and Lawrence too."

"This is messed up, Johnny."

Coombes supposed she meant Booth looking for the same woman over and over, rather than the cosmetic similarity of a handful of actors. He said nothing and instead took out his cell phone and opened Facebook. Unlike the DMV or other official databases, social media companies had fresh data, not up to five years old.

Since she had a shorter name, he searched for Stone first.

His screen filled with results, page upon page. Choosing Stone had been a mistake, there were hundreds of them. Despite this, and a slight name change, it took him less than thirty seconds to pick out the actor's smiling face.

According to an hours-old post, Jess Stone-Beck was topping up her tan on the roof of her Hollywood home while on a pandemic honeymoon. He scrolled down her feed and shook his head. Coombes was no prude, but within seconds he'd seen almost as much of her as her new husband.

He started another search, this time for Adrienne Strömberg. Coombes entered the name carefully, checking his spelling as he entered it.

Unsurprisingly, there were less than a dozen results.

He didn't recognize her from any of the thumbnail-size faces, so he selected the most likely candidate; a young woman in long shot, standing in front of the Chinese Theatre in Hollywood. Coombes cycled through the profile photographs to bring up previously-used images. After three clicks the familiar studio headshot appeared. It was her.

Strömberg hadn't posted since 2014.

Before she stopped, Strömberg had posted 8-10 times a day. In the time since, her friends had left worried messages on her timeline, pleading for her to respond. But to no avail.

No replies, no emoji, no likes.

An abandoned social media account was hardly evidence of anything, but it was a starting point. They had a name now, a face. He glanced toward Sato.

"What do you think, Grace?"

"It fits. The timeframe, the similarity in appearance, her proximity to Booth or whoever, they all match. She's your Jane Doe."

"Yeah," Coombes said. "Looks that way."

His mind returned to how the case started, with the Natalie Hahn ID.

Like Strömberg, Hahn was missing.

Logic told him she too was dead. Coombes realized that in the haze of disappointment over losing identification, a seed of hope had taken root within him.

If the victim wasn't Hahn, then her unborn child had survived.

"What's wrong, Johnny? This is a solid lead."

"I just realized Hahn is likely still dead, buried in some other hole. If she is, chances are the killer didn't stop there. Maybe Lawrence wasn't even the first, you know?"

"Let's get something straight, mister. *I'm* the negative one in this partnership. You're not even particularly good at it. So how about we run Strömberg through official channels and see where we're at before we go eating our guns."

It was an attempt to cheer him up, but it wasn't working.

He nodded and studied the headshot of Strömberg once again. If the killer was someone like the limo driver, then the Jane Doe being Strömberg made little sense. When would they have crossed paths? Not at the studio, not being driven home after late night trysts with Booth.

The only overlap he could see between the victims were key *Son of a Gun* personnel who worked on set and attended Strömberg's audition.

The door opened and Fran Knudsen walked into the room.

It wasn't the limo driver, he thought.

"How you guys doing? You want a coffee, a bottle of water?"

Knudsen wasn't here to offer refreshment; she was here to take the temperature of the room. Her earlier hard-boiled act hadn't worked, so she was trying something else.

"Actually," he said, "we're about done."

"You find what you were looking for?"

He didn't want to be drawn on the subject.

"We're just gathering background information, ma'am."

Knudsen nodded like she understood, her eyes drifting to the table behind him where the pictures of Strömberg and Stone still lay side-by-side.

Coombes saw her take a sharp breath in shock.

As far as she knew, they were investigating the Lawrence murder. If she was smart, and he was sure she was, then the only reason for the Strömberg and Stone headshots to be placed the way they were was if another body had been found.

The casting director glanced quickly back, all fake smiles like she'd seen nothing. The change in her expression was more telling for Coombes than the gasp a moment before. It occurred to him they'd only looked for a victim that matched the Jane Doe.

What they hadn't looked for were victims that *didn't* match.

There could, after all, be more victims out there. All actors marked as no shows would have to be checked, no matter the year or physical size.

He recalled Knudsen's penchant for destroying evidence.

"Look, there's a lot of information here and we don't have time to get through it all today so we're going to take these files with us."

"These are my work files, Detective. I need them."

He turned his back on her and began to pack up. Everything in front of him she'd printed out from her computer. If she needed anything, she could print it out again.

She's worried about something, he thought.

He put the lid on the first file box and began on the second. If she pushed him for a search warrant over the files, he knew he'd never get it. The only way to play it, was cool.

"You'll get them all back, ma'am, we'll give you a receipt."

Coombes finished and he and Sato took a box each and walked toward the door where the casting director stood, arms folded across her chest. Knudsen hesitated for a moment, then stepped to the side to let them pass. They made their way to the elevator. The boxes were heavy and he sensed that Sato was struggling with hers.

Knudsen had carried one effortlessly half an hour before.

Beneath her business suit, she was strong.

42

THEY SAID NOTHING AS they rode the elevator down to the street. Both had their heads directed straight ahead at the doors, waiting to get off. It was difficult getting through the street door with the large file box and they had to take turns to walk sideways through the revolving door with the door bouncing against their feet.

Coombes popped the trunk of the Charger and loaded the box inside.

Sato was still crossing the road, her face red behind the mask.

He should've carried both boxes. They were heavy, but he could've done it. She would never hesitate to ask him to get something off a high shelf but carrying something was different. Being tall was not the same as being strong, because being stronger implied the other person was weak. Whichever option he chose, it was always the wrong one.

It was now midday and the sun was high in the sky.

A smell was coming toward him from the front of the car, a smell he now recognized. Joseph Wright's brain. The vehicle had been professionally cleaned two days earlier, yet the smell persisted.

"Fuck, this shit is heavy," Sato said, approaching.

She dumped the box into the trunk next to his and pulled her mask off to let more air in. It looked like she was ready to lie down for a nap. He hustled her inside before she noticed the smell and decided to continue the conversation about the guilt he must feel over the death of the piece-of-shit that tried to murder him.

Coombes closed the tailgate and got into the car.

Sato turned to him.

"Is it just my imagination, or was that a bit weird back there?"

"It's not your imagination."

He started the engine and pulled out of the parking spot, waiting until air was moving over the car before cranking up the air conditioning.

"Could she really be the killer?"

He thought for a moment. Dakota Lawrence had been brutally beaten before she'd been bled to death. From minute one, he'd assumed that he was looking for a man. This level of violence against a woman almost never came from another woman.

Both he and Eddie Willard were old-school. They'd been raised to hold doors for women, carry heavy boxes.

Neither of them had ever considered the suspect was a woman, not even when a woman's shoe-print had been found at the scene. He wasn't just an asshole, he was sexist.

"I don't know, Grace. All I know is she's in love with Booth. Love makes you do crazy things, impossible things. I need to re-assess this from a whole new perspective."

They were silent for several minutes before Sato spoke again.

"That financial stuff; the IRS, the mob, where'd you get that?"

Coombes pulled to a stop at a traffic light and turned to her.

"Sullivan."

He held her gaze and saw her cheeks color with anger or embarrassment. Traffic began moving again and still she said nothing. The next time he glanced across he saw that her chin was sticking out a little, and that she was sniffing.

She turned away, looking out the side window.

"Nothing's going on, Grace. Not a damn thing."

"But it would, right? If I wasn't here."

"First I'm in love with a dead woman, now it's this journalist. If you still care, the person I'm in love with is in this car."

"Who? *Yourself?*"

Coombes laughed. Her comment was perfect. Sato smacked his chest with the back of her hand, then laughed herself. The mood in the cabin lifted and it felt like old times.

They were on Sunset now, heading west.

Despite the stay-at-home mandate, it was packed like nothing was going on. He realized that he hadn't answered her question, that he had in fact, avoided answering it.

"Tell me about Molly Walker," he said.

Sato winced.

"When my partner and I got to the ER that day, Molly was already in surgery. We knew it would be a long procedure, hours, but Ryan and I decided to wait no matter how long it took. While she cleared it with our lieutenant, I looked through Molly's purse.

"There wasn't a lot in there, cell phone, wallet, some make-up. All of it pretty busted up from the impact. Then I saw the vitamin container. I don't know why I opened it, I guess I just had a bad feeling."

He nodded. "They weren't vitamins."

"No, they weren't. Oxycodone, a high dose. I saw it straight away...attempted suicide. All I could hear in my head was Walker laughing. The pills would line everything up for the defense team, he'd never see the inside of a prison cell.

"I couldn't have that, Johnny, so I tossed them in the trash. My partner and I sat waiting on that surgery for 10 hours next to that trash can and not for a second did I feel any guilt."

Coombes stared through the windshield; teeth clenched.

He'd figured that it had to be something like this, but it surprised him how much anger he felt wash over him. She saw his reaction immediately and got angry in return.

"Don't tell me you wouldn't have done the same, because you would."

"You think *that's* why I'm angry with you, Grace? That you hid her pills? We could've tied this case up on *Monday* and not spent a week chasing our tails. I took time out of my investigation to help yours, time I don't have to spare."

"Don't you get it? I was embarrassed. First this guy tricks me, then I break the law. This isn't exactly my finest hour, Johnny. Not to mention Sara Ryan is dead because of me."

"No matter how things are between us, I'm still your partner. You can tell me this stuff and know that I have your back. What happened to Ryan is not on you, don't think that way."

Sato said nothing.

She knew it wasn't true.

———

THEY REACHED FRANKLIN CANYON Park just before 1 o'clock. A park service sign sat on the road stating that the park was closed due to COVID-19 and hoped to re-open soon. Coombes drove around it and a minute later came upon two staggered LAPD control barriers. Drake had been pretty smart shutting down the park like this, he thought. A casual visitor would turn back at the first barrier without ever encountering evidence of a crime.

They came to an LAPD SUV which activated its light bar.

Coombes was surprised that there was still an active police presence on site. He held up his badge and drew alongside, lowering the window so they could speak. The uniform closest to him had a tag that said Dillahunt.

"Coombes and Sato, RHD. Why you guys still here?"

"Drake found four more at the reservoir. Not in the ground, weighted down in the water. We've had divers working shifts to see if there are any more."

"How long?"

"Years. Man, they looked bad. I lost my breakfast."

"No. When did he start looking in the lake?"

"Oh," Dillahunt said. "Since Tuesday."

Drake had held it back all week, what a snake.

"Any information on the victims?"

"Three women, one man. That's all I know."

This surprised Coombes, killers rarely changed the sex of their victims.

"We're going to check out the grave site again, see if we missed anything."

"You got it."

He drove on past the West LA SUV.

Four more, he thought. It didn't seem possible and yet here he was, another serial. He parked on Lake Drive, not far from where he'd parked previously. The area was abandoned but there was still a band of yellow crime scene tape tied to the tree.

They got out the car and walked over.

Coombes felt different, now that he knew the victim was not Natalie Hahn, a person he'd met, interviewed. She'd lied to him, he knew it now for a fact, but she didn't deserve to die. Was Hahn one of the bodies recovered from the water?

The ground had been scraped back into a rough approximation of the way it had been before, minus the human remains. He turned to look at Sato next to him. She hadn't been here before, she had fresh eyes.

"What was the victim's name again?"

"Adrienne Strömberg."

"That's some name," Sato said, looking around.

"Northern European. Just as Sanchez predicted."

"You think Hahn's dead too because of the wallet?"

He shrugged. "What else?"

Sato bent down and ran her hand back and forth on the soil.

"I disagree, Johnny. The only way that makes sense is if both victims died at the same time and Hahn's jacket was put on Strömberg by mistake."

"That *is* what I'm saying. They were both the same size."

Sato stood and brushed her hands together.

"You're saying the killer had two bodies, dug a hole and didn't put both of them in? That makes no sense at all."

"Shit, you're right," he said. "I hadn't thought of it that way before."

Coombes moved to the other side of the tree, away from the work carried out by the dig team. Here his foot compressed the ground beneath his shoes like a luxury carpet. The soil was made from needles that had fallen over time from the pine tree above. It was over a hundred years old. Shade from the tree and the blanket of needles would've prevented the soil deeper down from turning into the baked, hard soil familiar to him from the trail paths.

Knudsen *could've* dug the hole.

She was strong, he'd seen it by the way she'd carried the box file filled with binders. He moved back to where Sato stood at the flattened earth.

"Let's say you want to get rid of a dead body and this is where you decided to put it. How would you do it?"

Sato angled her head as she thought about it.

"I'd find the best location during the day, pretend I was going for a run, you know, then come back when it was dark. I'd have your body in the trunk-"

"*My* body?"

"Maybe you left the toilet seat up, maybe you left your plate on the counter and didn't put it in the dishwasher, at this point it doesn't matter. Do you want me to continue?"

Sato's mood had improved.

"Sure, why not?"

"Ok. It's dark, so I use the headlights while I'm digging. When I'm finished, I turn the car around and back it up over the grass verge and under the tree. Then I just roll you into the hole. The taillights would give enough light to fill the earth in again. Done."

He sighed. This was the problem with working alone, you lost perspective. His simple mistake had removed more than half the population from the suspect pool.

"I imagined the killer carrying Hahn from the parking area because I knew how small she was, how I could've done it."

"That would never occur to me. Work smarter, Coombes, not harder."

He looked up at the underside of the tree and noticed that several of the lower branches had been removed. Bent back, twisted around and around. Not cut with a saw. It wasn't recent, from the dig team, it was old. The killer *had* reversed in to dump the body and the lower branches had been removed to allow access for an SUV with a high roof.

Like Booth's vehicle.

43

He drove to Little Tokyo, where they picked up late lunch at a Japanese place Sato liked. They ate in the restaurant's parking lot, the car windows down for ventilation. Neither bothered to make any conversation. It reminded him of meals he used to have with his ex-wife. Wordless. Nothing left to say. When they finished, he dumped the trash, then drove the short distance to headquarters, where they carried the *Son of a Gun* file boxes up to RHD.

His first task was to run Adrienne Strömberg's name through the system. He started, as he often did, by logging into the DMV's administrative portal. Driving licenses in California last for 5 years and Strömberg hadn't renewed hers when it expired two years before.

Since a potential reason for expiry was that she was incarcerated, he next checked the FBI's NCIC database, which also held missing person reports.

Here, he scored a hit.

Adrienne's sister, Hannah, reported her missing six years ago.

Coombes copied down her contact information and saw she lived in Sherman Oaks. He had no desire to drive to Sherman Oaks when he had already spent so much of the day on the road.

Being asked for a cheek swab to match DNA with a skeleton had to be in the same ballpark to getting a death notification and Coombes had never done one of those by phone.

Still, he wasn't going to drive to Sherman Oaks.

The line connected and he heard a burst of laughter.

"Hello?"

A woman's voice, light and filled with sunshine.

"Am I speaking to Hannah Strömberg?"

There was a long pause.

"She's dead, isn't she? You're with the police."

"My name is John Coombes, I'm a detective with the Los Angeles Police Department. I'm sorry to say we've found someone who might be your sister and we need to arrange for you to give a cheek swab for DNA comparison."

He liked to avoid the words *body* or *remains* with relatives.

The woman said nothing and instead began to sob down the phone. The sunshine was gone, her life was ruined, and it had probably only taken him thirty seconds. The sobbing went on, seemingly without end. To distract himself, he reached to the top of his head and pressed on the spot where his attacker had hit him with his gun.

"Ma'am, are you still there?"

Her voice came back small, like a child.

"Yes, detective."

"Do you mind if I ask how you knew this was about your sister?"

"I married four years ago and took my husband's name. I'm Hannah Johnson now. I never updated my name with missing persons so I knew right away."

"There's a chance it might not be her," he said.

"Please don't say that, I need this to be over."

"I understand."

He arranged for her to get a cheek swab.

If they were lucky, it would take at least a month to run the comparison, and that assumed the DNA in the victim's teeth hadn't deteriorated. When he was done, he went to the washroom and splashed water on his face and took some deep breaths.

This was the stuff he hated.

Blowing a Nazi's brains out, he could do that shit all day, every day.

When he returned to his desk, he saw that Sato had left a yellow Post-It on his keyboard with Japanese characters. Hiragana, not Kanji. He pointed his cell phone translator at it.

Even monkeys fall from trees.

Sato watching him over the partition, gauging his reaction.

"I like it," he said, sitting down.

With the Jane Doe situation handled for now, it was time to move on.

He propelled his chair around next to her and passed her the thumb drive of data from *Fletcher's*. His experience with databases and spreadsheets was close to zero, whereas she'd used both regularly when she'd worked at the Japanese Consulate.

Sato plugged it in to her computer and opened the file it contained. She studied her screen for close to a minute, then began to shake her head.

"This isn't right, Johnny."

"I can see the entries with my own eyes, Grace."

"All right, what we have here are two datasets spliced together as if they belong together, when they don't. It's called a...Cartesian product. Instead of narrowing a search, the second dataset has expanded it. Entries for *Son of a Gun* and entries for Lucas Dillon."

Sato meshed her fingers together to illustrate.

"Now, a lot of the time, it's the same thing. What we want is there, but there are these *other* entries that shouldn't be there. Work for another company by the same driver; and work carried out by a different driver for the same company."

"Shit," he said, understanding.

Sato was quiet for a moment.

"Why are we looking at this anyway? One minute it looks like you think it's Knudsen, the next you're back to Booth again, help me out."

"I wanted to look at the limo data because the driver said Dakota used her cell phone when I know for a fact that she did not. Either he's lying or-"

"Or she was using a burner cell. I *am* a detective, Coombes."

"Actually, no. I don't think so."

"What then?"

"That her last time in the limo *wasn't* the night Booth said it was."

Sato said nothing and they turned back to the screen.

The rows and columns seemed to impose an order on the data and he liked that. Because he hadn't limited when the data started, it went all the way back to when *Son of a Gun* first became a client, which he could see was before Lucas Dillon began working at *Fletcher's*.

The scrollbar at the side indicated a very long document.

Using Sato's mouse, he grabbed the scroll handle and scrubbed quickly down, over fourteen thousand rows. He stopped next to the dates corresponding to when *Fallen Idol* had been in production. The movie had taken two months to complete, dates Coombes knew off by heart. He inserted blank rows before and after to create a visual break.

Of course, it was the *last* rows that were of interest to him.

The spreadsheet hadn't frozen the top row so he could no longer see what each column represented, but it didn't take long to figure it out.

Date, client, driver, pick-up time, drop-off time, mileage start, milage end.

The mileage was a long number that served to hide the difference.

"Do you know how to show just the mileage used?"

"Sure, Johnny, just a sec."

Sato typed a formula into the end box then dragged it down to populate each row. He was now looking at milage per trip. He saw that each of Lucas Dillon's nighttime drives was within a couple of miles of each other, except the last one, the night Dakota Lawrence disappeared and was never seen alive again. That one was 15.87 miles shorter. It was what he expected.

"Booth's alibi is bullshit," he said.

"I don't get it."

Coombes pointed at the number.

"Dollars to doughnuts, this number represents Dillon driving somewhere close to Booth's home, where he listens to audiobooks while he waits to be summoned. Only that night, Booth calls and tells him he's not needed, so he drives back downtown to return the limo."

"Right."

"I couldn't understand why Booth would have this in his back pocket all this time and not tell me. I think he just didn't remember. After my last visit, Booth probably called *Fletcher's* and asked if he used the limo that night and the guy takes a look. The data says he did, when all the guy was looking at was Dillon's drive to nowhere and back."

Sato thought for a moment.

"Or Booth *knew* it wouldn't stand up to scrutiny so only told you when he felt you'd already ruled him out and wouldn't dig too deep."

He nodded. One final push in the right direction.

"It's possible," he said.

"I don't understand you, Coombes. You've had a hard-on for this guy for days, now you're playing down the significance of his alibi being garbage. What's going on?"

"Booth and Knudsen have a complicated relationship. They love each other, but he can't face it, so he uses these actresses as surrogates."

"Another man terrified of commitment," Sato said.

Coombes left that alone.

"*Anyway*, I think both of them suspects the other of killing Dakota and by trying to protect the person they love, each appears guilty when in fact..."

He let Sato finish.

"Neither of them did it."

"Correct."

Sato sighed.

"All right, what about the creepy limo driver?"

He again pointed to the screen.

"The day driver and the night driver use the same vehicle. We can see that, because the search included the day driver data by mistake. The end mileage for Lucas Dillon becomes the start mileage for Hector Ramirez. There's no scope for Dillon to hide the mileage of picking up Dakota, taking her to wherever she was killed, and then back across town to the studio lot."

"You do realize that you've started to refer to the victim by her first name? I don't think I've heard you do that before."

"She's been part of my life for a long time, Grace. I owe her."

"Where does this leave us?"

"Let's check Knudsen's files again, see if we can identify other victims that might match the four in Franklin Canyon Lake."

He put one file box on top of the other and carried them both through to an unused meeting room with a long table. He didn't look at Sato while he did this, in case she felt the need to scowl at him for overstepping.

Coombes laid out the binders as before, in chronological order.

He knew now what he was looking for: actors who were marked as 'no-show' on the call sheet and who had since disappeared from public life.

On a legal pad, he wrote the name of each movie, separated by a blank line, then went through each binder, noting down the names of all no-shows next to the title.

In total, there were thirty-six no-shows, the majority occurring during Booth's early years before he was an established player.

While he worked his way from one movie to the next, Sato began to process each name. Her personal laptop couldn't access official databases; however, social media websites allowed her to whittle the list of the missing down to six women and two men. For these, they would have to check from their computers in the detective bureau.

This list included Scott Peters, who he'd forgotten about.

He stared at the name on the page.

Between the Walker case and his attempted assassination at the hands of a Nazi, Peters had disappeared from his radar.

Did that make him a victim, or a person of interest?

He photographed the studio headshot of each of the remaining potential victims with his cell phone, then re-packed the binders into the file boxes.

It was nearly five o'clock, he'd lost himself to the work.

They split the list of names in half, each taking three women and one man, and began to do the same check he'd done already for Adrienne Strömberg.

Sally Fenn, who'd been too tall to pass for the Jane Doe, was alive and well with an active profile on LinkedIn. She was now a paralegal at a large law firm, which probably explained her absence from other social media sites.

Scott Peters and Natalie Hahn had both vanished without a trace. Neither had an active social media account, driver's license, were incarcerated, or were filed as a missing person. That left him with Naomi Holbrook.

The DMV found 42 matches, none of them matching the actor. No hits on NCIC left him scrolling through social media search results. None was the Naomi Holbrook from the casting director's binder.

He stood and looked over the partition at Sato.

"How are you getting on with yours?"

"I've cleared three. The other one, I don't know, it's almost like she-"

"Never existed?" Coombes offered.

"Yes!"

"I have the same damn thing."

Coombes couldn't explain it so decided to put it aside for now.

He was hungry, tired, and liable to make mistakes. The bottom line was that including Hahn and Peters, they had four missing actors to match the four bodies Drake had pulled out the lake. Coombes thought again of the ultrasound image from Natalie Hahn's wallet.

Another victim, one a lot of people wouldn't even count.

44

BACK AT THE APARTMENT, they ordered dinner through the building's restaurant. While he waited for it to arrive, Coombes decided to have a shower to clear away the day's failures for what he was sure was going to be a long night re-reading the murder book.

After washing, Coombes lost himself for several minutes in the sensation of the hot water pounding against his skin. Some days, standing in the shower was as close as he got to peace until he was asleep.

He found himself thinking about Lucas Dillon, the limo driver. The immediate hostile look that he'd given them, the powerfully-built body.

It was no stretch to imagine him as a killer.

You get to know the best spots, where you'll be left alone.

Coombes had written Dillon's line into his notebook, but he had no problem recalling it now. Something about the way he'd said it had seemed off. Taking pride not in his driving, but in finding places where he could be alone.

Dillon had pushed for the night shift, when he could move around the city unseen and do whatever he wanted. Did he really just use these isolated spots to listen to audiobooks, or did he kill his victims there?

The idea persisted and Coombes turned off the water and stood dripping in the stall, the screen door still closed. He imagined it from the point of view of the driver.

Booth had these beautiful young women, one after another. Each one somehow the same, yet different. To Booth they were disposable, trash to be taken away at the end of the night.

Drunk, tired, perhaps high on drugs.

An easy mark for a predator.

Coombes got out the shower, dried himself, and dressed in fresh clothes.

Dillon would know from experience that Booth replaced each woman after every movie was completed and from that point on, would not be missed. After collecting his victim he'd return to his favorite spot and pull to the side of the road. Perhaps say there was some problem with the car he needed to check.

The Town Car's rear windows were tinted almost black.

At 2 a.m. there would be little traffic, few witnesses.

Once he forced his way into the back with them, he could have whatever sick fun he wanted. Dillon's heavily-muscled body would easily over-power the vulnerable women that were his prey.

Dressed, Coombes walked into the living area and saw Sato watching TV in pajamas, a glass of red wine in her hand. It was eight-thirty and she was in for the night.

Sato looked at him, surprised.

"You're going out?"

"I need to check we didn't miss something with Dillon."

He saw her glance at her wine, the TV, then back to him.

"I thought we were finished. This is my second glass."

Sato drinking alcohol was a reminder that her case was closed.

"It's probably nothing," he said. "Just me being paranoid."

"You've not eaten your food. It's gone cold."

"I'll eat it later; I don't want to lose my focus."

She turned back to the TV, her face unreadable.

"Don't be a cowboy, Coombes."

He nodded to himself, then turned and made his way out the apartment. As he rode the elevator down to the street, he realized that for the first time in days he hadn't had his guard up for any of Walker's skinhead friends.

Coombes' mind returned to Dillon as he drove onto South Hill.

His plan was simple; drive to *Fletcher's,* note the mileage, then drive to Booth's former property in Silver Lake and check the mileage again and double it to work out a rough round trip. If the total distance was close enough to the logged mileage, then Dillon was innocent, just as he originally thought.

He figured that Dillon would park close enough to Booth so that he could arrive within five minutes of a call, which would be a mile or two at most.

The only thing that had changed since he'd first viewed the data, was the realization that Dillon didn't have to drive Lawrence to his home to kill her, though a question still remained about where he could have bled her out, he hadn't done that in the Lincoln.

He pulled up at *Fletcher's* and used his cell phone to photograph the odometer, clock, and date. This wasn't for evidence, just his own records. As he closed the camera app, he saw that he had five missed calls and had two voicemail messages.

Coombes began his drive toward Silver Lake using the shortest, most obvious route. He supposed that Dillon could've padded his route from the start of the Lawrence pick-ups to hide the extra at the end, but he wasn't too worried about that. His own drive would show any extra mileage Dillon may have had to play with.

If Lucas Dillon was his killer, he needed to have enough range to add the trip to the studio lot within the stated milage.

He thought about the calls and the voicemail.

They had either come in while he was in the meeting room at headquarters, which had a notoriously poor reception, or while he was in the shower. He played back the first voicemail.

Sullivan's voice came at him fast, with no space for air.

"We had a goddamn deal, Coombes! I sit on the story and you give me the juice. You've given me nothing but eye bangs since we first met."

He heard her take a breath. She was really angry.

Eye bangs. He was glad Sato wasn't sitting next to him.

"A contact of mine says the LAPD has been fishing at a certain lake all week and I was surprised I hadn't heard about it from you since we have this great deal together. Give me something good, Coombes, and I mean in the next hour, or I'm running the story about bodies in the park *today* and screw the consequences for your case."

The message ended. Coombes saved it and move to the next.

He was coming up on the exit for Silver Lake.

"Forget the last message! Those background packets you asked for came in and I've got a hot lead. Call me when you get this, Coombes, I'm going to run it down."

Another crisis averted.

He took the exit onto Silver Lake Boulevard.

During the original investigation, he and Willard had spent several days at Booth's home and he could locate it now with his eyes closed.

Compared with Booth's current $20 million mansion, the place in Silver Lake was modest. From the road he saw lighted windows and two cars out front. A Mercedes-Benz and a Porsche.

Coombes slowed to a stop and took a second picture of the odometer.

The street terminated in a dead end.

As he did a three-point turn, it occurred to him that Lucas Dillon could easily have parked the Lincoln at the end of the road as he waited to be called. He didn't need to find some magical isolated spot in order to listen to his audiobooks, it was right there.

But he couldn't kill people at the end of the street.

For that, he'd need something different.

He'd spent a couple of minutes thinking, so he took a fresh picture of his clock and odometer, then set off in the direction of the studio. The photographs were a simple way to log the time it took him to make the journey and he didn't want that skewed by any delays.

The tight spot was the mileage, it was the only metric that counted to determine if Dillon was innocent. There was no log of when the Town Car had been returned to Fletcher's lot. All that mattered, was that it was there before the day driver took over.

If Dillon wasn't innocent, then the time became relevant.

He was on the Hollywood Freeway when his cell phone rang, and he saw from the display that it was Sullivan again. The journalist was beginning to get on his nerves. He accepted the call using the car's hands-free connection.

"*Coombes.*"

He heard rustling and the roar of a car engine. After a couple of seconds, she still hadn't replied. Coombes shook his head. She'd butt-dialed him. Pressed a button accidentally, and redialed the last number called. Him. He was about to hang up, when he heard a grunt. It was the kind of grunt someone made when they were winded by a surprise impact.

In his mind's eye, Sullivan jumped from driving her car to lying semi-conscious in the trunk of a killer's. The hair on his forearms stood on end. He cranked up the volume on his cell and listened, deciding what to do next.

The roar of the engine faded, then stopped.

Wherever Sullivan was, she had reached her destination.

The car's cabin filled with the white-noise hiss of the other vehicle. He heard a door open, then a *crunch, crunch, crunch*. Finally, he heard Sullivan speak, her voice distant and confused.

"*Booth?*"

His cell beeped, then went silent. The call had disconnected.

Coombes' skin bristled like a static charge was passing over his body and he shivered in the car's warm cabin.

Booth.

It had been hours since he'd blown up the director's alibi and he'd done nothing about it. He should've brought him in for questioning immediately.

Instead, he'd done nothing.

Believed the man had made an honest mistake while trying to help him.

Coombes nailed the throttle to the floor. His eyes were jacked wide with adrenaline, the taillights of other vehicles smearing into light trails as they pulled to the side to let him pass.

He knew where Sullivan was, he'd heard that crunching sound before.

It was Joshua Booth's driveway.

45

It took him twelve minutes to get to Holmby Hills, using lights and siren to cut through the already thin pandemic traffic. His hand had reached out several times for the car radio, but each time it drew back, no call for backup made. Sullivan was in trouble, he knew it in his gut, but what if she *had* just butt-dialed him? How would he explain her presence at Booth's mansion without mentioning their information-sharing deal?

It would be everything Block wanted for his bogus investigation.

The last eighth of a mile took Coombes another five painful minutes, until finally he was turning into Booth's driveway.

His headlights washed over the side of the building as he pulled around the turning circle and slotted in next to Booth's Navigator. He stamped on the brakes and felt the Charger ruck up a tide of stone chips. Coombes shoved the selector into park and ran out of the vehicle toward the door, not even bothering to kill the engine.

A knot of tension filled his chest.

Sullivan was dead.

He knew it like it knew the sky was blue, but he refused to believe. Coombes drew his gun as he ran toward the building. The mansion's heavy front door was ajar.

Not that he cared, but he figured that was probable cause to enter.

He moved into the entrance hallway, his trigger finger straight, Glock aimed down at the floor. Loud music came from the direction of the swimming pool. It had a strong beat that came in fast, like a heartbeat.

Coombes shot a glance up the staircase, then along the hallway.

Up to the bedroom, or along to the swimming pool?

He ran toward the music. Nobody played music this loud if they were somewhere else. If Sullivan was still alive, he might only get one chance to save her.

The hallway scrolled past, a long blur.

Coombes held his gun and flashlight together in front of him. If he came upon Booth cutting Sullivan with a blade, he knew with cold certainty that he'd be unable to stop himself from shooting the director.

Booth's swimming pool opened out in front of him, huge and dark.

"Sullivan!"

His voice was swallowed by the relentless thump of the music. His ex-wife would be tripping listening to this. It felt like there was a hand holding his heart, squeezing. *For Sullivan.* The pressure in his chest made him want to throw up. He shouted her name again as he moved his sidearm and flashlight around.

"MONICA SULLIVAN!"

There was no reply, or if there was, he couldn't hear it.

He directed his flashlight toward the bar, then across to the far side of the swimming pool where he'd interviewed Booth the previous day.

No sign of life, no sign of a struggle.

The only lights in the huge room were some blue-white LED strip lights illuminating the bottles of spirits behind Booth's bar. He ran toward it, thinking there might be controls for the overhead lights and some way to shut off the damn music.

Coombes stopped, suddenly understanding.

He'd chosen the wrong option.

Booth wasn't here. Sullivan wasn't here. They were in the bedroom, or wherever Booth took his victims.

If he shut off the music, Booth would know, no matter where he was in the house. The purpose of the music wasn't just to drown out the sound of screaming, it was to lure any potential rescuer away from Booth's location.

He turned back the way he'd come, running back into the mansion.

No longer looking around to clear the room, just flat-out running. The music covered the slapping sound of his leather-soled shoes on the tiles. The hallway whizzed past once again. This time it seemed shorter, as return journeys often did.

Sullivan was only here because of him; he had no doubts about that. If she was dead, he might as well have killed her himself. He reached the polished marble entrance in front of the stairs. He was moving too fast as he came around the corner and his right foot came out from underneath him.

As he fell, he glimpsed a figure on the staircase.

He landed hard on his right hip and shoulder before his head snapped back and hit the marble. It was like a light went out for a second and then he was looking up at the ceiling. A face appeared in front of it.

Sullivan.

"You're alive," he said, his voice no more than a whisper.

"Why wouldn't I be?"

"Booth. He took you. How did you get away?"

Her eyes crinkled in amusement.

"Booth never had me; I came here looking for him."

A wave of peace rolled through him and his eyes closed.

"Oh my god. You were worried about me."

Coombes said nothing and sat up.

He didn't feel good. It was the second time in two days he'd lost consciousness. The third time in a year. Sullivan squatted down next to him, her face in front of his. She touched his cheek and held her wet fingertips between them.

A tear.

"What do I mean to you, Johnny?"

He didn't think she'd ever called him *Johnny* before and now didn't seem like a good time to start. He got to his feet, then bent to pick up his Glock and his flashlight.

"I hit my head, it's not all about you, Sullivan."

"Too late, Coombes. The genie's out the bottle. There's no putting it back until you make your three wishes."

At least he was back to being *Coombes*.

"We need to find Booth."

"Well, he's not in any of the rooms upstairs and he's not taken anything with him. His closet's full of clothes and his cell phone's sitting on his night-stand. I don't know if he has another vehicle, but nobody goes anywhere these days without their cell phone."

"They do if they're wanted for murder. You going to tell me why you're here? What was the big break that led you to Booth?"

"The background packet you asked for on Lawrence was a bust. No dark secrets, no crazy ex. Anyway, I kind of figured you were spinning my wheels, giving me busy-work to keep me out the way, so I wasn't too surprised."

Coombes said nothing.

"Still though, I thought it was a good idea. What is the idiom? *Coming events cast their shadows before them*. Something like that. I pulled everything we had on Booth. Did you know he's fascinated with the Black Dahlia case?"

"That's why you drove across town, because of the Dahlia?"

"No, asshat. Because I found a picture of Booth's mother. These guys all have problems with their parents. Guess what color his mom's hair is?"

"Blonde?"

"*Right.*"

It didn't mean much. When you got right down to it, hair only came in four basic colors. Five, if you include gray, which was more of a lack of color. His eyes drifted past Sullivan to the floor behind her. There was something on the marble that hadn't been there before.

Instinctively, he knew it was blood.

"Stay here," he said.

Coombes headed back down the hallway toward the pool. There was a trail of blood all the way back, getting gradually darker and more obvious. Again, the large swimming pool room opened out around him. He swept his flashlight around quickly to check for any threats. He found lighting controls on a wall panel that also controlled the music.

Coombes killed the music and turned on the lights.

Eight big lamps came on over the swimming pool, filling the room with light. He saw Booth immediately. He was fully clothed and floating face-down in the water.

Coombes sighed.

"*Shit.*"

There was blood on the tiles next to the water's edge. It was smeared with shoe prints that he knew would be his. He'd blown right past it in the dark, looking for Sullivan.

Coombes leaned over the edge and looked into the water.

A revolver lay on the floor of the pool. Black, with brown wood grips. He recognized it immediately, it was a Smith and Wesson Model 36, also known as a Chiefs Special.

He ran the obvious narrative in his head.

Booth, realizing his number was up, put the gun to his head and shot himself. He then fell into the water, taking the gun with him. The suicide a de facto admission of guilt for the murder of Dakota Lawrence, Adrienne Strömberg, and the four others in the lake.

The only problem with it, is that Coombes knew it was bullshit.

"Oh wow, is he dead?"

He turned to see the journalist walking toward him.

"This is a crime scene, Sullivan. You need to go before I call it in."

She ignored him and kept coming, her head craning to get a better look.

"For the record, Coombes, women don't like being told to sit and stay like a dog. I'm going to give you a free pass this time on account of how sweet you were back there."

Sweet. And here he was thinking he was hard-boiled.

"Thanks for the tip, Sullivan, but you need to go."

"All this time on the crime beat...this is my first actual dead body."

"If you're still here when other cops arrive, you become part of this. You will be detained and interviewed, perhaps seen as a person of interest. I can't protect you."

She'd stopped now, about five feet away.

"It's a suicide, Coombes, even I can see that."

"Then let me put it in a way you will understand. If you're *part* of the story, you can't *write* the story. I'm sure the *Times* has a rule about that."

"Why d'you have to be such a bunghole?"

"Yeah, yeah," he said, turning back to Booth.

The chlorine in the water was so strong he could smell it hanging in the air without having to bend down. It was strong enough that his eyes were starting to water. When he'd been here the day before he hadn't noticed any chemical smell. Almost like someone had dumped chlorine into the water to explain the lack of gunshot residue on Booth's hand.

"My story's done then? Booth's the killer?"

He didn't turn to face Sullivan.

"I'd hold off on that if I were you."

His focus shifted from the director's body, down to the firearm.

The S&W Model 36 had a two-inch barrel, making it small and easy to conceal. Before automatics became standard-issue in police departments, revolvers with six-inch barrels were the norm. Criminals could tell from a distance when those old-school cops were armed and when they weren't, so many looked for something more subtle to fill the gap.

As a backup, or as a throw-down to justify shooting an unarmed man.

For the throw-down play to work, a backup piece could never be a legally registered weapon. There had to be no way to trace it back to the owner, or it was pointless. Which brought him to his main problem with this suicide.

Eddie Willard owned a Model 36.

He'd worn it strapped to his left ankle the entire time they were partners. Willard carried the gun so long, that he'd named it *Patricia* after the first girl to break his heart.

It seemed unlikely that Willard would discard his Model 36 when he retired. An argument could be made that without the protection of his shield, he had more need than ever for an untraceable weapon.

Or perhaps, one *specific* need.

Willard's wife was dead, his career over. The two guardrails that kept him on the straight and narrow were gone. Coombes thought his ex-partner might find a meaning for his life in the hunt for Lawrence's killer.

He remembered the portrait of Dakota Lawrence in the center of the other man's evidence wall. Untouched by her killer's blade, perfect in every way. A face that looked down on him, day after day, as he worked the case.

Had he fallen in love with her?

Did Willard need to *see* justice done, instead of leave it to someone else?

When he looked around, Sullivan was gone.

After he called in the body, Coombes gloved up and began a quick search of Booth's home. If there was a security system, he wanted to know about it before he made his official statement. Explaining the presence of Sullivan on a recording later would be difficult.

He checked the area behind the bar first and found a MacBook sitting open, a screen saver moving around. Coombes brought the screen back to life and saw that the laptop had been the source of the terrible music. He minimized the music window and opened the apps folder, looking for anything that sounded remotely like a security system. Nothing.

Next, he looked at the photo album and saw it contained over twelve thousand pictures, all women. No pets, no pictures of his car, or meals he'd eaten. Perhaps nearly eighty different women in all. All young, beautiful.

All disturbingly alike.

He saw Dakota Lawrence and Natalie Hahn, as well as early, lower-resolution pictures of Fran Knudsen. Many of the pictures appeared to have been taken while the women slept. Covers pulled back, their bodies exposed like crime scene victims. Full length, then close-ups. The director at work. Their eyes were closed, their skin pale.

Like Booth was imagining them dead, drained of blood.

Regardless of the circumstances, Booth still looked good as the killer.

He checked his watch. Eight minutes since he'd called it in.

Coombes moved on, exploring the lower floor of the mansion. He found an office, a gym, a shower room, and a media room. The walls of the latter were lined with display cases of rifles, pistols, and revolvers. Some looked like museum pieces. He walked back out to the entrance hall where he'd fallen on the floor and double timed it up the staircase.

Why had Sullivan chosen to go upstairs first, not toward the music? He considered the journalist to be a solid investigator and he wanted to understand the difference in approach.

At the top of the stairs, the landing opened out into a wide hallway. A large square canvas was leaning against the wall, the painted side facing inward. He remembered the empty picture hooks he'd observed during his previous visit.

Coombes tilted the canvas so that he could see the front.

It was a painting of Orson Welles.

The director was large and threatening, with soulless dark eyes and a Rasputin beard. Not something Coombes would want to come home to every day, but definitely well executed. He set the canvas back against the wall and moved down the hall to an open doorway.

The master bedroom.

Booth had a large four-poster bed with a covered top and floating see-through silk curtain hanging down. The covers were neat and tidy. It was not the bed that had appeared in any of the photographs on Booth's laptop.

All those beds had been different. Smaller, more feminine.

Their own beds.

Did those women know they were being photographed, or had Booth broken into their homes and taken the pictures while they slept?

Coombes studied the round wooden posts of the bed, looking for the polished wear caused by rope movement, or gouges caused by handcuffs. As Sullivan had stated, Booth's cell phone sat on the nightstand charger. He thought about that. Booth might have been in the water for hours, so why would his cell be here and not in his pocket, submerged in water?

Doors slammed on the driveway. The heavy sound of a patrol SUV.

Coombes turned to leave the room, when his eye caught on something pushing out from under the drapes. It was round and black, and about the same diameter as a champagne bottle.

He lifted the fabric up and saw the world-famous golden figure appear.

Coombes squatted down to read the Oscar's engraving.

ACADEMY AWARD

TO

JOSHUA BOOTH

BEST ORIGINAL SCREENPLAY

"LAST NIGHT, BEFORE I DIED"

2008

There was a dark residue of what he assumed was blood on the statue's upper base.

It was the murder weapon.

———

It was approaching eleven p.m. when Coombes pulled up outside Eddie Willard's bungalow in Fairfax. His lights were on, his car was parked outside, and jazz was playing. Coombes left his suit jacket unfastened. To off-set this, and the obvious reason for it, he pulled down his tie and undid the top button of his shirt to present a casual end-of-the-day appearance.

Willard answered the door wearing a long-sleeve T-shirt covered in corn chip crumbs. He laughed when he saw Coombes standing there.

"John!"

It seemed like Willard had been hitting the booze. A celebration?

"I'm here to see Patricia."

Willard laughed again in apparent confusion.

"*What?*"

"You know what I'm talking about. Your throw-down piece."

His old partner's face lit up.

"Patricia! My god, I forgot I named it that. You've got some memory, rock star."

Coombes clenched his jaw and glared at Willard with years of built-up aggression caused by the *rock star* jibe. The message cut through the other man's alcohol haze.

"All right, John. Cool your jets, eh? It's in the garage."

Willard let him in, then shut the door behind him.

"I suppose from that face of yours that someone's dead. If you think I'm good for it, I'm guessing it's De Luca. Can't say I'm sorry about that, but it wasn't me. Probably one of his gangster buddies from Vegas."

Willard walked through to the back of the bungalow, then paused to unlock the door into his garage. He was smirking again, either because he was drunk, or at the idea that De Luca was dead.

"I'm not even offended by this, Coombes. You know why? Because I must've thought about killing that son-of-a-bitch a million times. What he did to that poor girl, fuck him, you know? He deserved it, whatever it was. I hope he went slow."

Coombes said nothing.

Willard nodded in a *so that's how it is* fashion and opened the door. They went inside as the florescent tubes flickered on above them. Willard walked to the workbench pressed against the end wall and reached out to open the second drawer down.

"That's far enough," Coombes said. "Step back toward the door."

Willard looked at the Glock that was now between them.

"Now *that* I am offended by, Coombes. You're like a brother to me, I would never pull a gun on you. In fact, I would've taken a bullet for you."

"Over by the door. If Patricia's here, you and me can hug and make up."

Willard laughed, sarcastically. "*Yeah, right.*"

The other man moved as instructed, and Coombes pulled out the drawer. Inside was an oil-stained cloth wrapped around something. He could see it was the gun even before he unwrapped it. The .38 was in perfect condition and looked well-maintained.

Coombes relaxed and holstered his weapon.

"Sorry, man."

He supposed that Willard could've had a *second* throw-down piece that he didn't know about and that this one was little more than an alibi, but it seemed unlikely. That didn't fit with the man he knew. If Willard had killed Booth and left the gun, leaving the gun would've been part of an admission of guilt, with the next step a full confession.

Willard would've *wanted* him to know.

"What you said before; about thinking of killing De Luca a million times. I understand that, believe me. I did too. In more and more grotesque ways. It took years to get past it."

He turned to Willard and saw his face had softened.

"If it wasn't me, then who?"

"I have no idea, Eddie."

And it was true, he didn't. People with egos like Booth often couldn't face the prospect of being revealed to the public as a monster and put in prison.

They had to be worshipped like a god, or nothing.

Two things told Coombes that Booth hadn't taken his own life.

The first, was the extra chlorine in the pool water and the second, was the gun that fired the fatal shot had had its serial number removed. Booth's guns were all legal. He was a collector of classic weapons, he wouldn't choose a street gun to end his life, it would be something that made a statement.

They walked back out the garage and into the house.

Coombes kept going, toward the front door.

He didn't want to waste an hour mending fences with Willard over beer and jazz. It was unlikely the two of them would meet again after this until one of them was in a box.

Outside, a cool wind had picked up and Coombes glanced at the night sky like at a person whose name he could no longer remember.

"You know who I think did it?"

He returned his gaze to Willard.

"Who's that?"

"Booth. That guy's a classic sociopath."

Coombes nodded.

"There's just one problem. Booth was the victim, not De Luca."

46

COOMBES MET FRAN KNUDSEN in the parking lot next to the Medical Examiner's building. Her Mini was there waiting when he arrived, so he parked alongside and killed the engine. They got out their vehicles and nodded wordlessly at each other. Knudsen's eyes were red, her face puffy. She'd had the worst night of her life.

It was ten a.m. on a Sunday morning, but they still had to wait ten minutes inside the building before he was able to walk her down to the morgue where Booth's body had been set up. Less than 24 hours had passed since Booth's death and the M.E. had yet to get to him.

As a perceived suicide, he would be the lowest priority.

Coombes turned to Knudsen.

"Remember, this isn't necessary. It's not too late to change-"

She held up her hand to cut him off.

He understood; she had to be here, to see the truth for herself. Coombes nodded to the medical examiner's assistant, who pulled back the sheet covering the director's face. At his request, a second sheet had been placed underneath to cover the top of Booth's head to hide the damage caused by the gunshot.

Sometimes when a body was exposed, the person identifying it would take a header onto the floor. He positioned himself to catch her if she fell, but Knudsen was made of stronger stuff. A single tear was all Booth got, a man she'd loved since first grade.

"Oh, Josh. Why did it have to be you?"

Knudsen reached out her hand to touch the body, then drew it back again. Nobody wanted to touch someone they loved after they turned cold. Coombes let a moment go by, watching her body language. He had anticipated a more extreme reaction, perhaps even sobbing.

"All right," he said. "Let's go back outside and get some fresh air."

Coombes walked her back out through the building, the smell of death and disinfectant chasing them all the way. One day he'd be back, only that time he'd arrive on a steel gurney and he'd be cut open, his organs lifted out and weighed. It could be five days' from now, it could be fifty years. The mistake was to think that the rules didn't apply to you.

Death came for everyone, there was no escape.

"Do you think he...did that to himself?"

Knudsen's tone was flat and it was hard for him to gauge why she was asking; if she wanted to be reassured that her great love hadn't killed himself, or if she wanted to know if he suspected her of pulling the trigger.

"No, I don't."

In the parking lot, the temperature was already in the high eighties with no cooling breeze to take the edge off. For once, he welcomed the heat after the chill of the morgue.

Coombes opened the trunk of his Dodge and pulled a bottle of water from a plastic-wrapped 6-pack. There was a conversation they needed to have before she left.

"When we talked before it seemed like you wanted to tell me something."

Knudsen sighed.

"I guess it doesn't matter now, not anymore."

Coombes said nothing, letting the silence build.

"Josh...killed a woman while he was at USC. An accident."

"He told you this?"

"After he finished film school we met for drinks. Instead of being on top of the world and excited about the future, he was depressed. It was obvious that something had happened but I couldn't get it out of him. I figured he'd tell me when he was ready.

"Anyway, a couple of weeks go by and we started to date again. He was working on a screenplay and it was going well. His darkness seemed to lift during the day as he worked, then return at night as he grew tired."

She was delaying telling him what he wanted, but that was ok.

"Go on."

"Josh had issues with sleep, like his brain didn't fully turn off."

Coombes had an idea what was coming next.

"What kind of issues?"

"Parasomnia. Sleep walking, nightmares, sudden movements like seizures, he even made love to me once, totally asleep."

Not what he was expecting, but he could see where she was going

"And he talked?"

"Yes." She looked at her hands. "Most of it was nonsense, but some words came again and again. *Gloria, eyes, fall*. Night after night it was the same. It scared me. I fed the words into Google with *USC* and got over a hundred hits. Gloria Stratton, another film school student, had been blinded and thrown out a window."

Coombes thought of the slow motion shot in *Fallen Idol* where the camera went out over the edge and followed the old man down onto his Ferrari.

"Did you challenge him about it?"

Knudsen nodded.

"Josh said he and Gloria had a *friends with benefits* arrangement. One night, he woke to the sound of screaming. When he woke up he found himself on top of her, his thumbs buried in her eye sockets. Blood was everywhere. He got off her and could only watch as she jumped out of bed and ran blindly across the room and through her tenth-floor window. Josh knew no one would believe him, so he got his stuff together and left."

Coombes sat back and sighed.

He could see it play out in his head, like a Joshua Booth movie.

The hapless hero, unjustly cast as a villain by events beyond his control.

"But you believed him?"

"Of course. I knew what he was capable of while he slept. You might think it strange, but his confession brought us closer together. Our relationship had never been so good. I thought he was going to propose to me that night at *The Biltmore* when he met De Luca."

"You weren't worried he would attack *you* in his sleep?"

"No, why would he?"

Coombes found this answer hard to understand, but decided to let it go rather than lose the momentum they had achieved.

"Ok, so your relationship comes to an end and he starts dating women that were nothing but cheap knock-offs. Why do that if he could have the original?"

Knudsen's face colored.

"That's the nicest thing anyone has said to me in years."

"Explain it to me."

"Josh was inspired by the death of Gloria Stratton. When he was writing he would submerge himself in the events of that night over and over. His responsibility, the guilt, the thrill of getting away with it. He said that knowing I knew about it prevented him from submerging, even if I was across town. He wished he'd never told me, we both did."

"And the lookalikes?"

A hard look came over Knudsen's face.

"I thought it meant that he still loved me and if I gave him time he'd come back. Then one day I saw him with one of them on the Venice Beach Boardwalk and realized I was the farthest thing from his mind. He had simply re-created our setup to the last detail."

Coombes nodded.

"And that made you angry."

"Of course."

"And the woman you saw him with was Dakota Lawrence?"

Knudsen met his eye. The hatred was pure, unblinking.

"Yes."

"Dakota wasn't like the others, was she? Josh was in love with her."

"It looked that way. Holding hands in public, kissing. This just days before the movie was about to wrap. Normally by that point he's getting ready to end things. It worried me."

"That you'd lost him."

She shook her head a little, like a dog drying itself.

He'd seen Sato do the same in the past, he'd missed something.

"I knew Josh. If their relationship had progressed that far, the next step was sleeping overnight. He promised me he wouldn't do that, but I saw that was now in the past. Once *Fallen Idol* was done, he'd begin work on his next screenplay. Which meant he'd re-submerge himself in Gloria's death. The nightmares would come again and Dakota would know what he'd done."

"That's why you started following her back to her house?"

"Yes."

"What happened on their last night together?"

Her lip curled, knowing he already knew.

"I was outside his home all night, she never left."

"So you killed her."

Fran Knudsen stared at him; her eyes wide.

"*What!?*"

"You knocked her out, beat her repeatedly, then slit her throat and made her watch herself die in the hand mirror."

Knudsen doubled over and vomited on the asphalt.

There went *that* idea.

When Knudsen straightened up, her face was pale and her hair wild. She wiped her mouth with the back of her hand and glared at him angrily.

Coombes had a feeling their conversation was about to end. He opened the bottle of water he was holding and passed it to her. While she drank, he filled the dead air, hoping to extend the conversation a moment longer.

"All right. Let's rewind. You saw the two of them together and began to worry. I assume you shared your concerns with Booth?"

"That's right."

"And? What did he say?"

"He laughed in my face. Called me paranoid, jealous, and pathetic. Then he told me to move on with my life and find someone new. Josh had never treated me like that before, he always valued my opinion. I was heartbroken, my hopes of him coming back to me were gone. I knew he wasn't going to change his mind."

"What did you think when Dakota was found dead?"

Knudsen shrugged.

"I thought she found out about Gloria and was unwilling to keep his secret...that he killed her to keep her quiet. I felt no surprise at all."

"How could you continue to work with him if you thought that?"

"He cornered me at the *Son of a Gun* office. I couldn't look at him and he guessed what I was thinking. He denied it. What can I say? I believed him. Josh said someone was trying to frame him. It sounded like he knew who, but he never told me a name."

This sounded desperate to Coombes.

"Miss Knudsen, we see this all the time in Homicide. The some-one-else-did-it defense. It's what every school kid says when they're caught."

"I know he was innocent. Not just for what he said, but because of what he did. Or rather, what he *didn't*. Josh didn't try to restart our relationship in an attempt to manipulate me. In fact, he did the opposite. He hooked up with the first witch he met in a bar."

Natalie Hahn.

She was right.

If Booth had killed Dakota, the obvious next step was to keep Knudsen sweet at any cost, at least until the LAPD lost interest in the case. It confirmed what he already knew, that Booth hadn't killed himself, and was most likely a victim of the same killer as Dakota Lawrence and Adrienne Strömberg.

The killer was tying off loose ends to cover their trail.

"Why did you give Booth a black eye?"

Knudsen glanced at her hand.

"He was being an ass."

47

COOMBES WATCHED KNUDSEN LEAVE, then sat listening to the white noise of the air conditioner as he tried to put together what he'd just learned. It had taken Booth's death to free up the information inside Knudsen. Had she been more forthcoming earlier, maybe he wouldn't have died. She'd been loyal to him until the end, until it didn't matter anymore. Perhaps hoping right up till then that he'd take her back.

Using his cell phone, he did an online search for Gloria Stratton. His screen filled with results, page after page of newspaper articles. The murder of a beautiful young white woman from a privileged background, it was practically the press corps reason for existing.

The casting director's story checked out; it was all true.

Coombes decided to continue his investigation elsewhere. His near-death experience with the Nazi made him wary about sitting in a parked car without his full attention on his surroundings.

Any other day, he would've had his ticket punched.

He stopped at the roach coach where Monica Sullivan had hijacked him and picked up a large cup of coffee. It was time to re-connect with the journalist, he thought, keep her on-side and the story about Franklin Canyon Park out of the *Times*.

Back at PAB, he was unsurprised to find the detective bureau empty. It was Sunday, and the caseload was almost nonexistent due to the pandemic and the stay-at-home order.

Coombes logged into his computer and took a long drink of coffee.

He expected to find the Gloria Stratton case listed as *open-unsolved*, but instead found that it was *closed by conviction*. Rather than be disappointed, he felt his interest sharpen. If what Booth had claimed was true, then not only was he responsible for a woman's death, but he had caused someone else to pay the price.

It was perfect.

He opened the file and felt his heart rate kick into a higher gear.

Soon after Joshua Booth left the crime scene, Billy, Gloria Stratton's sixteen-year-old brother turned up. Close enough, that the two may have swapped places on the elevator.

Billy, who shared the apartment with his sister, decided to take the edge off things with some crystal meth. When responding officers worked out where the smashed body in front of the building had originated from, they made their way up to the apartment. There, they found the front door open and Billy covered in blood, muttering incoherently about the window.

Coombes sighed.

It was easy to see why no effort had been expended elsewhere to find who might be responsible. Being caught literally red-handed and out of his mind on drugs, Billy had no chance. Under questioning, he had no memory of events, a condition known to addicts as a *blackout*.

Billy Stratton was unable to say he didn't do it, because he couldn't remember. When asked about the blood on his hands and clothing, he said he didn't know where it came from.

He had no motive, but also no alibi.

In a deal with the District Attorney, Stratton admitted to the lower charge of involuntary manslaughter and was given a four-year vacation at Lompoc and a $10,000 fine - the maximum sentence available.

Whenever Coombes saw an involuntary manslaughter charge, he smelled a rat. And, reading between the lines, he found it.

Looking at the chronology, it was clear to him that at the time of his questioning, Billy Stratton would still have been strung out on drugs and unable to tell when he was implicating himself. This was technically the same as receiving no Miranda warning, and everything that came out of Stratton's mouth would've been inadmissible.

The case was weak, and the DA had known it.

He opened the DMV portal and brought up the most recent driver's license for Stratton. The face that appeared was devoid of life. In contrast to his booking photograph, Billy Stratton now looked every inch the killer the files said that he was, plus some.

Prison changed a man, even if it was just four years.

Coombes leaned in close to the screen.

Something about this new Stratton seemed eerily familiar. The look of defiance in the eyes, the line of the jaw. He felt certain that he'd seen it recently, in a different context. But where? After a minute, the answer still wasn't coming to him so he left it.

His thoughts turned to Booth's confession.

There were two interpretations to the front door being left open. The first was that Stratton was already wasted when he returned home and hadn't closed it; the second was that Stratton had been in the apartment when Booth had his nightmare and it was Booth who left it open as he fled the scene.

Neither possibility moved the needle much for Stratton, but did affect how close Booth might have come to discovery.

The problem for Coombes, was that it was just as likely that Stratton *had* attacked his sister under the influence of the drugs, as charged, and that Booth had made up his story to explain a couple of weird dreams about a dead girl he used to see around campus.

Booth was a storyteller, a bullshit artist, an unreliable narrator.

Nobody had unearthed Booth's name during the investigation, nor did he appear in any of the many news stories that touched on her friends at the film school. To further muddy the waters, Billy had been staying with his sister in the first place because he was said to be 'troubled' and his father had thrown him out.

Coombes sat back in his chair.

He stared over the top of his divider at the distant ceiling to give his eyes a rest from the computer screen. Booth had described his relationship with Gloria Stratton to Knudsen as *friends-with-benefits*. Conceivably, this could explain why no one knew about their sex-based relationship, but in Coombes' experience, women always talked to their best friend.

A story would've come out.

Best friends were like flight recorders, filled with data, surviving the disaster to provide details to investigators about what happened.

If no one knew about Booth, why would Stratton?

The truth was, if Stratton *had* known about Booth, he would've mentioned him under questioning and the fact that he hadn't meant that Stratton was not the man he was after.

Billy Stratton was a dead end.

48

Sato wasn't in a talkative mood so they resumed their re-watch of a TV show about an L.A. fixer who solved a lot of problems with a baseball bat or his fists. Coombes kind of loved the show, and had probably seen it all the way through about six times.

As he watched, he found himself thinking about Gloria Stratton and the story about Booth waking up in the process of blinding her. If it hadn't happened that way, and if Billy Stratton was responsible, then why did the story ring true?

After three episodes, Sato decided to call it a night.

Booth had partially confirmed the story by claiming he had a fear of being blinded himself. Coombes could imagine such a phobia developing from a personal experience.

There was a problem with Knudsen's story, if it was just a story.

He had made a note of the investigating detective's name on the Gloria Stratton case and he looked it up in his notebook. He checked his watch. Almost 11 o'clock.

Late for a call, but not if you were a cop. He called the number.

"Torres."

"This is Coombes, RHD. Apologies for the lateness of the hour. I'm working a murder that might link to a case you worked in '06. A young woman who was thrown out of her tenth-floor apartment window."

"Oh, man. Gloria Stratton. What's your intersect?"

Coombes ignored that for now.

"The brother, you ever have any doubts he did it?"

"None, whatsoever."

"All right, here's my intersect: I have a guy who confessed to a third party, only he's now in a drawer with a hole in his head. I'm looking at your guy as the trigger man."

"Who's the stiff?"

"Joshua Booth."

"Booth, huh? Said on the news that he cleaned his own slate."

"It's bullshit."

Torres thought for a moment.

"I don't know what to tell you, Coombes. We dusted that whole apartment. The only lifts we got belonged to Gloria, Billy, and the father. Far as we could tell, Gloria had no boyfriend, girlfriend, whatever. She kept everyone away, because she knew her brother was a psycho."

It was hard to argue with forensics.

If Booth had this friends-with-benefits arrangement with Gloria like Knudsen claimed, then he would've left plenty of evidence of his presence behind. Fingerprints, hairs, fibers, even DNA. Torres hadn't just grabbed up the first suspect, he'd grabbed the *only* suspect.

"Tell me about this *involuntary manslaughter* crap."

Torres sighed.

"They said I questioned him while he was high, that I breached his Miranda rights. The DA took the first deal the defense attorney offered. Four years, what a joke."

Coombes nodded to himself; he'd nailed it.

"Do you think he was good for murder one?"

"We think he had a psychotic break under the influence and threw her out the window. That's it. No malice aforethought, no motive. He was probably waiting for her to fly back in the window when the uniforms arrived."

"All right, Torres. Thanks for your time."

"Just a moment. I assume this *third party* told you this story after Booth was already dead?"

"Correct."

"Did it occur to you that this person might've made the whole thing up?"

"Kind of why I'm asking," Coombes said.

"*Right.* Happy hunting, Detective."

They disconnected.

The forensic evidence suggested Booth had never been in Gloria Stratton's apartment. This suggested to him that Booth made up a story to impress a woman he assumed wouldn't be part of his life for long, then had to live with it when he realized she was his only muse, his only real love.

His story seemed authentic because he was a gifted storyteller.

Coombes walked onto the balcony outside the master bedroom and alternated between taking in the view, and making notes about his phone call. The view was incredible and he didn't often take the time to appreciate it. If he'd lived here while he was still married it was his belief that he'd still be married.

He knew someday he'd be asked to leave by the owner of the apartment, but until that day came, he was going to enjoy it as much as possible.

His cell phone rang and he answered without looking at the display.

"Coombes."

There was a long pause and he wondered if the caller hung up.

"I wasn't sure if you'd take my call."

He froze. That voice, he *knew* that voice.

"I was just thinking about you," he said.

His ex-wife laughed without humor.

"All good things, I'm sure."

"Why are you calling me, Julie?"

"I saw the *Times.* I wanted to make sure you were all right."

The shooting, he'd forgotten all about it.

"Do you care?"

He heard the surprise in his own voice.

"I guess I don't want...you're ok, right?"

"I'm ok."

"Good," she said.

The line went quiet. After a beat, he heard a car drive past her. He pictured her on the street outside their old bungalow.

"These are the conversations I miss," he said.

This time, her laugh was natural.

"It wasn't all bad, was it? There were some good times."

Julie sounded happy, more at ease than he could remember. It was a long time since he'd heard it, but he realized this was what she sounded like when she'd been in love with him. She was in love with someone else now, of course, but her voice was the same.

"Yeah," he said. "It wasn't all bad."

"If this happens again, will you take my call?"

"Depends."

"On what?"

"If I'm still alive," he said.

After the call finished, he looked at his cell phone in his hand, as if looking at it could explain the conversation that had just taken place. Why had she really called him? Sullivan's puff-piece in the *Times* made clear that he was alive and uninjured.

The penny dropped.

Julie hadn't called to ask about a physical injury, she was asking about his mental health. Asking him how he was dealing with the fact that he had killed someone. Or since she knew him so well, killed *another* someone.

Coombes looked over the rail at City Hall framed by other buildings.

He felt nothing about it at all.

49

He awoke to the sound of his cell phone ringing and vibrating. The ringtone was set to kick in after an increasing level of vibration; it had rung a few times. He answered and held it zombie-like to his head. The clock told him he'd been asleep for an hour and a quarter.

"Coombes."

"This is Detective Sands, RPD. Do you know an Edward Willard?"

He sighed and closed his eyes. The old fool had been arrested. He couldn't place the letters RPD. Some kind of police department outside L.A.

"What's he done?"

"Look, there's no easy way to say this. He's dead."

Coombes sat up in bed.

"Jesus Christ! What happened?"

"We're just getting started here, but it looks like he was shot through the front door of a residence with a Heckler & Koch MP7. There's thirty or so shell casings in the hallway. Needless to say, the shooter's in the wind."

He swung his legs onto the floor and walked through the main living space to the breakfast bar where he kept a pen and paper.

"Give me the address."

Sands gave him a location in Riverside. As he wrote it down, Coombes realized he knew the address. He'd given it to Willard.

It was Robbie Ellis' address.

"I'm on my way. Can you hold the scene for me?"

"You know how it goes, Coombes. That shit isn't up to me. It's a safe bet I'll still be here, but your friend might be gone. One more thing, this is *my* crime scene, not yours."

He was about to tell the detective that he was working a related case, when the man disconnected. It was doubtless part of a power play by Sands to highlight the fact that he was an outsider and was little more than a civilian in the matter.

Coombes considered waking Sato to tell her what was going on, but changed his mind at the last second, reasoning that she'd want to be fresh for court the following morning, and the arraignment of Stephen Walker. He wrote a note and left it under an LAPD-branded coffee mug in the kitchen in case she woke early and wondered where he was.

It took him an hour to get to Riverside.

He could've made it sooner, but for a reluctance to get there and see Eddie Willard's body shot through with bullets. To his shame, he spent the majority of the journey time relieved that it was Willard he'd sent to interview Ellis, not Sato.

The end of his trip was guided not just by his GPS unit, but by the flashing strobes of emergency vehicles in the night sky. Coombes parked the Dodge well clear of the scene and walked the final 50 yards.

Yellow crime scene tape was staked out around the front yard of a standard two-bed bungalow. Coombes could see four men and three women working the area inside the tape, and four uniforms standing around the edge looking out. It was a response Willard was unlikely to have received from the LAPD.

He approached the tape, his eyes on the crumpled figure on the footpath. A tall black man came over. He appeared to be in his 30s, but his hair was white and was beginning to recede at the temples.

"You Coombes?"

He nodded.

"I assume that makes you Sands?"

"That's right. We held the scene for you like you asked. I figure you can officially ID him, get that all squared away, one less box to tick."

Sands nodded to the closest uniform who lifted the tape to let Coombes pass underneath. As he dipped his head, Coombes fixed his gaze on Willard and noticed he was wearing his old suit like he was still on the job. It told him everything he needed to know and that he needed to be careful with Sands.

They walked to where Willard lay on a footpath.

Willard was on his back, his head facing straight up at the cloudless night sky. His arms were thrown wide and his right leg was folded up under his left. It reminded Coombes of depictions of Jesus on the cross, only it was his alcoholic ex-partner that had been sacrificed.

"Were you working together?"

Coombes ignored Sands and crouched down next to Willard, carefully avoiding the body and the pool of blood that had seeped out around the sides. The small amount of blood told him that Willard had died almost instantly, that his heart had stopped before he hit the ground. It was the reverse of what had happened to Dakota Lawrence, whose life had been preserved longer in order for her own heart to pump the blood from her body.

Willard's chest was riddled with bullets, it was a mess.

Coombes moved his hand above the body, trying to count the impacts. Over his shoulder, Sands spoke again.

"Twelve to the chest, two in his left arm, one on the right."

Coombes nodded. At least Willard's face was untouched.

Poor Eddie. Coombes rose stiffly and turned to Sands.

"Well, it's obviously Willard. What made you call me?"

"We checked his wallet to get outline ID from a driver's license. Your friend had your business card next to it. You were also the only saved contact in his cell phone."

Sands indicated an evidence bag containing a 20-year-old flip phone. It was the second time Sands had called Willard his *friend* and the lie cut deep.

"Look, he wasn't my friend, ok? Until recently, I hadn't seen him for years. Eddie was my partner when I first made detective. Everything I know about being a cop, I learned for myself, you know what I mean? He didn't deserve this, but he was an asshole."

"That's not a nice way to speak about the dead, Detective."

"I said it to his face often enough, he just laughed. He wouldn't take offense at my saying it now, that's not who he was."

"All right," Sands said. "Why do you think he was here?"

"I'm working a murder that links to a case we worked together six years ago. An unsolved. Last week, I go to his home to talk to him about it, only to discover he's been working on it as a retirement project-"

Sands held up one hand to stop him.

"Woah. Back up. He has a shield wallet on his belt. Neighbors heard him shout *police*. You're telling me he was retired? What am I supposed to do with that?"

"The badge is a duplicate or a phony. I saw his actual badge in a cube of resin. I assume he was representing himself as a cop in an attempt to muscle the resident and got blown away for his troubles."

Sands nodded and wrote that into his notebook.

"What do you mean by a *duplicate?*"

"Guys like him, they got nothing except the badge. One day they wake up and realize they're staring retirement in the face. No badge. They figure they *earned* it; they should be allowed to keep it. So before pulling the pin, they claim they lost their badge and get a replacement, so when it comes time to hand their badge in, they still have the spare."

Sands said nothing, his gaze hard to read.

"Shit," Coombes said, "I guess *I* think we earn them too."

"Did you know he was still investigating?"

"I knew it. No matter what I told him, he was never going to stop. That's how it was with him. Say *leave it alone*, he'd do the opposite. So I had him run surveillance on a guy he liked for the murder. I knew the guy had nothing to do with it, but it made Eddie feel involved and kept him out the way."

"That wasn't *this* guy, was it?"

"No. A producer in L.A. called Anthony De Luca. That said, the two men have met. Ellis is an actor. He connected with De Luca at a party trying to get noticed. Hustle a part, you know? Afterwards, the lead actress was tortured and murdered."

Sands looked sharply up from his notebook.

"You're talking about Dakota Lawrence."

"That's right."

This was the tricky part, Coombes thought. If it came out that Willard died doing unsanctioned work for him, he knew he was looking at a sharp exit from RHD, perhaps even the LAPD.

It would be everything Block wanted.

"You think Willard followed De Luca here?"

"I'll be sure to ask him. The way De Luca spoke, their meeting was a one-off, memorable only by association with what happened later to Lawrence."

"Why else would he come here at this time of night?"

Coombes smiled a little, from a memory of Willard.

"Eddie had this theory that it wasn't just *what* you ask someone, but *when*. He thought if you show up at lunchtime, bad guy figures you're just passing the time. But pound on their door when they're in bed, that person thinks you've got something good, they panic."

"And pull out a submachine gun," Sands said.

Coombes' mood dipped. "Right."

Silence fell between them and he turned just in time to see Eddie Willard's body being lifted onto a gurney and carried across to an unmarked van. Willard had called his technique *the midnight knock* and they'd used it at least four times during their time together, always with positive results. It worked.

Coombes wondered if Willard had time to think about Dakota in that brief moment as the bullets tore through him, that his death would seal the other man's fate.

That he had solved the case.

"Does he have family I can contact?"

"His wife's dead, there's no one else. Just brothers in blue."

Sands closed his notebook and returned it to his suit pocket.

"You think Ellis is your killer?"

"I'd hate to think he's just a dope slinger with his wires crossed."

The other detective said nothing and instead put his hands on his hips. It seemed to Coombes to be a blocking gesture and that he was now being invited to leave.

"You realize I have to see the inside of the house, right?"

Sands shook his head.

"Can't do it, Coombes. It's a crime scene. I told you on the phone this was my case. You have no jurisdiction in Riverside."

"Give me a break. This waste of skin has now killed nine people. Eight in L.A., one here. Whose party does that make it, mine or yours? This guy is in the wind. Gone. The most likely place he'll reappear, is back in L.A. I need to see if there's evidence in there that will help me find him or convict him."

"I told you, Coombes, it's my crime scene-"

"I am *already in* the crime scene, Sands. The crime scene is *outside* the property; all you have inside are spent shell casings. I know how to preserve evidence. I'll glove-up, put on shoe protectors, I know the drill. Just give me ten minutes."

Sands' teeth clenched together and they stared each other out.

"You got five."

"All I'll need," Coombes said.

50

THE FRONT DOOR OF Ellis' property, what was left of it, was propped open with a silver coffee can. Coombes studied the damage to the door, which was substantial. It gave him a visual of the gunfire Willard faced standing two feet beyond the wood. He could picture Willard leaning in, pounding on the door with the base of his fist.

It made no sense to him why his ex-partner had taken this approach with Ellis, there was nothing to indicate he was their guy. He had only sent him here to verify De Luca's alibi.

Why do *the midnight knock* for that?

Coombes stepped over the threshold, into the hallway.

The shell casings still lay there, scattered all around. Forensics had finished processing the scene. Despite this, he was careful to place his shoes in their Tyvek covers carefully, so as not to disturb the evidence. He sensed Sands behind him in the hallway, supervising his search. Coombes spoke without turning his head.

"Did you serve, Sands?"

"Yeah. Afghanistan. You?"

"Same. Ever use the MP7?"

"Can't say I did."

"It holds 40 rounds, but there aren't 40 in this hallway, I make 26. The thing about the MP7 is the ejector sticks really easily. I'll bet this clown didn't maintain it one day in his life. Anyway, I figure it jammed, hence, the 26 shell casings. Maybe he clears the chamber but by then the spell is broken and he realizes the job is done."

Sands grunted, as if to say that no amount of small talk would lengthen his stay in the property, or repair the damaged relationship between them.

Combes got to where he figured Ellis stood and turned back toward the entrance and Sands advancing toward him. He held out his right hand, dummying the gun shoot.

He looked to the side.

A framed movie poster was hung on the wall and glass lay broken on the floor. The glass broken by repeated impacts from ejected shell casings. He turned to Sands.

"I assume this is a fully-furnished rental?"

"Yeah," Sands said. "Why do you ask?"

Coombes pointed to the poster.

"I don't figure we're looking for a *Sound of Music* type of guy."

"The name on the lease came back to an Alan Smithee, that's Smith with a double e at the end. We haven't tracked him down yet, or established his link to Ellis."

Coombes laughed and stepped into the living room.

The place was a mess of empty beer bottles and take-out containers. There was a sofa and a chair and judging from a blanket on the sofa, it looked like he watched TV in the chair and slept on the sofa. A stack of Joshua Booth DVDs sat next to the TV, most had a discount label stuck to the cover.

The case for *Fallen Idol* was sitting open.

Sands walked in behind him.

"What's the big joke, Coombes?"

"Alan Smithee. It's a pseudonym used by directors when a studio messes with their movie. It prevents a studio using a director's name to sell the movie if it sucks. It's like a big middle finger. We think Ellis was trying to frame the director Joshua Booth for the killings, if this place was ever found he wanted that to point to Booth too."

"Shit. That was our only lead."

Coombes said nothing and moved into the kitchen.

After Willard was dispensed with, it was unlikely that Ellis would want to hang around. He'd want to get dressed, grab his car keys and go. That meant there was, potentially, a treasure-trove of evidence left behind.

The sink drainer was stacked high with pizza boxes.

If there was a treasure-trove here, he wasn't seeing it.

He opened the fridge. In the movies, that's where bad guys hid their money, guns, or drugs. A quick glance told Coombes that Ellis used his for holding beer. A *lot* of beer. He closed the door and sighed.

Then angled his head and frowned.

On the counter next to the fridge was a clear mark. Something had sat there, protecting it from dust and grime. He pointed it out to Sands.

"Have your forensics people photograph this clean spot here, get a ruler in shot to show scale, I need a size. I think I know what sat here."

"And what's that?"

"An Oscar."

Coombes left the room and went into the bathroom.

Sands went outside to find the photographer. For the moment, Coombes had the room to himself. He opened the medicine cabinet and found a bottle of pills. Seroquel.

Part of the label had been torn off, the part with a name.

He looked down at the floor and saw a wastebasket. He lifted off the lid and saw it was half-full. Empty sheets of anti-smoking gum, a squeezed-out tube of toothpaste, a cardboard box for a new toothpaste, an empty bottle of shampoo. No ripped label.

Through the wall he heard Sands talking to someone about the mark on the counter and the scale. Coombes turned the trash lid over and saw the partial label had stuck itself to the underside of the lid. He peeled it off and stuck it to the base of his thumb, then pulled his glove back down over it. He put the trash back as it was and stood up.

"Find anything?"

Sands was behind him now, his gaze on the open medicine cabinet.

"Pills. Antipsychotics. Looks like a full container. Our boy doesn't seem to have been keeping up with his dose."

"There's a surprise."

Coombes closed the cabinet. As the door swung closed, he noticed that the light above was briefly reflected on his forehead. It formed a perfect square cross. He moved the mirrored door back and forth to line the cross up in the center of his forehead.

Ellis had seen this cross every time he closed the cabinet door. If he closed it fast enough, it would be almost subliminal. He took out his cell phone and opened the camera app.

"Do me a favor. Take a photograph of my face in the mirror."

Sands took the offered cell phone.

"*Why?*"

"Because our killer has been marking this exact cross on his victims. Cutting it into the middle of their heads, right down to the bone."

Sands' face twisted with disgust.

"Aw, man! That shit right there, *that's* why I left L.A."

Sands took the picture and handed him the cell phone back.

He checked both bedrooms; a master and a spare.

Coombes could tell neither bed had ever been slept in by Ellis because they looked like they had just been made, with tight hospital corners. Whatever Ellis had going on, it caused him to be able to sleep only on the sofa in the living room. Given the medication in the bathroom, Coombes hypothesized this could be PTSD.

The only thing of note in either bedroom was a rectangular impression on the spare bed that likely came from a Pelican case holding the MP7.

Sands made a circling gesture with his finger. *Wrap it up.*

Coombes figured he'd seen all he needed and left the house without complaint. It made no sense to him that the other detective was pushing him out when he'd done nothing but help his investigation, but nothing surprised him anymore. Least of all how a man on antipsychotic medication got his hands on a submachine gun.

"I'll be in touch if I need anything," Sands said. "I've got your card."

This, he supposed, was a dig. His card being in evidence due to Willard.

"Send me a copy of that photograph from the kitchen."

"Oh, I'll get right on that."

His voice was thick with sarcasm.

What an asshole, Coombes thought.

He regretted telling Sands about Alan Smithee, he should've let the other man chase his tail looking for the mythical man.

Coombes left his gloves on until he was back behind the wheel of his Dodge. Then, with the driver door open and the dome light on, he peeled back his glove and looked at the name on the pharmacy label and smiled.

William Stratton.

The dead-end had evaporated.

Robbie Ellis and Billy Stratton were the same person.

51

THE CRIMINAL COURTS BUILDING was renamed *Clara Shortridge Foltz Criminal Justice Center* in 2002, but Coombes didn't know anyone that called it that, it was just *the CCB*. It sat on Temple, between Spring Street and Broadway, across from City Hall and a block from LAPD headquarters. A strict use of masks was being enforced inside the building and anyone that pulled theirs down was quickly told to put it back up.

Wearing a mask again was making Coombes irritable and he could think of little else but getting out of there and removing it. He glanced at the clock on the wall. It was 9:02.

Judge Beesley was running late.

Sato turned toward Reyes and spoke with her voice lowered to prevent her conversation from being overheard by those around them. Coombes struggled to make out much of it and quickly gave up.

He thought of Billy Stratton.

The actor had gone to ground and he had no idea where to find him. Stratton seemed to have no friends to fall back on, no place to go. His sister appeared to have been his only friend, right up to the point where he'd thrown her out a window.

Coombes took out his notebook and looked for something to jump out at him, a thread he could start pulling on to find Stratton. His notes for the Walker case and the Stratton case were mixed together, it was a nightmare.

Minutes passed and nothing was popping.

314

He had been through the notebook several times before, doing the exact same thing, he practically had it memorized. The pages were curled, the edges discolored from the oils on his fingertips.

There was nothing new here, it was already in his head.

Having exhausted his notebook for new leads, Coombes switched to his cell and opened his photo app. He often used pictures as a form of note-taking since a lot of information could be captured quickly. Unlike a notebook, a camera recorded everything in front of it. Depending where you were in a case, you saw different things in the same pictures.

Nothing was missed in interpretation.

The app stored the pictures first to last, so it opened on the last photographs he'd taken of his trip to verify the limo driver's story. Pictures of his dashboard clock, odometer, and external temperature. If the driver had become a plausible suspect, repeated drives along the route would've been required to establish average journey times.

But it hadn't gone that way.

He swiped on, back to the beginning of the investigation, and the pictures of the movie posters in Booth's office. A memento of the director's career and of all the women he'd slept with through the years.

What a douchebag, he thought.

Coombes zoomed in on each poster, first comparing the similarity of the female leads, then thinking about the victims dumped into Franklin Lake.

He came to the poster for *Carnival of Delights* and found himself staring at Natalie Hahn. The graphic designer who made the poster had given her a glow-up. All hints of darkness or her trademark scowl had been removed. It had the effect of making her look the same as the women on the other posters, her individuality had been erased.

Coombes preferred her the way she was, not as an airbrushed plastic doll. Hahn was a singular person in a sea of fakes and wannabes. She probably wasn't the girl you took home to meet mom and dad, but that was ok.

His attention shifted to the text.

Introducing Natalie Hansen.

He swore to himself for not studying the picture before. *A stage name.* It had been right there in front of him from day one. Natalie Hansen. He said it to himself again in his head. It sounded reassuring, trustworthy.

Like the name of a kindergarten teacher, or a bank teller.

Coombes realized that he'd only been using Hahn's correct name all this time because he interviewed her before she was in the movie.

He thought of the untraceable names that he and Sato had identified.

The names of people with no driving license, criminal record, or filed missing person's report. They were untraceable, he knew, because they were not real people.

But he knew *one* database where he'd find them.

He opened the IMDb app on his cell and searched for the missing actors. Each had an entry; each showed a different birth name in the biographies.

He looked at the clock and saw the judge was now close to fifteen minutes late. It was unheard of; Beesley was a stickler for punctuality. The voices in the courtroom were getting louder with each passing minute. Anyone could get caught in traffic, he supposed, but not during a pandemic.

Half the traffic was gone.

Coombes returned to his cell phone and plugged the actors' birth names into Facebook. He got three hits, all still alive. He saw pictures of home baked bread, positive COVID test strips, and endless selfies. None of them were still working in the movie business, but they still liked the look of their own face.

The profile for Skipp Pedersen, aka Scott Peters, was set to friends-only. While this setting hid most of his content, Coombes could still see Pedersen's profile picture, which were always publicly visible. His timeline was filled with updated profile pictures, and the most recent picture still looked like Peters. It was good enough for him.

The only one still missing, was Natalie Hahn.

Assuming she was one of the lake victims, who were the others?

Logically, they would not have been killed prior to the burial of Strömberg for the simple reason that dumping a body in water was a lot easier than digging a hole and carried no risk of animal discovery of remains.

Once a killer refined their disposal method, they never went backward. That meant either Stratton changed to lake burials in the last five years, or the bodies in the water had nothing to do with him.

Were they looking at the work of two killers, both drawn to the open space of the park as an isolated yet convenient graveyard?

He glanced up to see the door to the courtroom's holding pen swing open and inmates start to file in wearing Department of Corrections jumpsuits. It signaled to Coombes that the judge was ready to come out.

He scanned the faces looking for Stephen Walker.

As a white man in his late forties, Walker should've been easy to spot, but Coombes didn't see him.

They were three deep in the pen and it took him a moment to double-check each of the faces. Twenty-two men stood in the cage, none of them Walker. He saw a deputy glance back and Coombes followed his look, expecting to see Walker being led in last.

Instead, he saw another deputy come into view through the doorway, shake his head, then disappear again. The door to the holding pen closed. Coombes leaned close to Sato, who was staring at her hands with a fixed expression.

"Grace. Walker's not here."

She looked up, daring herself to look at the men in the cage.

"Where is he?"

Before Coombes could respond, the judge's clerk approached.

"Mr. Reyes, Judge Beesley needs to see you in chambers immediately, if you'd like to follow me. Detectives, you can wait out in the hall, you won't be needed today."

He watched Reyes get to his feet, suitcase in one hand, legal pad and loose papers flapping in the other. His suit was crumpled and at least a size too big for him. Coombes shook his head. The prosecutor was a clown, he thought. The man looked like a kid that had been called to the principal's office in the middle of class.

After twenty feet Reyes glanced back at him with an accusatory stare.

You convinced me to take this case.

Whatever's about to happen to me, it's on you.

Coombes got to his feet and followed Sato out the courtroom into the cool hallway. The moment the doors closed behind them he felt her iron grip on his left forearm through his suit jacket, and the fear that drove it.

"What is this, Johnny? The judge can't kick the case, can he?"

"I don't see how. Our warrants are good."

"What the hell's going on?"

If the judge had a reason to throw the case out, he'd have to do it in open court, not in-camera. Walker wasn't present. That was the only fact they had. Coombes found himself thinking about the conversation he'd had with the man with the skull mask.

A twitch started under his left eye.

"I think he's dead."

"Is this a *joke* to you, Coombes?"

It wasn't, but her shrill voice held him back from saying so. She'd probably been wishing Walker dead from the get-go and didn't like to hear there was a possibility her wishes had come true.

They stood in awkward silence, waiting for Reyes to come out and fill them in. At least ten minutes passed before the prosecutor re-emerged.

His composure was back, the flustered schoolboy was gone.

"I'm sorry guys, it's over. At six-thirty this morning, Stephen Walker was removed from the protected custody unit and taken to be loaded onto the prison transport. Somewhere between the two points, he was assaulted by another inmate and slashed by a blade. A single cut to the neck. They blue-lighted him to hospital in San Pedro, but he was dead on arrival."

Sato gripped his arm again, this time for support.

It was possibly the first time she'd touched him in front of someone in their food chain, but for sure Reyes wasn't reading anything into it, she looked like she was about to be sick.

It confirmed his view that she'd wished Walker dead.

Reyes gave Sato a friendly smile.

"If it makes you feel better, Detective, we were never going to get him. Walker had made a secret deal with the feds. In exchange for testimony on the Brotherhood, the new case was to be dropped and his remaining sentence vacated. We were supposed to find out today. I guess his Nazi pals somehow got wind of it first and shut him down."

Somehow, Coombes thought. That was one way of putting it.

Another, would be that he'd warned them.

"I suppose this *assault* took place in security camera blind spot?"

Reyes looked up at him, the friendly smile melting away.

"Uh...that's right."

"And the whole thing happened so quickly that the sheriff's deputies didn't catch the man responsible, or even get an ID."

Reyes frowned, confused.

"I'm not sure what you're driving at, Coombes, they couldn't chase down the assailant while holding Walker's neck together. They literally had their hands full."

"You can't be this stupid, Reyes. I'm saying the *deputies* killed him because they are in the Aryan Brotherhood. There *was* no other prisoner."

The prosecutor stared at him open-mouthed. It appeared Reyes had no comebacks and there was no sign of any arriving soon. Coombes turned and guided Sato down the hallway like she was sleep-walking.

They were almost at the elevator when Sato finally spoke.

"I knew he'd get out of it, Johnny. I *knew*."

"Yeah, well. This wasn't exactly what he had in mind."

Sato shot him a dirty look so he decided not to tell her it was his fault Walker was dead, even if it was the best result they could've hoped for under the circumstances.

Reyes was right about one thing: it *did* make him feel better knowing that the feds hadn't managed to give Walker a get-out-of-jail-free pass and a cushy witness protection life funded by the American taxpayer.

52

ANTHONY DE LUCA'S HOUSE on Willow Glen Road sat high in the Hollywood Hills off Laurel Canyon Boulevard. The road, and everything around it, was covered in a dry dust and the eucalyptus trees in front of the property looked like they hadn't seen a drop of rain all year. The temperature gauge in Coombes' dashboard said it was 114 degrees outside.

He saw De Luca's vehicle, a blood-red Lincoln Navigator with a *Son of a Gun* sticker on the fender.

Apart from the color, the Navigator was identical to Booth's. Doubtless leased through the production company and written off as a tax deduction, just like the limo service. It always seemed to Coombes that many of the nice things in life were only affordable to the rich, who found ways to get them for nothing.

Coombes killed the engine and stepped out of the Dodge.

He felt the heat hit him immediately, it was like opening an oven door. There was a slight breeze but it offered no respite, only a lower cook time.

Sato looked at him across the hood.

"Have you been here before?"

It was the first thing she'd said to him since the courthouse.

"Once, during the original investigation."

"With Eddie Willard?"

"Yes."

Sato gave a small nod, probably approving of the way his face fell at the mention of Willard's name. She needed to be reassured of his humanity, because he didn't care about Stephen Walker, or the Nazi he'd killed.

De Luca opened the door wearing a loosely tied purple robe, his hair wild and unbrushed. His eyelids were heavy from lack of sleep, seemingly only opening at the bottom. His gaze went to Coombes, then in surprise to Sato, whom he'd never met.

"This is Detective Sato."

"What can I do for you, detectives?"

"We have some follow-up questions that will only take a couple of minutes. We know this must be a difficult time for you."

De Luca waved them inside, a look of indifference on his face.

The interior had a cobblestone floor and rough untreated stone walls. In the middle of the space was a full-size orange tree which rose up out of the floor to the glass roof.

This was where the *Fallen Idol* wrap party had taken place. Where Natalie Hahn had come uninvited looking for Booth, and where she later claimed to see Dakota Lawrence and De Luca in a semi-compromising position.

In his mind, the location had fundamentally changed for one simple reason. He now knew that the killer had been here.

Everything he saw, Stratton had seen.

It was a crucial point in the investigation, knowing both a killer's true identity, and visiting locations where they had been. He had never failed to close a case after crossing both milestones. The investigation was now a manhunt.

He stood looking at the tree, and at the oranges on it.

"When I extended the property, I kept the tree. Beautiful, isn't it?"

"It is," Coombes said. "Are the fruit edible?"

"Yes. Please help yourself, I can never get through them all."

Coombes reached up and picked one off.

Taking the orange felt like accepting a bribe. The fact that De Luca was no longer a suspect didn't make the feeling go away. It was just a fruit, but he should've declined it, he thought. It was too late now, he'd picked it.

They walked to the right through a stone arch into a narrow hallway, then, after about twenty feet, turned again into a huge room that De Luca used for entertaining. A grand piano dominated the top of the room with its top open and the keys exposed.

There were clusters of chairs and tables, enough for thirty plus people to relax in during a party. De Luca walked to a set of chairs next to a window that faced Coombes' Dodge and indicated with his hand for them to sit.

They sat and De Luca sat opposite on a three-seater. Coombes put the orange on the table and took out his notebook. He started with an easy one.

"What do you remember about Robbie Ellis?"

"Robbie? Not much. Older than my usual type and more muscular. He spoke softly so I had to lean close to hear. I liked that; it made our conversation feel intimate."

"All right. What did you talk about?"

De Luca shrugged, a heavy frown creasing his face.

"Movies of course, he was looking for work. We talked about roles he'd played before. He was interested in Josh and was disappointed that he hadn't come to the party. I remember he had a lot of questions about Josh's private life, who he was dating. Obviously, he was into Josh and didn't realize he was straight."

That wasn't Coombes' takeaway, but he ignored it.

"And you told him about Dakota?"

"Sure. Everyone knew, it wasn't a secret."

It was likely this conversation had doomed Lawrence, but that wasn't on De Luca. He wasn't to know what was to come. If Stratton hadn't got the information from him, he would've asked someone else at the party.

"You never used him in a movie, did you?"

"No. I think he realized he was wasting his time, you know? He gave off the wrong vibe for our kind of movies. Josh gave me a lot of latitude, but final casting was his call. I knew he would never agree to cast Ellis."

"What vibe did he gave off?"

De Luca looked embarrassed.

"Like a gangster. If you check IMDb, you'll see the roles he gets, he's typecast. Assassin, nightclub security, hired goon number 4, you get the idea. He was a gym guy, all muscles."

Coombes wrote this down, then flipped back to his notes from their last interview and quickly skimmed it for a place to start.

"You said before you had to stop to buy gas."

De Luca's confusion intensified.

"*Right.*"

"I realized later that you'd mentioned that during our first interview six years ago, and I wondered why it stuck with you."

"I always go to my cabin after a wrap party, so I check beforehand that there's enough gas to get there and back. I had a Range Rover at the time. It didn't get great mileage, but you get to know your vehicle, right? How much is left, how far it will go. But the next day, the gas warning light came on almost immediately."

"Maybe you over-estimated your tank?"

"I've driven there for a decade. I never misjudged it before."

And you didn't this time, Coombes thought.

The answer had been right there in front of him and he'd missed it. Because he'd missed it, Willard was dead, Booth was dead.

"The night before; how did things go with you and Ellis?"

"Nothing happened. We had a lot to drink at the party, I barely remember the drive. I must've passed out, because when I woke up the whole night had passed and it was already after midday. I was still dressed and I had the worst hangover of my life."

And there it was.

"Why didn't you mention this to me before?"

"Because I obviously shouldn't have been driving at all. I have two previous DUI charges. If I owned up to a third, I thought I'd be looking at prison time. Three strikes."

"We have to *catch* you and get a record of your inebriation. Evidence. If we put people away every time they confessed, prisoners would be packed like sardines in the cells with no air left to breathe."

"Whatever. It changed nothing, so I missed it out."

Anger flared in Coombes' chest.

"Let me *tell* you what it changes, De Luca. Ellis drugged you. While you were blacked-out, he drove your SUV back to L.A., murdered Dakota Lawrence and posed her body at the studio lot before returning to Big Bear. *That's* why you ran out of gas."

"No!"

"*Yes.* He wasn't your alibi, you were his."

De Luca went pale and his chin began to wobble, then glanced at Sato, clearly hoping she'd give some sign it was all a joke.

"Why would he...do that to Dakota?"

Coombes said nothing and waited for the penny to drop. The truth hit De Luca hard and he had to steady himself with his hands on his knees.

"You can't blame me for that! We were just having a conversation."

"I *don't* blame you. This guy used you. I have no doubt that he would've done what he did no matter what. Someone else would've told him about Dakota. Like you said, everyone knew. As for a reason, I can't tell you that. Some people are broken, there is no why."

"I don't suppose Ellis said anything to you that might help us find him? Friends in L.A., relatives, somewhere he might go?"

De Luca shook his head, his thoughts elsewhere.

"That motherfucker killed Josh, didn't he? No way he took his own life."

"Certainly looks that way, Mr. De Luca."

A silence opened up and Sato took that as a changeover point.

"What happened to that Range Rover you had back then?"

De Luca shrugged.

"It was six years ago. The lease came to an end so I changed it. Next was a BMW 7 Series. I got out of that lease early. Once you get used to an SUV, you can't go back. Josh and I went for the Navigator. Josh thought it was funny, you know, him driving a Lincoln."

"How much longer did you have the Range Rover before you changed it?"

He knew she was thinking about broken branches in Franklin Canyon Park and the burial of Adrienne Strömberg. It seemed unlikely to him that Stratton would steal the Range Rover again to dispose of a second body, but he said nothing.

"Probably another year, I'd have to check my records."

Sato nodded and made a show of writing this in her notebook.

"I'm new to this investigation, Mr. De Luca, so I apologize if this has been covered before. Am I correct in saying that you never met Robbie Ellis again after that night?"

"Yes. There was no spark between us and therefore nothing more to pursue. If what you say is true and he used me to kill Dakota why would he have met me again?"

"Just procedure, Mr. De Luca."

Coombes almost smiled at that; she was learning all his bullshit.

"I'm curious why you feel the need to drive all the way to Big Bear Lake to relax when you have such a fantastic home here. Laurel Canyon isn't exactly South Central, it's remote, private. Surely the simplest thing would be to stay here? What do you need the cabin for?"

It was a question that Coombes had never considered and he kicked himself for it. De Luca's face twisted awkwardly and he dropped his gaze to the orange on the table.

"We have *associates* that we use to fund our movies, you understand? These people are very serious. The cabin is owned through a shell corporation that can't be traced to me. I feel safe there because these associates don't know about it."

"They don't know you're a homosexual?"

A pint of blood appeared to drop out of De Luca's face.

"I hate that word! I'm just me. This is who I've always been, I don't want this *label* like I'm sub-human. We're all different, like different things. I just want to be left alone."

Sato nodded to him, unfazed, indicating that she was done.

Coombes wanted to revisit something De Luca said before.

"Why did Josh think it was funny...him having a Lincoln?"

"Because of his family connection. His great grand uncle I think it was."

"You're saying Joshua Booth was related to John Wilkes Booth?"

"That's what I'm saying."

Coombes didn't buy it. Booth was a storyteller, an entertainer. He had to be the center of attention at all times and saying a predecessor killed a president probably achieved that.

He looked around the room, as if taking it in for the first time.

A lot of blacks and browns. Leather furniture with oversized studs and dark wood. Chrome details. The room was depressing, he thought. Like some kind of Vegas strip club. De Luca could have anything he wanted and *this* is what he chose.

"That painting in your office...the Bugsy. Where'd you get that?"

"It appeared one day on my doorstep, no sender's name. Later, I worked out it was from Josh because he has a painting of Orson. Same artist, same size. Dark, moody, retro. It was perfect, see? The gangster and the director. He was having fun."

De Luca crossed his legs and his robe fell open, exposing his bare left leg to his upper-thigh. The flesh was as white as any corpse Coombes had seen.

De Luca made no move to cover himself so Coombes angled his body toward Sato so he didn't have to look at it.

"You happen to know the name of the artist?"

"Amanda Watts. She's got a studio in Venice. I was impressed with the Bugsy so I commissioned her to do one of Capone. You passed it in the hall."

"Josh never said anything about it?"

"Not a word."

"That didn't strike you as unusual?"

"I guess a little, but that's just who he was."

De Luca didn't elaborate any further. Remembering Booth and using the past tense had caused him to shut down.

Coombes put his notebook away and stood up.

Something about the paintings bothered him. He saw no reason why Booth would give his friend a painting then not want to talk about it. De Luca got to his feet.

"Don't forget your orange."

Coombes picked it up.

It had a pleasant weight in his hand, like a baseball.

They walked into the hallway and paused to look at the painting of Capone. He hadn't noticed it on the way in, because the opposite wall was glazed and he'd naturally turned his head to look into the yard which had an outdoor swimming pool and a fire pit barbecue.

The three of them stood in front of the painting.

Capone looked utterly terrifying.

"What happens now with *Son of a Gun*?"

"Josh could write a screenplay in two months, but it took him eight to make a movie. As a result, we have thirty-odd screenplays ready to go when the virus lets us get back to work. Before the shutdown, we planned to double production with Fran directing, but that plan hit the bricks along with everything else. I'll give her a chance, see what she can do."

Something clicked into place and he turned to De Luca.

"Fran runs *Son of a Gun* doesn't she?"

"That's right. Josh and Fran were the heart and soul of the company, I was just the money. He was the talent, she was the brains. She's been by his side since day one, she knows how everything works."

He thought of Knudsen. She was strong, physically and emotionally.

"She'll do great," Coombes said.

They walked outside, the producer tagging awkwardly along.

The dead skunk smell of cooked brains was now gone from the hood of his car, baked out of existence by the relentless sun. Coombes got into the Dodge and started the engine, then thought of something and powered the window down.

De Luca was still standing there.

"It might be a good idea for you to get out of town for a while. *Not* the cabin. Somewhere Ellis doesn't know about. If he's tying off loose ends, you could be next."

"I can't. I have to stay for Josh's funeral."

"Then go to a hotel. I'll call you as soon as we make an arrest."

"Very well, Detective."

53

THEY DROVE IN SILENCE down Laurel Canyon toward Hollywood, the air between them dead. Coombes wondered how things might have gone had Booth attended his own wrap party and come face-to-face with Stratton. Would the actor have remained in the shadows, or would he have tried to kill Booth in front of 40-odd party-goers?

The latter seemed unlikely.

Since his release from prison, Stratton had poured his energy into acting, all to get close to a man that he believed had killed his sister. Someone who had gone to that effort would likely already know that Booth never went to any of his own wrap parties.

Stratton wanted what happened to him, to happen to Booth.

To feel the loss of a loved one, then to be blamed for it.

Stratton had gone to the party to find out who Booth was dating, then, within hours, had killed that person and set out her body close to where Booth worked.

"What now?" Sato said.

"Venice."

"You want to speak to the painter. Why?"

"A painting is a very personal gift. I don't see Booth having one created for De Luca then just dropping it at his door and running off like a school kid. That makes literally no sense."

"That's not why we're going, is it?"

Coombes sighed.

Sometimes he preferred working on his own, not having to explain his gut instinct. To having to show his work before it was ready, his thoughts half-formed.

"Do you know what Bugsy Siegel and Orson Welles had in common?"

"Tell me."

"Both men were suspects in the Black Dahlia case."

"Orson Welles, the director, was a suspect for Dahlia?"

"The very same. I won't be offended if you Google it. I'm not saying that means much, everyone with a grudge was calling in tips about people they didn't like. It was open season and those cops had nothing."

"All right, but what's Dahlia got to do with anything?"

"Booth was fascinated by the case; he once told a reporter that he'd worked out who was responsible. After Dakota was murdered, the *Times* re-published his bar room conversation. It didn't look good."

Sato thought for a moment, her head tilted toward him.

"You think Stratton gives both men a painting, knowing each will think the other gave it to him and that this frames Booth?"

Sato made it sound like a joke.

Because it *was* a joke.

Was Stratton relying on a cop making the same connection he had? The fact that Booth had recently taken his painting down suggested he had become suspicious about the painting's origin. It was the thinnest lead he'd ever pursued and he wondered if he was any different to the detectives that had interviewed Orson Welles.

"Actually," Coombes said, "frame Booth *and* De Luca. Booth believed two people were responsible for Dahlia, like the Hillside Stranglers. Detectives were looking for one person, so Elizabeth Short's real killers fell through the net. Put the two together and suddenly it looks like maybe Booth's interest is more than just an intellectual exercise."

"You're high, Coombes. Fifty bucks says the artist worked for Booth."

Coombes said nothing.

They were driving through West Hollywood now. The route down Fairfax Avenue would take him a couple of minutes' drive from his former home. It was the shortest route, but he wondered if he'd subconsciously chosen it due to a dormant homing signal, triggered by his ex-wife's call the night before.

Julie had betrayed him, broken his heart.

To his surprise, he felt no ill-feelings toward her. He hadn't been emotionally available to her anymore. What happened was as much his fault as hers.

Sato was talking to him and probably had been for a while.

Not listening, that had been his first misstep with Julie.

"Here's my point, Johnny. If Willard goes there and does this *midnight knock*, it's because he knew something, right? He didn't go all the way to Riverside at ass o'clock and pound on this guy's door because he was verifying an alibi for you."

"Right."

"Well? What did he have that you didn't?"

"I gave him the final piece of the puzzle and he didn't tell me what it meant because he wanted to be the one to get justice for Dakota."

"I realize that, Coombes. I'm asking how you think he did it."

He thought about it as he made the turn onto Venice Boulevard.

"Willard followed De Luca for a long time, like six or eight months. I assume he never once witnessed De Luca with a woman but often did with young men. Maybe he saw something that looked like intimacy. It wouldn't take much for him to get the picture.

"Scott Peters backed his friend's story about De Luca and Lawrence hooking up at the party but Willard might've figured we got it backwards. That Natalie Hahn created the story to give *Peters* an alibi. So Willard follows *him* around, trying to build a case. Only, Peters sees the tail, imagines him as a mob hitman and disappears himself."

"Then you give Willard the name and address of the man he's after."

Coombes nodded. "Exactly."

Sato considered it, checking the angles in her head.

He didn't need to wait for her answer. It fitted; he knew it did.

"It's funny. Eddie solved this using a false breadcrumb trail."

"What do you mean?" Sato said.

"He suspected De Luca, it wasn't him. He pivots to Peters, based on a lie. Neither Peters or Lawrence was at the party. Then he gets the right person because I give him the answer. He *knows* it's right, because Stratton fitted the person his mind had created. Without realizing it, Willard solved this using behavioral analysis. He profiled a ghost."

"He got lucky before he got unlucky, that's what I think. Who knows how many doors he's knocked on before now."

Coombes supposed her skepticism was justified. She'd only seen Willard once, walking half-cut across a street wearing nothing but boxer shorts. The old detective might've been living the dream, but it didn't inspire a lot of confidence in his abilities as a cop.

"How about you find out where Watts lives?"

"Right," Sato said, opening her tablet.

The artist's front door was an antique with stained glass panels set in wood, with thin lines of lead holding the glass together. Coombes imagined Stratton cutting the lead out then reaching inside to turn the latch.

Difficulty level: zero.

Amanda Watts opened the door. She was a black woman in her early thirties with an athletic frame and an easy smile.

"Cheese it, it's the cops!"

He had that kind of face, he supposed.

"Detectives Coombes and Sato. Can we come in?"

"It's that bitch next door, isn't it? Look, I need my music when I work, it helps me concentrate. She's deaf as a post anyway, what difference does it make to her?"

"Ma'am. This isn't a noise complaint, we're homicide detectives."

That hit her pause button.

Watts led them back through the property, up a narrow set of stairs toward a kitchen with a large window that overlooked the street. The air was hot and filled with paint fumes.

"Sorry about the heat, the AC's busted. Who's the stiff?"

Coombes ignored that and took out his notebook. He'd just met the artist, but already he'd had enough. Some people were like that.

"Several years ago, you were commissioned to produce two paintings for a client and we're hoping you still have some details that can help us. The paintings were of-"

"Bugsy and Orson."

He glanced up from his page, surprised.

"What makes you say that?"

"I'm right though, yes?"

"Yes."

"Client was real particular. He had photographs for me to work from. He said, *like that, but four foot square and dark like a motherfucker*. His words, not mine. It was new for me to have so little creative input, but also liberating to get such a clear idea what a client wanted."

Coombes' heart sank. She had to be talking about Booth.

"You think you'd be able to identify this guy?"

"I remember every face I've seen. Kind of goes with the territory."

He nodded, then brought up De Luca's photograph on Sato's tablet.

"Not him, although he is a client-"

Coombes changed to a picture of Booth. Her face dropped.

"Joshua Booth." She looked up from the screen. "Is he why you're here? I can't believe he's dead, such a great director. They say on TV he killed himself, I *knew* that was bull."

"Miss Watts. Did he order the paintings?"

"Are you *kidding* me? If Joshua Booth bought one of my paintings, I would've put it on my website. I could've jacked my prices by a factor of ten."

Coombes hadn't considered that. Lastly, he brought up a studio headshot of Stratton. He saw his answer in Watts' face before she could say a word.

"That's the guy! God, even a picture of him scares me."

"All right," Coombes said. "We're going to need any details you have for him. Name, address, cell number, payment details, everything."

Watts grabbed a ledger and began to leaf through it. Even upside-down he could see her handwriting was better than his, it looped and flowed artfully.

"No name or number, just an address to send them. That's how I knew you were here about that order, it seemed hinky from the get-go."

"He paid cash?" Sato asked.

"About a third of my clients do. Art can be a way to avoid tax."

"Why pay cash and conceal his name if he gave his address?"

"Because it's not a residence, it's a mailbox center. I drove the paintings there to save on courier costs. I expected to deliver to a home and instead find a store. I wasn't happy giving them my paintings, but what else could I do? It was the right address."

"There was no box number?"

"No, the number is formatted to look like an apartment number. I wanted to see where my paintings would *live*, you know? Instead, I see rolls of packing tape and shipping boxes."

"We'll need that address."

"Sure."

Watts copied the details onto a sticky note and passed it to him.

"You think this guy killed Joshua Booth, don't you?"

Normally he would evade such a question, but he figured Watts needed to wake up to the danger she was in. If he thought to come here, so would Stratton.

"That's right."

"He gave my paintings to Booth, didn't he?"

"Just the Orson."

Watts nodded like she understood who had the second painting.

They were done here. Coombes put away his notebook and walked over to the large window. The artist had several panels open in an attempt to chase the heat out of her apartment. Instead, it felt like more hot air was coming in the openings.

"Do you think he liked it? My painting?"

Amanda Watts was standing next to him.

"I guess so, he hung it on his wall."

To his surprise, she began to cry for Booth, a man she'd never met. The show of emotion made him uncomfortable, so he looked away, through the glass. He could see both sides of the street for some distance in each direction.

"I don't suppose you happened to look out your window that day and see what our man was driving did you?"

Watts sniffed and nodded.

"An SUV. Silver. I don't know the make. European, I think. It was pretty banged up. Marks on the doors, on the roof. Like that. Seemed odd to lay out all that money on the paintings and to be running around in an old car. Not that I was complaining."

"Describe the marks on the roof," he said.

"I don't know. It was like three scratches that went from the back toward the front. Maybe two feet long? They were *deep*, it wasn't someone in a parking lot with their keys."

He glanced at Sato and saw her nod.

From reversing under a tree.

54

THE ADDRESS AMANDA WATTS gave them was on Beachwood Drive on the other side of the 101, between the Hollywood Reservoir and Griffith Park. Which was hell and gone from Venice where the artist lived. Coombes sighed inwardly, and began to drive while Sato punched the address into the Dodge's GPS unit. She said nothing about the value in running down a lead that was years-cold. Stratton wasn't going to be at the other end of this rainbow and they both knew it.

Other partners he'd had in the past, Eddie Willard included, would've spent the whole trip telling him he was making a mistake. That they were wasting time. Telling him, not just like it was something he didn't already know, but like they were getting some kind of pleasure from it.

He got none of that from Grace Sato.

The journey took a modest thirty-eight minutes, despite the fact that it was approaching one in the afternoon. Coombes parked up in one of the slots out front and killed the engine.

To his relief, the store wasn't closed due to COVID like so many others.

Inside, a young man in his mid-twenties stood behind the counter wearing a tight pink shirt. He had a carefully manicured beard and hair pulled up on top of his head in a top knot.

The store was small with no other customers.

Coombes laid out what he wanted, his voice soft and conspiratorial. The soft sell. Telling the man they were in a jam and he was the only person that could help. Pink Shirt smiled and Coombes knew what he was going to say before it left his mouth.

"I can't give out client details without a warrant, sorry."

Coombes had imagined the conversation taking this turn during the drive. He didn't have time to get the warrant. Most likely, the age of the information would reduce the chances of a judge signing off on a warrant in the first place. Coombes held up one finger.

"Just a moment."

He opened his tablet and found a copy of the image that haunted his dreams: Dakota Lawrence's last public appearance, dumped on a studio lot like garbage. He avoided looking directly at the photograph and instead selected it while focusing on the images around it.

"The client you're protecting did this."

Coombes tilted the screen toward the other man who looked down as the tablet rotated the image to face the other way up.

"Oh, sweet Jesus!"

Pink Shirt put his hands on the the counter to steady himself.

Coombes made his voice harder.

"You ask me for a warrant. I assume that means you're a switched-on guy. You want to be on the right side of history, correct? I'm a cop, which makes me a fascist puppet. I'm not offended. I put my life on the line every day so you can ask for a warrant. It's your right."

Coombes leaned in closer.

"Now, this customer of yours, he's a serial killer. Nine people that we know of so far, including an unborn child. I ask you, does helping this guy put you on the right side, or the wrong side of history?"

The man swallowed.

It looked like a billiard ball moving up and down in a sock.

"I guess...I could take a look at our records."

Coombes closed the case on his iPad and took out his notebook.

"Perfect."

The counterman walked to a computer terminal and punched in the number the artist had given them for Stratton. Coombes moved with him so that he could see the screen.

"Okay," Pink Shirt said. "It's not a mailbox, it's a re-direct. The account is live and paid on the sixteenth of every month from a Wells Fargo bank account."

"How about you print that screen and we let you get on with business?"

The man was silent as he thought about a way to say no.

Coombes laid his hand flat on top of his tablet, fingers spread out, like the contents within it were under pressure and the terrible picture might come into view again. A second later, the silence ended as a printer began to spit out the information. Thirty seconds after that, they were inside the Dodge with the AC on.

Nobody wanted to see that picture twice.

Or even once.

Judging by the dates, the account was established not long before the start of Stratton's sentence at Lompoc, which suggested its initial purpose was to conceal his incarceration. After he got out and re-created himself as Robbie Ellis, Stratton would've realized that he could use the same address for both names since it was controlled by a number, not a name.

The forwarding address was on Creston Drive, which was close enough that he could see it on the car's GPS without zooming out the map.

Coombes put the Dodge in reverse and backed out of the parking space. His jaw was clenched and he began to think about how Stratton would react when they showed up.

"He's not going to be there, Johnny. This address pre-dates his sentencing. Maybe he visits to pick up mail, but he isn't going to be *living* there."

Coombes glanced at her, disappointed.

Maybe she *was* like his other partners after all.

"Everything about this guy is new or fake, but this address has been with him for over a decade. It's *real*. It's not changed. That tells me it's a family home. He thinks we don't have his real name, so where better to hide out than a place he belongs?"

Sato's face grew red. "I missed that."

"Grace, I should've worked this out years ago. Eight more people are dead because I didn't. If you're *embarrassed*, just imagine how I feel."

She reached across and lay her hand on his leg.

"That's just it, Johnny. I *don't* have to imagine."

Coombes sighed.

He'd never met Sarah Ryan. It seemed likely that the man who killed her former partner was the same waste of skin he'd shot through the forehead and given the front of their Dodge a new fragrance.

Why, then, was his lack of remorse eating away at her?

Her hand was still on his leg.

In the moment, she'd forgotten they were *hitting pause*.

Because he hadn't programmed the house number into the GPS it took him nearly ten minutes to locate the right address on the narrow, twisting street. The address was two houses from the point where Creston Drive came to a dead end.

Coombes pulled to the side of the road, the engine still running.

Two vehicles were parked outside Stratton's mail drop address.

The first was a blue Mitsubishi Mirage, a subcompact about the same size as Knudsen's Mini; the second, was a silver Audi Q7. Although he couldn't see any dents or scratches from where he sat, it was a match for the vehicle Amanda Watts had described.

"That has to be the SUV we want," Sato whispered.

"Agreed. Particularly since the blue car is Stratton's registered vehicle."

"Shit, Coombes. When you're right, you're right."

Coombes said nothing, his thoughts fixed on Eddie Willard's bullet-ridden body. It was a long time since he'd faced a heavily-armed opponent so he was happy to watch the property, thinking about the best way forward.

Following policy, there was only one move: call for backup, surround the property, and let weight of numbers and lack of obvious escape routes force the suspect to accept his fate.

The Audi's turn signals flashed and the tailgate powered open.

They had arrived just in time, Stratton was leaving.

Coombes unholstered his Glock and drew back the slide, then held it against his thigh, ready to go. He thought of the different ways a showdown with Stratton might go down and how in each scenario he would gain the upper hand.

All of the futures he imagined ended with him shooting Stratton.

Sato seemed to read his thoughts.

"We're here to arrest him, Johnny. I want you to say it."

Coombes didn't look at her, his eyes were pinned on the Audi.

"It takes two to tango, Grace, you know that."

Just then, Stratton walked out onto the street carrying two canvas bags which he loaded into the back of the SUV. He was wearing running shoes, cargo shorts, and a faded white T-shirt with the name of a high-end gym written on it.

Even from fifty feet back, Coombes could tell that Stratton was enormous. Like he'd spent the pandemic taking steroids, pumping iron, and eating chicken and raw eggs. The stats on his profile listed his weight at one eighty, but Coombes thought Stratton was now more like two fifteen, maybe even two twenty-five.

The actor turned and went back inside the property, leaving the Audi's tailgate open. He wasn't finished loading. At no point had Stratton lifted his head to look around. He felt safe here. Most likely, he'd spent a lot of his childhood here.

Stratton believed his false identity would hold.

"John, I want you to know something. If you kill him, you and me are done. I don't care what he does to provoke you, we're better than that. I won't be with a killer."

Coombes looked at her.

By her definition, he'd been a killer as long as she'd known him. Now, she was sensitized to it and was drawing a line in the sand. All without knowing about his twelve confirmed kills in Afghanistan before he joined the LAPD.

Sato wanted him to say something, to agree to her terms.

He said nothing, and instead turned back to the Audi.

Maybe he *was* a killer, but he was no liar.

A minute passed, then another. Silence like the Pacific surrounded them, endless and untouchable. Finally, Stratton reappeared. The actor now wore sunglasses and a baseball cap with the brim pulled low. In his right hand, he held a black plastic case that Coombes knew would contain a partially disassembled Heckler & Koch MP7.

Coombes smiled.

What an asshole, keeping a gun that killed a cop.

Stratton lifted the case into the back of the Audi and took a moment to position it, perhaps concealing the MP7 beneath the canvas bags.

The tailgate powered smoothly closed and their eyes connected.

They'd been made, Stratton was looking right at him.

He slammed the Dodge into gear and floored the throttle, directing the Charger at the front of the Audi, blocking its escape on the dead-end road.

Stratton turned and ran.

55

COOMBES BRAKED HARD, THE Dodge stopping inches from the fender of the German SUV, then swung the door open and stepped out, gun raised. Stratton had disappeared behind the bulky Audi. He stepped around the partial shield of the Charger's door and made his way forward in a wide arc around the SUV. He saw Stratton running toward the end of the road.

Coombes shouted at him.

"*LAPD! Freeze!*"

The actor kept going, no hesitation. Coombes turned to Sato.

"Get some uniforms up here. I want someone babysitting this car at all times until a judge signs a search warrant. Nobody opens these doors; nobody drives it away. And see if you can get an airship to keep track of this asshole."

"You got it, Johnny."

He ran after Stratton, who was using a neighbor's wall to climb up and around a chain-link fence that was fastened across a dusty earth track. The street wasn't the dead-end he had supposed. The quickness of the maneuver told him that Stratton had done it many times before and had perhaps counted on it as a last-ditch escape route.

Coombes put his Glock back in the holster, copied the fence maneuver and dropped down on the other side. The ground rose up to a summit with a round concrete structure. As he crested the rise, he saw Stratton duck under a cut section of fence and charge off down the slope beyond.

The actor was rapidly leaving him behind.

It was a fact that people who were running for their life had an advantage no amount of training could ever equal. There would be no point telling him to freeze again, it was clear what the result would be.

Coombes reached the second fence and ducked under the cut section.

Fresh cuts.

Stratton had planned for this, he was certain.

The hillside dropped steeply away beneath his feet and he found himself running faster and faster in an attempt to stay upright, his eyes shifting between Stratton and the terrain in front of him. He made it about half-way down the hill before gravity caught up with him and he fell onto the hard soil and rolled several times.

He cursed his dress shoes, which had no tread at all.

Coombes got back on his feet and continued his descent.

In front of him, the Hollywood Reservoir sparkled like diamonds under the early afternoon sun. Way over to the left, almost out of sight, he saw Stratton headed to the Mulholland Dam.

Like Franklin Canyon Park, this was a place Coombes had run on numerous occasions. Again, he wondered if their paths had crossed before; running past one another, lost in the moment. A small nod of the head to a fellow traveler as they passed.

He could see it clearly, like it had happened.

When he reached the trailhead, Coombes looked down Weidlake Drive. It was clear. His height and the elevation meant he could see a good stretch of the road, even after it folded back on itself. He ran onto the Mulholland Dam and saw Stratton immediately. He was about a third of the way across, with a lead that was close to a minute's run.

Despite the stay-at-home order, there were close to a dozen tourists on the dam, taking photographs of the distant Hollywood Sign, the reservoir, and of their own stupid faces. As he ran past, several of them grinned, like whatever was happening was some kind of joke.

At the end of the dam, Stratton turned downhill and disappeared behind the guard wall. Losing sight of a suspect was a depressing moment in any chase, and time seemed to elongate as ran on with no visual on Stratton.

Coombes took the same route and found himself on an unpaved track.

Still no sign of Stratton. Coombes pressed on.

The huge wall of the dam towered above him on the left; to his right were trees, shrubs, and vines. Although Stratton was nowhere to be seen, he'd left a trail in the dust and stones that was hard to miss. Coombes followed the trail, eyes darting between the shoe marks and the track ahead of him.

After a short distance, the marks veered off into the trees.

A good spot for an ambush, he thought.

He drew his Glock and followed.

Moving slower now, more carefully.

Several minutes had passed since he'd last seen Stratton. A part of his brain seemed to have dedicated itself to counting the minutes. He told himself that it wasn't like a chase on city streets where if you lost someone for five minutes they were gone forever.

Stratton was simply hidden from view.

After pushing through branches and vines, he found himself on a twisting path through the trees. The ground was uneven with a steep downhill slope, but it was a path at least, and he could now see up to fifteen feet ahead of him.

Coombes increased his speed.

In darkness, Stratton might have attempted to hide and double-back but in full daylight his best option was to get as far away as possible. That meant taking the same path he was on, a path heading south toward Hollywood.

He thought about the location.

Billy Stratton had grown up nearby. It was fair to assume that he had been here before. Perhaps he had come here with his friends to drink alcohol, get high, or get laid.

In movies, criminals always made a run for Mexico or Canada, but in real life, most fugitives were arrested a matter of miles from their home. People fell back on what they knew best; either believing this gave them an advantage, or from a subconscious desire to re-visit parts of their childhood one last time before they were caught.

The trees thinned out and he finally saw Stratton again, his head moving from side-to-side as he ran. His early lead had fallen away to no more than fifty yards. As Coombes broke through the tree line into open scrubland, he saw Stratton run along the back of a property, trying to find a cut into the road below. Coombes shouted at him.

"Stratton!"

The other man glanced back, then disappeared into some bushes. Coombes was able to take a more economical line, cutting the actor's lead in half. A set of steps cut into the hill that led down onto the street.

Coombes pushed through the foliage and saw Stratton standing in the middle of the road, hands on his knees. His face was scarlet, his massive shoulders visibly heaving as he struggled to catch his breath.

Stratton had nothing left, he'd sacrificed duration for speed. Coombes, in his dress shoes, hadn't had that option and had been forced to take it slower.

The actor looked around desperately for a place to go.

"It's over, Stratton. I can shoot you from here. Right between the eyes."

He was less than forty feet away and getting closer.

About the distance he'd taken out the Nazi. Coombes imagined the pink mist that would surround Stratton's head and decided he could live with it. He was discovering that there was a lot he could live with these days.

"You can't shoot me, you're a cop!"

It was the second-funniest thing Coombes had heard all week, and his sides pinched as he laughed. Stratton's eyes bugged as panic began to take hold. Coombes looked one way, then the other. The street was empty.

"I tell you what," Coombes said. "Run toward me."

"*What?*"

"Run at me as fast as you can. I'll make it quick."

A torrent of abuse flowed from Stratton's mouth.

"Last chance, Stratton. Now or never."

"*Never.*"

Coombes resisted the urge to smile.

"All right. Turn around."

Stratton didn't move, didn't speak.

"There are two ways off this street, you know what they are."

Stratton sighed and turned away from him. Coombes came forward and stopped ten feet back, gun aimed at Stratton's head. The closer he got, the more muscular the actor appeared.

"Down on your knees."

Stratton got down. One knee, then the other. His head twitched from side to side, looking for a way out to the very end. This was the pinch point, and he wished Sato was with him.

"Interlace your fingers behind your head."

Stratton did so and Coombes stepped forward.

To his right, a door slammed shut. Coombes' eyes went to the sound.

A middle-aged woman was coming down the path of the house next to him with two young boys. The woman stared up, open-mouthed, at an approaching helicopter.

He looked back at Stratton just as the other man smacked the Glock out his hand, sending it spinning away onto the road behind him. Stratton launched himself at him and sent a fist like a locomotive into Coombes' stomach.

The punch sent him backward, but Stratton kept coming, sending blow after blow to his head. Coombes fought to maintain his balance, but the momentum continued to push him backward and his legs went from underneath him and he went down on the asphalt.

Rather than kick him on the ground, Stratton jumped on top of him, knees on either side of his chest, and began to work on his face. Coombes could taste blood.

Stratton had caught him half-asleep, but he was awake now.

Billy Stratton was laughing. He wouldn't have recognized the sound he was hearing as laughter; it was like a sound from a slaughterhouse. His face was right in front of his, mouth in a bizarre rictus, eyes wild.

This is what Dakota Lawrence had seen. What she'd heard.

The thought sent a burst of anger and energy through him.

Coombes whipped his head forward into Stratton's nose.

He heard the crunch of cartilage against his forehead, the mashing squash of flesh, and the liquid squelch of blood. The sounds seemed separate, distinct, though logically they had to have happened at the same moment.

Stratton's high-pitched laugh became a deep-chested howl of pain and he rolled off Coombes, blood pulsing thickly out his nose onto the dusty road. Coombes got to his feet and looked down.

His suit and shirt were covered in blood.

Stratton shakily stood and squared off in front of him.

The laughter and confident smile were gone and the front of his t-shirt was soaked in blood. Coombes had taken twelve solid blows and delivered only one, yet it was Stratton who looked like he was in trouble.

Fist fights were not a huge part of his skillset but he had the measure of Stratton and he could see the other man knew it. To help him understand his situation more clearly, Coombes punched him on the neck, just below his left ear.

Stratton reeled, his legs sagging at the knees.

That would be the vagus nerve, he thought.

Out of his peripheral vision, he saw that the slamming-doors woman was holding a cell phone in front of her face. Instead of getting her children to safety, she was getting a video for her socials. Probably missed the start of him being attacked by Stratton, getting only some questionable use-of-force footage of him.

It was how these things went.

No context, just police brutality.

Stratton had spent a lot of time in the gym in an attempt to land roles and had an easy thirty pounds on him, all of it muscle. The longer any fight went on, the more likely the actor would gain the upper hand.

He had to shut the fight down as quickly as he could.

Coombes stepped back from a wild right hook, then stepped quickly forward again and brought his knee up into Stratton's crotch. The other man folded in half.

"That was for Dakota," Coombes said.

He grabbed the actor's shoulders to straighten him up and drove his knee again into the other man's groin using all the power his leg had left. Stratton collapsed to the ground and vomited onto the road.

"That one was for Adrienne."

He knocked Stratton to the ground, grabbed a fistful of his hair, and pressed his face into the asphalt.

Cuffing an unwilling suspect while trying to pin them down was notoriously difficult. Since he'd lost his gun and three civilians were in harm's way, he didn't have much choice.

He grabbed the actor's right arm and pulled it back, twisting the arm around the shoulder joint. Stratton yelled and flattened out face-down on the ground. Coombes trapped the wrist under his knee to hold it, then reached back and grabbed his handcuffs.

"My shoulder! My shoulder!"

Yeah, your shoulder, he thought without concern, putting on the first cuff. He then brought the left arm around and down, deliberately twisting and extending the tendons in Stratton's other shoulder and snapping on the second cuff.

Exhausted, he rolled off Stratton and sat next to him in the dirt sucking air. After a beat he looked up and saw the woman finish her video, a big smile on her face.

Great.

Coombes got to his feet, picked up his Glock, and approached her. She shrank away from him. Through the lens of her eyes he saw himself, covered in Stratton's blood.

He'd been to hell, and brought back a demon.

"Forget it," she said. "The footage is in the cloud and I got witnesses."

He supposed that she meant her two children.

"Well, before you go posting that online for nothing like a *sucker*, how about I give you the name of someone at the *Times* who will pay you for exclusive rights?"

The woman's face brightened.

"Sure!"

He gave her Monica Sullivan's details and hoped he had enough juice with the journalist to neutralize any problems. This would be where he found out the true nature of their relationship.

Was he a friend, or a means to an end?

"Tell her it shows John Coombes making an arrest. She'll want it."

The woman returned her gaze to the helicopter. It was what had drawn her out her home in the first place. It rotated 90 degrees and he saw LAPD markings. He held up his badge, then four fingers to indicate *code 4*, no assistance required.

The airship rose and banked over his head, back toward Hollywood. When his head dipped down, he saw Sato driving toward him. She parked the Dodge and got out.

Her eyes took in the fresh damage to his face, then his clothes.

"I hate to tell you this, Coombes, but that suit's ruined."

"A price worth paying. What about the Audi?"

"Don't worry," she said. "I've got uniforms sitting on it."

Sato turned to Stratton who lay on the street like a bag of trash ready to be thrown into a garbage truck. She snarled in disgust and for a long moment he thought she might actually spit on the actor. The moment passed, and the tension left her face.

It took both of them to get Stratton onto his feet and perp-walk him toward the Dodge. Coombes held Stratton's shoulder in his right hand and a folded-over little finger in the left.

A small amount of pressure would cause Stratton a lot of pain.

When they got to the Dodge, Sato released Stratton to open the rear door. The actor's body became tense, his huge shoulder muscles fanning out.

Coombes leaned in close.

"It's not my style to shoot a handcuffed man, Stratton, but I've *done* my cardio for the day. Make a break for it again, and it's two in the chest, ok?"

Stratton said nothing, so he gave the man's finger a squeeze.

"All right!"

They loaded him into the back seat, Stratton folded awkwardly into the space, arms like glazed hams cuffed behind him.

Stratton looked at him through the window.

His face was calm. He'd know this day was coming for years, today was simply *that day*. Coombes stepped away from the car and tilted his head up to face the cobalt-blue sky. He closed his eyes and took a deep breath.

It was done.

After six years, the nightmare was nearly over.

56

WHEN HE OPENED HIS eyes, he saw Sato watching him. She gave him a small nod. Some cases became personal, she knew it as well as he did. They got into the Dodge and shut the doors. Inside, the car was like a furnace.

Instead of starting the engine and dialing up the air conditioning, he took a long moment to adjust the driver's seat and rearview mirror from Sato's settings to his. Thinking about his next move. He turned to face Stratton and saw he was already sweating.

"That wasn't a Heckler & Koch MP7 we saw you loading into that Audi, was it? The exact same type of pistol that was used to kill a policeman outside your Riverside home." Coombes paused for a beat. "Here's what we're going to do. We'll get a nice, juicy, search warrant. Everything above-board. Then we're going to search that vehicle from top to bottom, going to take our time, make no mistakes.

"You know what I think? I think forensics will find fingerprints all over that pistol, not to mention on the unfired rounds in the magazine. What are the odds they will be *your* prints?"

Stratton glared at him with the high beams on.

Coombes nodded and continued.

"After processing it for prints, they'll test-fire it and compare rifling marks with the bullets recovered in Riverside. You think they'll match up? I mean, maybe it's a *different* pistol. It could be a total coincidence. Someone else shot a cop outside *your* home and by sheer chance you own that exact model of gun. That's possible, right?"

The death stares continued.

It was all the man had left, and he knew it.

The heat in the car's cabin continued to climb and Coombes' skin prickled with sweat. He ignored it, and leaned between the gap in the front seats, his right hand on Sato's head restraint to push himself closer to Stratton.

"We have you for murdering a cop, jackass. That's capital murder. It gets you life without the possibility of parole. Which means you're going in a hole forever, just like you thought you were doing to Adrienne Strömberg. Only, you'll still be alive."

"Get out of my face, man."

Coombes turned to Sato.

"He's worried about my *face*."

Sato laughed.

"Wait till he finds out what happens at Pelican Bay."

"That's right," Coombes said, turning back to Stratton. "Piece of fresh meat like you. I hope you're open-minded, because your *outlook* is about to be seriously widened."

Sato laughed again. *Ha, Ha, Ha.*

She was laying it on thick, and the acoustics of the car seemed to amplify it, making it come at you from all directions. Stratton's eyes went to her.

They were wild, white visible all around the iris.

"Shut up, bitch! Shut! Up!"

The outburst came as no surprise to Coombes. You didn't do what Stratton had done without being a misogynist. Maybe Stratton believed Booth was to blame for everything, but this was his real driving force: his utter hatred of women.

Still, winding the man up wasn't his goal here.

"Do you want to go down as a coward who shot a man through a door? Or a serial killer who struck fear into Hollywood? Who do you think gets the rolling news coverage; the magazine covers; the summer blockbuster movie? The door guy, or the serial killer?"

"Why would I tell you shit?"

"There's no death penalty in California anymore. It's a psycho dream deal. Buy one, get eight free. Here's the thing; we don't need to prove *anything* on those other murders, the cop is enough. What's it to be? Do you want to be legend or..."

His voice trailed off and he glanced at Sato.

"Loser," she said.

Perfect.

"Legend or loser," Coombes said, nodding. "You might not care about fame, but it will affect how the boys treat you at Pelican Bay. Cop killers. Serial killers. Those people get respect on the inside. Think about it."

Stratton said nothing.

"Guys like you," Coombes continued, casually. "They always talk in the end. You need people to know what you did, why you did it. Why else would you sign a kill that you were burying in the ground?"

The high beams dipped and Stratton's gaze appeared to turn inward.

Coombes faced forward and he started the engine.

It had taken him a long time to get to this point and he allowed the feeling of peace to spread out inside his body. Sometimes wins could be short-lived and he'd learned to take each victory while he could in case it all turned to shit later.

57

A HIGH-RESOLUTION CAMERA WAS set up on a tripod in the interview room ready to capture every word that might come out of Billy Stratton's mouth. The room also had two security cameras mounted high up in the corners: one facing the door, and the other facing the back wall. High-angle cameras captured everything that happened, but made for sterile viewing. Juries always responded better to eye-level footage and a quality fit for a true crime show.

Stratton had been in holding for five hours.

There was a sweet spot for each criminal, how long to let them marinate before you put them on the grill. Not long enough, they had too much fight left; too long, they went right out the other side and closed down completely.

Judging how long to leave someone was an art form.

As Stratton was led into the room in handcuffs it was obvious to Coombes that he'd mis-judged it and he should've waited another half hour at least. He decided to begin slowly and build the lines of communication between them.

Coombes started the camera recording before Stratton sat down so it didn't look like the footage had been edited to remove a section damaging to the prosecution. When Stratton was seated, one of the two uniforms that was escorting him removed the handcuff from his right hand and fastened it around a bar on the table.

The uniforms filed out and closed the door behind them.

Coombes sat where the camera could see him.

Both of them had been cleaned up. The actor's nose was taped and splinted while Coombes' lip, left eyebrow, and forehead were all sutured closed.

"Interview of William Stratton by Detectives John Coombes and Grace Sato. Today's date is Monday, July 27th 2020. Time is 6:24 p.m."

The other man gave no reaction.

Not fully marinated, Coombes thought.

If Stratton sat there in silence the interview was going nowhere. Sometimes when this happened, it was impossible to get the flow of conversation to start no matter how long they spent in holding, the damage was done.

There was no use worrying about it, so he kept going.

He began by reading Stratton his rights off a laminated card.

The card was a prop, he knew the Miranda Warning off by heart. He spoke slower than usual to be sure that he could be understood by Stratton, and heard clearly by the camera recording him six feet away.

While preparing for the interview, his thoughts had returned again and again to Detective Torres' disastrous interview with Stratton over the death of his sister. There would be no procedural mistakes this time around.

When he finished reading, Stratton remained silent.

"I need you to confirm that you understand your rights, Mr. Stratton."

The killer's eyes moved first to Sato, then to him.

"I *heard* you."

"And you understand what I said?"

"Yeah, man. I understand."

"Do you currently wish to invoke your right to an attorney?"

Again, Stratton glared at Sato.

He didn't like her, Coombes realized. *This* was the friction he'd seen in the other man's eyes as he came in, it was nothing to do with his time in holding. Sato had mocked him in the Dodge and he was still angry about it. To a man like Stratton, a woman with a gun and a badge was too much.

"No lawyer," Stratton growled, his eyes now fixed on Coombes.

Although the interview was being recorded, Coombes was taking nothing for granted. He placed a folio down in front of Stratton with a legal document and a pen in the fold.

Stratton's face screwed up. "What's this?"

"A document waiving your right to counsel. I need a signature on the line. For the record, Mr. Stratton, legal representation is not just a right, but a recommendation."

The *last* thing Coombes wanted was for the other man to lawyer-up, but saying this on the recording prevented Stratton from later claiming he was denied his constitutional rights, was unlawfully coerced, or that he had been purposefully misled.

It was his experience that criminals often liked to do the *opposite* of what you appeared to want as a way to re-balance the power dynamic and give them back a measure of control. Seconds ticked by. Ten. Twenty. It looked like Stratton was actually thinking about it.

Shit, Coombes thought.

The actor stared at the camera, then down at the sheet of paper.

His face was blank, emotionless. Finally, after almost a minute, Stratton picked up the pen and signed by the cross without reading the text. Coombes picked up the folio, checked that Stratton had used his actual name, then returned the pen to his pocket.

"A copy of this document and the interview will be made available to you or to any future legal counsel at a later date."

Stratton let out a blast of fetid breath that rushed across the table at him.

"What difference does it make? I killed them all. I *liked* it."

Coombes kept his face calm, professional.

"Before we get to that, Mr. Stratton, I'd first like to ask if you are currently under the influence of drugs or alcohol."

"No."

Coombes decided to start things off tangentially, with how he'd been caught. Once a pattern of easy answers built up, there would be less friction when the difficult questions came along.

"Those paintings, the Orson and Bugsy, how was that supposed to work?"

"*Work?*" Stratton asked, frowning

"You were trying to frame Booth, right? Trying to turn his interest in the Black Dahlia case into something that would look suspicious."

"I wasn't trying to frame him. The picture was a gift. I had forgiven him for what he'd done to Gloria. For the longest time, I hated him and that hate had sustained me. *Defined* me. Then, almost overnight, it was gone. It was like clouds opened up and the sun came out. I didn't feel it anymore."

Coombes knew exactly what Stratton was talking about.

He'd forgiven his ex-wife for her betrayal. He'd heard happiness in her voice and he hoped she stayed that way. After forgiving her, he'd felt physically lighter, like an actual weight had been lifted from his shoulders.

"Why give De Luca a painting if the gift was for Booth?"

"Booth would only accept it if he thought it was from his friend. I didn't mind that. It was enough for me to know it would be in his home, that he would look at it sometimes and maybe smile. I had come to respect him. The darkness in his movies spoke to me."

Coombes leaned back in his seat.

"All right. Tell me about Dakota Lawrence."

Stratton's eyes lit up, remembering what he'd done to her.

"Ah, Dakota. So beautiful...not too bright though. I went to her home at two in the morning and said Booth needed to see her. She didn't question it for a second, she just turned to go change out of her pajamas. I hit her over the back of her head and she went out like a light. It was easier than picking up dry-cleaning."

Coombes was glad he'd left his sidearm in a locker outside.

"You hit her with Booth's Oscar?"

"Yeah. That was when I *was* trying to frame him."

"How did you happen to have his Oscar?"

"I was at a party in his house once. I stole it."

He was getting lost in the weeds when he needed to focus.

"All right," Coombes said. "What happened after you knocked her out?"

"I loaded her into the back of De Luca's SUV and drove to a vacant rental property my dad had in Echo Park. He didn't know I was using it; I knew the code to the key safe."

"We'll get the details later, stay with Dakota."

Stratton nodded, his focus on Coombes.

It looked like he'd forgotten about Sato.

"When she came around, it was like she didn't come all the way back. She wasn't right, I'd hit her too hard. Sometimes she'd be there with me, having my fun, the next she looked like she was comatose. Kind of ruined the mood to be honest."

Coombes couldn't hide his surprise.

"You had sex with her?"

Stratton looked disgusted.

"God, no! She was Booth's whore. I couldn't go where the devil had been."

He decided to steer the conversation away from god and the devil.

"Then what did you do?"

"I strangled her until her face went blue. I did that over and over for about an hour. There were bruises on her neck. She'd had it before from Booth, those bruises were *old*. I did other stuff. Punching, slapping. I bit her left breast."

The bite evidence had been held back; the press didn't have it.

Coombes clenched his jaw. "*Then* what?"

"You know, Detective, you saw her."

"I need you to say it, Mr. Stratton."

"I cut her throat and slaughtered her like an animal."

There was nothing in Stratton's eyes, they were as soulless and vacant as the painting of Capone. Pure evil, no humanity.

Coombes found he missed the routine of making notes in his notebook. With the camera recording everything, he had no reason to look away from Stratton, not even for a moment.

"There was a mark on her neck like you'd tied something around it."

Stratton laughed, like he'd forgotten that detail.

"Lamp flex. I wanted Dakota to watch her blood cover our naked bodies. To make that last moment stretch out as long as possible for her, not just black out." Stratton's eyes closed, a sick smile curling his lips. "It was hot and thick against my skin. It went everywhere; up my nose, in my mouth. I could smell her death. I could *taste* it."

Coombes let the other man's words hang in the air, both to let his anger subside, and to let the words sink in to the jury that would later see it. He wondered if the camera would capture the evil that he was seeing, or if it would be as hollow as a cooking show.

"Where in the property was this? The bathroom?"

"The garage. There's a drain in the floor. I planned to give her the Dahlia treatment, you know? The mouth cut, the bisected torso, but I didn't have time. I had to get back to De Luca before he noticed I was gone."

Coombes sensed that Sato was about to ask a question and he fanned out his hand under the table where only she could see it. *Stop.* He didn't want Stratton to shut down again now that he'd got him talking.

"Tell me about the cut on her forehead."

"I don't know where that came from, I just did it."

"How did you gain access to the studio lot?"

"Easy. I was in De Luca's ride so security waved me straight through. At night you can't see shit through tinted glass, less when you've got headlights in your eyes."

It was exactly what he'd assumed.

There were a lot of details still to flesh out, but he wanted to cover each of Stratton's kills while he was talkative and they had been at it already for half an hour.

"Let's skip ahead to Adrienne Strömberg."

Stratton's face fell.

"My big mistake. I scooped her up on the street coming out of Natalie Hahn's apartment. I got her all the way back to Echo Park and it was only when she's on the garage floor half-naked that I realize there's something wrong. That her face wasn't quite right. They were like twins. Same hair, same clothes. She even had Natalie's wallet. I couldn't believe it."

"But you killed her anyway."

The smile came back.

"You still get the pleasure, Detective. I was able to take my time with her, I had nowhere else to be. I didn't hit her as hard as Dakota, I was getting better. She lasted two days, we did everything. Booth hadn't been with her, so the gloves were off."

Coombes' heart sank.

"You had sex with Adrienne."

He didn't call it what it really was because he wanted Stratton to keep talking. It made him feel sick to pander to the other man's fantasy in this way, but he had to get to the information that was locked inside Stratton's head.

"I took what I needed, sure. She hoped that's all I wanted and I'd let her go after. I think in her heart she knew the truth; there was a smell of death in there I couldn't get out."

Coombes thought about the dig site. About the rivets from Adrienne's jeans, about her leather boots, the jacket.

"You let her get dressed again, didn't you? She thought it was all over, and she was going home, and *that's* when you killed her."

Stratton's face filled with joy.

"She was *so* surprised; you have no idea. I had to sacrifice the clothes I was wearing to make her believe it, but it was totally worth it for the moment when I opened her throat."

Coombes felt contaminated being in the same room as Stratton. The man was a monster. Feeling no irony at all, he wanted to launch himself across the table and end the man's life.

He could do it.

He *wanted* to do it.

Stratton's posture changed, like he'd seen something familiar in the way Coombes was looking at him. He decided to move things on.

"You buried Adrienne in the woods, why was that?"

"She wasn't linked to Booth, so displaying her like Dakota wouldn't blow back on him. I figured I'd get to Natalie later and do my thing with her but I never did. It was like she'd disappeared off the planet."

Again, just as he'd figured.

"Tell me about the four in the water. We don't even know who they are, perhaps you could help us out?"

"They're nobodies, I don't know their names. The first was a girl who came to my door with a pizza I hadn't ordered. She had the wrong house. *Boy, did she have the wrong house.* She was cute, so I thought, why not? That was when I realized I didn't care about Booth anymore, that I had my own needs now. I'd enjoyed the mistake as much as Dakota."

When Coombes said nothing, Stratton continued.

"The next two were together, I picked them up in a bar. I told them I had blow at my place and they got straight into the Audi and laughed all the way. I thought two at once would be a challenge, but it was almost tedious. I didn't even have to buy them drinks."

He couldn't face asking Stratton what he'd done to these women, although he would have to eventually. Listening to the actor talk conversationally about the impossible was taking something from him, he could feel it leaching out his body.

Was this how Sato felt when he talked about the dead Nazi?

"We found a man in there too, who was he?"

"Some PI working for the missing girl's parents. He was going door-to-door asking questions. Houses she might've gone to with the pizza, I guess. He took one look at me and I knew he'd seen me, the *real* me. I killed him in the kitchen with a bread knife."

Stratton shook his head, remembering.

"A bread knife is *not* a good weapon. It was brutal. I was trying to pin him to the floor and saw away at his neck with the knife at the same time. People can get real strong when you're doing that. Took me three days to clean the mess up. After that, I decided to return to my place in Riverside and focus on acting again."

"Because you still planned to get Booth?"

"No, because I like it. Pretending to be something I'm not is what I do all the time. The PI saw through my act, but most didn't."

"Did you continue to kill after going back to Riverside?"

"Not until that cop came sniffing around, pounding on my door. I wasted him on general principal. I was asleep, the man nearly gave me a heart attack."

"*His name was Eddie Willard!*"

Coombes said it sharply, with anger he couldn't control. Both Stratton and Sato jumped at his mood change.

"I didn't stop to check his wallet, man. I blew him away and hit the road."

It took Coombes a moment to realize what had happened.

"Wait, you missed one out. There was one before Willard."

Confusion crowded Stratton's face. He'd been enjoying talking about what he'd done and suddenly something had gone wrong. It was a curious omission, Coombes thought.

"Who...who did I forget?"

There was a wobble of uncertainty in the actor's voice.

"Joshua Booth. I'm a little surprised he slipped your mind."

Stratton glared at him, his face impossible to read.

Static energy filled the gap between them but Coombes did nothing to stop it building. He could stay here all night if he needed to. Stratton's head dipped down to look at his hands on the table in front of him. When his voice came it was slow, world-weary.

"That's right. I killed that pig. He killed my sister, so I shot him in the head and left him floating in his stupid pool. I got justice for Gloria, since you people weren't interested in getting it for her. If you guys had done your job none of this would've happened."

If he'd been taking notes, he would've let some time pass while he wrote down gibberish to create a gap and to get under Stratton's skin, but the camera prevented that.

"I thought you'd forgiven Booth, grown to respect him?"

"I *had*. It didn't stick. Killing that cop brought the rage back. Nobody cared about Gloria but a couple of whores die and I'm getting hunted for it? Where's the justice there?"

Stratton's obsession with Booth had taken over his life. His hatred had given him strength, given him a purpose. With Booth dead, his life was meaningless. It was the real reason he was here, and why he was admitting to everything.

"How did you gain entry to Booth's home?"

The question surprised Stratton and he had to think for a moment.

"The security gate was shut. I was thinking about coming back when it was dark and climbing over the wall when suddenly the gate opens and he drove out. I got past the gate before it closed and hid in his yard until he got back. While he unloaded groceries, he left the front door open as he carried stuff inside. I slipped in behind him."

Coombes felt heat spread out across his chest.

"Between Booth leaving and coming back, how long did you wait?"

"An hour, maybe longer. I don't have a watch and I'd ditched my cell."

What Stratton didn't realize, was that he'd just admitted to lying in wait to murder Booth. Lying in wait was a *special circumstances* add-on, making Booth's killing a capital murder.

It was unlikely to Coombes that the DA would push for capital murder in the death of Eddie Willard for the simple reason that Willard should not have been pounding on Stratton's door in the first place. The law covered retired officers pursued by criminals after leaving the Department, not retired officers *pretending they were still cops.*

That part, the DA would want to disappear.

Coombes glanced at his watch.

They'd been at it now for over two hours and he needed a break to de-louse himself and get something to eat. When they came back it would be time to fill in the large brush strokes.

Details made cases. With enough details, they could make the case without the confession.

"Let's take a break, get you something to eat."

"Look," Stratton said. "I'm beat. Do we have to go through this? Type up a confession and I'll sign it. I'm going to plead guilty anyway. I just want this all behind me."

Coombes nodded.

"We're almost done, Mr. Stratton."

He stood, walked to the camera, gave the time and shut it off.

58

WHEN COOMBES STEPPED INTO Gantz' office four days later, he saw that Detectives Kennedy and Stills were in the room already, sitting on the only available chairs. It had been exactly a week since he'd last seen them but it felt like nearly a month. The two detectives looked pretty pleased with themselves, which he figured wasn't a good thing.

Coombes saw his service weapon sitting on Gantz' desk.

"Is this the part where I give you my badge?"

Gantz checked her fingernails.

"I'm hoping we can work something out, John."

Solving a serial case didn't get you as much as it used to.

"You want me to quit, is that it?"

"There's going to be a hearing into the fatal shooting. I've got no worries how that's going to shake out, but these two assholes want me to suspend you until it's-"

"Hey!' Kennedy and Stills said in unison.

"Shut up and sit down, this is MY office."

The two FID men glanced at each other, then sat back down.

"I'm *not* suspending you, John, fuck these assholes. However, you've got a pile of unused vacation time so you are taking the next rotation off, which covers the period leading up to the hearing. Any court dates you have scheduled will go ahead as normal."

Kennedy and Stills looked like they were about to explode. That worked for Coombes. He nodded at his gun sitting on his lieutenant's desk.

"Does this mean I'm getting that back?"

"Of course," Gantz said. "I can't have you facing Nazi hitmen with just your dick in your hand, no offense to what you're packing downstairs."

"This is outrageous!" Kennedy said.

"No," Gantz said. "It's called due process. Innocent until proven guilty. You ever hear about that in the rat squad, Kennedy? I won't have your bullshit threaten the career of one my best detectives or the viability of his cases. You got what you wanted, he's off-rotation. The two of you can get the hell out my office and fall under a bus. Make sure you get your heads under the back wheels where the weight is; front wheels might not get the job done."

Kennedy and Stills jumped out their chairs and came toward Gantz.

Coombes stepped forward to intercept them.

"We could file a 1.27 complaint for that," Kennedy hissed.

"Not without looking like a pussy," Coombes said. "The two of you should leave before she cuts you off at the knees. It's just embarrassing watching you go down in flames."

Kennedy stormed out, trailing Stills behind him like luggage on wheels.

"Thanks L-T," Coombes said, picking up his gun. "What about Sato?"

"I won't pair her with Wallfisch, John. You have my word."

"Look...she wants to become a D-II. If I'm out of circulation and it's quiet here anyway, maybe you could encourage her to take the tests. Now might be a good time."

"I'll do that. About time she advanced."

At the door he stopped and turned back.

"See if you can't get her to a shooting range as well. Sato's never had to use her weapon and I want to know she's got my back."

"Let me guess. She still thinks scumbags are humans?"

"Something like that."

"I'll take care of it," Gantz said.

When he got back to his desk, he saw Sato playing solitaire on her iPad. Klondike, with a three card draw. Running out the clock, hoping no new corpses would turn up.

A cop's life.

She glanced up, bored.

"You have visitors in the meeting room."

"Yeah? Who?"

Sato rolled her eyes like she was asking if she was his *secretary* and passed him a Post-It with LOCKE written on it, then turned back to her cards.

The name meant nothing to him.

Coombes supposed Locke was the name of an Internal Affairs detective and that he was facing fresh charges arising from the FID investigation. Fishing for problems ahead of his hearing.

He walked to the meeting room but instead of a pair of grizzled IAD detectives, he found a beautiful woman with long blonde hair and a young girl with headphones around her neck.

He recognized the woman immediately.

"It's weird seeing you again, Natalie. I thought you were dead."

"I'm feeling much better now, thanks."

She smiled and her eyes seemed to sparkle.

This would be the dark sense of humor that Booth had spoken about. Natalie Hahn, alive and well. Her insolent smolder had matured into a knowing smile, something she could actually pull off.

Normally, when he suspected someone was dead, they *were* dead. From his point of view, it was like she'd come back to life. It felt good. Despite the problems she'd created for his investigation six years before, he had to fight an urge to embrace her.

Sato had set him up.

Coombes took out his notebook.

"I have a couple of questions."

She glanced at his notebook. The notebook made it official.

"Look, I came in after reading my name in the *Times*. You thought this other woman was me, but she wasn't. I thought I should let you know I'm ok and not in a hole somewhere."

He popped the nib of his pen out.

"So, you're Natalie Locke now. Why the name change?"

"It's no big mystery," she said. "I got married."

"I found no evidence of a marriage in county records."

"My husband's Canadian, we got married in Toronto."

He sighed. Sometimes the truth could be mundane.

"And your passport and driver's license?"

"My car died and I never replaced it. I work from home and shop online; Uber is all I need now. No maintenance, no high gas prices, no parking nightmares. I'm *done* with cars. As for the passport, I hated flying even before the virus."

If he was to believe her, circumstances had conspired to remove her from the grid. She wasn't dead in a hole; she was in a blind spot.

"I never took you for the type to change her name after marriage."

Locke nodded.

"When the movie came out, I got a lot of hate from Booth's fans. They thought the movie sucked because of me. I got death threats. I shut down my socials after two days. Taking my husband's name was the easiest decision I ever made. All my problems went away."

Coombes noted this down.

"Did you know the victim, Adrienne Strömberg?"

"Sure. Addie was on the party circuit, same as me. Another actor trying to catch the eye of some mover and shaker, get a role."

Coombes glanced at the girl. Natalie got the message.

"Lily, put on your headphones. Listen to some music."

The girl sighed, then did what she was asked. Coombes waited until he heard the buzz of music playing before resuming his questioning.

"The two of you traded sex for access?"

"If you're trying to upset me, you're wasting your time. Yes, we slept around. I'm not proud of it, but it's tough out there. My first month in acting I did sixty auditions, all for nothing. You don't know what emotional damage that causes, you have to really put yourself out there. After that, sleeping with a couple of guys was easy. Booth was different. I had a crush on him, I always had. His movies were why I wanted to act in the first place."

"Your wallet was buried with Strömberg. How do you explain that?"

"Addie and I met often enough at parties that we became friends. After a while, we decided to share an apartment to cut costs. We were the same size, so we wore each other's clothes. Last time I saw her she was wearing my jacket. I guess my wallet was in the pocket."

A tear rolled down her face and Coombes watched it.

This was the first sign of emotion from her, perhaps the first real thing she'd ever shown him. She let it roll down her cheek, without wiping it away.

"What's the significance of that to you?"

"Isn't it obvious? Our hair was styled the same way, we were the same height and build. With my jacket on…"

Locke's voice trailed off.

"You think the person that killed her thought she was you?"

"Yes!"

She was right, but he wasn't going to tell her that. She might find out from press coverage anyway, but that was a problem for another day.

Coombes tilted his head toward the girl.

"Lily is Joshua Booth's daughter?"

"That's right."

"Did he know about her?"

"No. By the time I found out I was pregnant, Josh and I had already parted ways. I knew his track record with female leads, how he got rid of them after a movie finished. I thought it wouldn't happen to me, that I'd be the exception."

"Why would you think that?"

"On account of how good I am in the sack."

Coombes smiled and she sent it right back to him. *The sack.* He hadn't heard that expression in years. His gaze drifted down to the floor as he asked his next question.

He saw she was wearing running shoes. Nikes. She jiggled her foot when she saw him looking. A lot of women didn't like men looking at their feet, he didn't know why. Coombes didn't figure Locke for the shy type.

He wan't be a hundred percent, but they looked size 9.

Coombes thought about the shoe print recovered from the Lawrence crime scene. It was a loose end he'd been unable to tie off. Stratton hadn't left it behind, nor had any of the first responders. He glanced back up.

Natalie was looking at him, her dark eyes like pools to infinity.

It was the most common shoe size for women in the US, Lawrence herself was a size 9. Without unique tread marks and a matching shoe in the suspect's closet, it meant little.

Over the years, he'd come to believe that the print had been at the scene before the crime. In the right conditions, a shoe print could last for weeks, even months.

The baking sun, the lack of rain. Earth became like concrete.

"Everything all right, Detective?"

"I totally forgot what we were talking about, I'm sorry."

Who benefits.

With Booth dead, his daughter had a claim to his entire fortune. If he and Natalie had married, Booth would've insisted on a pre-nuptial contract to protect himself in any divorce. But dead, with no other descendants, his estate would pass to Lily and her mother.

"You asked if I planned to have children. I did, but not with Josh. It was something I thought I would do when I was maybe 30, not when I was 22."

"Booth told me you took contraceptives. He said he saw them."

"The pills messed me up. I wanted to be authentic on set."

Coombes said nothing, thinking of her erratic on-screen performance.

She mis-read his silence and spoke again.

"I didn't think it would matter, ok? It took my sister five years to get pregnant, and that was only after treating it like a science project. All the coke Josh did, I thought his swimmers would be going around in circles."

Coombes smiled and nodded. Locke was in good spirits.

The print being hers didn't line up with the chronology, he realized. Locke didn't meet Booth until *after* Lawrence's body was found. She'd had her sights set on Booth before that, but only because she wanted a job.

The shoe print was nothing, it always had been.

Locke glanced at her daughter and smiled. It wasn't for his benefit, he could tell. This was something she did all the time. She loved her daughter; this was her life now.

Coombes decided to give her a second chance.

"Are you making a claim for Lily?"

"A *claim*? For what?"

"For Booth's estate. Far as I know, Lily is his only heir."

Locke looked at him, astonished. She hadn't thought about it.

He'd seen her act before, this wasn't it.

"What would I do?"

"You need to prove Lily is his with a DNA test. Josh is in the morgue but he won't be for long. You'll need to file an emergency petition to run a DNA panel before his body is sent for burial or cremation. Then Lily will need a cheek swab for comparison. I can't do this, you need a lawyer."

Her eyes were wild, excited.

Natalie was no actor, but her emotions were right there on the surface. Looking at her face he could feel her emotions. *This* was what Booth had seen in her, he thought, why he'd cast her in the movie. What Booth couldn't have known was that she was unable to turn it on and off on camera like Dakota Lawrence.

He wrote down the name and address of an attorney he'd heard good things about, tore the page out his notebook, and passed it to Locke.

"Go directly to this address, explain the situation and the need for urgency. I'll call the morgue and put a hold on things there, buy you some time."

"I don't know how to thank you, Detective."

"You mentioned something before about a sack?"

Locke burst out laughing.

"You're a riot!"

He nodded somberly and put his notebook away.

She'd think him the lamest sap going if he told her that seeing her and her daughter alive was all the thanks he needed after spending time in Billy Stratton's world.

"I don't suppose you know what happened to Scott Peters?"

Locke looked surprised at this name from the past.

"Scott? Last I heard, he was living with his mom in Chatsworth."

Not dead then, but close.

59

AFTER HIS CALL TO the morgue to put a hold on Booth, Coombes sat staring at his computer screen. His conversation with Natalie Locke had shifted some of the pieces of the jigsaw around in his mind. Where before the picture on the puzzle appeared complete, he now saw that there was a missing piece.

He opened his notebook to the notes he'd made after talking to Torres, the case detective on the Gloria Stratton murder.

Stratton has no memories of events due to drugs (blackout).
Stratton never mentioned Booth under questioning.
Torres has no doubts about Stratton's guilt.
No forensic evidence to support Booth's presence in apartment.
No mention of Booth by any of Gloria's friends.
Fran Knudsen is the only -

The last line he'd left unfinished, his train of thought derailed by the call from his ex-wife. It was this thought that interested him now. The lack of forensic evidence was damning, it sealed the whole thing up. Booth could not have been in Gloria's apartment, not the night of, not ever.

Coombes took out his pen and completed the last line.

Fran Knudsen is the only link between Booth and Stratton.

Booth's fear of being blinded in his sleep convinced him that the recurring nightmare about Gloria Stratton was true. The part that *wasn't* true, was that Booth was involved in her death in any way. That part came from Knudsen.

He sighed deeply and Sato's voice came over the partition.

"I *know* that sound, Coombes. What did you miss?"

"Everything."

News reports had described Gloria as beautiful.

It was likely that Booth had noticed her around campus. Noticed, and perhaps forgotten. There were a lot of beautiful women around campus, a factory somewhere was churning them out. It wasn't Gloria's looks that captured Booth's imagination and invaded his dreams, it was the manner of her death.

Coombes turned and saw that Sato had shuffled her chair around next to his, her bored look replaced with one of interest.

"I very much want to hear your tale of woe, Johnny."

"I'll bet."

He didn't roll it out for her yet, instead, he opened the DMV portal and brought up Fran Knudsen's driver's license. It was four and a half years old, almost expired. He brought up a copy of the previous license, issued in 2016. The image of Knudsen was nine and a half years younger, yet she looked almost the same.

"Damn," Sato said. "She's barely aged."

Dirty-blonde hair framed a naturally beautiful face that, save for lipstick, was free of cosmetics. Knudsen had the pink bloom to her cheeks of a teenage girl and prominent Nordic cheekbones.

It was a familiar look, all Booth's women looked this way.

Coombes rolled it back again, to the 2011 issue.

For the first time, she looked visibly younger. Her jawline was more defined, her eyes brighter. It seemed impossible to Coombes that Booth had a woman like this interested in him and he'd kept her at arm's length instead of marrying her like she wanted.

He saw that the previous issue date was 2006.

It was the year Gloria died; the year Booth graduated and moved in with Knudsen; the year he met De Luca in *The Biltmore*; and the year he wrote *Last Night, Before I Died*.

He brought up Knudsen's 2006 license and sat back.

A different woman seemed to look back at him.

Chestnut-colored hair, plump face, and heavy use of cosmetics. Additionally, Knudsen's ears stuck out more and her nose looked a little different.

Even natural beauties needed a helping hand.

Sato leaned in.

"Bring up Gloria Stratton's license."

"You read my mind," he said.

There was a single license for Gloria, issued in 2004. Her likeness was not a surprise to Coombes, he'd seen a cropped high school class picture in the articles on her death.

Blonde hair, high cheekbones, no cosmetics.

He'd got it wrong.

Booth's muse wasn't Knudsen, it was an unattainable dead girl.

The director had *Laura Syndrome* long before he did.

"What am I missing here, Coombes? We know Stratton's the killer, he even confessed to the whole nut. Where does Knudsen fit into this?"

"Stratton kills his sister while he's high on drugs. He has no memory of it, he has a blackout. After his release from Lompoc, he meets Knudsen who tells him he was framed, that Joshua Booth is Gloria's real killer. Who wouldn't believe that? It had to be everything Stratton wanted to hear."

"*John-*" Sato started.

"I'm not finished," Coombes said. "If he looked up Booth, he would've seen that they were both the film school at the same time. The information would appear to check out. So he does what Knudsen wants, he kills Dakota. An eye for an eye, a tooth for a tooth.

"But Knudsen's plan doesn't work. Booth didn't come running back to her, he hooks up with Natalie Hahn. Meanwhile, Billy Stratton realizes how much he enjoys murder and goes on a killing spree. She's lost control of her weapon."

Sato was silent for a moment.

"Even if every word you just said is true, we've got nothing to prove it and the only way we could is to offer Stratton a plea deal to roll on Knudsen. The DA's never going to sign off on that. Better to have the killer behind bars than someone who told a lie."

"It's more than *telling a lie*, Grace. She's responsible for-"

Sato put her hand on his leg under the table and he fell silent.

"We've got nothing," she repeated, softly.

It would've been risky, he thought, to tell Stratton that Booth was responsible for Gloria's death. How could Knudsen be sure that his rage wouldn't be directed at Booth himself? That would've been the normal reaction.

He sighed again.

There'd been nothing in Stratton's confession of Booth's murder that hadn't been in the news. The pool; the type of gun; the impact to the side of his head. He'd said nothing about adding extra chlorine to the water to hide fingerprint evidence, or about the loud music.

Coombes realized he'd been greedy.

"Knudsen killed Booth. *Not* Stratton. It explains how his killer got into the mansion without challenge. The gun's small, easy to hide. He trusts her. She's his oldest friend, his confidant. After it's done, she returns to the office and starts clearing house."

"She *was* acting pretty squirrelly when we turned up."

He nodded. "For sure."

"Why would Stratton confess to a murder he didn't commit?"

He thought about the look on Stratton's face when he mentioned Booth.

Up till that point, the confession had rolled along smoothly, then, suddenly, this hole in the road. His face had filled with fear and confusion. Stratton couldn't remember killing Booth. A normal person would deny it, but this wasn't the first time he'd been in this position.

"His biggest fear is that he killed his sister. He constructed his life around the idea that he was framed. I tell him he killed Booth, it all falls apart."

"It forces him to see himself," Sato said.

Coombes nodded.

"Another blackout, another death. The obvious conclusion is that he killed Gloria. How can he deny it, if it's happened again? He decides he'd rather take responsibility for Booth, a man he hated for years anyway, than confront his guilt for his sister."

Sato tilted her head over as she thought about it.

"I see what you're saying, Johnny, but it's academic isn't it?"

"*Excuse me?*"

"Stratton confessed to killing Booth along with all the others. If we charge someone else with Booth's murder, the confession is toast. Worthless. We can't pick and choose the parts we like or dislike. It's true, or it isn't. Another killer equals reasonable doubt. You *taught* me this. They'd both skate. Justice for seven is better than justice for none."

Coombes swore loudly.

Stratton's confession about killing Booth, which he had apparently made up on the spot, would ensure he spent the rest of his life in prison.

He sat looking at the picture of Gloria Stratton's first and only driving license on screen. She was the original, the prototype for all the others. But her beauty was no match for Dakota Lawrence, who was perfection.

He couldn't jeopardize the trial of Dakota's killer.

Eddie Willard had given his life to make the case.

Knudsen had beaten him.

60

COOMBES ARRANGED TO MEET Monica Sullivan at the roach coach they'd met at the week before. While he waited for her to arrive, he took out his cell phone and read the texts that she'd sent him after the shooting. He'd avoided doing so before and he quickly wished he'd stuck with that decision, because they were not the messages of one casual acquaintance to another. His face grew hot reading them.

Right at the bottom, was his reply to her, short and to the point.

I'm fine, cell phone was muted.

Though his message was true, he couldn't deny it was insulting after what had come before. She'd been worried about him and he'd thrown it back in her face.

He wished he could take it back.

Coombes put his phone down and drank some coffee.

His mind returned to the Academy Award in Joshua Booth's bedroom. It was the one thing that didn't fit. How could it be there if Stratton hadn't been there?

Knudsen couldn't have left it there.

The blood on the edge was old and had turned black.

To the untrained eye, it looked like dirt.

The easiest explanation, was that Stratton had simply mailed the statue back to Booth and the director hadn't noticed the black mark or taken the time to clean it off. He had no reason to think that the object had been used to kill the woman he loved. All Booth could see when he looked at it, was a plate that said *Best Original Screenplay* instead of *Best Picture*.

Coombes saw Sullivan step out her car and look around.

He watched her face closely as it took in the food truck, then the tables around it. As her eyes fell on him, she smiled. It was easily one of the top five smiles he'd ever received, it lifted him up after a really grim week. He watched her walk over, full of attitude.

"What are you smiling about, Coombes?"

"You," he said, and laughed.

She smiled again at this, but in bemusement, one side of her mouth angled down. If he was being honest with himself, the main reason he'd selected the location was because nobody around the truck wore masks and he wanted to see Sullivan's face again.

He had a disturbing amount of time for her face.

Coombes slid her coffee across the table.

"Wait," she said. "Is this the same table we sat at before? You aren't getting sentimental on me are you, Coombes? Are we going to grow old together, is that it?"

"For the record, Sullivan, I've *always* been sentimental."

She lifted her coffee as if in a toast and drank some.

There were two reasons why Stratton would give Booth the statue back: to frame him; or because he'd forgiven him. No such reasons existed for Knudsen. She wanted to direct and Booth's unused screenplays would become toxic if it came out he was a serial killer.

Sullivan watched him in silence. When she turned off the *femme fatale* act, she was easy to be around.

"I read your stuff in the *Times*. It's good."

"You didn't have to say that, but thank you."

"Makes a change reading news that isn't anti-police."

Sullivan shrugged.

"If it's not *part* of the story, it doesn't go *in* the story. I've got no axe to grind. Besides, a friend of mine's a cop."

She smoldered a little, to let him know she meant him. Sullivan knew how to smolder; Natalie Locke could take a lesson.

"Just to be clear, I can't help you with parking tickets."

"*Speeding* tickets."

"Right."

Her eyes moved over his face, taking in the fresh damage from his fight with Stratton. He'd forgotten all about it, but he could tell that the cuts and bruises didn't bother her.

"I wanted to thank you for sanitizing the arrest video."

"Shit, Coombes, I watch the unedited video ten times a day. You *destroyed* him. I only wish it could've been me doing it."

"Thanks...I guess."

"I make you uncomfortable, don't I?"

He stared at his hands. This was not a conversation he wanted to have.

"I feel the same way, Johnny. You make me blush like a school girl. That's not who I am. Didn't used to be anyway."

He first met Sullivan before his relationship with Sato had started. A twist of fate had sent him one way, and not another. From an objective standpoint, a relationship with the journalist made more sense than one with his partner and all the problems that created.

"Things could've been different between us," he said.

"You never asked, Coombes, but you're not the only one in a relationship."

That explains all the flirting, he thought.

"I guess we're both happy then."

Sullivan laughed.

"You've got such a dry sense of humor, I love it."

He used to see signs in shopping malls that read *pickpockets operating in this area*. It was intended as a warning to shoppers to take care; however, it led many to subconsciously pat the pocket where their wallet was located, thus identifying it to the very pickpockets they were being warned about.

A similar thing happened whenever he saw Sullivan, that he would mentally check if his feelings for Sato were still strong. And they were, every time.

Yet, there he was checking.

"That night at Booth's mansion...what was your plan exactly?"

"My plan?"

"You thought he was a serial killer so you go to his home?"

"I figured he'd feel safe in his own property, that his guard would be down. He'd answer questions for me that he wouldn't answer for you. He'd think I was just like one of those girls but he would've been wrong about that. I have a taser."

Coombes said nothing.

"Can I ask you a question?"

"Shoot," he said.

"How come you never asked if *I* killed him?"

He said nothing for a long time. The question came as no surprise, it was something he'd thought about before.

"Because I didn't want to know if you did."

She smiled.

"That's better than any Valentine I ever got."

Coombes nodded, but his thoughts were elsewhere.

He'd hoped he could tip her off to the situation with Booth, that maybe she could do what he couldn't and turn the spotlight onto Knudsen. She already had half the pieces; it wouldn't take much of a nudge to get her to the finish line.

But in that moment, he saw it didn't matter where the information came from, removing Booth's name from Stratton's case would deal it a death-blow.

Joshua Booth was a first-rate director and a third-rate human being. Despite this, Coombes' memories of Booth were positive. Perhaps it was just the NLP mind games, but he'd enjoyed sparring with the other man and wanted to get him the justice he deserved.

But there was no path forward, he saw that now.

Knudsen was untouchable.

Coombes allowed himself one last look at Sullivan's freckles. They were beautiful and somehow wholesome. Then there was that *city mouth* right there underneath, all pouty and high-gloss. It was like a glazed doughnut, and though the wholesome look was more of a draw for him, he couldn't deny the way his eyes kept going to her mouth.

He stood and picked up his cell phone.

"I guess I'll be seeing you around, Sullivan."

"We're sharks in the same water, Coombes. You can count on it."

———

As he was entering his apartment, he heard the shower running through the wall. He'd always speculated if it was possible to hear his shower from the doorway, but this was the first time he'd been able to confirm it. He walked inside and swung the security bar across.

Coombes left his tablet, keys and notebook on the breakfast bar and pulled off his suit jacket as he walked into the living area. The room was in darkness, with just the light spilling out from the bedroom to light his way.

He walked to the window and stood looking at the building opposite.

Coombes could see inside two dozen apartments.

Nobody had shades drawn. Shades would defeat the purpose of owning an apartment in this zip code. It would be like owning the *Mona Lisa* and covering it with a cloth.

Checking the view had become part of his nightly routine. The stay-at-home order had not been for everyone. The small lighted rectangles were like thumbnails for different streaming shows that were awaiting selection. He'd seen people close to the edge, throwing plates or glasses at each other. One day, maybe he'd see a murder.

No dramas were playing out, so he turned and walked into the bedroom.

He hung his jacket over the back of a chair and threw his tie over it. At the end of the room was a corridor to a walk-in wardrobe that linked on again to the bathroom. He unbuttoned the top two buttons of his shirt and was about to wash his face at the sink when he remembered that Sato was in the shower and stopped himself.

She had five different soaps lined up on the shelf behind the sink. Coombes wondered why more than one might be required. Next to them, she had cleansers, scrubs, moisturizers, and a pair of tweezers he wasn't allowed to mention. Sato didn't wear a lot of cosmetics, yet there were enough to fill a different shelf.

He had a toothbrush, a razor, and a floss harp. That was it.

Five different soaps, he shook his head.

She's not even that dirty.

He smiled to himself, then felt it dissipate as he recalled Booth talking about Hahn's contraceptive pills. Frowning, he opened the medicine cabinet and studied the contents. Pain killers, supplements, dental products.

No contraceptives.

He closed the door again. Sato was discreet. They were somewhere else, either because she didn't want to start a conversation with him about it, or because it would confirm to any snooping third parties the true nature of their relationship. Any guest could be in here, it was the only bathroom in the apartment.

But they were both adults, they needed to talk about it.

"Grace?"

A moment passed before his voice reached through the glass door and the pounding water of the shower and she shut it off. The door opened and Sato looked at him. The stall was raised out the floor, bringing her face close.

"Did you say something?"

Her cheeks were pink from the heat of the water.

There *were* no contraceptives, he knew it in his bones.

Not in the medicine cabinet, not in her purse. They weren't hidden under a squeaky floorboard, or in a box of cornflakes with a snub-nosed '38.

She was rolling the dice.

A shiver went down his spine and the hair on his arms stood on end.

You didn't roll dice because you didn't want to play, you rolled them because you did. If they had a conversation about it, that end goal would be finalized.

It would define their relationship, or end it.

He wasn't sure he wanted a child; he hadn't thought about it for years.

He remembered the way Natalie Locke had looked at her daughter, the love that he'd seen in that moment. Having a child had transformed Locke, made her a better person. The world was ugly and his job rubbed his face in it. Every day he was losing parts of himself to the abyss, he could feel it. Pretty soon there wouldn't be anything about him worth saving.

"Johnny? What is it?"

He had to say something.

"If you're breaking up with me, I'd rather you just say that rather than try to let me down easier. I don't want false hope, I want the truth."

"I'm standing naked in front of you. What do *you* think?"

"You're in the shower. I'd be surprised if you were wearing clothes."

"I'm not breaking up with you."

"Then stay. Don't move out. Do you know anyone that ever got back together after separating? It's just leaving by a different name."

A bead of water dropped off the end of her nose.

"I'll stay if you do something for me."

"Name it," he said.

"I want you to talk to a therapist about the shooting. A real one, not one employed by the Department. One you can be honest with, without worrying about your job. Let all that toxic stuff come out. I want my funny Johnny back."

This again.

"Look, Grace, I might as well tell you...Joseph Wright was never the problem. No amount of therapy will make me care about some dead Nazi."

She did a slow blink and sighed.

"*Dakota.*"

He nodded.

"A complete stranger broke my heart; I can't explain it."

She patted his chest with her hand.

"That's because underneath this bullshit macho shell, you *have* a heart. It's not broken. Your heart makes you the cop you are, John. You care about victims. This...I can work with."

He kissed her on the nose.

"Finish your shower, we'll talk more later."

She looked at the handprint on his shirt, then into his eyes.

"I got you wet. Why don't you take these off and join me?"

"Only fair," he said.

"And how about we *don't* talk later? I've been saying all the wrong things lately."

He kissed her again.

"I can do that."

NEXT IN SERIES: Johnny Coombes will return. Follow me on Amazon to receive updates.

About the Author

I LIVE ON THE outskirts of Edinburgh with my fiancée and young son. I would like to thank my family for their support and encouragement, it means the world to me. If you enjoyed The Final Cut, please consider writing a quick review, it would be greatly appreciated. I am the author of four novels: Night Passenger, The Dark Halo, The Scapegoat, and The Final Cut. To stay up-to-date on new releases, click Follow on my Amazon author page.